A Life of

Seizing Opportunities

Kayla Danoli

A sequel to the novel *A Life of Tea and Sugar*

Copyright

Cataloguing-in-publication data
Creator: Danoli, Kayla, author

Cataloguing-in-Publication details are available from the National Library of Australia www.trove.nla.gov.au

ISBN: 978-1-7635109-1-3 (paperback)
ISBN: 978-1-7635109-2-0 (digital)

Cover design: T A Marshall, Mackay, Queensland, Australia
Cover Image: Majella Geddes, Mackay, Queensland, Australia
(*Aquarius* at anchor in Upstart Bay)

Disclaimer
This novel is a work of fiction. All characters and events are the product of the imagination of the author. While some of the characters might remind you of people you know, they are fictitious and any resemblance to anyone living or dead is purely coincidental. Although some locations also may seem real and familiar, most places referred to in this work constitute a collage of places the author has known. But they are fictitious, and any resemblance to an existing location is coincidental.

Introduction

Previously....

Sarah (Erskine) Wallace's life growing up on the family's tea plantation was idyllic until, aged sixteen, she was sent 'home' to Glasgow to live with her grandmother and great aunt while attending finishing school. A little over two years after leaving India, completing finishing school, and making her entrance into Glasgow society, Sarah married into Glasgow's wealthy Wallace family.

Douglas Wallace made his fortune from import/exports, shipping, and two Caribbean sugar plantations. Sarah married Douglas's elder son, Robert Wallace, on New Year's Eve 1841 and a week later was on a Wallace Shipping Line vessel bound for the Caribbean.

Robert and his younger brother, Cameron, ran the family's sugar plantations. While Robert, as the eldest son, managed the family's overall Caribbean sugar operations. On a day-to-day basis, Cameron oversaw the running of the smaller of the two plantations and their sugar milling factory. Sarah's transition to Caribbean life was not easy.

In the absence of a wife on the plantation following their parents' return to Glasgow, Robert's sister set herself up as 'the lady of the house', and she was not about to relinquish that position to a new young bride. It wasn't until after Douglas Wallace recalled his daughter to Glasgow that the situation improved. Sarah settled in and won over the staff. In 1843, as dark clouds began to gather over the future of the Caribbean sugar industry, leaving his wife at home, Robert spent some months with his father in Glasgow, working on a financially viable strategy for a successful Wallace family exit from the Caribbean sugar industry.

The end came in mid-1845 when the new owners warned Robert, whom they had kept on as manager, that they were about to abandon the plantations and walk away. Robert and Sarah sailed for Glasgow on the next available Wallace ship. Still childless, Sarah had mixed feeling about returning to Scotland and, to compound the situation further, she found Robert's plans for his future did not include Sarah. With no intention of remaining in Glasgow to work with his father, Robert became a consultant to the sugar industry in Java, employment that did not allow for a wife to accompany him to that country. Sarah continued to live alone in a cottage on the Wallace Estate.

Soon after Robert left for Java, Sarah accepted Douglas Wallace's offer of a position helping him run his enterprise. After a number of years, Sarah decided it was more convenient to accept her father-in-law's offer of an apartment in the 'big house' than having to commute between the cottage and the big house every day. Sarah's part-time marriage continued with increasingly less frequent contact with Robert until 1858.

Cameron, on his way home one night just before Christmas, noticed a light on in the cottage and discovered Robert had been staying in the cottage for a couple of days but had not contacted Sarah while there. Any doubts she had about the state of her marriage were replaced by the realisation it was over. Then, around Easter the following year, a chance encounter with an old acquaintance from the Caribbean changed her life.

Jimmy Fraser came to visit Douglas Wallace. Sarah hadn't seen or heard from Jimmy since he left the Caribbean before she and Robert did. Jimmy also had come directly from Java, where he had been working in their sugar industry. But, the infant Australian sugar industry appealed to Jimmy and he had come to Glasgow to update his knowledge of machinery and processes before heading to Australia. During Jimmy's visit, Sarah discovered Robert had developed quite a reputation in Java as he went about increasing the country's population. In a private meeting with Jimmy, Sarah questioned him about the new sugar industry being established in Australia.

She learned of Jimmy's interest in an area of the new colony of Queensland that he believed offered excellent growing conditions for sugar cane. He thought his sugar industry experience might be worth something there. By the end of their meeting, Sarah knew her destiny lay in Australia. What Sarah also took away from that meeting with Jimmy was his philosophy: If something presents as an opportunity, seize it.

Over the next few years after Jimmy departed for Australia, Sarah and Jimmy regularly corresponded. Then, in 1862, Jimmy's glowing reports of the new lands being opened up on the banks of the Pioneer River in Queensland further fuelled Sarah's interest in Australia. She arranged a passage on a Wallace vessel sailing the company's new shipping route to Australia, but had to delay her departure when tragic news reached the Wallace family.

Douglas received word that his elder son, Robert, had died when the ship on which he was a passenger went down in heavy weather off South Africa. According to reports, Robert was on his way to meet with Dutch Government officials to discuss the sugar industry in its colony of Java. All on board the Netherlands-owned ship were lost when the vessel went down. A few days later, Douglas admitted privately to Sarah that the loss of Robert had simplified the company's future. Now, in the event of Douglas's death, Cameron would inherit without risk of any challenge.

Days later and with mixed emotions Sarah boarded a vessel bound for Australia. Cameron refused to allow her to sail alone and accompanied her.

It was late in 1862 when Sarah arrived in the embryonic settlement of Mackay. After ensuring she was safely settled, Cameron returned to Glasgow... and only after receiving a solemn undertaking from Jimmy that he would keep watch over Sarah.

No time wasted; both Jimmy and Sarah applied to take up holdings along the south bank of the Pioneer River as soon as lands became available for selection. Although women were not entitled to apply for Selections, Sarah exploited her widow's status to circumvent the rule. Both hers and Jimmy's applications were successful. Then it was full-on hard work completing necessary improvements on their blocks and within the specified timeframes as required under the conditions applying to their Selections.

Then, it was 1864, and a year of surprises followed. Late in the year, a letter from Cameron told Sarah he would again be in Mackay by January of the following year. To further compound the surprise, it was only late in December when he arrived. He was accompanied by Philip Robert McCabe Wallace, whom Sarah learned was the illegitimate son of Sarah's one-time best friend in Glasgow, Jane McCabe, and Sarah's husband, Robert. Philip was conceived in 1843 while Robert was back in Glasgow developing a strategy for the disposal of their Caribbean plantations. Jane brought her illegitimate child up alone and far away from Glasgow. Towards the end of 1862 and shortly before her untimely death, Jane gave Philip a letter to deliver to Douglas Wallace. The letter explained Philip's parentage. Douglas accepted the nineteen year old lad as his grandson... and then set about taking the necessary steps to attach the Wallace surname to the lad.

While Philip's story and his arrival in Mackay were a shock, Sarah welcomed him as her stepson. It was while Jimmy showed Philip around the settlement that Cameron proposed to Sarah. On their return, Jimmy and Philip were shocked to find Cameron and Sarah in a firm embrace.

Chapter 1

Wedding Plans

"So, how do you go about getting married in this place?" Cameron asked, not for the first time over the last few days. "I can't say I've noticed a Kirk anywhere in the settlement."

As night dropped its heavy, dark cloak over the landscape, Jimmy Fraser sat smoking his pipe alongside his current housemate, Cameron Wallace. Relaxed under the awning at the front of Jimmy's house, for some minutes, they felt no need for conversation, but after a day of heavy showers, the leaden sky and moisture-laden breeze warned of more rain to come.

Then, "More rain tonight…," Cameron murmured, breaking the companionable silence shared with his longtime friend as they drained their wee bevies of rum.

"Aye, the monsoon season has announced its arrival. Although, now some time removed from the Caribbean, neither of us has forgotten what tropical wet seasons are like. If you had forgotten, today's heavy showers were a timely reminder."

"Hmm… I do remember, and that's what concerns me. I don't want to find myself out here and cut off from town by the rain, not until I've sorted out how I am to be married. If there is no Kirk in the settlement yet, how does one go about getting married in this village?" Cameron repeated.

"Ah, well, it's like everything else in this new world we have chosen to inhabit. Nothing is easy."

"That's not exactly helpful, Jimmy. I plan to go into town tomorrow to search for answers. Sarah has left it to me to organise our wedding and I know she is becoming anxious about my lack of progress on the matter. It's not that we want a big, fancy event. We just want to do the 'right thing' and make it legal before… before… you know what I mean."

A further period of silence ensued as Cameron, and presumably also Jimmy, gave the matter some thought.

"I suppose…," Cameron began again hesitantly. "I suppose I could arrange for the captain of the Wallace vessel currently in port to conduct the ceremony."

"Aye, I suppose you could, but it would *nae* be legal, and the captain probably would refuse. He can legally marry you only when out on the high seas."

"Okay, so we will be on the ship when it leaves port, and he can marry us as soon as we are out to sea and heading south."

"Cameron, I appreciate your predicament, but you need to think it through a bit more. If you leave port on your next ship out of here as you suggest, where do you plan to leave the ship again? And, how would you then return here with your new bride? Or do you plan to continue to Scotland and maybe spend a honeymoon in Glasgow before returning here?"

"What? No, of course not… And Sarah would never agree to such an arrangement. All right, come on, Jimmy, any useful suggestions would be most welcome about now, thanks."

"*Dinna fash* yourself about it, lad. Tomorrow, we will ride into town and make enquiries at the courthouse," Jimmy replied as he tapped out his pipe after realising it was no longer alight.

"I don't know, Jimmy. Maybe it would be better if Sarah and I travelled north to Port Denison to be married. That place has been established longer, so I'm guessing they might already have a Kirk there."

"You will do no such thing… not until we've explored other options first. We will take a wagon into town tomorrow to find out what can be done here in this settlement before you come up with any more rash ideas."

The arrival of the next big shower on the tin roof curtailed any further discussion.

Cameron stood in the doorway, watching the heavy rain create huge puddles outside the house and along the track out to the road. He felt sure Jimmy would refuse to go into town in such conditions and would advocate waiting for a fine day before they set forth. He soon found he had sold his friend short.

"Well, don't just stand there, lad. If we are going into town, you had better put on an oil skin, unless you intend turning up at the courthouse looking like a drowned rabbit. While you deal with that, I'll hitch up the wagon. Do you need to confer with Sarah before we head out?"

"No, and it's as well I don't. She would only argue against our making the trip today."

"Aye, she's a wise woman that intended wife of yours. Get a move on then, or it will be time to come home before we've even left."

After sitting in silence for some time as they bumped and splashed their way into what passed for 'town' in the embryonic settlement on the south bank of the Pioneer River, Cameron's curiosity won out over his better judgement.

"Why are we going to the courthouse? Surely, the answers I need are available from the locals. Someone like the publican probably could provide the information I need."

"Lots of people might offer you advice, but why wouldn't you go to the place where you know their information will be accurate and legal? Trust me, Cameron. I know what I'm doing."

"It's obvious you know more than you are telling me, so why aren't you sharing all of it?"

Jimmy sighed. This was going to be a long ride into town. "Because I don't *know* much. All I know is that it has something to do with a visiting cleric, and the courthouse is where you need to find answers to your questions. Now, when we get there, just ask that basic question about how to get married and then listen to whatever they tell you. It will be best not to make suggestions about all the other alternatives you have mentioned to me. Keep it simple; don't complicate matters."

While not happy about being spoken to like a child, Cameron took on board Jimmy's comments. After all, it wasn't hard to understand how Jimmy couldn't possibly understand how desperate he was to arrange his wedding. It turned out Jimmy was right. The courthouse was indeed the right place to ask questions.

Since 1863, Anglican church services were held in the courthouse whenever Bishop Tufnell was able to visit the settlement, and he conducted marriage and baptismal ceremonies while he was in town. The Bishop was expected to be in town in five days' time. If it suited Cameron and his bride-to-be, they could be married at ten o'clock on the morning of the Bishop's visit. Paperwork needed to be completed and lodged at the courthouse in advance of the event. Cameron was urged to complete the necessary documentation while he was there.

After being handed the forms to fill in, Cameron was directed to a small table and chair in one corner of the room where he could attend to the paperwork in comfortable privacy. Jimmy peered over Cameron's shoulder as he perused the paperwork.

"Will you be able to fill in all that information?" Jimmy whispered. "I mean, do you know all those details?"

"As soon as we decided to get married, I gathered together all the documents I thought might be necessary to organise the event. So, yes, I think I should have everything I need."

Continuing to stand at Cameron's shoulder, Jimmy scrutinised all the groom's details as Cameron wrote them. The groom's part of the forms completed, Cameron sat up, flexed his shoulders, and then, on the remaining part of the document, wrote in the bride's name: Sarah. He was about to write her surname when Jimmy grabbed his hand.

"Erskine… Write 'Erskine'," he hissed at Cameron.

"But, that's not…."

"Write Erskine. Don't fuss, just do it. I'll explain later."

Cameron shrugged and did as he was told. There was something about the urgency – the insistence – in Jimmy's voice that persuaded him.

Once the paperwork was completed, handed in, and received the nod of approval, the two men made their way to the pub in search of lunch. The first topic of conversation as soon as they sat down at a table came as no surprise to Jimmy.

"What was all that nonsense regarding Sarah's surname? Erskine was her maiden name, but she became 'Wallace' when she married my brother."

"Aye, I know all that, but I'm not so sure about some of the Rules of the Marriage Act of 1835, or if there has been a new Act with different rules since then. The Act I know about contains rules about who can marry whom. I don't really know or understand them, but I believe it includes something about a widow not being allowed to marry his sister-in-law."

"Sarah is not my sister-in-law. Well, I don't think she is. She is my brother's widow, but I don't think that makes her my sister-in-law, does it?"

"As I said, I don't know those rules, and I'm no expert on such matters. But I thought it wise to use Sarah's maiden name to avoid awkward questions that the same surname for both of you might raise."

"Good thinking, old friend, and besides, in this colony, we are a long way from Scotland. I doubt anyone here has the time or inclination to check on such trivialities."

"Well, now that we know you are to be married in five days and all the necessary documentation has been submitted, how is this event to play out?" Jimmy watched Cameron wrinkle his brow and shake his head in confusion before offering a reply.

"I'm not sure I understand the question. As you stated, we are to be married at the courthouse in five days. What else is there to worry about?"

"Right you are, lad. That's the main detail taken care of, but what about the rest of the event? Is the wedding to be followed by some sort of feast, and where might that take place? Who are you inviting to this wedding? And, the big question: what are Sarah's thoughts on how her wedding day should be?"

"Oh, God, I had nae given the rest of it even a passing thought. As we are to be married at mid-morning, perhaps a lunch to follow would be appropriate. But where to have it? In town or at the property....?"

"Perhaps this hotel might lay on a lunch for guests," Jimmy suggested. "You could organise that, too, while we are here in town, but you will need to tell them how many guests they will be feeding on the day."

"Since I don't know who we will be inviting or how many of them will come, all I could give the publican would be an approximation of the numbers. Although, I suppose I should draw up a rough guest list anyway."

With prompting and suggestions from Jimmy, a list proved less difficult than Cameron expected.

"Let's see now. There would be Sarah's housemaid, Orla, Sarah's stepson, Philip, and me of course. Then there's Roddy McDonald, who built Sarah's house, and his wife, and a couple of the neighbours and their wives. Who else can you think of who Sarah might want to invite?" Jimmy asked.

"We would have to invite Sarah's gardener, Cheng Li. I think he might come to the courthouse, but I'm not so sure about the luncheon. He's more likely to want to spend the extra time in town chatting to his own people before returning to the property. Ah, and there are another couple I feel obliged to invite: the captain and his wife on the Wallace vessel currently moored in the river. It doesn't matter if they don't want to attend the wedding, but the luncheon might compensate for the few extra days in port that I've delayed their departure to allow Philip to attend the wedding."

"It will still be early after the courthouse stage of proceedings is over," Jimmy suggested. "Perhaps it might be best to ask the publican for an early luncheon. That way, everyone could come back here to the pub for a celebratory dram before sitting down to lunch."

After further deliberation, it was agreed to book a luncheon for fourteen, or maybe fifteen, people to be served at about 11.30AM after guests had enjoyed a drink.

"Well, lad, apart from a quick word to the publican about the catering on our way out, I think we have everything in place for the big day. Is there anything else we need to attend to before heading home?"

"No-o, I think we've covered everything," Cameron agreed but, after a moment's thought, changed his mind. "Uhmm… there is one other thing, but I will sort that out when I talk to the publican on my way out. Oh, and I should have a word to the captain of our ship before I leave town. If there is nothing more you need to do here, Jimmy, perhaps you might hitch the wagon while I organise things with the publican."

Jimmy was about to argue that he would wait with Cameron before realising Cameron did not want him hanging around while he discussed private matters with the publican.

Cameron looked exceedingly pleased with himself as he climbed up beside Jimmy on the wagon after speaking to the captain. Without comment, Jimmy flicked the reins, and the horses headed for home. They were outside the main town area before Jimmy spoke.

"So, no problems organising everything with the publican, I assume?" he asked.

"He saw no problems with anything I asked for. I will be able to assure Sarah everything is in place for our big day. I can't tell you what a load off my mind that is. I suppose my only disappointment about the day is that it will be so much a lesser event than a proper Scottish wedding would be – and to which Sarah might feel entitled. After all, there will be no pipers, a pub luncheon is not a major feast, and there will be no dancing afterwards."

"And, the 'no dancing' bit might be a good thing as far as me and Roddy are concerned," Jimmy chuckled. "There probably are some additional minor details you still need to work out with Sarah."

"What details? I think I have everything organised."

"Let's see. Both wagons will need to be in town on the big day, but who will ride in which wagon?"

"Sarah and I will go in Sarah's wagon, and Orla and Cheng Li can travel with you. I don't see a problem with that."

"Ah hah, see… You're forgetting a few protocols, my friend. On the day of the wedding, the groom is not supposed to see the bride before they are married. It's bad luck and all that. Even if you don't pay any regard to the superstition, a groom hanging around before the wedding is only going to be in the way.

There is another big thing I'm sure Sarah will acquaint you with. When will be the best time for the bride to go into town? I doubt she will be happy to ride into town on a wagon on the morning of her wedding, only to arrive looking a bit bedraggled. She is likely to prefer to spend the night before the wedding in town at the hotel. That means your wagon would need to go into town the previous afternoon … without you on board. Maybe Philip could take Sarah into town and spend the night at the pub as well or, instead, maybe on board your ship. You could accompany Orla, Cheng Li and me on my wagon the next morning."

"I see your point. And, it could be raining on the day. It will be hard enough for Sarah to move from the hotel to the courthouse without being soaked. She would not want to ride into town in such weather, and there is nothing fetching about an oilskin. As you say, Jimmy, there are a few points still to tidy up with Sarah."

The heavens opened up again as the men reached the outskirts of the township, making the trip home slow going. Huddled in their oilskins in a bid to remain as dry as possible made conversation difficult. Silence reigned between them until they were almost home, and a terrible thought occurred to Jimmy.

"Argh, Cameron, we have overlooked something important. What about a ring?"

"Not overlooked, Jimmy... taken care of well in advance. In the hopeful anticipation Sarah would accept my proposal, I purchased a ring prior to leaving Glasgow. I know she wasn't able to choose it, but at least we do have a ring.

It's a shame we will be so late arriving home tonight, Jimmy. It will be too late to apprise Sarah of the arrangements I put in place today. I will have to leave it until tomorrow."

Cameron was right. It was too late. Sarah's house was in darkness by the time the wagon drew up outside Jimmy's place. What Sarah didn't know as she went to bed that night was that, by the time she knew of Cameron's efforts, she would have less than four days left to prepare for the event.

Later, both men, feeling mellow and generally pleased with their morning's efforts, were settled under Jimmy's front awning when the next wave of heavy showers arrived. As they scrambled back inside to avoid becoming soaked, Cameron started to chuckle.

"First thing tomorrow, I'll go across to tell Sarah how little time she has to prepare for her wedding. That should prove entertaining for a moment or two."

Chapter 2

Marriage

Cameron timed his arrival so as to have breakfast with his bride-to-be, and his prediction the previous night was right. Sarah's reaction to his news about their forthcoming wedding did cause a brief panic. What would she wear? Who to invite? What remained to be organised? She fired what felt like a continuous barrage of questions at Cameron, later admitting some of them were not his to answer. This was a side of Sarah he had never seen before, and he was enjoying it.

Then, almost in desperation, she demanded, "There remains so much to do. What must I do first?"

"Invitations, Sarah… write out the invitations so they will be received in time."

"Right… Yes, invitations first – but who do I invite?"

Taking her by the hand, Cameron led Sarah to her small writing desk and motioned for her to ready herself with pen and paper before he recited the tentative list of invitees he and Jimmy had developed.

"You should add any others you would like to attend, but give me the number of names you add to the list. I gave the publican tentative numbers for the luncheon, but that can be amended if needed," Cameron told her.

"I'm not sure about Cheng Li," Sarah commented as she tapped the gardener's name on the list. "I'm unaware of his views on such matters as religious wedding ceremonies. I wouldn't want to place him in an awkward position by inviting him."

"He must be invited. It would be seen as a slur if you do not. Speak to him about it when you hand him his invitation. Explain that, while it's not compulsory, you would welcome his attendance. Jimmy and I discussed the matter and agreed that

14

he might see fit to attend the courthouse, but probably would decline lunch in favour of pursuing personal interests."

"Of course, you are right. Cheng Li is as much a part of this household as Orla. I now realise it was remiss of me not to have gained a better understanding of his beliefs and his culture before this.

I will pen the invitations immediately so they can be delivered as soon as possible. There is one name on the list I wanted to ask about: Philip. Will he and his ship still be here at the time of the wedding? I would be disappointed if my stepson couldn't attend."

"Once all the arrangements were in place, I spoke to the captain before leaving town. I have delayed the ship's departure to allow Philip and Captain Billings and his wife to attend the wedding. Again, I'm not sure whether the Billings will attend the courthouse, but I don't doubt they will accept the luncheon invitation.

By the way, where is the youngest member of the Wallace family this morning? I expected he would be at breakfast with you."

"No, last night, he requested an early breakfast. He is spending the morning with Jimmy. I think the intention is for Philip to learn a little more about what it is we do here."

"Right… I'll leave you now to deal with the invitations while I go in search of Philip to tell him of our wedding arrangements, and I hope Jimmy hasn't already done so."

Cameron, with Philip in tow, returned to share morning tea with Sarah. Any thoughts he had of spending the rest of the morning sitting on the verandah watching the rain come down were dashed when Sarah shoved a pile of envelopes into his hand.

"You might like to deliver these before lunchtime. Don't worry if it takes a while. We'll wait lunch until you return," Sarah told Cameron.

Then, as Cameron struggled into his already damp oilskin, Sarah turned her attention to Philip.

"I assume Cameron has acquainted you with our wedding arrangements?" Philip nodded, and Sarah continued. "Good. Now tell me, how was your morning with Jimmy."

"Oh, so interesting. Jimmy is so knowledgeable about the sugar cane industry. He showed me where you will be planting sugarcane in the near future to grow it in preparation for planting as a crop the following year. I didn't want to show my ignorance, but I am a bit curious about the pair of you being so interested in sugarcane when Jimmy tells me there is so little interest so far amongst property holders in this area. Can you, please explain why you and Jimmy, and maybe a couple of other planters around here, have such an interest in starting this industry? Does it relate to the time he spent in the Caribbean? And, did sugarcane have something to do with your coming here in the first place?"

"It is fair to say the Caribbean had everything to do with my moving to this country. The Wallace family was friends with Jimmy when we all lived in the Caribbean. I lost touch with him for some time until a chance meeting in Glasgow. He was putting his sugar industry knowledge to good use in Java when a chance trip to Australia excited him. He saw a better opportunity to exercise his industry knowledge in a fledgling sugar industry being established south of here. But, he also recognised that where they were trying to grow sugarcane at that time was not the best growing area."

"How did he get to hear about the attempt to start a new sugar industry in this country?"

"On a visit to his sister in Scotland, he took the opportunity to visit the various suppliers of the latest sugar industry equipment and technology so as to better serve his clients in Java. In talking with those suppliers, he learned of attempts at an industry in Australia and saw that as a better long-term proposition. Although, once he arrived here, he set up as an advisor to the new industry in the southern colony of New South Wales, it was the land up here that caught his attention. He believed the land

and climate here were ideal sugar country, and he moved here as soon as possible.

Prior to that, when I spoke with him in Glasgow, he quoted a philosophy that struck a chord with me: *when an opportunity presents, seize it.* From my conversation with Jimmy, I realised Australia was an opportunity for me to make something of my life… And so, here I am."

"Now you are here, have acquired land and stocked it, are you still convinced about the future of the sugar industry here? I suppose what bothers me is that there is no industry yet. What's the point in growing a crop of this stuff if you can't do anything with it?"

"Well, rumour has it that the government is keen to see a sugar industry established in this country. We are hopeful that it will come to fruition, and major opportunities will open up for Jimmy and me if it does."

"And, should an industry become established here at some time in the future, might it be to the benefit of the Wallace Shipping Line?" Philip gave Sarah a mock innocent questioning look as he posed the question.

"Ah, your question confirms for me that you are indeed now a fully-fledged member of the Wallace family. Yes, should a sugar industry be established here, it would present opportunities for the Wallace's shipping operations. Since the decline of opportunities with the American colonies, the family's shipping is now a Pacific region-based operation. Hence, it's beneficial to have Cameron running that shipping from here."

Philip appeared to lapse into thoughtful silence for a few moments before sharing those thoughts. "Before talking to Jimmy this morning, I thought starting a sugar industry was no more involved than a matter of planting bits of cane and waiting for it to grow. Now I realise it appears to require significant knowledge of more than just how to plant sugarcane and which varieties to choose. How does anyone go about learning this? How did Jimmy and the Wallace family learn about it?"

"You are right about the industry being more complicated than just planting bits of cane. As for how people go about gaining the requisite knowledge, it's like everything else. It comes with experience. The experience of having been involved with every aspect of the industry, and through that, gaining an understanding of all the intricacies involved."

"So, did Jimmy and Cameron also acquire the knowledge from their experience in the Caribbean industry?"

"Douglas Wallace established two plantations in the Caribbean and the children grew up on those plantations. Then, when the offspring reached adulthood, the parents returned to Glasgow, leaving the two sons to manage the plantations while Douglas set about establishing his business empire in Scotland. Your father, Robert, as the elder son, managed their overall Caribbean operations. He lived on and had direct management of the larger of the two plantations. Cameron was responsible for the smaller plantation, which also was where their sugar mill was situated.

So, over their many years in the Caribbean, the sons gained a sound knowledge of not only the agricultural side of the industry, but Cameron also understood and was responsible for their milling operations. Jimmy Fraser already had spent some time on plantations in the Caribbean before coming to work for many years as an overseer on the Wallace plantations."

Cameron had been right when he claimed Philip was a bright lad, and Sarah could see why Douglas had been keen to have the lad enter the family business. Although it was something she would never mention to Philip at this stage, Sarah couldn't help wondering if, at sometime in the future, Philip also might consider relocating to join her and Cameron in this new country. She had no doubt she would revisit this morning's conversation with Philip many times in the coming months.

For Sarah, those four days until her wedding flew past in a blur. As originally planned by Cameron and Jimmy, Philip loaded Sarah and her trunk onto her wagon and drove her into the hotel where she would spend the night before her wedding. Although tempted to spend the night on board the ship, Philip elected to stay in the hotel so as to keep an eye on his stepmother and be available should she require assistance with anything.

Early in February 1865, and despite the monsoonal wet season, the gods still chose to smile on Sarah and Cameron's wedding day. Although the sky remained leaden and threatening, the rain stayed away until early evening. It remained dry for most of the day, allowing guests to attend the wedding and travel home later without being drenched. Jimmy, who considered himself *au fait* in such matters, saw it as a good omen regarding the future of the marriage.

The hotel provided an excellent luncheon spread of cold cuts and salad, including a wonderful bowl of heart-of-palm salad. It resulted in guests lingering at the hotel longer than anticipated, and then only making a move to depart when they realised there was barely enough time for them to arrive home before dark. When Jimmy, Orla and Philip walked out into the pub's horse yard, they found a morose-looking Cheng Li waiting on Jimmy's wagon. He had been ready to leave as instructed and then spent about an hour waiting before the others finally appeared.

It was a sheepish looking newly married couple who dined alone as they shared the hotel's dining room with a few other patrons that evening. After finishing their meal, no time was wasted in abandoning the dining room in favour of their room.

Next morning, after an early breakfast, the newly married couple were on their way home to start their new life together on Sarah's Selection.

"My first task today is to move my belongings from Jimmy's place and into your house. Perhaps Philip might spend his last twenty-four hours here ensconced in my former room in Jimmy's house," Cameron announced as the wagon ploughed through the puddles, spraying muddy water in all directions.

Orla had been busy in her mistress' absence. With a little help from Philip and Cheng Li, a large pitcher occupied pride of place in the centre of the table in the front room. It was filled with sprigs of poinciana flowers and other flower heads from some of the plants in Cheng Li's vegetable garden. Someone had created a 'welcome home' sign and hung it along the wall opposite the front door.

"Perhaps a pot of tea might be nice before we move on with the rest of our day," Sarah suggested to Orla.

With the kettle having been put on the fire the moment Orla saw the wagon coming along the track, only a few minutes later, Orla carried in a tray laden with cups and saucers and a plate of freshly baked scones. As she turned to return to the kitchen for the teapot, Sarah called after her, "Best bring another cup when you come back. Jimmy has just arrived."

None of the four people indulging in morning tea appeared in any hurry to move on with the rest of the day. It came as no surprise when the prime topic of conversation was about 'the future' and who planned to do what in the next little while.

"That's easy," Philip announced. "I'll be joining my ship tomorrow to return to Glasgow. What about you, Jimmy? What big plans do you have?" he asked, although he suspected he already knew the answer.

"We-ell, I believe I am booked on a ship that sails tomorrow night. So, I will be accompanying you, young Philip, as far as Java."

"Java?" Sarah echoed. "Why Java, Jimmy? You haven't changed your mind about establishing a sugar industry here, have you? I know we talked about a trip to Java, but I didn't expect it to be so soon."

"Nothing has changed, Sarah, except perhaps the timing. Cameron, perhaps you might be available to take Philip and me to board our ship tomorrow?"

"Of course… Sarah and I were going to take Philip into town and say goodbye to him. So, you can join us on our wagon."

"What will happen to your place while you are gone, Jimmy?" Philip asked.

"Cameron and my headman will keep an eye on things while I'm gone. Cameron, if you would keep an extra eye, please, on that small corner of my land that needs to have the clearing finished and then be worked up ready for planting." Cameron nodded, and Jimmy continued. "I made it my priority today to start some of the workers on clearing it."

"How long will you be gone, Jimmy?" Sarah asked.

"I anticipate spending a week in Java before returning on the next Wallace vessel bound for Mackay. And, while we are on this subject, Sarah, have you given any further thought to which part of your land might be put under sugarcane when the time comes? I know there is plenty of time before anything needs to happen on your land, but we do have to plan ahead."

"Forgive me for speaking out of turn, please, Sarah, but it appears to me all your land already is being used for other purposes. Where are you going to find spare land for cane without robbing some of your grazing areas?" Philip asked.

"Good question, Philip," Cameron interjected, "the answer to which I also am interested to hear."

"It is not my intention to disrupt that which is already in place on my block. But, if the need arises, there is a small area of pasture I might sacrifice. As Jimmy said, there is plenty of time before I need to make such a decision. In the meantime, it depends on what happens in another direction, whether any such sacrifice might be necessary."

"Perhaps you might care to expand on that," Jimmy suggested.

"Yes, please, Sarah. I also would like to know more about what you are hinting at," Cameron added.

"There is some suggestion that the block across the road from this Selection might become available for reselection again in the near future." Sarah reluctantly answered.

"Tell us more, please." Cameron's tone of voice suggested it was more of a command than an invitation.

"Rumour has it that the couple who selected that block failed their last inspection. They hadn't completed the necessary improvements, and already had been a little behind at the previous inspection."

"In such cases, the selectors are usually given some period of grace in which to complete the necessary work before a further inspection is carried out," Jimmy said.

"Ye-es, that is the practice," Sarah agreed. "But word has it that, in this case, there is little prospect of any further progress being made before the next inspection. Failure of that inspection will result in the Selection being forfeited and the selectors being forced to walk off the land."

"Hmm… Isn't there a loophole that's sometimes employed in such situations?" Jimmy asked as he gave Sarah a hard look. Sarah confirmed he was correct.

"Am I to understand you propose investigating whatever that loophole is?" Cameron asked.

"Before I can answer that question, I would need to learn more about what is possible and how it might be applied. I'm just not sure who to ask about it," Sarah admitted. "Of course, I could do nothing and sit patiently until what appears inevitable happens, and then try my luck in securing the property."

"You want more land…?" Philip asked in disbelief. "How much more do you need, and how expensive will it be? Argh… I do apologise. That was most indelicate of me."

"Sarah, we need to discuss this matter later. All I will say at this juncture is that I do not wish to see you become financially embarrassed. You have achieved too much here to risk losing it all." Cameron's concern was evident in his voice and body language.

"While your business decisions are none of my business, Sarah, in this instance, I feel compelled to agree with Cameron," Jimmy told her.

"Gentlemen, thank you for your concern, but I can assure you this property is safe. I have already taken the necessary steps and my Selection is now freehold. If anything should come of my interest in the land across the road from here, I would seek to lease it for the remainder of the ten years before freeholding that block as well. Jimmy, if I am successful in acquiring that land, you are free to initiate discussions if you should be interested in the use of some portion of it."

A stunned silence descended over the gathering and only ended when Orla came to clear away after morning tea before laying the table for lunch. "Excuse me, Mrs Wallce, how many will there be for lunch?" she asked, eyeing off Jimmy and Philip.

"We will be four, I think, thanks, Orla… Unless you have to be elsewhere, Jimmy?"

Straight after lunch, Jimmy and Philip returned to Jimmy's house to make preparations for their departure the following day. The four would meet again at Sarah's table for a farewell dinner that evening.

An emotional day followed for Sarah. Jimmy had been her rock since her arrival in the new colony and now he wouldn't be around for a while. It wasn't as though she couldn't manage on her own. After all, what did she have to do apart from ensuring everyone else did the job they were supposed to do? And she wouldn't be alone. Cameron would be with her. While she loved him dearly, and he had become the focus of her life, he wasn't Jimmy. Her bond with Jimmy was something different, something secure and supportive while not being intrusive or controlling. He made no demands on her, but was always there when she needed advice and in times of trouble.

Her feelings of insecurity – feelings of loss – at Jimmy's departure were not something she could share with Cameron. Cameron had always been there for her as well, but in a different way and he would be deeply hurt were he to learn of her insecurity at Jimmy's departure.

Further compounding her despair that day was Philip's departure. He was only her stepson, but Sarah was fond of him from the moment they met, and they had grown close in the short time he was with them. Now, he, too, was about to sail away. Would she ever see him again? They had agreed to correspond but, somehow, she felt letters would not provide her with sufficient insight into his life and how he was progressing with his transition from young lad into manhood.

Although their ship didn't sail until around midnight, Sarah's wagon, with its four passengers on board, arrived in town at about lunchtime. The publican at their favourite hotel welcomed them into his dining room. Sarah noted, mercifully, that they were the only lunchtime diners that day. It would not be so embarrassing should her resolve to remain strong crumble at the last minute.

While Sarah remained somewhat withdrawn, conversation over lunch was non-stop and excited. The ship they were to sail on was to spend a couple of days in port once they reached Java before heading home to Glasgow. Jimmy offered to take Philip with him when he went in search of sugar cane to bring back to the colony. The prospect of exploring somewhere new and exotic had Philip almost bursting with excitement. Jimmy was also excited – although a little more subdued than Philip – about taking the first positive step towards their new sugar industry venture.

Lunch stretched on until almost three o'clock, only coming to an abrupt end when Cameron realised how late it was.

"Come on, gentlemen, we need to see you on board your ship," he announced. "If Sarah and I don't head home soon, we will be finishing the trip in the dark… and it looks as though there will be more rain tonight."

It was some comfort to Sarah that, as they shared a final hug, their parting also appeared to cause Philip some distress. She didn't want him to be upset, but somehow, it was comforting to know he was sorry to be leaving her.

After watching the two men march up the gangplank and on board, Cameron and Sarah climbed aboard their wagon and headed home. They had travelled some way before Sarah felt sufficiently in control of her emotions to be able to speak.

"How long is Jimmy likely to be away, Cameron?"

"Are you concerned about what his absence might mean for the properties?"

"No, of course not. Everyone knows what they have to do, and between us, we will ensure everything continues as it should. But, when Jimmy returns, the sugar cane he brings back will need to be planted immediately. It will already be distressed by the voyage. We want to save as many stalks as possible."

"Yes, that will be a concern. I expect Jimmy will be away for maybe five or six weeks at the most. I'm sure we will manage splendidly in his absence."

Sarah knew there was nothing to worry about, but she continued to sit glumly perched high up on the wagon next to Cameron for the rest of the journey.

Chapter 3

Surprise Announcement

Over dinner that night, Cameron revealed that the first Wallace vessel to call at Java since Jimmy's arrival there was due to moor in the Pioneer River tomorrow.

"As part of my duties, I will meet the ship when it arrives, and if Jimmy is on board, I'll return here with him and whatever he has brought with him. Exactly when we will arrive home depends on a number of factors, but it might be late, and we may even have to spend the night in town."

"Am I not to be included in your arrangements?" Sarah demanded.

"I hadn't thought on your accompanying me but, if you wish to ride into town with me, there will be plenty of room on the wagon, as long as there isn't too much shopping to bring home with us. We likely will have Jimmy and a supply of sugar cane stalks to fit onto the wagon. If you have much to bring home, it might prove prudent to take both wagons into town tomorrow."

"What I might wish to load onto the wagon will not be a problem… And before you mention it, nor will staying in town for the night be a concern."

As they made their way along beside the river, Sarah expected to see the ship moored and Jimmy pacing the deck impatiently as he awaited their arrival. That wasn't the case. Sarah stayed on the wagon while Cameron went to make enquiries. He returned after about fifteen minutes.

"The vessel is not expected to enter the river until sometime between two and three o'clock. By the time they have tied up and unloaded, it will be quite late, too late to return home tonight. In the meantime, we might see if Mine Host at our favourite hotel has a table for two for a late lunch."

While they didn't deliberately dawdle over their meal, by the time they left the hotel to return to the river, it had just gone two o'clock. As they drove out of the hotel's horse yard, Cameron said, "We shouldn't have too long to wait to see the ship come up the river."

They didn't have to wait at all. The vessel was being made fast as Cameron drove the wagon onto the dock. Jimmy waved to them from the deck as the gangplank was being lowered. Moments later, he was standing beside the wagon.

"Might be in for a bit of a wait, I'm afraid," he told them. "The boat has a hold full of cargo to unload and, as the cane travelled as deck cargo, it might take them a while to get around to unloading it."

"Let's see how it goes before we become too concerned," Cameron suggested. But, shortly before three o'clock, he went in search of the captain to persuade him to free up a couple of men to unload the cane – now.

Not easily persuaded, it wasn't until Cameron 'pulled rank' and emphasised the delicate nature of the cane that the captain agreed to send two men to unload the deck cargo. It was almost four o'clock by the time the last of the ropes securing the cane on the wagon was tied off. While Cameron and Sarah climbed onto the wagon, Jimmy checked the ropes yet again before climbing up to join the others.

"Right… Let's go and see about a couple of rooms at the hotel," Cameron said as Jimmy climbed onto the wagon.

"If it is all the same to everyone, I'd rather head for home," Jimmy suggested.

"Oh… All right, if you insist, Jimmy," Cameron replied, "but it is becoming a bit late to be setting off for home. Is there a reason you're anxious to be home?"

"If we stay in town tonight, by the time we are home tomorrow, most of the day will be lost. There will be little of that cane in the ground by nightfall. If we spend tonight at home, an early start in the morning can be made on planting the cane and the work finished by the end of the day. That way, the cane will not suffer much further stress before it is planted."

When Orla saw the lantern coming along the track, she rushed to move the stew she had prepared back onto the fire to reheat. A few minutes later, Sarah strode into the kitchen and announced there would be three for dinner… and the stew smelled divine. About twenty minutes later, hungry and tired, the men joined Sarah in the dining room.

"Thanks for the dinner invitation, Sarah," Jimmy said as he wiped his plate clean with a thick wedge of bread. "It would have been slim pickings at my place tonight, and that stew was just what was needed after not a lot to eat onboard that ship. It seems they weren't able to take on all the provisions they had intended before leaving Java."

"I must speak more with you about the provisioning issue at Java, but that is a matter for another time. We've all had a big day, and I suspect none of us wishes to be out of bed for too long tonight," Cameron said.

"Aye, Cameron. It is time this old-timer laid his weary head down to rest. Thank you again for dinner, Sarah, but I'll be off home now. See you in the morning bright and early, Cameron."

Early next morning, the business of growing sugarcane began in earnest. The canes Jimmy brought home from Java were cut into roughly footlong lengths, each length containing at least one joint from which a plant would shoot in due course. While horses ploughed a shallow furrow, several workers followed behind on foot, dropping the billets of cane into the furrow. Off to one side of the small block and enjoying a warm feeling of satisfaction, Cameron and Jimmy stood watching the planting progress.

"I'm a bit surprised Sarah hasn't come to witness this for herself," Jimmy confided to Cameron. "It has been so long in the planning and been discussed so often, I felt sure she would join us here on the sideline this morning."

"She showed no inclination to come and watch," Cameron said rather flatly. "Once we start seeing green shoots come up out of the ground, I'm sure it will re-ignite her enthusiasm for this project."

"No doubt she will be wanting to go to the church service on Sunday," Jimmy suggested. Cameron looked confused, so Jimmy explained. "This Sunday is April 16, is it not – Easter Sunday? I overheard some of the crew talking about it. It seems the town is abuzz with the news that the Bishop is hoping to conduct a service here over Easter, probably on Easter Sunday."

"Oh, I see. No, I don't believe Sarah plans to attend the service. Well, she hasn't made mention of it at all. Actually, I'm worried about Sarah. She says she is okay but, to me, she doesn't seem to have been well lately. I admit I'm probably not in a position to judge what the situation is. The shipping business has kept me in town a lot lately."

Jimmy nodded knowingly, but kept his own counsel. It was not his position to comment on what was happening in Cameron's marriage, but if Sarah were ill, he would be as equally concerned as Cameron. He realised Cameron had only paused for a moment before continuing to discuss Sarah,

"If I'm honest, Jimmy, I would say it is almost a relief to be spending so much time in town. Sarah has been difficult to live with for weeks now, and civil conversation has almost become a thing of the past. It has become impossible to have a reasonable conversation on any subject."

With a silly grin plastered across his face, Jimmy asked, "What have you been up to, lad? What have you done, eh?" But he allowed the matter to drop when Cameron had no answers and appeared genuinely at a loss about it.

Easter came and went without as much as a ripple on the flow of life on Sarah and Jimmy's selections. Occasional light showers of rain kept everyone hopeful for a good 'strike' from the recent planting of cane on the small area of Jimmy's block.

One morning, about a month after Easter, Sarah was up earlier than usual. Over breakfast, she announced she would be taking the wagon into town for the day.

"I'll drive you. There are a couple of matters I could attend to while I'm in town today," Cameron offered.

"Why do you need to take care of them today? Could you put it off until tomorrow?"

Something of a debate ensued for a few moments as Cameron tried, not too successfully, to smooth down the feathers he appeared to have ruffled. But Sarah was adamant she was going alone.

"There is shopping I wish to do, and it could take a while. I don't need you hanging about all day and making me feel as though I need to rush through what I have to do. If you must go into town today, ask Jimmy if you may borrow his wagon for the day."

With no room to move on the matter and no real need to go into town that day, defeated, Cameron slunk off nextdoor to Jimmy for consolation.

"For God's sake, lad. *Dinna fash* yourself about it. Sarah is a capable and independent woman. She doesn't need you to be getting in her way. She probably plans to visit her dressmaker or do some other womanly-type thing while she is in town, as well as whatever shopping she needs to do. You don't need any part of that. Think yourself lucky you have been excluded." Later, Jimmy would discover how insightful his words were.

Although Sarah did a little shopping before leaving town to back up her story to Cameron, shopping was not the reason for her trip to town that day. A comment in passing by Cameron a couple of weeks after Easter had captured Sarah's attention and stayed with her:

Our Pacific operations have picked up a secondary source of income. As more people move into this region, more are travelling on our vessels as paying passengers. For example, one of our ships that will spend a few days in port here has a doctor on board. He's on his way to work with the natives on one of the Pacific islands.

"It would be worthwhile if someone managed to persuade him to remain here when the ship sails again. The settlement is in need of a doctor," Sarah had said.

"That's true, but at least we have one here while the ship is in port. He has arranged a room at a hotel and will see patients during the few days the ship is in port."

Armed with that information, Sarah's 'shopping' trip became about something other than shopping. It was in the hope of seeing the doctor. When she made enquiries about an appointment, she was surprised to be told she would be able to see the doctor 'in a few minutes'. Sceptical about what a 'few minutes' might amount to, she sat nervously in the chair provided outside the doctor's room. Her fear that someone might see her there was ill-founded. She saw not a soul, and it was only after sitting there for a couple of minutes that the doctor ushered her into his make-shift consulting room.

Stunned but to some extent reassured after visiting the doctor, Sarah hurried out of the hotel and across the street to the general store to give her 'shopping' story credibility. After purchasing a few items for the kitchen, Sarah turned her attention to what amounted to the haberdashery corner of the store. She added several items of sewing paraphernalia and several yards of fine white cotton fabric to the foodstuffs she already had purchased, and told the storekeeper she would return with her wagon to collect it all.

About half an hour later, after the lad at the store had loaded her purchases onto the wagon, Sarah was on her way home. It's as well the horses knew their way home. For the whole trip, Sarah's mind was in turmoil. She was vaguely surprised when she discovered she was already halfway along the track to the homestead.

It took her a few days to come to terms with the news she had been given in town that day, but she knew the time had come to share it with Cameron… But when and how to go about it? After much deliberation, she realised there was no perfect time, and she told herself she must do it as soon as he returned from his current trip to town. After dinner that evening, Cameron announced he might go across to update Jimmy on the rumours circulating in town.

"No. Please, Cameron, leave that until tomorrow. Come and sit with me a while. I have something I wish to discuss with you."

Cameron acquiesced but felt the tension mounting in him as he made his way out to sit on the verandah with Sarah. After the way his wife had been for so many weeks, he had no doubts the conversation Sarah wanted to have would amount to nothing more than the delivery of bad news. As soon as they were comfortably settled, and before her courage deserted her, Sarah launched into the discussion they needed to have.

"Dearest Cameron, I need to start this conversation with a confession," she began, and Cameron felt his grip tighten on the armrests of his chair. "While I did shop when I went into town a few days ago, shopping wasn't the reason I went to town. I took advantage of the fact there was a doctor in town for a few days and went to see him."

"Argh, Sarah, I knew something was wrong. You haven't been yourself for days. We must face whatever the doctor told you together, no matter how bad the news. Please tell me what he discovered and what you have been trying to deal with on your own since that trip."

"Well, my Love, he didn't tell me anything I didn't already know. He simply confirmed it for me. Cameron, I am with child."

"What?... What are you saying?"

"We are going to be parents. By my reckoning, we should be welcoming a baby into our midst around mid-November." Stunned, Cameron sat blinking at Sarah for a moment before she said quietly, "Please, Cameron, say something. I know it is a shock, but please say something."

"I'm stunned, too stunned to speak. This is wonderful news. I can't wait to tell my father. He will be beside himself at the news of another grandchild."

"Perhaps you should wait for a while before sharing our news with Douglas. We don't want him to be disappointed if something should go wrong."

"What could go wrong? Did the doctor say something to give you cause for concern? Don't hold back, Sarah. If there is something, I, too, need to know about it."

"No, the doctor didn't say anything to cause concern, but I am old, Cameron. I had accepted I would never have children and that the reason we never had a child was my fault, not Robert's. After all, Philip is proof the fault did not lie with Robert. If more proof is needed, it appears there is plenty to be found on Java."

"You are not too old. That's rubbish. The fact that it has happened proves you are not too old. I refuse to have negative thoughts about what will be a wonderful event in our lives happening later this year. Sarah, what are you concerned about? What do you think might go wrong?"

"That you would ask that of me comes as a surprise, particularly after your loss of Elizabeth and your baby son following a difficult birth. I do not want to put you through that again. My age must count against me. If childbirth can be so risky for someone so much younger, what are the chances of survival for my child and myself? And all of that is based on the supposition we will still be expecting a birth in November, and that all has gone well during the rest of these intervening months."

"This is an exciting time. A time for celebration, not for dark thoughts. The past is behind us, Sarah. This is our life. This is the future of *our lives*. It is not about those other lives we left behind, or about those people who no longer are part of our lives today. I am not suggesting we should forget those people. They will remain in our memory but in a quiet, back corner of our memory. They should not influence what we do with our lives today."

"Everything you say makes sense, Cameron, but I do worry and I will continue to worry until we safely hold our child in our arms."

"Good… That's a good start. For my part, I am thrilled and excited beyond words, and I know I will remain that way. Now, unless you have more to say on this subject, I am off to tell Jimmy the good news."

"Jimmy…? Jimmy is likely to have taken to his bed by this hour of the night. Should you at least wait until the morning to tell him?"

"The morning be damned. If he has taken to his bed, I shall roust him out of it. I will burst if I can't share this news with someone before the morning."

While neither of them knew how Jimmy might react to the news, they hoped he might share something of their joy and excitement. In the event, Jimmy's reaction was not at all what Cameron expected.

Although not yet in bed, Jimmy was making moves in that direction when Cameron arrived. After pouring both of them a tot of rum, Cameron led Jimmy out to the chairs on the verandah. Once they were comfortably settled, Cameron shared his good news… and was taken aback when Jimmy laughed so hard he was almost rolling on the floor.

"Well, I had hoped you might share my excitement. I didn't expect you'd find it quite so laughable," Cameron said indignantly. "Perhaps you might share the humour with me?"

"Oh, no. No, Cameron, I am truly thrilled for you and Sarah. You must be so thick. The thing I find hilarious about all this is that you appear to be the only one around here who wasn't aware of her condition. When Sarah was not her usual self, everyone else guessed what was happening – and why."

Several more wee drams of rum were consumed before all was put right between the two friends, and Cameron at last returned home much later and a bit under the weather.

At the end of May, two things of note were happening. The first of those, Cameron reported on his return from one of his trips to town.

"The hot news around the settlement is that John Spiller has set sail for foreign shores in search of sugar cane. It appears to be common knowledge that he has sailed for Java."

"Okay. It is good to know we might have beaten him to it," Jimmy chuckled.

"Why so?" Sarah asked.

"Er, well, I'm not sure how to explain it, but sometimes it pays to do things without fanfare or advertising what you are doing. Sometimes, stealth is the way, and I feel that might apply in this case. But we will watch what Mr Spiller does on yon property across the river."

Spiller's hunt for sugarcane aside, Jimmy was again planning a trip on a Wallace vessel. This time, his mission was to go in search of coffee beans. He hoped to smuggle a quantity of them into the settlement without the authorities being aware of it and imposing various import duties on the beans.

The Sugar and Coffee Regulations of 1864 allowed for the cheap purchase of land for the establishment of both sugar and coffee industries. While Jimmy and Sarah had taken the first steps towards being a part of a fledgling sugar industry, Jimmy was keen to explore the possibility of a coffee industry. Sarah was more ambivalent about coffee, although not completely opposed to the idea. Nevertheless, she told Jimmy that she thought it might be wiser to concentrate on sugar and the long-term rewards that might accrue from such an industry, rather than diversifying too much. She heard nothing more about coffee again until the night before Cameron took Jimmy to the port to join a Wallace Line vessel, and then it was only about why he would be away again. In Jimmy's absence, another small area of ground was cleared and worked-up in readiness for Jimmy's return.

It appears all went well with Jimmy's expedition. Although Sarah never did discover where he went, Jimmy did return with a small quantity of coffee beans. By the end of the day after he arrived home, most of the beans were planted on Jimmy's land, while a smaller area of Sarah's land also was put under coffee. That evening, Jimmy joined Sarah and Cameron for dinner to celebrate having entered what they hoped would become a local coffee industry. Cameron regaled the diners with tales circulating in the settlement about others attempting to exploit the conditions relating to coffee in the new Regulations.

"From what I've heard told," Cameron announced, "a few others have taken an interest in coffee. While few have shown an interest in the sugar aspect of the Sugar and Coffee Regulations, interest in coffee is far greater. But, there appears little chance of an industry developing as a result of their endeavours. They have bought and planted – in great quantities in some instances – the only coffee beans readily available … and they already had been roasted."

"So, there is little chance of those beans producing coffee bushes?" Sarah asked. "I mean, if they were roasted before they were planted, there is little chance they will germinate, is there?"

"Of course not," Jimmy confirmed. "But they have planted coffee beans, and the Regulations don't stipulate whether they should or should not be roasted. So, in effect, they have complied with the Regulations and are able to take advantage of its conditions relating to cheap land prices."

"Hmm… It sounds as though there is little chance of establishing a viable coffee industry, at least not in this area," Sarah observed.

No further mention of coffee occurred for quite some time after those first beans were planted. That suited Sarah as she had become even more convinced she should concentrate on sugar and not proceed further with coffee.

"There is one other thing I forgot to mention, Jimmy," Cameron began. While you were off in search of coffee beans, John Spiller returned from Java with a supply of sugarcane stalks. Rumour has it that quite a bit of his load perished before it reached here. The other thing of note in relation to Spiller's Java trip is that he reputedly sold half of his remaining supply of cane to Fitzgerald."

"Fitzgerald?... Thomas Fitzgerald, the surveyor chap that's supposedly drawing up the town plan?" Jimmy asked in disbelief, and Cameron nodded. "What on earth does he want with sugarcane, and where does he plan to plant it?"

"Ah, well, it's already in the ground. Fitzgerald planted it on that block he owns near the river in town."

"In town…!" Sarah echoed. "Surely he can't be planning a plantation in the heart of the settlement."

"I guess we will have to wait to see what develops. I believe Spiller has planted his half of the cane he brought back from Java on his riverbank Selection." Cameron added as his final piece of information.

"Now that is most obliging of him," Jimmy grinned. "We will have a bird's eye view of how things progress there.

Chapter 4

1865-1866

Late in August, on his return that evening, Cameron rushed to share with Sarah some exciting news he had picked up in town.

"John Davidson has arrived in Mackay," he announced.

"Should I be particularly excited about his arrival?" Sarah asked. "I doubt I've heard of him before this."

"Did you not meet him during your time in the Caribbean? He is a fellow Scot who became well known in the sugar industry in the West Indies."

Sarah confirmed she had never met Davidson and couldn't remember having heard mention of him before then. Somewhat deflated by Sarah's lack of interest in his news, as soon as dinner was over, Cameron excused himself and rushed across to Jimmy's house. As expected, Jimmy did recall Davidson.

"Interesting, Cameron, very interesting," was Jimmy's initial response to the news. "Now, why would John Ewen Davidson choose to come here? That's a question worth pondering for a moment or two."

"I'll warrant he is here for a sneak look at what's happening with our local sugar industry. We should keep an ear to the ground to know what he gets up to while he is here," Cameron suggested.

A week later, on his return from town, Cameron again shared his latest news with Jimmy and Sarah over a drink before dinner.

"My surprising news from town today is that John Davidson already has left the settlement. Rumour has it that he was heading up north, but nobody appears to know exactly to where or why."

"Is that a bad sign?" Sarah asked. "Why would Davidson see fit to stay here only so few days? Did he assess the area and a possible sugar industry here not worth his time or interest?"

"Good question, Sarah," Jimmy murmured. "I suppose there wasn't much to see at this point, but his departure after so little time here does intrigue me."

"Ah, well, I think not only his visit to this settlement, but the fact that he is in this part of the country, is interesting," Cameron said. "And, I think it might pay us to keep an ear out for any future references to our Mr Davidson. It could well be in our best interest to know what he is up to."

At the start of November, Sarah went to call on Frida McDonald. They had discussed the matter earlier on several occasions, but Sarah now needed reassurance from Frida that the arrangements they had put in place previously still held.

Sarah had first met Frida when her husband, Roddy, was building Sarah's house. Since then, a strong friendship had developed between the two women, and Sarah planned to take advantage of her friend's reputation as a midwife in the area. After having given birth to six children of her own, and since settling in Mackay, Frida's services as a midwife had been called for by a number of women in the settlement.

"I know we've discussed this several times already, Frida, but I just need to be sure that you will be available later this month when I expect to give birth. Is there anything we need to put in place beforehand to facilitate that? I'm afraid I have so little experience of such matters, I'm not sure if there is anything I need to do."

"Rest assured, Sarah, I will be there when you need me. There is little to do beforehand, other than having a few things on hand and made ready for the big event. Do you have any thoughts about a date when the birth is imminent?"

"Not really, but I think it might be sometime during the last week of this month."

"Good, that gives you about three weeks to prepare for the event. I'm sure there isn't much for you to do, as everything we'll need on the day, you probably already have to hand. While you drink your tea, I'll fetch some writing material and make you a list of the things you'll need."

Frida's list mirrored her words to Sarah. Everything that was needed to cope with the birth was already in place. It was with a triumphant flourish a couple of weeks later that Sarah showed Frida everything ticked off on Frida's list.

"So, Frida, unless you've changed your mind or thought of something else we might require, we are ready for the big day," Sarah told her friend.

"Ah, well, there is one more thing we need to think about. If your calculations are correct, sometime in the next week or so, your baby should make its arrival. I assume the nursery is ready for the occasion?"

"Yes. Yes, we have provided everything we could want or need in the nursery extension. Maggie, the new nanny, started work this week and has busied herself preparing everything ready for the baby's arrival."

"The only other thing that needs to be dealt with is me. With your approval, of course, I should move in sometime during the coming week to stay with you and be on hand when I'm required. Babies have a habit of turning up in the middle of the night and often when least expected. Having to send someone to fetch a midwife at that time is not a good thing. It is much better that I should be on hand when things begin to happen."

Of course, Sarah did not argue with Frida's moving in to live with her prior to the birth, and two days later, Roddy delivered his wife to take up her midwifery duties.

Sarah had been restless all day and had spent much of the evening pacing through the house and checking on the new nursery. Although she joined them at the table for dinner, she ate virtually nothing, claiming she did not feel like food at all. As they left the table after dinner, Frida drew Cameron aside for a quiet word.

"I don't know if you had any plans for this evening, Cameron, but it might be best if you went across to Jimmy's house. Better still, it would be good if you planned to spend the night at Jimmy's place."

Stunned and confused, Cameron eyed Frida up and down before demanding, "Why would I want to do that? I have a perfectly comfortable bed here."

"An anxious father-to-be is the last thing we need hanging around at this time. Please, take my advice and go to Jimmy's house and spend the night there. It is likely that sometime during tonight, your baby will make its arrival. Sarah and I will be occupied with that event and you will only be in the way."

A few minutes later, a stunned and pale-looking Cameron stepped up onto Jimmy's verandah and announced he would be staying the night. Taken aback by this development, Jimmy carefully sought an explanation.

"The baby is coming, Jimmy. It's going to arrive tonight. Well, that's what Frida gave me to understand before she tipped me out and told me to come here for the night."

"Ah, well then, lad, you'll be in need of something to settle your nerves. We could be in for a long wait, so maybe we need to pace ourselves a bit, but a dram about now would probably go down well."

Meanwhile, at Sarah's house, events progressed much as expected and much to Frida's relief. There was no getting away from it. Sarah was an older first-time mother. That was something Frida had not encountered before. Nanny Maggie's job was to assist Frida as required and to keep Orla, hovering expectantly in the sitting room, updated on progress. Cheng Li, the gardener, was strategically placed out in the kitchen in readiness for his role in the event.

At about 2.00AM, Maggie emerged from the bedroom to exchange a few hurried words with Orla. Those words sent Orla to the kitchen. It was time for Cheng Li to play his part. Moments later, he was racing along the track to Jimmy's house. A light still burned inside the house, but the place was silent. Cheng Li thumped on the door, stepped back and took a couple of deep breaths before preparing to attack the door again. As he lifted his arm to pound the door, the door flew open, surprising Cheng Li.

"Has it happened?" Cameron croaked as Jimmy peered over Cameron's shoulder at the shocked gardener.

"No… Still coming… But soon, Miss Orla say. Miss Orla say you must stay awake now. She will send word when the baby is here." Cheng Li was thanked and then sent back to resume being on standby ready to deliver the next, and most important message.

As the gardener made his way back to Sarah's house, the two men moved again to take up their seats on Jimmy's verandah. In silence, they watched the lantern Cheng Li carried swinging from side to side as he ran back to Sarah's kitchen. Both men claimed not to be sleepy, but Jimmy secretly hoped the bairn wouldn't develop 'stage fright' at the last moment to delay its appearance any longer than necessary.

Then, at three o'clock on the morning of 26 November 1865, the faint cry of a new born carried on the still night air to the men on Jimmy's verandah. For a few moments, Cameron was too stunned to move. Not so Jimmy, who bounded up out of his chair and grasped Cameron's hand.

"Congratulations, Papa," Jimmy said as he vigorously shook Cameron's hand. "But, why the hell are you still sitting here? You have a new baby to meet."

Without waiting for the lantern that Jimmy went to fetch, Cameron set off at a flat-out gallop along the path towards home. Bounding up the stairs and through the front door, he was brought to a sudden halt by Frida, waiting in the front room. Cameron felt himself turn cold. Where was the baby? No, this can't be happening – not again.

"Where are my wife and child?" he demanded of Frida. "I need to see them now."

"Stop, Cameron. Relax. Maggie will bring the baby out to you in just a moment. Just as soon as she has attended to some last-minute matters for both mother and child."

Frida had barely finished speaking when Maggie came into the sitting room carrying a small bundle. Holding out the bundle towards Cameron, she asked, "Would you like to hold your son, Sir?"

"It's a boy…!" Orla squeaked. "Oh, congratulations, Mr Cameron, Sir… Our congratulations to both you and Miss Sarah, Sir. Oh, I had better go and tell Cheng Li the good news." With that, pulling back a corner of the shawl the baby was wrapped in, Orla gazed at the sleeping child. "Aye, and what a fine looking young chap he is and all." Then, she was striding off to the kitchen and Cheng Li.

"Is my wife all right?" Cameron, at last, plucked up the courage to ask Frida.

"Aye, she is right fine, although a little tired."

"Can I see her, please?"

"Uhmm… Well, I suppose it will be all right. Sarah is sleeping at the moment and must not be disturbed. She needs her rest now, but you may see her… As long as you promise not to wake her. The bairn probably will do that soon enough."

"He seems contented to sleep," Cameron observed.

"For the moment," Frida replied. "He'll be squawking soon enough to let everyone know he is hungry. Well, come along. I'll take you through to your wife."

Cameron, still holding his son, stood by the bed, looking down at his wife. As Frida predicted, about a minute or so later, the little fellow bellowed to be fed. Frida rushed to take the baby from Cameron as Sarah groggily tried to work out what the noise was.

"Right, Cameron, he needs feeding now… And it's time you weren't here. Go and share your news with Jimmy while we take care of things here."

"What is that noise?" a groggy Sarah managed to ask as Frida shoved the baby into Sarah's arms.

"Come on, Mother. Your baby needs feeding. The sooner he is fed, the sooner he will stop bawling," Frida said as she checked over her shoulder that Cameron had indeed left the room.

Maggie hustled Cameron out of the bedroom as soon as she heard Frida say he should leave. After offering him her congratulations, she also urged him to go and share the good news with Jimmy. Muttering something about 'knowing when I'm not wanted', Cameron followed the women's advice and again tread the path to Jimmy's.

The sun was high in the sky next morning before either of the men saw the light of day. When he checked after breakfast, Jimmy found the level in his demijohn of rum had dropped considerably overnight. Neither man felt much like breakfast, instead each opting for his favourite hangover cure.

"So then, Laddie, what's the name of this latest addition to the Wallace family?" Jimmy asked after they eased themselves into the comfortable cane chairs on Jimmy's verandah.

"Good question, my friend. That's the first thing to sort out… as soon as I'm allowed more than five seconds with my wife. It appears to me that in this whole procreation thing, once the initial deed is done, the male involved is relegated to the sidelines and barred from any participation or involvement."

"We-ell, now, I'm no expert, of course, but it seems to me there is little for you to do in all this … other than to go and throw yourself into whatever work needs to be done around the place. Don't you have some shipping business to attend to in town about now?"

"I tell you now, I will not be going into town, not until after I have spent some time with my son and my wife."

"A game lad's famous last words…," Jimmy muttered as he refilled his pipe.

It was lunchtime when Cameron returned home for lunch. After a quick check on who was where, he felt brave enough to sneak into the bedroom to spend some time with Sarah. His attempt was foiled when Frida met him at the bedroom door and demanded to know where he thought he was going.

"I've a mind to speak to my wife on an urgent and important matter. Please step aside, Madam."

"I'll do no such thing – and nor will you be annoying your wife at this time."

Frida, with her hackles well and true raised, was a formidable opponent, but his hangover headache made Cameron a little short on patience.

"Madam, I will spend some time with my wife and son. And, if you persist in being obstructive, I will personally carry you out, load you on the wagon, and have one of the men drive you home. I'm sure that, with the aid of the other women in this household, Sarah, independent woman that she is, will manage perfectly well without you. Now, will you take lunch out in the dining room, or will I summon one of the men to drive you home? They are your only options." A voice from the bedroom brought the matter to a halt.

"Cameron, there is no need for that. Frida, please step aside and allow him to come in. No… On second thought, Cameron, please allow me a private word with Frida before you enter." Sarah's voice was so strong and commanding that both parties felt compelled to comply with her request.

It was only a few moments later when the bedroom door was flung open, and Frida flounced out. On her way past Cameron, she announced, "I'll take lunch, and then, if you would be so kind as to arrange transport home for me, I'll take my leave."

"I'll do no such thing. I will see you home safely myself. It's the least I can do after all your help with Sarah's birth of my son." With that, Cameron stepped briskly into the bedroom and closed the door behind him.

"I do hope that, between us, we haven't managed to ruin a valued friendship," Sarah said with a wry smile as Cameron approached the bed. "Wait a moment while I retrieve our little bundle for you to hold while we talk," Sarah suggested as she scrambled out of bed and went to lift the baby from his bassinette.

"Now, Cameron, what are we to name this little mite who has entered our lives?"

"That is the exact nature of the conversation I came to have with you. I know we have talked in vague terms of possible names, but do you have any more definite ideas now he is here?"

"He is your son. I feel it is your privilege and right to name him. So, what say you?"

Their discussion did not last long before Cameron's thinking became clear enough to offer a firm suggestion.

"Angus Douglas Wallace… How does that sit with you?"

"It's a grand name for the wee bairn, and one I know will please his grandfather. And, unless my memory fails me, I believe Angus was *your* grandfather's name. So it would appear an appropriate name in every way."

After a few more minutes with Sarah, Cameron left the bedroom and joined Frida and Maggie in the dining room. Orla bustled in and set his lunch down in front of Cameron as he took his seat at the table. With a silly grin on his face, he looked at each of the women in the room in turn.

"Angus Douglas Wallace is sleeping peacefully," he announced before picking up his cutlery and attacking his lunch.

The trip to take Frida home began in stony silence. Cameron allowed it to stretch on for some time before he felt moved to do something about it. His apology and explanation were received with the same stony silence. It took another couple of miles, and until they were turning onto Roddy McDonald's Selection, before Frida relented.

"It appears I might have overstepped the mark a bit with Sarah. I meant no ill by it. It came out of my concern for her as an older first-time mother. I suppose I overlooked the fact that Sarah is a lot fitter and stronger than many women half her age. It's to be hoped I haven't done irreparable damage to our friendship."

"I doubt that will prove to be the case. I'm sure Sarah will continue to look to you for advice as she settles into motherhood."

Peace having been restored, the trip home felt as though it took no time at all. As soon as he had unhitched the wagon, Cameron went in search of Jimmy, who was found inspecting his block of young cane.

"Looks good, doesn't it?" Jimmy commented as Cameron rode up to him. "We will have plenty of plant stock by the time we are ready to start planting up the paddocks next year."

"Aye, it's a good crop. You did a great job with those initial canes. Few were lost on the voyage from Java, and it appears just about every billet planted here has struck. Let's see if the next phase of our entry into a local sugar industry goes just as well."

"We will need to wait until the annual wet season is over before we consider planting any of this out into the paddocks. And, by the way the weather feels lately, a wet season is about to be upon us again. Now, my friend, did you come to see me about something specific, or is it that you were chased out of the house by one or other of the women who seem to be in charge there at the moment?"

"Neither really… But I can update your information while I am here. Frida McDonald has returned to her own home, and Sarah once more reigns in ours. No, I came to tell you we had decided on a name for the new arrival: Angus Douglas Wallace."

"It has a good ring to it, and it is bound to go down well with his grandfather. It is late enough to retire to my verandah. Why don't we go and indulge in a bevy in honour of the naming of the wee chap?"

Two days later, an invitation was finally issued for Jimmy to join Cameron and Sarah for dinner and to meet the new bairn.

The weather continued hot and humid for the next month, but still it refused to rain. A different Christmas was celebrated in 1865. Although Christmas Day was always a low-key event in the Wallace household, that year, there was a new baby in the house… and he was most unhappy about the hot, sticky days and nights. About a week after he was born, Maggie insisted his bassinette be moved from his parents' bedroom to the nursery so she could begin settling him into his new surroundings. Then, while Angus spent much of his time bawling, Maggie was kept busy sponging him down to keep him cool.

On Christmas night, as Sarah and Cameron sat on their verandah after dinner in the hope of finding a cool breeze, Angus's incessant howling continued in the nursery.

"If only it would rain," Sarah said and sighed.

"It might cool things down a bit. I suppose it will come soon enough, and then we will be wishing it would stop," Cameron said.

"We are stocked up and ready to be cut off, so it can start raining as soon as it likes. And then, maybe with any amount of luck, young Angus in there will be a little happier, and we might be spared a few minutes without his continuous bawling. One thing has been confirmed. Your son has an excellent set of lungs."

"What does Maggie have to say about him? Does she think it is just the weather making him so unhappy, or is it possible there is something amiss with him?"

"Relax, Cameron. I am assured by both Maggie and Frida that he is in fine health and that his behaviour is only to be expected in this heat."

A further lifestyle change was experienced come Hogmanay in 1865. There was no major celebration, no pipers, no dancing, and no first-footing. Orla went all out to prepare a special feast of sorts, and Jimmy and Roddy and Frida McDonald came to help Cameron and Sarah dispatch it. By what Sarah thought must have been nothing short of a miracle, Orla had even managed to produce a haggis, which turned out to be the highlight of the evening.

The traditional monsoon season arrived in tandem with 1866. The heavens opened on New Year's Day, and the heavy rain continued for most of the next two weeks before a couple of grey but dry days broke the monotonous cycle. A traditional wet January, February and March followed before the rain tapered off to occasional showers during the early part of April. For weeks, everything had sprouted mould, and the kitchen was continuously festooned with baby's clothes drying in the heat from the fire as Maggie struggled to maintain a supply of clean, dry garments for Angus.

Chapter 5

Increases

At the end of April, Cameron and Jimmy agreed the wet season appeared over for the year, and it was time to start working up ground in readiness for planting out the cane. The news was relayed to Sarah, who immediately went into a minor panic.

"No, it is too soon to think about planting yet," she told Cameron. "I'm not ready for it."

"What's to do, Sarah? All you need do is to select the area where the cane is to be planted and then send some of your men to start working up the ground."

"Yes, it sounds simple, does it not? But there is more to the story than that. No, I don't want to discuss it now, but there is something I must do – today. If you would be so kind as to hitch up the wagon for me, I'll attend to the matter forthwith."

Wanting to avoid an argument, Cameron attended to the wagon and then stood looking bemused as Sarah drove off the property. Completely mystified by her comments and actions, he sought out Jimmy in the hope his friend might shed some light on what Sarah had to do that was so urgent.

"Well, now, that is interesting," Jimmy mused. "I'll be keeping an eye out for her return. There is a conversation I think we'll be needing to have."

"Be that as it may, Jimmy. What I want to know is what the hell is going on, and I suspect you know more about it than I do."

"I'd only be guessing, mind you, but I think it might have something to do with that Selection across the road from yours. As I hear tell, the selectors there are in dire straights and likely as not will be forced to walk off their block. In the recent past, Sarah has expressed an interest in it. As most of her present

Selection is already allocated to various production, I suspect she would prefer her sugar interests be based elsewhere. In that way, she wouldn't have to change the way things are set up here."

"More land…? Christ, between you and Sarah, you already own the equivalent of more than half of Glasgow. Why could she possibly think she needs more land?"

"Ah, well, Laddie, that's something you'll have to be asking your wife. But, whatever her thinking, the arrival of a new heir possibly has galvanised her to pursue the matter further."

Cameron returned home, still shaking his head in disbelief and confusion, and collapsed into a chair on their verandah to await Sarah's return.

By the time Sarah returned home, Jimmy had joined Cameron on his verandah, and that's where Jimmy remained when Cameron went to meet his wife and deal with the wagon.

"I am unaware of what it is about, but Jimmy insists he must speak with you. He has awaited your return but has not been inclined to enlighten me as to his business with you."

Sarah noted the edge to Cameron's voice and knew she would be spending time placating him later. As Sarah strode resolutely to meet Jimmy, she tried to prepare exactly what she would say, for she knew what his 'business' with her would be.

"Jimmy, how fortunate you are here. It saves me having to look for you, so we might discuss something we have touched upon previously. Do you have time to discuss this matter with me now, or should we wait until after dinner?"

"Now would be fine, thanks, Sarah. But, if there is to be an invitation to stay for dinner, I should be delighted to accept."

At that point, Cameron strode up onto the verandah and made to drag a chair closer to where the others were sitting. Sarah had other ideas.

"Cameron, if you wouldn't mind and before you sit down, would you please advise Orla Jimmy will be joining us for dinner tonight. Thank you, Dear."

As Cameron stomped off, Sarah turned to Jimmy. "Now, quickly, while we may speak alone… As you no doubt have guessed, I went to visit the selectors across the road. I believe I have negotiated a deal with them for the acquisition of their Selection without having to bid for it should the Land Board put it up for reselection. Are you still interested in participating in this endeavour?"

"Aye, I could be, but I would need to know more about the deal you struck before I can give you a definitive answer."

"Right… The selectors are in arrears with their lease payments and with the improvements required. I suggested a scheme I heard about in town that others have employed successfully. I would advance them sufficient money now to pay out any monies owed on the selection and to convert it to freehold. Then, once the land is freehold and they are legally able to sell it, I would pay them a sum to compensate for the existing improvements on the property. That last payment would constitute the final part of the sale. They would be free to relinquish the land and move on with their lives with a small sum of money in their pockets."

"So, the money you give them up front, plus the small amount you pay them at the end, constitutes the total sale price for the Selection?"

"That would be the agreement we would enter into. It would be a signed contract to avoid any 'mishaps' or 'misunderstandings' along the way."

"I assume the figures you have discussed are in our favour and not so much the other way?"

"Of course, and it would be much less than we might expect to pay to acquire the land through any other means."

After Sarah outlined the figures she had discussed with the neighbouring selectors, Jimmy took a few moments to consider the matter before responding.

"You appear to have negotiated a favourable deal. Please count me in. How soon are we able to implement these plans?"

"Our neighbours are as keen as we are. I agreed I would be prepared to go into town tomorrow to take care of the necessary arrangements. They will come into town as well. As soon as the money was available to them, they would undertake the necessary dealings with the Land Board. Are you available to go into town tomorrow?"

"I shall drive us in first thing in the morning. So, if all goes well, by tomorrow evening, we should own the Selection across the road?"

"Not quite… The exact timing of the handover will depend on how swiftly all the Land Board processes are completed. The selectors are unable to sell the property until it is declared freehold. In past instances, that has taken a week or so, depending on when the Land Board next meets. My information is that the Land Board is due to meet the day after tomorrow."

"So, if all the necessary paperwork is completed tomorrow, and the Land Board approves it the following day, the sale could proceed within the next few days. Such a short timeframe will not adversely impact preparations for planting our cane," Jimmy said and added a satisfied nod.

Cameron had ventured out within earshot towards the end of Sarah and Jimmy's conversation and wanted to add to the discussion before it ended.

"As the acquisition of this extra land appears to be a joint venture, I was wondering whether I, too, might be allowed to be a party to the purchase. It would mean ownership rested with the three of us, and my cash contribution of one-third of the price would reduce some of the strain on both of your cash reserves."

Discussion flowed back and forth between the three parties for a couple of minutes before Jimmy made his position clear.

"A three-way ownership sits comfortably with me, Cameron, but it also depends on Sarah's position on the matter. How say you, Sarah?"

"Well, I will say up front that I was happy to pay whatever was required to acquire the property. Now both you, Jimmy, and Cameron have expressed interest in becoming partners, I have no problems with the land being bought by a three-way partnership."

"Right then, we will proceed accordingly. Jimmy, you will have two passengers accompanying you to town tomorrow," Cameron announced.

Sarah giggled, and both men demanded to know what she found so amusing. "Oh, I was thinking about the bank. I'm not sure they will be able to cope with so much happening all at once tomorrow."

By the middle of May, all appeared aright with the world. Purchase of the extra land occurred without problems, and all the cane that was to be planted was in the ground and starting to shoot. Just as the two men were congratulating themselves on a job well done and being on top of everything, new issues emerged.

The first of those was Sarah, who, for the second morning in a row, felt unwell and remained in bed rather than having breakfast with Cameron. When she still looked pale that evening, concern drove Cameron to enquire after her health. Sarah refused to enter into a discussion about it, but later that evening, relented and shared her concerns with her husband.

"I fear I am again with child. The way I have felt for the last two days is quite reminiscent of how things were a little over a year ago."

"Are you sure?"

"No. Of course, it is not confirmed, but I am quite sure enough to bring it to your attention. This time, I am worried about it. I believed I was too old last time. Now, I am more than a year older than I was then. How does the thought of a second child sit with you?"

"A second child…! I would be delighted to welcome a second child into our family, but not at a heavy cost to your health. Perhaps we should wait a little longer before we become too concerned."

Sarah's concerns deepened over the following fortnight, and Cameron had occasion to revisit his last words on the subject several times during that period. Sarah became sicker by the day. By the start of June, both she and Cameron were aware she was much sicker than she was with their first child. Sarah had developed a firm conviction that it was a sign that all would not end well. While Sarah refused to do anything about it, Cameron took it upon himself to seek the advice of Frida McDonald on the matter. Frida was not about to waste time with advice. She insisted Cameron drive her back to Sarah immediately.

Within minutes of Frida's arrival, Sarah was tucked up in bed and threatened with dire consequences if she did not stay there. Frida, in command mode, was a force to be reckoned with, and on this occasion, Sarah was not up to the challenge. About half an hour after her arrival, Frida sought out Cameron to deliver an update.

"Your wife is in bed and will be staying there for some time to come. I will stay tonight. First thing in the morning, you can take me home to fetch a few things before I return to continue looking after Sarah. I may be a guest in your house for some weeks to come. We shall have to wait to see how things progress before we know how long I might be here."

When no argument was forthcoming from Cameron, Frida marched through to the kitchen to instruct Orla on the menu Frida required for Sarah for the immediate future. After dinner, and with Frida and Sarah ensconced in the bedroom, Cameron, feeling a bit superfluous to needs, took the opportunity to escape to Jimmy's house.

Over a wee bevy on Jimmy's verandah, Jimmy asked, "Did my eyes deceive me, or has Frida McDonald moved in?"

"Aye, she has, and it is more like she has taken up residence for the foreseeable future. I don't know what Roddy will make of it. I don't imagine he will be too pleased."

"Och, now, I wouldn't go worrying about that. Knowing Roddy as I do from way back, he will probably be happy for the respite, even if it is only for a few days," Jimmy said with a grin, before another thought struck him. "Hang about. Cameron, why is Frida here? You never said. What has happened?"

"It appears we are on the way to adding another member to our number, but it is not going well for Sarah. Although I'm trying to be positive around her, we both are concerned about how this might end. I didn't know what else to do other than ask for Frida's help."

"My, my… What have you been up to, lad?" Jimmy chuckled.

"Regardless of what has been done in the past, I can assure you we will be more circumspect in future."

After about three weeks, Frida reported Sarah's condition was much improved. Having gained an undertaking from Sarah that she would continue to remain in bed, Frida judged it safe for her to return home, although she would return periodically to check on Sarah. Cameron drove Frida home the next morning. Immediately on his return home, Cameron went directly to Sarah and implored her, for both their sakes and the baby's, to comply to the letter with Frida's instructions.

By the beginning of August, Frida judged Sarah's condition to have improved enough to be allowed out of bed for short spells during the day. Cameron felt confident Frida's assessment was right as, unlike earlier, Sarah was not of a mind to object to being ordered about by Frida. And she was intelligent enough to agree to all Frida's demands – while Frida was there with her.

Other issues, of which Sarah remained unaware, had emerged during the weeks of her convalescence. One came as a surprise, while another one was the cause of some discussion when she learned of it.

Sarah took herself out to spend a few minutes enjoying the fresh air as the sun was sinking one afternoon, and was just in time to greet Cameron and Jimmy as they returned home from the paddocks. Both men joined her on the verandah. It was Sarah's opportunity to ask questions about something she noticed as soon as she sat down.

"Jimmy, what is happening at your house?" she asked. "It looks as though major construction work is about to begin."

"Aye, they've made a start. Roddy and his men came and marked it out and have now completed all the foundation works. We should see wall timbers starting to go up in the next day or so."

"I realise it will be an extension to your house, but Jimmy, it looks huge. What has prompted this?"

"Of course, you are unaware… Forgive me, but I haven't spoken to you for a few weeks, so you don't know about recent developments. My sister, Annie, for some time now, has been hinting at coming to join me here. I figured it was just so much talk, so I never encouraged – or discouraged – her from doing so. Then a letter arrived, giving me the name of the ship, the date it would depart Glasgow, and probable date of arrival here. She is coming to join me here at Mackay."

"Oh, Jimmy, that will be lovely for you. I know you value your independence, but to have someone for company and to look after you will be good for you. But that is a huge building extension you have happening over there."

"Well, the fact that Annie is coming is only the half of it. Her daughter, Elspeth, is coming with her. So, now my house needs to accommodate two more people, and needs to include a few more civilised touches… such as a proper dining room and a sitting room. When I first discussed it with Roddy, I thought that was the extent of the extension required. Then Frida became involved and insisted the extension needed to include more, if a woman was to be running the household. At that point, had there been time, I'm almost sure I would have written Annie not to come."

"Nonsense, having her here will be wonderful for you. I look forward to enjoying her company and her daughter's as well."

At that point, Cameron took advantage of a pause in the conversation to ask a question. "How old is… What's her name? Elspeth, is it? How old is she, and is she likely to be happy here?"

"Uhmm… Good question, Cameron. Now let me think on it. Now, I know she turned eighteen a while ago, but I don't know how long ago that was. Off the top of my head mind, but I would guess she might be nearly twenty by now. She was training to be a teacher, but I remember Annie wrote that Elspeth had completed her training and had found employment as a teacher in an upmarket girls' school. I can't say I know what she is like now, as I haven't seen much of her since she was a little girl. How she might settle into a place like this has me concerned. I'm sure Annie will be okay, but I don't feel quite so sure about Elspeth."

"Don't sell her short, Jimmy," Sarah counselled. "It sounds as though coming here was of her choosing, and as we all know, this settlement will be in need of well-trained teachers. So, perhaps she might not live out here on the property with you and her mother. She might board in town somewhere and teach at a school there. Even if she can't find a position as a teacher in town, soon, I will have two children in need of a teacher."

The conversation about the imminent increase in Jimmy's household having run its course, Jimmy took the opportunity to introduce another discussion he'd been wanting to have for a while but had avoided while Sarah was incapacitated.

"While we are all here, this might be a good time to discuss a few things about our future sugar plantation. I know we have planted two sound varieties of sugarcane that should do well in this climate and on the rich alluvial flats where we've planted it. I can't help harking back to the lessons that were hard learned early in the industry in the Caribbean."

"Which particular lessons were they, Jimmy?" Cameron asked. "There were so many lessons to be learned, so many problems to be solved, and I remember most of them from those early days on our plantations."

"It seems to be the habit of people entering a new sugar industry to look for a 'golden' variety of sugarcane. By that, I mean one that promises everything they could hope for – long, heavy canes and high sugar content. Then, having found what they believed to be such a variety, the whole plantation is put under that one variety. In some cases, a second, not quite so fantastic variety might also feature in a small way." Jimmy paused to think about how to say the next part, and Cameron jumped in.

"There's nothing strange about that. Why wouldn't you focus on something that was going to give you the best results and create the best cash flow?"

"Aye, lad, the motivation is clear enough, but earlier experience has taught us it is foolhardy. Those fantastic varieties are often susceptible to diseases and other vagaries of weather and soil conditions. The hard lesson that was learned early in the piece by the likes of your parents and others, Cameron, was not to put all your eggs in the one basket. If you do, and a problem develops with that fantastic variety, the whole crop can be lost. We know how long it takes to re-establish a crop from scratch."

"So, what are you suggesting, Jimmy?" Sarah asked. "Am I to understand that you have become a bit nervous about the fact that we have only two varieties, Bourbon and Ribbon, planted on our blocks?"

"That is my concern. I feel we should look further afield than Java to source other promising varieties that might provide some resilience if the two varieties we have planted let us down. My answer has to be that I believe we will be better served in the long term if we diversify more from the outset. If I were to bring back new varieties now, it would be a couple of years at least before we would know how they might perform here in this environment."

Although the discussion of possible additional varieties stretched on for some time and continued again after dinner, the night ended without any firm decisions on the matter. Nevertheless, Jimmy was determined to push ahead with his idea of sourcing other varieties – as soon as a possible opportunity presented. He also resolved he would pursue the matter with or without Sarah's approval or involvement.

Jimmy wasn't the only one whose thoughts frequently revisited the idea of sourcing other varieties. Sarah, although remaining ambivalent about the matter, also found her thinking returning from time to time to the benefits or otherwise of additional cane varieties. Nevertheless, the matter remained in abeyance for a while longer before being addressed again.

When the trio dined together a few weeks later, Jimmy announced his sister, Annie, and niece, Elspeth, were on their way to Australia. Everyone at the table expressed their concerns that the women would be arriving at the start of summer and would have no time to acclimatise. Jimmy ended the discussion by saying he warned them about the heat and had suggested they delay their departure to ensure they arrived in winter, but Annie had said their minds were set and their bookings were in place.

Discussions then moved on to how well their crop of sugar cane was coming along. It prompted a discussion of their future agricultural pursuits. Sarah took the opportunity to state again that, in future, she would concentrate on sugar and not worry too much about coffee. Jimmy also agreed that sugar was the way forward and confirmed he, too, probably wouldn't worry much about coffee. That revived the topic of additional varieties, and Jimmy again warned of the folly of concentrating on only one or two high-performing varieties.

A week later, Cameron informed Sarah that Jimmy would leave in a couple of days to search for new cane varieties. He said Jimmy possibly could be away for as long as a month, depending on how shipping from that part of the world was running.

"A month? What about Annie and Elspeth? Will Jimmy be home again by the time they arrive?"

"Yes, but it's possible it won't be much before their arrival. If he shouldn't make it back in time, I'm afraid we will be introducing them to their new home and looking after them until he returns."

"Of course, we will look after them if Jimmy has not returned by then. I have to admit, I am looking forward to having another woman around. In my present condition, it will be something of a comfort to know there is another woman close at hand.

Chapter 6

New Arrivals

Jimmy's search for new cane varieties kept him away for just over three weeks. It left him a week after his return to prepare for the arrival of his sister and niece, and to plant the stalks of Rose Bamboo and Raphoe varieties of cane he brought back from New Guinea.

On his return, over dinner one night, Sarah again expressed her concern at the folly of Jimmy's sister and niece arriving in summer.

"They will be here only days before Christmas. This year, summer has arrived early and with a vengeance. I don't recall such a hot, sultry Christmas in my time here."

"Perhaps we should pray that the wet season sets in before they arrive. It would cool it down a bit for them," Cameron said.

"Heaven forbid! The horror of constant heavy rain for days on end, and everything becoming covered in mould, would be enough to have them boarding the next ship back to Glasgow," Sarah replied. "No, I'm afraid there is naught to be done about it. Along with the rest of us, they will have to suffer the weather. In the meantime, I am so looking forward to the arrival of this baby. I suspect Maggie is a little less eager for it."

The heat and humidity continued until after Christmas. For Sarah, it was a Christmas to remember. Her baby weighed heavily on her, and the weather made her condition almost unbearable. She was not sleeping and had little interest in food. Amidst all her bustling about reorganising Jimmy's home, Annie noticed Sarah's distressed state and took time out to visit her.

"What can I do to help you, my dear?" Annie asked as Sarah waddled out onto the verandah to greet her.

Sarah wrinkled her forehead and shook her head before delivering a confused reply. "Why do you think I need help, Annie? Has Cameron been saying things?"

"No, Sarah. I only have to look at you to know you are struggling with this baby of yours. How much longer before it is likely to make an appearance?"

"Oh, not for ages. Mid-January at the earliest, I should think."

"You might be well advised to take to your bed for the next couple of weeks."

"It is far too hot to be lying about in bed. Besides, in my present condition, it is almost impossible to be comfortable. All I know, Annie, is that there can be no more after this one… And I pray I'm still around to see that is the case."

Later that afternoon, when Cameron, on his way home from town, called to see Jimmy, Annie made a point of inserting herself into the men's get-together on Jimmy's verandah.

"Cameron, I spoke with Sarah today. She is not in a good way. I know that is not uncommon at this late stage of her condition, but she tells me she believes she still has two or three weeks before the birth." Cameron nodded and confirmed that also was his understanding. "Well, I think she is mistaken. In my opinion she has more like days to wait, maybe as long as a week, but not more."

"Both Sarah and I will be pleased to see a healthy baby delivered as soon as possible. I confess I am concerned for her wellbeing and am alarmed by how much she has slipped in the last few days. I truly hope your assessment of the situation is correct, and it will be over sooner than she expects."

Two days before the dawn of the first day of 1867, the rains finally arrived and continued to bucket down relentlessly. Roads and other tracks along the valley became impassable. Although the rain cooled the place a little, Sarah now admitted to another concern.

"All the roads are flooded, Cameron. You told me that yourself. What if this rain doesn't let up and the roads remain impassable? How will Frida McDonald be able to come for the birth of this baby? I already have a bad feeling about this birth. Without Frida, I'm terrified to think what might happen."

Late in the evening of the second day of January, there was no further wondering to be done. Sarah went into labour. Almost as if she had some premonition, after retiring to her room for the night, Annie was compelled to wander out onto the verandah. Something about a light still burning in the bedroom end of Sarah's house told Annie she was needed. Grabbing her sewing box and a lantern, she donned an oilskin and strode through the rain to Sarah's house.

Almost beside himself, Cameron met Annie on his verandah. "What are we to do, Annie? Sarah's time has come, and she has no one to help her. Maggie, our nursery maid, is with her, but she admits she is not up to the task ahead. There is no hope of Frida McDonald being able to come to assist with the birth."

"The only thing for you to do, Cameron, is to step aside and let me go through to Sarah. I might not be as experienced as Frida, but I'm no novice at such things. Now, while Maggie and I attend to matters here, you should rouse Jimmy from his bed to keep you company. If we are to be awake this night, it won't hurt for him also to lose sleep."

Sarah's nervousness and ill-boding about the coming birth were well justified. It proved a long and difficult birth.

"Advice I've been given in the past is that the second one comes easier and quicker than the first," Maggie whispered to Annie as she dumped down the extra towels she had fetched.

"Aye, lass. Most times, that is the case, but Mrs Wallace is no longer a young woman. Most of those 'rules' you've heard along the way probably don't apply in her case.

Sarah was exhausted and had almost no strength left by the time the baby decided to venture out into the world. Just before nine o'clock in the morning of 3rd January 1867, Sarah was delivered of a son.

Orla was sent to dispatch the gardener, Cheng Li, to tell the father. Surrounded by a cloud of rum and tobacco fumes,

Cameron raced home – and fell up the front steps in his haste. Cheng Li was told only that the baby had arrived. That was the extent of the information he passed on to Cameron, although Cameron had demanded more details before rushing home. Orla met him in the dining room and walked through with him to the sitting room to await further news.

"Annie still appears to be quite busy in there with Miss Sarah and the baby, but I think everything has gone well. I heard the baby cry before," Maggie tried to reassure Cameron. She didn't mention that it had seemed a tiny, weak cry that she heard.

It was a good half hour later when Annie came into the sitting room with a tiny bundle in her arms. Cameron noted with alarm that Annie looked exhausted.

"Here you are, Cameron," Annie said as she held the bundle out towards Cameron. "It's time to meet your son."

"Ooh, another son…," Orla whispered. "Congratulations, Sir. May I see him, please?" Cameron nodded, and Orla gently lifted a corner of the shawl to expose the baby's face. "Ah, he is so beautiful, Sir. You must be so proud."

"Perhaps we could all do with a cup of tea, Orla. Do you think you might manage that?" Annie said as she gave Orla an encouraging smile.

As Cameron stood gazing down at the face of his new son, Annie watched the retreating housemaid until she disappeared into the kitchen. Then, it was time for a stern word with the proud father.

"Sarah did not have an easy time of it. But, apart from being exhausted, she has come through it reasonably well. It is likely to take her some time to recover this time. She might find she needs to take things easy for quite some time – much longer than last time. She is resting but you may go in to see her. Please don't wake her. This wee chap will do that soon enough. He's had a little feed but was too stressed and exhausted to take much. He will wake again as soon as he decides he is hungry."

"Annie, I hear what you say, but I suspect there is more you are not telling me. Please tell me the whole story. Are my wife and child really all right?" Annie heaved a sigh and considered his question for a moment before answering.

"Truth is, the birth has left both of them weak and exhausted. In itself, that is not cause for alarm – if they are afforded everything needed to help them recover. Maggie knows what is required to see the bairn develops properly, and I will keep a check on Sarah to ensure she is recovering as she should."

A moment later, Maggie seemed to materialise from out of nowhere to stand beside Cameron. "I'll put him to bed now, Sir, if you don't mind," she said as she held out her arms to take the baby.

At that point, Orla arrived with a loaded tea tray. "Shall I pour, or would you prefer to do it?" she asked Annie. The question was unnecessary. Annie had already taken command of the teapot. As she poured the tea, Annie addressed Cameron.

"There is something you need to consider, and it needs to be done now. Young Angus still demands much of Maggie's time. She will struggle to manage two such small children, especially when the new baby may well demand special attention for some time to come. Maggie must be given an assistant if she is to manage the increased workload, and the children are to receive the best care."

"Surely that is something for Sarah to consider? The household staff are Sarah's concern, and I doubt she would appreciate my interference. Apart from that, I would not know how to choose the best person for the job. I will promise you, though, that as soon as Sarah is up to having such a conversation, I will bring the matter to her attention."

It was a couple of days later before any such conversation was possible. Sarah spent almost all of that time sleeping. But at last, Cameron was at home when Sarah was awake. No one prevented him from seeing her. He laughed when she opened their meeting with an apology for not having spoken with him since the baby arrived.

"Well, now I'm here; what are we to call this new addition to our family?" he asked, his eyes straying to the bassinette.

"Where is the baby?" he demanded in shock. "He's not in the bassinette."

"No. Maggie has moved him to the nursery already and only brings him to me when necessary."

"Why? He is too young to be moved away from you already."

"He is proving a difficult baby, hard to settle and cries a lot. Maggie has had her work cut out with this one and is quite exhausted. She had been crying when she brought him to me. She eventually explained that the two babies, being only fourteen months apart, and with this new one being such a handful, she can't cope."

"I was going to talk to you about that, but I didn't want to trouble you until you were up to dealing with the matter."

"Thank you for your concern, but the matter is well in hand. I offered to find an assistant for Maggie but wouldn't be able to do anything about it until I was up and about again. She asked to see me the next day. Maggie knew of a young girl who was looking for a similar position. The young girl is coming to see me this afternoon. If she measures up as well as Maggie thinks she will, I will ask her to start as a trainee nursery maid at her earliest convenience."

"On an equally serious matter, Sarah, what are we to name this new bairn? While I had the privilege of naming our first son, I believe you should choose the name for our second son."

"Of course, I have been giving the matter some thought so that I might make some suggestions when the time came. If you are sure you are comfortable with my choosing his name, I would suggest Lachlan Michael Wallace... Lachlan after my uncle, my mother's brother, who died in Egypt, and Michael after my maternal grandfather. How does that sit with you, Cameron?"

"Perfectly... A good, solid name for a lad. Now, if he will start behaving himself a little better, he might live up to the standards of those ancestors after whom he is named. Sarah, are you sure you don't want to give him your father's name? I mean,

I am perfectly happy with the names you have chosen, but I am a little surprised Thomas wasn't one of those suggested."

"Thomas was never a name I considered. I assure you I am perfectly happy with those names."

"Right then, that's how he shall be known, and one day he will be baptised accordingly."

By the end of January, Sarah was back on her feet again, although both Cameron and Annie believed she was putting on something of a brave face and wasn't as fully recovered as she would have them believe. Nevertheless, Cameron at last felt comfortable leaving her home alone while he went into town to attend to shipping line business. As he expected to be away from home for a couple of days at least, he asked Annie to keep an eye on Sarah in his absence.

On Cameron's return three days later, when Cameron went to relay Sarah's invitation to dinner to the members of Jimmy's household, Annie was pleased to report Sarah appeared to be exercising common sense as she went about her days. Although attending to everything required of her, Sarah allowed herself rest periods. And the new, young assistant nursery maid, Maisie, appeared to have made a difference in the overall running of the household.

That night at dinner, Cameron was keen to share with the others all the news from town.

"John Ewen Davidson is back in town," Cameron announced. "Rumour has it, he is sniffing around for land to buy in the area and plans to start a plantation."

"Och, I knew he was up to something when he was here last time. You mark my words. That's not the last we will hear about him," Jimmy snarled.

"Does it matter if he buys land and starts a plantation?" Sarah asked. "Is it likely to have any adverse impact on our operations?"

"No, of course not," Cameron replied quickly.

"*Dinna* be so sure, Laddie," Jimmy warned. "I *dinna* trust the man."

"Who is this man Davidson you speak of?" Annie asked. "Should I know the man from back home?" Jimmy jumped in to answer.

"Mebbe not, Annie. I don't recall him from my days in Glasgow. We knew him from the Caribbean. But, aye, he is a Scot like the rest of us here. Educated at Oxford, I believe, but I *dinna* know in what. His was a well-known name in the West Indies sugar industry in its heyday, but he gained a bit of a reputation."

"What sort of reputation? I was unaware of it," Cameron said.

"Oh, nothing real bad… just that he was a bit of a mover and shaker, that's all."

After considering Jimmy's comments for a moment, Sarah said, "Well, maybe a mover and shaker might not be a bad thing in the establishment of a sugar industry here. He might be just the person to get an industry up and running in this part of the country."

Over the next couple of weeks, and after each trip into town, Cameron managed to keep everyone abreast of interesting developments from town. The first update came about a week after he alerted them to Davidson's return to the settlement.

"It appears the rumour is confirmed. The latest news is that Davidson has gained a half interest in the new Alexandra Plantation Fitzgerald is establishing just a short ride up the valley from here."

A bit later in February, the next news Cameron brought home from town, taken at face value, seemed a little encouraging.

"It seems almost common knowledge that Davidson is soon off to see this colony's Colonial Treasurer to discuss the current excise duty on rum."

"Like I said, a mover and shaker," Jimmy reminded them. "If he is to be involved in a sugar industry in this colony, you can bet Davidson will be doing his utmost to make it as comfortable as possible for him to be a part of it."

"Perhaps that's true, Jimmy, but I, for one, won't mind if his mission meets with some success. If he manages to initiate some change, it could benefit not only what we do here, but also Wallace Shipping's operations," Cameron pointed out.

No news of any consequence was gathered from Cameron's trips to town over the next little while. It was late February before he brought home his next interesting snippet.

"Before I left town this afternoon, I had quite a surprise. On concluding my business in town, I had lunch at the pub before heading home. As I walked towards the pub, I thought I recognised a face coming towards me, but I couldn't put a name to it. As it turned out, the man was of a similar mind and followed me into the pub."

"Was that man up to no good and a threat, Cameron?" Sarah demanded. "I do worry about the look of some of the people amongst the recent arrivals in the settlement."

"Of course, he wasn't a threat. He was just another hungry man looking for lunch, but I had to appease my curiosity. In the few moments while we waited to be shown into the dining room, I asked the man his name."

"Go on. Don't keep us in suspense," Jimmy barked.

"It was John Dow. Jimmy, you will remember Dow from the Caribbean sugar industry. As soon as we exchanged names, we realised we had both been trying to fathom out who the other man was. Anyway, I asked him to lunch with me, and a pleasant and interesting interlude it proved to be. He said he met with Davidson in Brisbane when Davidson went down to talk to the Colonial Treasurer. Davidson has now engaged Dow as his sugar milling engineering expert for the Alexandra Plantation."

"That John Dow is a good man to have. Davidson isn't wasting any time. We are likely to see a sugar milling factory established at Alexandra before long. Trust Davidson to get in ahead of everyone else."

"Well, Dow admitted his immediate focus will be on Alexandra, but he remains a free agent and able to accept work from other quarters if it comes along."

"So he dropped you a wink, did he?"

"Aye, that he did… And I'll be keeping him in mind for when the time comes. It seems interest in a sugar industry is increasing. Word around town is that Holmes has planted a small plot of some variety – probably Bourbon – on his Pleystowe Plantation."

"The gold discovery at Gympie also might generate more interest in a local sugar industry. Apart from being the saviour of an almost destitute colony, the gold has people swarming into the colony. It will likely create a healthy home market for sugar – and perhaps rum," Jimmy suggested.

"And it may be just what's needed to save the colony's struggling pastoral industry," Cameron added. "More population also requires more beef and increases the need for other cattle-related products."

During a lapse in conversation, Sarah asked, "By the way, Jimmy, where is Annie tonight? I expected she would join us for a drink before dinner."

"Ah, well, things are a bit hectic in the Fraser household this evening. I'll be taking Annie and Elspeth into town in the morning. There's talk of a position for a governess in town. Annie will go with Elspeth to meet the people and check out everything before she agrees to allow her daughter to take the position. I'll have to collect them from town the next day."

"Jimmy, please don't feel I'm prying into family secrets, but I find myself treading carefully around Annie because I know nothing of her past," Sarah told Jimmy. "Is there anything you might share with me without breaching her confidentiality?"

"It's not a happy tale. Annie married a much older brute of a man. Between them, they established a successful business, produced a son, and then nine years later produced Elspeth. The husband died about fifteen years ago, leaving the business jointly to Annie and his son. At the time, the boy was too young to be much involved, but Annie built the business up into something quite remarkable. The son left school as soon as he could and came to work in the business. That's when the rot set in. His drinking and gambling almost ran the business into bankruptcy, and his involvement with a rough element of the community eventually saw him receive a lengthy gaol sentence.

Annie continued with the business and gradually built it up again, better than it was before. Then, the son was the victim of an 'unfortunate accident' and was found dead in a prison workshop. That was two years ago."

"She is an amazing woman. Not only did she survive and conquer those setbacks, she did it all while also caring for a young daughter," Sarah said. "What happened to her business when she decided to come here?"

"Coming to join me was something she wanted to do for quite a while, but Elspeth had a long-time beau. Annie wanted to see them married and settled before she left Glasgow. An unbelievable offer to buy the business meant nothing would hold her back once Elspeth was married. She told Elspeth of her plans, and that's when things changed. Elspeth said she would never marry that man as she saw too much of her father in him. After a couple of days to think on it, Elspeth announced she would be accompanying her mother to Australia. She had finished her teacher training and felt sure there would be a need for governesses and teachers in this colony."

"I admire the bravery of both those women," Sarah murmured.

"Much like that of another woman I know, who seized an opportunity when it presented and also ended up in this settlement," Jimmy commented, making Sarah blush.

Chapter 7

Sugar

After accepting the position of governess to the two young children of a successful businessman in town, Elspeth settled in well in her new surroundings, but admitted she missed life on the Selection with her favourite people. Then, in December 1867, her employer and his family were off to their summer retreat to escape the heat. Elspeth was happy there was never any suggestion she should join them.

It was that family's practice to visit the wife's parents in Sydney briefly before taking to the cooler climate of the Blue Mountains until the end of January. The arrangement allowed Elspeth two months at home again. The imminent return of the family from the summer retreat plunged Elspeth into a fit of despair.

Sarah felt for the lass and offered a few words of encouragement. "It might not have to be for too much longer, Elspeth. The Wallace offspring will soon outgrow the nursery and will be in need of a governess. There will be a position waiting for you here at home when the time comes."

At the end of the 1868 wet season, as was now his custom, Cameron brought more news of the settlement's fledgling sugar industry.

"More news from up the valley," Cameron announced on his return from his latest trip to town. "It is confirmed the small plot of cane Holmes has planted on his Pleystowe Plantation is the Bourbon variety and will be used as the plant stock when he puts more ground under cane."

"Nothing too surprising in any of that," Jimmy commented, "but it is good to keep abreast of what's happening around us."

"Aye, and that's not all I heard whispers about. Rumour has it that Pleystowe Plantation might be on the market."

"Hmm… I always suspected Joseph Holmes might be undercapitalised for what he hoped to achieve. I believe family money might have gone bad. Pleystowe would be a good buy for someone with the right financial backing to develop it to its full potential," Jimmy suggested.

By mid-year, it was an excited Cameron who, on his return from town, announced, "Holmes is believed to have sold his Pleystowe Plantation to the partnership of Hewitt and Romilly."

"Ah hah, me thinks it has deep pockets to take Pleystowe forward now," Jimmy said with a sly grin.

"Should we worry about that development?" Sarah asked. "Is it likely to impact our operations?"

"Nah, I don't think it likely," Jimmy said. "In fact, depending on how the new partnership progresses, it might be to our advantage. Let's wait to see what happens there."

"I noticed some interesting activity on Spiller's place recently," Jimmy commented. "Any mention about town on what might be happening there?"

"Well, yes… But I'm not sure how much truth there is to the rumour. There is some talk that Spiller is installing a mill of some sort to crush his crop this year. Some suggest it might be nothing more than a horse mill." Cameron said and shrugged. "As I said, I don't know how much truth there is to the story."

"Perhaps we should find out. It's only neighbourly to ask if the man needs some help with whatever he is doing," Jimmy told them.

"Right then, Jimmy, you are charged with the task of offering assistance and finding out what John Spiller is doing on his Selection," Cameron told him.

A couple of days later, Jimmy reported back to Cameron and Sarah. "I offered our assistance to Spiller with his construction work, but he assured me everything was under control. It is indeed a horse mill Spiller is installing. He plans its imminent first crushing will be his block of Ribbon variety cane. He lamented that it was a small block. Although that might be a good thing for the first run through the new mill, he would have liked a bit more 'to run it in properly', as he put it. I might have spoken out of turn, but once his mill is up and running, I offered to sell him the cane we will have ready for crushing."

"Did he accept the offer?" Sarah chirped. "It would be so satisfying to have our cane starting to pay its way."

"Aye, he did accept the offer… And I have negotiated a good price for our cane from that first small block we planted."

"That will take care of this year," Cameron began. "We will have more cane ready for crushing come next year. We need to devote some time to planning how our crop will be crushed."

With the matter of the crushing of that year's crop settled, the question of future crushing arrangements remained in abeyance until September, when Cameron next brought news from town.

"The word around town on the latest development in this settlement's sugar industry is that Davidson's Alexandra Plantation has completed its first crushing. The rumour is they crushed the Bourbon variety."

"By the way, I meant to update you on Spiller's achievements," Jimmy remembered. "I caught up with Spiller a few days ago. He crowed about having produced about half a ton of sugar from his Ribbon variety."

"How much of that quantity was from our cane?" Sarah demanded.

"He assured me it was from just his Ribbon variety, but I doubt that be the case. Nevertheless, he bought our cane fair and square, so it is not for us to question what he did with it."

"As we agreed earlier," Cameron reminded them, "we must try to plan now for our next year's crushing. Does anyone have any ideas, or are we just going to go back, cap in hand, to Spiller again next year?"

It was close to the end of 1868 before anything akin to a firm crushing arrangement was in place for the coming year.

Another couple of major changes took place during 1869 to impact the lives of Sarah and Cameron Wallace and Jimmy Fraser. Cameron and Jimmy kept a close eye on progress on

Pleystowe Plantation. It was anticipated the plantation's first crushing season would commence around September. An arrangement was in place to sell that year's cane crops from both Sarah's and Jimmy's Selections to Pleystowe for crushing.

After a visit in March to check on progress with the erection at the sugar milling factory at Pleystowe, Jimmy seemed troubled. One evening, after dinner, he was persuaded to share his thoughts with Cameron and Sarah.

"Everything is in place for this year's crop of cane that is ready for harvest, but it is the future that bothers me. Are we to constantly look to others to buy and crush our cane, or should we consider a more permanent approach to the matter?"

"Are you unhappy with the arrangement we have with Pleystowe Plantation?" Sarah asked.

"Argh, no, it is fine – for this year. But Pleystowe continues to expand its area under cane. They will have more of their own cane to crush next year and might not want our cane or, indeed, might not have capacity to crush more than their own crop. Likewise, the size of the crop we have to crush will continue to increase every year for a few years to come. I believe it behoves us to look ahead and plan accordingly before we find ourselves in the embarrassing situation of having excellent cane ready to crush and nowhere to process it."

"Jimmy, are you advocating we look at acquiring our own milling factory?" Cameron asked quietly.

"I suppose that is the nature of my thinking. Although I haven't given the matter any real thought to date, I believe we must do so, and soon."

"While I admit to nothing to add to this conversation, what you suggest makes sense to me, Jimmy," Sarah confessed. "Cameron, you are familiar with the milling side of the industry. What are your thoughts on this?"

"Like Jimmy, our situation has been at the back of my mind for a while. Perhaps, Jimmy, you and I should work out what we might need to process our crops over the years to come. Things – equipment and technology – have changed since our days in the Caribbean. As a first step, maybe we should investigate current trends before much more time elapses."

Over the next few days, the two men revisited that conversation on several occasions. When it again was discussed one evening, Jimmy announced, "I feel a visit to the Old Country coming on in the near future, including perhaps a detour to Java along the way."

By mid-April, Jimmy was on his way back to Glasgow to talk to equipment suppliers there followed by a quick trip to England to talk to other suppliers. Before departing, he had obtained a list from John Dow of the equipment they were likely to need for their factory. It helped shorten the time spent talking to suppliers, and Jimmy was soon on his way home via Java.

As Hewitt and Romilly also discovered, much of the equipment and machinery required was available from the industry in Java. Jimmy also paid special attention to what might be acquired from that country.

With the trip to Glasgow taking the best part of four months, by the time Jimmy returned, it was almost Christmas. During his absence from the settlement, Pleystowe's first crushing commenced early in September, progressed reasonably well, and saw all of Jimmy's and Sarah's crops for that year processed as arranged.

The other event of note to happen while Jimmy was away occurred early in December. The family employing Elspeth as their governess announced they would leave the following week for their annual retreat in the Blue Mountains. That was the moment Elspeth had waited for. She handed in her notice, effective the day before the family departed, and said she would not be returning in the new year as she had secured other employment. That 'other employment' was as governess to Angus Wallace from the start of 1870.

By the end of the year, and with the imminent employment of Elspeth, Sarah was forced to consider her current staffing arrangements. From the start of the next year, only one staff member would be required in the nursery to care for young

Lachlan, and by the end of that coming year, Lachlan would also begin his formal education under Elspeth's guidance. Sarah didn't have to devote much thought to the situation to realise the young trainee nursery maid would no longer be required. She hated the thought of what she must do.

Sarah's dilemma disappeared when Maisie, the trainee nursery maid, asked to be let go as she wished to travel with her parents to New South Wales, where the family planned to purchase a small farm. The timing was perfect, and it allowed Sarah to avoid the unpleasant situation of having to fire the lass. But Sarah knew she would have to revisit the situation next year when a fulltime nanny no longer would be required. In the meantime, the boys would have to adapt to the change and become used to calling Elspeth 'Miss Winter'.

Following Jimmy's return from his fact-finding mission, the matter uppermost in the minds of all those involved was whether or not to proceed with the erection of a milling factory. To that end, a couple of days before Christmas, the three parties gathered for a formal meeting to (hopefully) arrive at firm decisions on the matter. Once they were settled, Jimmy was asked to present his findings from his trip.

"I'll start at the end of the trip instead of at the beginning, if I may?" Nods from the other two present encouraged him to go on. "Having kept a keen eye on what happened at Pleystowe, and following John Dow's advice, I investigated what might be available from Java. The industry there appears to be going through some form of decline. As growers turn to other crops, some mills are becoming redundant. Various bits of equipment and machinery would be available and at reasonable prices from that industry."

"Do we want used equipment that its owners no longer require, as opposed to new equipment?" Sarah asked.

"Good question, my dear," Cameron said. "What are your thoughts, Jimmy? After all, you also looked at the latest equipment and technology available from suppliers."

"That rather depends on the size of our milling factory," Jimmy replied thoughtfully. "We need to estimate what our required future milling capacity might be, as that will inform our purchase of suitable equipment."

"As opposed to wasting money on superfluous capacity that we might never require?" Cameron asked.

"Exactly… And I understand your concerns about second-hand stuff, Sarah, but I inspected everything of that nature that Pleystowe installed and found no fault with any of it," Jimmy said.

"Perhaps, Jimmy, you and I should devote time to resolving the issues of capacity and type of equipment required, and we also need to consider where such a factory might be located." As Cameron finished speaking, he looked to his colleagues and found them both nodding their agreement.

Sarah, who had no wish to be involved in such technical discussions, was surprised when another meeting of the trio was scheduled between Christmas and New Year to discuss the outcome of the sugar milling factory planning. She was surprised to learn how much the two men had achieved in so few days. Their report started with something they believed Sarah might understand, as opposed to talking about the details of the equipment and machinery to be installed.

"We've selected a site over on the second block where the cane is planted and have measured it and checked it for accessibility. Of course, we would require your approval of our choice before any progress occurs," Cameron opened the discussion.

"There seems to be so much cane planted over there. I'm surprised you found a vacant area large enough to hold a sugar mill. But, if you believe you've identified the most suitable location, I doubt I'll have much argument with your choice – after you show me the site," Sarah assured them. "Now, what goes in the factory? Have you reached any conclusions regarding equipment and machinery?"

It was Jimmy's turn to explain. "We looked at both importing new material from Scotland and acquiring redundant equipment from Java. After discussions with John Dow, and a chat with Hewitt from Pleystowe Plantation, we believe what is available from Java will be satisfactory for our needs. We think that, in the near future, both Cameron and I will travel to Java with a view to sourcing the required plant for our factory. After Java, we will be in a position to know whether we might still need to import some new equipment from Scotland."

"I see… Have you decided on a likely date for your trip to Java?" Sarah asked, the edge to her voice quite noticeable. "And, how long do you anticipate that trip to Java might have you absent from here?"

"Sarah, dear, I detect you are not entirely happy with our proposed trip to Java," Cameron began tentatively. "Perhaps you might share your concerns to allow us to put your mind at rest. Regardless, I can assure you we would be absent for no longer than necessary to achieve the task we set ourselves."

"Yes, I believe that to be the case, but my concern is for the continued efficient running of our properties here during your absence. With both of you away, the continued management of all three of our properties will fall to me. As I suspect I have not been kept up-to-date with everything in that regard, your absence does not bode well for the continued effective running of our properties. You have not indicated how soon you might undertake such a trip to Java, or given me an estimate of how long you might be away. I wish to make it clear that, without time and appropriate involvement for me to be brought up-to-date with what's happening on the Selections, I will not be happy to take over the reins while you're away."

A stony silence settled over the group for a few moments while the men considered Sarah's statement. For her part, Sarah sat with her jaw set, watching the men struggle to absorb her comments. For a while now, Sarah had felt sidelined when it came to the running of the Selections. While she accepted that her pregnancies had contributed to that situation in no small way, she was not about to accept it as being the way of things. This house where they were all gathered this evening was on *her* land. While she would never deny Cameron his say in matters relating to the running of the property, decisions about *her* property were *hers* to make.

While Sarah accepted that the current forum was not the place to air such grievances, she had no qualms about giving warning of conversations that might follow. And, yes, some of those conversations Cameron might well find uncomfortable. Nevertheless, she pushed such thoughts aside when she realised the silence had lasted long enough.

"There is another matter of which I've heard no mention so far this evening. What is the likely cost of such a sugar milling factory? Have you agreed on some theoretical figure for the erection of such a facility? While I might not be funding it alone, my contribution would be equal to anyone else's. I believe that entitles me to more than a little say in any such planning – even in whether the project goes ahead or not. And, in case you feel inclined to argue, I am quite resolute in this matter. So, gentlemen, unless you can produce here tonight a detailed proposed costing for the project that I may take away and scrutinise, you have more work to do before you receive my approval for any of this project to proceed."

With her position made clear, Sarah flounced back inside, leaving the men on the verandah stunned and unsure about what to do next. After a few moments, Jimmy again found his voice.

"This appears an appropriate time for me to take my leave… and to leave you to whatever awaits you inside. My friend, I suspect yours will not be a happy evening. I hope there is somewhere comfortable in the stables where you might spend the night – if necessary."

Jimmy had assessed the situation accurately. Cameron found the bedroom door firmly closed. Sarah ignored his requests to speak to her, clearly negating any chance of conciliatory conversations that night. While there were other beds available in the house, Cameron felt so stunned – and shunned – by

Sarah's actions that he took Jimmy's suggestion and made himself as comfortable as possible for the night on the tray of the wagon. Next morning, Cameron discovered he was still non grata when he breakfasted alone, Sarah having requested a tray in her room. Straight after breakfast, Cameron went in search of Jimmy and found him inspecting their block of plant cane on Jimmy's property.

"Not having spent too much time in the paddocks over the last few days, and with another deluge threatening, I thought I should have a quick check on everything while I could stay dry while about it," Jimmy chattered before becoming serious. "I was going to wish you a 'good morning' as you rode up, but by the look of you, that seemed an unlikely situation. Things still a bit frosty this morning…?"

"I wouldn't know. I haven't spoken to or even seen my wife since she left us on the verandah last evening. This is so unlike Sarah. I don't know what to do. How to repair the situation between us. Perhaps you are lucky, Jimmy. Being unmarried, you are immune to such situations."

"That wasn't always the case, my friend. I was married once, but not for long, I admit. That was before one too many such occurrences after some transgression or other on my part convinced her to abandon me as a lost cause. She was right to do so, of course. Some of us men are just not cut out to be married. Now, in your case, that's not true."

"Until last night, I thought I had a wonderful marriage."

"Aye, and you do, lad. But I wonder if you might be able to help me understand what it was that set Sarah off… With what she found such grievous fault regarding our plans."

"Not sure I can, Jimmy. Sarah always was an astute business woman, and she sharpened her skills further while working with my father. We were tasked with a job and we did it. I believe we did what was asked of us. But, when we told Sarah what we planned, it was obvious we hadn't done something right."

"Ah, well, lad, therein lies the problem. We *told her* what we planned. We did not *consult her,* or seek her input into the planning process. We don't know if she might have ideas of her own about where to locate the mill or what to buy. I suspect she sees our behaviour as something of a male takeover of her rights and business. While there is many a husband who believes he has the right to dictate how his wife leads her life and might not even allow her an opinion on anything, you are not that sort of husband… And Sarah is not one of those wives who allows it to happen. The only part of our operations here that you may lay any claim to is one-third of that Selection across the road. Everything else here is either owned by me or Sarah."

"Are you suggesting she felt as though I was trying to take over what is rightfully hers? Take over her life, maybe?"

"Perhaps that's a reasonable assessment of the situation, but only Sarah can confirm whether that be the case or not. So, Lad, best you talk to her."

"Chance would be a fine thing. She won't even acknowledge my presence, let alone talk to me."

"Talk to Cheng Li. See if he can rustle up a large bunch of flowers to take to her when you go, cap in hand, to try to apologise to her."

Nevertheless, despite his scepticism and foreboding, Cameron sought out Cheng Li and politely requested a large bunch of flowers for Miss Sarah, please. Happy to be given something different to do, Cheng Li sprang into action. Ten minutes later, he met Cameron at the stables and handed over an impressive bouquet. Then, it was the moment Cameron had dreaded. It was time to try his luck at re-establishing a rapport with Sarah, and he realised it would take a special approach if he were to have any hope of success.

"No point delaying the inevitable," he told himself as he strode off towards the homestead. Orla was on her way through the front room as he stepped inside. The sight of her gave rise to an idea.

"Orla, please be so kind as to take these flowers to Miss Sarah and tell her I am truly sorry I have upset her… and that I wish to apologise personally."

"Right you are, Mr Cameron. I'll take them through to her now. By the way, will you stay for morning tea?"

Bless the woman, Cameron thought as he watched Orla stride towards Sarah's private little sitting room. Orla never as much as blinked an eyelid when I made my request, although she must already have been aware of the situation in this house. About a minute later, Sarah emerged carrying the flowers. She paused when a couple of paces away from Cameron and eyed him up and down.

"Perhaps we should talk," she said quietly. "I'll ask Orla to put these in water first," she added as she lowered her face and smelled the flowers.

Later that afternoon, when Cameron encountered Jimmy on his way home from the paddocks, he was able to report to Jimmy that peace was restored on the home front.

Chapter 8

Philip

Once life settled back to normal in the Wallace household, Sarah called the two men to a meeting to again discuss their plans for a sugar mill. This time, she led the discussions and asked questions, some of which the men couldn't answer, and still no budget had been prepared.

"Well, gentlemen, if we are to proceed with this project, I suggest we meet on a regular basis – say, every evening before dinner – to process any further thoughts, suggestions or ideas. I see our first task as the preparation of some form of costing for the project. I will undertake the production of that, but I will be asking for information from you as we proceed. So, gentlemen, I strenuously advise you to set your mind to all and every last detail we need to consider if this project is to result in what we want and at a price we can afford. Is there any argument with any of what I have said?"

No argument forthcoming, Sarah moved to set things in motion. "Jimmy – and Cameron, if needs be – I will require a list of the machinery and equipment we need to install in the factory, and the likely cost of each piece on your list. To allow time to produce such a list, perhaps we won't meet tomorrow night, but will meet again the following night. Does that present any problems?" Two heads shook in unison.

The following night, although there was to be no project meeting, at the first break in conversation during pre-dinner drinks, Sarah launched a question that had plagued her all day.

"This isn't a project meeting, but I thought I might put this to you for consideration. I wondered whether there might be benefit in organising a meeting with John Dow for him to cast an eye over our plans and offer suggestions. What are your thoughts on that?"

Despite feeling slightly affronted by their competency being called into question, both men agreed it would be a valid move to have Dow involved.

"First thing in the morning, I'll ride over to see what I can arrange, " Cameron volunteered.

"If he is available, don't organise anything before sometime next week. We will have nothing to show him if he comes sooner than that," Sarah said.

"Next week means we will have to be busy in the meantime, but at least by then, we should have some firm plans on paper for him to consider," Jimmy said. "By the way, Sarah, I should have those costings for you to look at by tomorrow evening's meeting."

At their meeting the following evening, Cameron reported John Dow had suggested they meet around mid-morning on Wednesday next week. While Sarah and Jimmy were happy with the arrangement, Jimmy continued to appear disgruntled about something. Despite trying to ignore him, by the time their meeting drew to a close that evening, it had gotten the better of Sarah.

"Jimmy, before you go… I've noticed you are not entirely happy about some aspect of our project. What is bothering you?" Sarah asked. "This project involves all of us. Any facility that results from it will be of significance to the three of us. We all must have our say in what happens and how and when. So, whatever does not sit comfortably with you, Jimmy, now is the time to air it. Share your concerns with us, please."

After initially refusing to be drawn on the matter, Jimmy eventually opened up about it.

"All right, all right… I am concerned that time is fast away and we haven't progressed far, if at all. I believe there is little chance we will have our own factory ready in time to crush our 1870 crop. As a consequence, we are again faced with finding an alternative way of turning our crop into cash."

"Are you of the opinion that Pleystowe may not be inclined to purchase our cane again?" Sarah asked as she tried to control the feeling of alarm rising in her.

"Argh, I hadn't considered the situation," Cameron began, "but Jimmy paints an accurate picture of our potential situation this season. Thank you for alerting us to the problem, Jimmy."

"Tomorrow, I will ride to Pleystowe to try for a few words with Hewitt regarding our crop. If he *canna* see his way clear to take it, we might have to try Davidson at Alexandra. It is vital we have a firm arrangement in place as soon as possible."

"Let's pray for encouraging words from Pleystowe," Cameron suggested. "I much prefer to deal with Hewitt, or even Romilly, than Davidson. Besides, I think Alexandra Plantation's crop looks about sufficient for their current available milling capacity until their new works are completed."

"In that case, let's hope Pleystowe's response is in our favour," Sarah agreed.

"By the way, Sarah, what is the nature of that new extension to the house that now looks almost complete?" Jimmy asked.

"It is to be the boys' school room where Elspeth will deliver their lessons. Well, where she will teach Angus this year until Lachlan joins him at the start of next year," Sarah explained.

"I understood this year's lessons had already begun," Jimmy said. "Without a school room, where are they taking place?"

"Until the school room is ready for use, Elspeth is delivering lessons in my private sitting room. It is a little inconvenient for me. As it will only be for a short time, I can work around the arrangement."

"Annie tells me Elspeth is happy in her position here, something she never managed to achieve in her position in town." Jimmy sighed and continued. "It is good to have them both here and so settled. I wasn't sure how it would work out for them, or me, if truth be told. I was so used to living alone, but it feels as though it's where we all belong and as though we've always been together."

"My only comment is that I hope it remains that way. Elspeth appears a capable teacher and the boys have taken a liking to her. That's probably half the battle won when you are trying to educate young boys. Apart from that, it is wonderful having

Annie living so close. We regularly take morning tea together, and she should join us more often for our pre-dinner drinks. I hope she doesn't think she is excluded from our evenings together."

"For the next little while, as we work on planning our factory, perhaps it is as well if she doesn't join us," Jimmy suggested. "I'm sure she would find these sessions boring."

Sarah doubted that would be the case, but chose not to say so at that juncture. Sarah had kept Annie updated on everything discussed regarding the erection of a milling factory. Annie displayed a high level of interest in every detail, and asked the most intelligent and thought-provoking questions.

After dinner that night, Sarah invited Cameron to join her in the sitting room. She was hoping for a conversation on what she considered a delicate matter. Cameron suggested the verandah might be cooler than the sitting room on such a humid night. Sarah followed him out to the verandah. As soon as they were settled, she launched into the conversation that, for more than a week, she had been trying to pluck up the courage to have.

"Cameron, have you had news from your father lately?"

"Not for two or three weeks. Father writes every week. Then, his letters go into the mailbag with any other business documents and arrive here when the next Wallace vessel comes into port. Argh, that reminds me. I collected a mailbag the other day when I was in town and made a point of leaving it on the table in the hall so I wouldn't forget to deal with it. In one of her cleaning frenzies, Orla must have shifted it and I forgot about it. Out of sight, out of mind, I suppose. Allow me a moment to hunt for it. It probably contains mail for you as well."

A couple of minutes later, Cameron returned. "I do apologise for the late delivery of these," he said as he thrust several letters at Sarah. "Should we go inside to read them where the light is better?"

"Yes, I'm keen to see what Philip might have to say."

"Is there something amiss back home that I don't know about?"

"Uhmm… I don't know. I suspect Philip, in his last couple of letters, has hinted at something. I might be imagining it, or maybe Philip only suspects something is afoot, but isn't sure."

"What sort of 'something' did he hint at, and did he appear concerned?"

"As I said, I don't know. Maybe it was something to do with Douglas himself, or possibly about the business… Or perhaps I just imagined the whole thing."

"Well, whatever it was seems to cause you some concern. So, I suggest we retire indoors to read our mail. Maybe at the end of that exercise, we might know more about what's afoot, or your concerns might be put to rest."

Sarah sorted her letters into chronological order before opening the first of two from Philip. She read the first one, then went back and read it again before considering its contents for a few moments. Cameron looked up from his reading and felt a jab of alarm when he saw the concerned look on Sarah's face as she stared off into the distance.

"Was it bad news?" he asked quietly. The sound of his voice startled Sarah.

"Er… Why? Does yours contain concerning news?"

"I'm not sure I'm concerned – yet. But I admit to being a bit apprehensive and reluctant to open the next letter. Now, what about yours? Does it contain concerning news?"

"Let's leave such discussions until after we've read all mail from Glasgow. That way, we'll have a better idea of what it is we're going to be discussing," Sarah suggested, and Cameron agreed.

It felt like an eternity before they laid aside their mail and exchanged meaningful looks.

"Right, I suspect we both have plenty to discuss. Shall I tell you about my news first?" Cameron asked. Sarah nodded and motioned for him to go ahead. "When your father's opening comments are to remind you that he is an old man and that he is tired of the life he is living, you know it is time to be concerned."

"Oh, dear, that's worse than I expected."

"Things did clarify a little as the letter progressed. He complained that it was almost impossible to run a business in Glasgow any longer since the government again introduced new excise duties and rules about to and from which countries goods might be imported and exported. Somewhere else in his letter, he claims money is becoming tight. Some of his long-term, previously sound clients are now either defaulting or struggling to meet their financial obligations. He claims he is now looking for suitable buyers to enable him to dispose of much of his business enterprise, but he claims their shipping operations will continue."

"What was the date on his last letter?" Sarah asked. Cameron read it to her. "Right… So Douglas's last letter dates from prior to Philip's second letter in this dispatch. In his first letter, Philip talks about Douglas looking for buyers for some of his business operations. Then, in his second letter, Philip says sound contracts were now in place for the sale of much of the business."

"Ok-ay, so matters are progressing much as Douglas hoped. Do Philip's letters contain anything else I should know about?"

"Yes, there is a major development you need to be aware of, and I suspect your next letter from Douglas will explain it. With all of the business in Glasgow being wound down and only one small enterprise continuing for the moment, Douglas is sending Philip to join us here in the settlement with a view to helping you run shipping operations. From the comments in Philip's last letter, I suspect he might already be on a Wallace ship bound for Mackay."

"How do you feel about that, Sarah? One assumes he would move in with us, as Jimmy's house is at capacity with Annie and Elspeth living there."

"It will be wonderful to have Philip here again, but it does mean we need to think about appropriate accommodation for him. I think that might entail a small apartment attached to the homestead where he will have his own bedroom, sitting room, and other facilities. Oh, it just occurred to me… Would you prefer he resided in town? What are your thoughts on this?"

"In truth, I don't have any thoughts yet, but as you say, once we sort things out here, it might be better if he resided in town. Although, if he resided in town, I imagine he'd still spend quite a deal of time out here with us. That means he still would require an apartment here."

"You are right, Cameron. Whatever happens, Philip will need an apartment here. It seems I need to talk to Roddy McDonald again and soon, if we are to have anything even nearly ready by the time Philip arrives."

As they prepared for bed, another thought occurred to Sarah. "Cameron, is it likely Douglas is not well, and hence his decision to sell off the business? In any case, as he says, he is an old man now. Might a visit to Glasgow by you be in order as a matter of some urgency to spend some time with your father?"

"That is something to ponder. I think I will leave it in abeyance until I speak to Philip to gain a better understanding of how things are in Glasgow these days. There is another possibility, of course. As planning our new sugar mill progresses, it might transpire we need to acquire some vital piece of equipment from Scotland. That would provide the perfect excuse for a trip back home, without its appearing I've made a special trip just to spend time with my father."

"Knowing Douglas as we both do, he would not condone any visit unless some other matter necessitated it. Nevertheless, I agree. Once Philip is here and before we do anything else, we should acquaint ourselves with the facts relating to the Glasgow situation. Until we possess all the facts, we could be concerning ourselves unduly over nothing other than a sound business move."

"Well, here's something for you to think about in the meantime. If Philip is already on his way here, he will be here much sooner than you might expect. Since the Suez Canal opened last November, and since the start of this year, 1870, when our vessels started using the new canal, sailing from Glasgow to here now takes only 35 to 40 days."

"So, quickly…? My goodness, I must talk to Roddy McDonald tomorrow."

Next morning, as Roddy McDonald supervised his men putting the finishing touches to the school room, Sarah drew him aside to discuss the next –urgent – extension to the homestead. Within no more than a matter of minutes, Sarah had told him what was required, and Roddy had drawn for Sarah's approval a rough sketch of his proposal in the dirt with the toe of his boot. After some discussion, agreement was reached, and Roddy went to tell his men about the new work they were to begin as soon as they finished the school room.

A couple of days later, amid the hammering and sawing that started earlier than usual that morning, Cameron announced over breakfast that he had a ship to meet when it tied up today, but he should be home in time for dinner that night.

"It's the first of our vessels to come through that new Suez Canal. I'm hoping it might be bringing more mail from Glasgow. My curiosity and concern about what is happening over there will kill me if I have to wait until Philip arrives to know more."

Sarah took the pre-emptive measure of cancelling that evening's project meeting on the basis that Cameron might not arrive home until late. Jimmy seemed disappointed but accepted the situation. When Cameron did arrive home a little before their normal meeting time, Cheng Li was dispatched to tell Jimmy the project meeting was on again.

With the revised plan and budget now documented by Sarah, at least in rough form, the project meeting was brief.

"Right, that leaves two more events to tick off my list of things to be done: our meeting with John Dow tomorrow, and discussions with Pleystowe Plantation regarding the sale of our current crop. I take it both of you will be available when Dow arrives," Sarah asked her two companions and received affirmative nods.

"Sarah, there is one thing I would suggest," Jimmy began. "There might be merit in leaving discussions with Hewitt at

Pleystowe until the current wet season is ended." His suggestion hit a nerve. Both Cameron and Sarah sprang upright in the chairs.

"Are you expecting problems with such discussions, Jimmy?" Sarah asked.

"No, but I have heard gossip that suggests it might be to our advantage to wait. Talk around these parts has it that Pleystowe has a small crop this year as a result of poor strikes after planting last year. Adding to their woes is a large area of one paddock where the cane is already poor-looking after being waterlogged for several weeks as a result of the constant heavy rains and poor drainage. Once the rain ceases and they have a chance to assess their situation, they may realise they have not much cane of their own to crush this year and will be eager to buy ours."

"I had heard something similar," Cameron admitted, "but I put it down to no more than idle gossip. Of course, it may prove to be just that, but I agree there is merit in waiting before we approach them."

With the business of the meeting dealt with, Sarah took the opportunity to alert Jimmy to Philip's imminent return to the settlement and the likelihood that it would be permanent.

"That is great news. It will be good to have the lad here again. It might be a bit crowded in my house, but I suppose it will be all right if he isn't too fussy about his accommodation," Jimmy told them. Sarah eased his mind by explaining the next extension to her homestead.

"By the way, Sarah, I collected a mailbag from the ship while I was in town," Cameron announced. "I haven't opened it yet, but it might contain information regarding Philip's likely arrival. Straight after dinner, I'll check the bag."

Both had received letters. Sarah received one from Philip, and Cameron received one each from his father and Philip. In both Philip's letters, he confirmed his travel arrangements. Douglas's letter to his son outlined the recent sale of various components of the Wallace business empire and what he saw as the future for the remaining components. He also explained his vision for Philip's ongoing role in the family's enterprises after becoming permanently based in the settlement of Mackay.

"If Philip did depart as indicated in his letter," Sarah began thoughtfully, "he could be here in as little as two weeks or maybe three. I must say, I am excited about seeing him again, even if the circumstances making that possible are perhaps not the greatest."

"I don't agree with your assessment of the circumstances. By the sounds of the way the business world is going in Glasgow, I think the family, and particularly my father, are well out of it now while good sale prices can be achieved," Cameron said.

When they met later that day for their usual pre-dinner drinks, the project team agreed their meeting with John Dow went exceptionally well. Annie joined them at Sarah's invitation. Nothing other than their proposed sugar mill had a chance of being discussed that evening. Dow had made several suggestions and provided some recent information regarding Java that required a redraft of their project plan. Due to other commitments, it was the start of the following week before the revised plan was available for discussion.

Plans for Jimmy to visit Java to source various plant and equipment for the new factory were put on hold for a while due to the imminent arrival of Philip, but a tentative date of the end of March was agreed.

On the morning of Philip's arrival, Sarah had planned to travel into town with Cameron to welcome him, but Cameron had vetoed her plan.

"Philip is bringing a mountain of material with him. There will be quite a few crates and trunks to load on the wagon. There won't be sufficient room for an extra passenger. You will be able to give him a proper welcome when he arrives here. Besides, I need to discuss a few business issues with him. The trip home will be an ideal time for that."

Although Sarah sulked when he drove into town, Cameron wasn't concerned. He knew the thought of Philip's arrival later that day would snap her out of it before he returned that evening. And he was correct on all counts. All the material Philip brought with him almost overloaded the wagon and even meant his small personal luggage had to be stacked at their feet for the trip home. Aware of how anxious both Sarah and Jimmy were to welcome Philip, Cameron wasted no time before heading home once the wagon was loaded.

Their arrival at the homestead a little earlier than anticipated allowed Philip enough time to be fussed over by Sarah, unpack a few things in the homestead's spare room, and freshen up before pre-dinner drinks. During Cameron's absence in town, Sarah went across and invited Annie and Elspeth to drinks with Jimmy that evening to meet Philip and then stay on for dinner with the rest of them.

Then, when Orla served lunch, Sarah advised Orla there would be six for dinner that night, and for the foreseeable future, there would be three for breakfast in the dining room every morning unless she was otherwise advised.

The sounds of merry conversation filled the night air as six people enjoyed their drinks. Although not a project meeting night, it was inevitable that mention of planning for a new sugar mill would occur. Philip was fascinated by what was planned and how it was going to happen. He kept the conversation focused on the project for much longer than intended as he launched question after question about almost every aspect of the project.

At last, the topic appeared to have run its course when Philip asked one last question. "When shall I see the first of all these works happening here?"

"Well, there will be nothing happening here," Jimmy told him. "But, by the middle of the year, quite a bit will be happening on our other Selection across the road. I hope to travel to Java at the end of March to purchase the first of the machinery for the factory. Then, once it arrives at the port, we will have to transport it to the site. In the meantime, the foundations and other necessary parts of the factory building will need to be prepared in readiness for the equipment."

After dinner, the ladies retired to the sitting room and the men escaped to the verandah to smoke and down a nightcap or two. Cameron later reported to Sarah that Philip's interest in the new factory had him talking about nothing else while they sat with their pipes and wee drams on the verandah.

Chapter 9

The Mill

Over the next few days, Philip spent most of his time with Jimmy as well as in meetings with Cameron regarding the running of their shipping operations. Cameron later told Sarah that Philip seemed reticent about the idea of being located in town, claiming the additional cost of such accommodation was an unnecessary expense.

"He is right about the expense. I would suggest you let it sit while you sort out how the two of you will manage the shipping business. There's always a chance Philip will decide it might be more convenient and effective to be located in town."

Cameron was still working his way through everything his father had sent with Philip, and trying to establish what future his father intended for Wallace Shipping.

"I did discover something surprising in the small portion of his documents I've read. He travelled to London to open an account with the London branch of the Bank of New South Wales. He thought it the safest place to put the operating capital for Wallace Shipping as it was an Australian bank already with branches in the colony of Queensland," Cameron told Sarah.

"But it doesn't have a branch here, does it?"

"Not as far as I am aware. If it had been my decision, the money would have gone into the Australian Joint Stock Bank (AJS Bank). With Maryborough the busiest port in the colony, the AJS saw merit in establishing a branch there. It also was to establish one at Gympie to meet the needs of that area following the gold discovery there. One or both of those banks will likely open a branch here in Mackay, especially after the settlement was declared a municipality last year."

"Quite a few people suggested you should stand for election when the first election to form a council was held. Did you ever consider it?"

"No, not for one minute. I like my life the way it is, thanks. Besides, being an elected councillor best suits those who either live or spend most of their time in town. I don't, and I wouldn't change my life for something I lacked passion about. If I were to be elected, but continued to live here, it would still require me to spend increasing amounts of time in town to deal with the duties and expectations attached to the position."

At that point, Philip arrived home after spending the morning in the paddocks with Jimmy. He bounced up the stairs, announced he would freshen up before lunch, and disappeared inside. At a more sedate pace, Jimmy followed Philip up onto the verandah where Cameron and Sarah were seated.

"This might be out of order, but it is something for you to think about before our next project meeting," Jimmy said by way of a greeting. "Young Philip seems besotted with our plans to build a factory. He wistfully commented this morning that he wished he was involved in the project."

"Aye, I had noted his high level of interest. Is it causing a problem?" Cameron asked.

"Not at all. But it makes me wonder whether it might be worth his accompanying me to Java when I go in search of plant for the factory. It's not what he came here to do, but if you could spare him for a while, Cameron, I think his assistance would be an asset to me. You know how I hate paperwork and how notoriously bad I am at it. Philip could take care of that side of things for me. While I concentrate on doing the inspections and deals, Philip could keep a record of everything I've done and any purchases agreed."

"It sounds like it could be wise for him to accompany you," Sarah conceded. "But it is your decision, Cameron. Philip is supposed to be assisting you with the shipping operations. Can you spare him to go tripping off to Java with Jimmy?"

"Uhmm… Let me think on it until the next project meeting. As I managed everything on my own previously, I can't see his absence being a problem. But, once he returns, it will free me up to spend more time developing our new factory."

Jimmy dropped Sarah a wink as he took his leave and headed home for lunch. Later, he confided to Annie he was reasonably confident Philip would be accompanying him to Java.

At the next project meeting, Cameron confirmed Jimmy's prediction. When asked about it, Philip made all the appropriate noises about not wanting to leave Cameron in the lurch in terms of the shipping operations, but everyone noted how he struggled to control his excitement. Cameron put the young man out of his misery by suggesting it would be a great assistance to Jimmy if Philip could see his way clear to go to Java. At the conclusion of the meeting, Jimmy advised the others he again had discussions with Hewitt at Pleystowe.

"We now have a firm arrangement in place for Pleystowe to buy all of this season's cane. I decided we needed to have something definite in place, and they would be aware of the nature of their crop by now. They made it clear it was only the poor nature of their crop this year that made it possible to buy our cane. They warned that they might not be in a position to purchase our crop next year."

A week later, Jimmy and Philip boarded the next Wallace vessel scheduled to call at Java. As Philip went in search of their cabin, Jimmy had a last few words to Cameron before following his companion on board.

"I have high hopes for the outcome of this trip and hope we are not disappointed. But first, I have to survive the voyage to Java. Philip is so excited; he hasn't stopped talking about it and the new factory. I suspect he will have talked my ears off long before we reach our destination."

A scant four weeks later, the pair were on board a Wallace ship when it made fast alongside the Wallace Shipping Line's wharf on the bank of the Pioneer River. It had been a rough voyage home. Both men had been thrown about their cabin so violently that neither had managed much sleep for the entire voyage. After exchanging perfunctory greetings with Cameron, the pair climbed aboard the wagon in silence and spoke little on the way home. When dinner was about to be served that evening, and Philip still had not emerged after disappearing into his apartment when he arrived home, Cameron found Philip sound asleep and chose to leave him that way. Later conversations recounted a similar occurrence at Jimmy's house on his first evening back home.

First thing after breakfast the next morning, Jimmy went to Sarah's house. He was not inclined to wait until pre-dinner drinks or a project meeting to share news of the Java expedition. Sarah laughed as Maggie ushered Jimmy into the sitting room where she and Cameron were about to have Philip share the highlights of his trip with them.

"Jimmy, you are just in time to keep this young man's story honest and true," Sarah said as Jimmy settled into the nearest chair.

"Perhaps we might need to collude in that endeavour," Jimmy replied.

"No, you have the floor, Jimmy," Philip grinned. "You will provide a much better report than I might."

"Right… Well, the first and most important thing I have to report is that our trip was most successful. All items on our shopping list were procured and at excellent prices. With some mills going out of production in that country, the quality of the plant available was excellent, and the amount to choose from was amazing. Philip has done preliminary work regarding transporting the equipment."

"I will need to finalise the shipping arrangements with you, Cameron, but that won't be needed until Jimmy's agent advises that all the plant has been delivered to the warehouse at the port."

"What timeframe is likely for the various stages of bringing the plant here?" Cameron asked Jimmy.

"Hard to say, but inside three months by my reckoning. Some of it is a little hard to estimate as it is still in situ in the factory and must be removed before it can be transported to the port. Nevertheless, we now have all of the relevant details of all the plant acquired, so we can proceed with refining the drawings for our new factory, and establishment of a plan for installation of the major components and completion of the building."

"How does our budget look after this shopping trip of yours?" Sarah asked.

"Ah, I think that's something Philip might answer. He kept meticulous records of everything… and I do mean everything."

"This initial stage of equipping the new factory has come in well under budget. Only one item cost the price we had estimated for its purchase. Everything else was under our estimation and by quite a bit in some instances."

"If I understand our current positions with this project," Sarah began hesitantly, "and all the plant and equipment we need has been sourced, am I correct in assuming there is no need to visit Scotland to acquire any essential equipment?"

"Your understanding of the situation is correct, Sarah," Jimmy replied. "No further trips abroad for the sake of the project are needed."

Sarah appeared disappointed by Jimmy's reply and became a bit subdued. After a few moments, Cameron felt compelled to investigate.

"You seem disappointed by something, Sarah. May I know what bothers you about Jimmy's report?"

"Oh, no. I'm delighted with the way everything turned out. I just… Well, I felt a little disappointed there is no reason for you to visit Scotland. I suppose I hoped a visit to Glasgow to see your father again would eventuate as part of this project. Now, it appears such a trip is unnecessary."

"Would you have accompanied me to spend time with Douglas?" Cameron asked.

"I hadn't thought on that. Perhaps we might discuss this in private later," Sarah suggested. Cameron agreed, although a bit intrigued and bemused.

The next few days slipped by in a constant flurry of sale contracts, budget figures, discussions with Roddy McDonald, and factory building drawings to amend and approve. The machinery already received at the Java port warehouse needed to be paid for. After a couple of frustrating days of trying to achieve that, Cameron grudgingly announced he would be on their next southbound vessel to deal directly with the bank in Brisbane. A few similar trips occurred over the ensuing several months.

Then, at pre-dinner drinks following Cameron's return from his latest Brisbane trip, Jimmy noticed Cameron looked exhausted and enquired after his friend's health.

"No cause for concern, Jimmy. My health is fine. Life has been hectic lately, and I have had my fill of getting on and off ships and dealing with bank managers. Tell me, please, is there anything more from Java we are yet to pay for?"

"Nothing more…," Philip replied on Jimmy's behalf. "All sales contracts are now finalised. Equipment will begin arriving here next month."

"Thank God, and thank you. And thank you also, Philip, for running the shipping operations in my absence."

Several more consultation meetings with John Dow occurred to confirm the proposed layout of the building and location of machinery within it were satisfactory. Jimmy and Cameron also sought Dow's advice on what to do with the equipment when it arrived from Java. The factory would not have progressed sufficiently to have the machinery installed as soon as it arrived… and there was the problem of how to move it from the port to its intended installation location.

Dow drew their attention to how John Spiller had brought the various components for his horse mill up the river from the port to his plantation.

"Boats, lads... Boats are what you need or, at least, barges of some sort. The only alternative available is to employ teams of horses to haul loaded drays to the site."

"Some of our cargo from Java will be large pieces of machinery," Jimmy said. "I'm not at all sure horse teams and drays will safely transport it to here. In fact, I can't get my mind around the size and style of boat that would be required."

"Still, Jimmy, we do have to move it from the port to the site," Cameron reminded him. "Others have done it. Others besides Spiller, that is – like Davidson at Alexandra and Hewitt at Pleystowe."

"Yes, I suppose it must be possible. I'm just not sure how."

"Perhaps you are unaware of how the machinery will arrive, Jimmy," Dow suggested.

"I know how it better arrive: on a ship and undamaged."

"No. No, that's not what I meant. Yes, it will arrive at port on a ship, but the machinery will most likely not arrive fully assembled as it was when you last saw it. It will be broken down into its components for easier handling and shipping."

"Broken down...." Jimmy and Cameron exclaimed in unison as they exchanged an alarmed look.

"Does that mean re-assembly on site when it arrives?" Cameron asked, and Dow nodded.

"Did the machinery we bought look familiar, Jimmy? I mean, does it still look like the machinery and equipment we knew in the Caribbean?"

"Aye, to some extent, it does, but technology and design have moved on since then. Some looks quite different from what we were used to seeing in factories."

Cameron groaned. "We'll never manage," he said, shaking his head at the thought of what lay ahead. "It's going to be a disaster."

"There is no need for concern," John Dow assured them. "I will supervise the re-assembly and installation, and I have put together a small group of men who I trust to work with me."

Jimmy gave Cameron a hard look after Dow's comments, but Cameron missed its meaning and it wasn't until later that Jimmy explained.

"John Dow and his merry men won't come cheap. Just wait until we tell Sarah about that. We might have saved some money on the purchase of the machinery, but it could end up costing us more by the time it is installed."

"Oh, God, yes. The Chancellor of the Exchequer will not be pleased if we have ruined her budget. I'm not saying she is tightfisted, Jimmy, but she does keep a firm hand on spending."

"It occurs to me, Cameron, that we will have a problem once machinery starts arriving from Java. Where do we store it until the new factory building is ready for it to be installed? We can't leave it sitting out in the weather, but what alternatives do we have?"

"Let me think on it for a while. I have been so focused on everything else, I hadn't thought about once things started arriving. I suppose, in the first instance, and until we work out what to do, I could instruct our ships' captains not to accept any of the machinery as cargo until further notice. At least, that way, everything will be under cover, although still at Java, until we work out something here."

"Right you are. That sounds like the best move while we sort something out here."

Cameron took almost a week to come up with a possible solution to the problem. "As promised, I gave some thought to the storage of the machinery once it arrives here. I believe I can make a small area of Wallace Shipping's warehouse at the port available. It won't be a big area, not big enough to hold all the gear to come from Java, but it will be a start."

The two men, with some input from Philip, then turned their attention to the practicalities of unloading the various heavy pieces of equipment from ships, moving them to the assigned space in the warehouse, and unloading them from whatever was used to move the equipment. After some discussion, it was Philip who suggested he might know of a way and would investigate. That resulted in Philip making an unscheduled trip into town the next morning. The following day, he reported he might have solved the problem.

"I had noticed a group of men – wharf labourers, I suppose they would be called – servicing various ships tied up along the river. After managing to track down the chap in charge, I learned they are a gang of men available for hire for work in the port area. I told him of our possible requirements in the near future. He considered the work I outlined to be within the scope of his gang and also said he had a couple of horse and dray teams they could employ when necessary. He seemed happy to continue our discussion, so I asked whether his teams and drays might be available later to haul the same equipment out to our construction site. He assured me that also was within the scope of the work they undertook."

"If I might comment," Cameron said. "That man and his gang sound almost too good to be true. How did you assess the man himself, Philip? Did he appear honest enough?"

"He struck me as being honest enough, maybe a bit rough around the edges, if you know what I mean, but honest nevertheless."

"Right then, Jimmy, we should talk to his other employers to check out his credentials. If the word about him is all good, we should proceed with moving at least some of the machinery from Java to Wallace Shipping's warehouse."

By late November, the allocated space in the warehouse was crammed with pieces of sugar milling machinery. Cameron estimated it would be another four to six weeks before the site would be ready for installation of any of the machinery. A further delay was encountered that year when the monsoonal wet season set in early and, long before Christmas 1870, roads were cut everywhere, and the construction site was a quagmire. Progress on the new factory halted until the wet season made a belated departure around April the following year.

Despite every available ounce of manpower and any other resources being thrown into the project, by the end of May, there was no avoiding the truth. Their new mill would not be operational in time to crush their 1871 crop. Although not holding out much hope of success, Jimmy again approached Hewitt about the possibility of their cane being sold to Pleystowe. Hewitt, although at first reluctant to accept any of the cane, after discussions with his partner, Romilly, agreed to purchase about a quarter of the cane available.

While Cameron continued to drive those working on their new factory to the limits of their endurance in the wild hope they might have the mill operational in time to handle at least some of the remainder of the crop, every day, that possibility diminished. John Dow suggested discussing the matter with Davidson at Alexandra Plantation. Jimmy was reluctant as he had always found Davidson distant and uncooperative. Nevertheless, after plenty of encouragement from Cameron, Jimmy did approach Davidson. It came as a surprise and a relief in equal measures when Davidson agreed to purchase the remainder of their cane – but at not quite the price they had hoped for.

Before the close of 1871, the small group gathered on Sarah's verandah to celebrate the completion of construction of their new sugar mill. That day had come too late to be of any use with that year's crop, but it would stand ready for the 1872 season's milling operations.

Sarah's project budget was in tatters long before then, but they all agreed they now had an excellent milling factory standing ready for operation and that the finished project exceeded their expectations. Of course, the factory itself was only the start of things to come. Manning and operation of the factory were among matters that remained to deal with before the start of the 1872 crushing season. The one definite aspect agreed and in place was that Cameron would oversee the operation of the factory.

Chapter 10

Douglas

It was as well the mill was ready when it was. The wet season began in earnest on Christmas Eve 1871 and continued with little respite into early April. Continually surrounded by flooded roads and inundated paddocks, all eyes frequently turned towards the heavens.

"If it doesn't stop raining soon, our mill's first crushing will extract nothing but gallons of water from our cane," Cameron moaned as they sat on Sarah's verandah one evening.

As usual, the rain did stop, the roads became passable again, and paddocks dried out. By delaying the start of their first crushing until early September, their 1872 crop had plenty of time to develop a high sugar content over the unusually cold winter. While the first couple of days of the mill's first crushing season were a 'bit ragged' (to use Cameron's description), milling operations soon settled down. The factory gradually stepped up to run at its intended crushing rate without encountering any problems. Maintaining a constant supply of cane to the mill rollers meant the cane cutters and the drays bringing the cane from the paddock to the factory were forced to increase the speed at which they worked.

The first batch of sugar produced was celebrated in fine style with a dinner at Sarah's house. After dinner, they broke with the usual tradition of the ladies retiring to the sitting room while the men retreated to the verandah. On that occasion, everyone adjourned to the verandah, where talk of their achievement and the sugar industry generally continued well into the night.

"That gold discovery at Charters Towers last year has given the industry added impetus," Jimmy commented at one stage late in the evening. "There's nothing like an influx of people wanting to try their luck for increasing the demand for staples such as meat and sugar."

"And that puts us in an ideal position to capitalise on this opportunity that has presented," Sarah added and dropped Jimmy a wink.

"I imagine most would also be looking for a wee dram of rum, whether to celebrate their success or drown their sorrows," Cameron suggested. "Should we move our rum production up the calendar a bit?"

"Probably wouldn't hurt to look at that as soon as we have a reasonable supply of molasses available," Jimmy replied. "We will need to purchase a few barrels as soon as possible before kicking off the fermentation process. Any thoughts on that?"

"Is there any particular type of barrel you need?" Philip asked. "I know of a supplier who might have what we need."

"Right… Philip, talk to Jimmy about the barrels we will need. I'll set some men fabricating the couple of pot stills we will need for fermenting the molasses to produce the rum."

"So, it's made from the molasses and not the juice?" Philip asked.

"It can be made from fresh juice, but molasses is the more traditional way and is quicker and easier. Jimmy, you and I need to start growing the yeast we will need."

"No point in having barrels on hand if we have nothing to put in them, I suppose," Jimmy replied. "Cameron, you and I should chat about that in the morning straight after you check on things at the factory."

Next morning, Cameron returned from the factory in time for morning tea. Jimmy saw him arrive and came over to share morning tea with him and continue their discussions about rum production.

"I saw Philip heading into town as I rode home. He seemed in a hurry. Is everything all right here?" Cameron asked.

"Aye, as far as I know, all is well. Now you mention it, I suspect he might have gone off to do something about barrels. We discussed the barrels required and the numbers we might need in the first instance. I gave him a rough estimate of the puncheons and hogsheads that might be needed. He didn't mention going into town when I spoke to him. Now, about the yeast we might use, what are your thoughts on this, Cameron?"

"Well, we could use the dunder left behind in the vessels after the sugar is made, or we could use the pot skimmings removed during the sugar boiling process. Based on your experience, do you have a preference?"

After a moment's thought, Jimmy replied, "Dunder, I think. I always liked the rum it produced better than anything else, and it's easy to scrape out of the pots every time they are cleaned after a batch of sugar is produced."

"Good; that's the yeast sorted out. Now we need to see what Philip comes up with in terms of barrels."

At pre-dinner drinks that night, it was obvious rum production had been high on everyone's minds during the day. Cameron reported that John Dow visited the factory at his invitation. He had discussions with the men tasked with fabricating the pot stills required for the rum production.

Then, it was Philip's turn to report on his progress. "I used the electric telegraph to send an order to the supplier for the barrels we require. What an invention that is, and we haven't used it hardly at all since it arrived here several years ago. The next time someone goes into town, they should check at the telegraph office for a reply from the supplier. I don't anticipate a delay, but you never know. With the sugar industry increasing in such a big way, he might now be extra busy."

Philip was shaking his head in amazement as he finished speaking. "So, we already have everything needed to produce rum right here in our own factory? We don't need to buy anything else to produce it?" Philip asked. "Except for the barrels, I suppose," he added as an afterthought.

"Now that's a good point the lad has raised," Jimmy said. "Should we look to employ a good cooper to produce our own barrels onsite?"

"Let's see how our rum production goes for a while before we look at setting up a cooperage," Cameron suggested.

As Cameron reported at drinks one evening, results for the first two weeks of crushing operations were surprisingly good.

"I have to admit to being more than a little impressed with our efforts over the whole production process. We have produced good heavy crops of canes, particularly with the Bourbon variety, and the sugar yield is excellent. I had not expected it would be so good or so soon." They raised their glasses in response before he continued. "When one of the boiling pots was cleaned out today, I had them set aside a good amount of dunder from the bottom of the vessel. I have set it aside in a small, open tub to allow the yeast to grow."

"How does that smelly stuff out of the bottom of the pot become yeast?" Philip asked.

"It attracts yeast spores out of the atmosphere that quickly grow on it," Jimmy replied.

"But how do you know they are the right spores, and not something harmful, or ones that won't make good rum?"

"Because it stays within the mill environment, it attracts the spores from the air in there, the right spores we want for rum making."

"As it will take at least a couple of days or so before the yeast is ready to use, Jimmy, it gives us time to clean out a couple of those old hogsheads lying around in our outbuildings. We can use those for our first batches until those Philip ordered arrive," Cameron suggested.

A couple of days later, Philip collected a wagon load from the port. "It's all the puncheons I ordered and about half the hogsheads. The supplier's note said the remainder of the hogsheads will be ready for the first ship to sail next week," Philip told Cameron.

"Should we consider getting a few quarter casks or barrels to cater for possible future local sales?" Jimmy asked.

"Worth a thought," Cameron agreed, "but not until after it has matured for a while."

Early one morning the following week, Sarah was preparing to head into town as Cameron headed off to check on operations at the mill.

"I see Jimmy is hitching his wagon for a trip to town," Cameron told his wife. "Perhaps you could ride in with him this morning."

"Last evening, when Jimmy mentioned he was going into town this morning, I told him I also needed to go today and suggested that we ride in together. He politely declined, saying that it wouldn't suit the day he had planned in town, and it would be better to take my own wagon."

"Oh, I see. That does sound a bit unusual, but I suppose it's fair enough. Okay then, I'll see you again later today." With that, Cameron rode off, and Sarah continued preparing to head into town.

It was after five o'clock when Sarah returned. Cameron rode up to the wagon as she gathered up her shopping and handed the wagon over to the stable hand. Cameron gave the same man his horse to unsaddle and put into the yard along with the team from the wagon, before he helped Sarah carry her shopping into the house. On his way through to his office, he dumped her shopping on the dining room table.

"Have you seen anything of Philip today?" he asked.

"I thought I saw him heading into the paddocks as I drove out this morning. Jimmy might've assigned him a task to undertake while Jimmy was in town. Is there a problem?"

"No… It's just unusual for me not to have seen him at all. He didn't even visit the mill today and that is unusual for him."

"He's probably all right… Might have spent the day attending to matters in his room. Let's wait to see what happens before we worry about him. I don't want to do anything that makes him think we're intruding on his privacy. If he doesn't front up for dinner this evening, then we should check if he is in his apartment and whether he is all right."

Cameron shrugged, but nodded his agreement before continuing to his office. Sarah went to attend to a matter that caught her attention when she first arrived home. She had noticed her two boys playing outside. They had managed to get themselves covered in mud. It was almost their suppertime, and Maggie would be beside herself if they fronted up for supper in their present condition. After taking her shopping inside, Sarah marched out onto the verandah and called to the boys.

"Angus, Lachlan! … Look at the state of you. It's almost your suppertime. Get yourselves cleaned up before Maggie sees you looking like that. And make sure you remove every speck of that mud before you even think about coming inside. Now, hurry and get yourselves cleaned up."

While she had been addressing the two boys, she heard a wagon draw up out front of the house. As she finished speaking, Jimmy called to her.

"I've brought you something from town."

Not wanting to take her eyes off the boys to be sure they did as they were told and didn't scamper off to get into more mischief, Sarah replied to Jimmy without turning to look at him.

"I've just come from town. What could you possibly have brought to me that I didn't collect while I was there?"

At last, the boys had removed most of the mud from themselves and were scampering up the back stairs, where Maggie waited with a disapproving look on her face. Sarah chuckled. The boys would be hearing more about their muddy adventures this afternoon before they were fed supper tonight. The matter of the boys dealt with, Sarah turned her attention to Jimmy. As she turned on her heel to face him, she let out a strangled yelp.

"Douglas! Douglas… I don't believe my eyes." Rushing down the stairs, she scolded Jimmy. "Oh, you rogue! You were in on this and kept it secret. Cameron! Cameron, come quickly."

In response to the urgency in his wife's voice, Cameron rushed out onto the verandah and came to a sudden halt as his eyes fell on Jimmy's passenger. Then, Cameron was bounding down the stairs two at a time.

"Father?… I can't believe my eyes. How wonderful is this? Thank you, Jimmy, but we will talk about this later. Now, where the hell is young Philip?"

"Right here, Cameron," Philip answered from the top of the stairs before bounding down to hug his grandfather.

"Grab hold of the other end of this trunk, please, Philip, and we will take it through to Douglas's room for him," Jimmy said.

Philip took hold of one handle of the steamer trunk. As they moved with the trunk towards the stairs, Philip said, "Follow us, please, Grandfather, and we will show you to your room."

"Thank you. It will be good to freshen up a little before we all sit down to catch up."

"Oh dear, that's a problem," Sarah murmured to her husband. "Because I didn't know Douglas was coming, Orla hasn't prepared the spare room for him."

"Don't worry about it, Sarah," Philip replied, having heard her words to Cameron. "All is in order."

After seeing Douglas safely to his room and leaving him to freshen up, Jimmy went down the back stairs and around to his wagon to go home. Philip spent a few moments alone with his grandfather before joining Sarah and Cameron on the front verandah. Sarah began berating him as soon as he joined them.

"You knew he was coming. You knew Douglas was coming to visit us and you didn't tell me. Now I'm embarrassed because I hadn't prepared his room for him. What must he think of me as a housewife?"

"He'll think of you as highly as he always has done. Yes, I knew he was coming and Orla and I have spent the day preparing for his arrival. For the foreseeable future, I have taken up residence in the spare room, while Douglas is ensconced in my apartment out the back. Orla even had Cheng Li fetch a bunch of flowers to put in a vase in the room for him."

Once Douglas had settled into a comfortable chair in their midst on the front verandah, Sarah put on her sternest face. "Now, Mr Wallace, after having dealt with everyone else, it is now your turn. How naughty of you not to let me know you were coming to visit us. I was in town this morning. I could have collected you from the ship."

"Dear Sarah, where's the fun in that? The surprise my visit caused was wonderful, but there is one other thing I need to do. I need to make the acquaintance of my other two grandsons. Is that possible, do you think, before they are shunted off to bed?"

"How remiss of me. Of course, you must meet the boys. I'll fetch them for you," Sarah said as she scrambled out of her chair, before returning a few moments later.

"Boys, we have someone for you to meet. Grandfather, these are your two grandsons, Angus, the elder, and Lachlan. Boys, say hello to your Wallace Grandfather."

Formal introductions completed and a few words exchanged, Sarah shooed the two boys back inside to a nervous Maggie waiting just inside the front door.

"They are two good-looking young lads you have there," Douglas said as he watched the boys retreat into the house. "I suspect they have very different personalities," he added as an afterthought.

"Aye, they do," Sarah responded. "Angus is quieter and more studied in his approach to life, whereas Lachlan is something else and needs a tight rein kept on him."

Douglas chuckled. "Very much like my two Wallace offspring," he observed. It was obvious he was about to say more, but changed his mind.

Then, Orla called them all to dinner and that proved a most enjoyable time. Orla had excelled herself with the meal she prepared, and the conversation and occasional banter the diners shared made for a memorable evening. Believing the senior members of the family might need time alone, as soon as dinner was over, Philip made excuses and went to his room for the night. Cameron was about to take the others through to the sitting room when Douglas suggested they might adjourn to the front verandah again.

"It is such a balmy night. It seems almost disrespectful to sit indoors."

"We tend to spend more time sitting on the verandah than in the sitting room," Cameron admitted.

"Jimmy showed me something of what you have here as we came home this afternoon. He pointed out his property and yours, Sarah, and told me the land across the road now under cane belongs to the three of you. It appears, between the three of you, quite an empire has been created. Exactly how much land does each of you own?" Douglas asked.

"Well, now, Father, I could tell you, but it would be almost impossible for you to get your head around. It would be better and easier, if I took you on a tour of inspection tomorrow. How say you to that?"

"Sounds good to me, and will I get to see this new sugar milling factory Jimmy tells me you recently brought into operation?"

"Of course, no tour would be complete without visiting the mill."

At that point, Douglas chose to move the conversation onto a different topic. "Sarah, how old are the boys now? And what do they do for schooling in this part of the world?"

Sarah took her time answering Douglas's questions, particularly in regard to the roles Maggie and Elspeth played in the boys' upbringing and education.

"It does an old heart glad to see more young ones coming along to carry the next generation of the Wallace family forward. And it's as well the whole burden of that undertaking doesn't fall solely on young Philip's shoulders. By the way, Philip appears to have grown into a fine young man, a grandson I can be proud of. How has he settled in here?"

"Your assessment of the young lad is spot on," Cameron assured Douglas. "As for how he settled in, I believe him perfectly happy here. Philip has been a great help to me in maintaining the shipping operations, especially in the last while when we have been so busy erecting the new factory. He has shown a great interest in both the cultivation of sugarcane and the operation of the mill, but I think he might be equally keen on the pastoral pursuits we run here as well. He and Jimmy established a firm friendship almost from the moment Philip arrived. In simple terms, Philip is a joy to have around."

"What about you, Sarah? How do you find having Philip around?"

"I can only echo Cameron's words. He is a much loved part of this family."

"That is good to hear, but I must commend you on your acceptance of him, given his origins. Perhaps the less said about Robert here, the better. But I must say that I have nothing but praise for the way your best friend, Jane, brought up my grandson, and have nothing but gratitude to her for referring him to me when she knew she would no longer be able to care for him. Philip's letters home to me confirm what you have told me. He loves it here and is happy in this family. That is not only a relief but a joy for this old man to know."

"Father, I have heard 'this old man' uttered several times since we've come out here this evening. Why have you really made this trip? And what are you not telling us? If there is bad news to be shared, this might be the time for it." Cameron gave his father a hard look as he finished speaking.

"There is no ulterior motive, Son," Douglas began. "I finally disposed of the last of my business interests in Glasgow. That allowed me the freedom to do what I had wanted to do for the last few years. I wanted to see this new country that you call home, and I needed to see you all again and meet the children. We none of us know how long we have left on this earth, but I know I can't have too many more years available to me. So, if there are things I want or need to do, now is the time to do them. And so, here I am."

"And it is wonderful to have you here, Douglas," Sarah said, her voice cracking a little as she did so. "I have missed your company, missed your guidance on so many occasions, but the training you gave me stood me in good stead. Given other circumstances, I might have run to you to discuss a problem or situation that troubled me, but in your absence, the training you gave me allowed me to work my way through whatever it was that needed to be dealt with. For that, I can't thank you enough... And I can't tell you enough how delighted I am you are here."

"While I am a little reluctant to bring this up at this time, there is one thing I would like to ask you about, although I know it might be difficult for you to discuss," Cameron said. Douglas shrugged and indicated he should continue. "I have heard nothing of my sister, Cecily, since soon after she departed the Caribbean. I know you and she became estranged, but may I ask what became of her after she returned to Glasgow?"

"Argh, yes, Cecily... On her return, she did not want to be anywhere near me and, if I am to be quite honest, I did not want anything to do with her either. My days of sympathising with Cecily's unfortunate life were long gone. The reality of what she had become was not something I wanted around me. On her return to Glasgow, within a couple of days she had relocated to the Highlands to a small property we owned, and there she made her home. About three years ago, I received word that she had passed away. We had not reconciled, and I had not known she was ill. Later, I learned she had developed a close friendship with the ghillie we employed there, but I believe it was only a friendship and nothing more. Nevertheless, the knowledge that there had been someone in her life right to the end was a comfort to me."

"You never told me of her passing. I would have come home if I'd known she was ill or... whatever. You didn't need to deal with it on your own," Cameron told him.

"Son, part of being estranged is not knowing what's going on in that other person's life. I was unaware... No, I am still unaware if she had been ill before her death or not. In fact, I did not know of her death until more than a month after the event. It appears she had sworn the ghillie to secrecy and insisted he not advise me of her demise, but eventually, ignoring Cecily's instructions, he followed his conscience and contacted me."

"So, now, I am your last remaining offspring. What a sad, and at times dysfunctional, family we have been. My hope is not to repeat that."

"Cameron, my son, that is highly unlikely. With Sarah by your side, that is not likely to occur. But, if I might give a word of warning, your younger son, Lachlan, is very much as your brother, Robert, was at his age. My advice for what it's worth is to take a firm hand there, Sarah."

Chapter 11

A Wedding

Douglas appeared in no hurry to return to Glasgow. His occupation of the apartment at the rear of the house stretched on for months, prompting concern that there might be more behind his sudden jaunt to the antipodes than he would admit. As the weeks turned into months, Cameron's concerns for his father grew. Sarah remained more pragmatic.

"Douglas appears healthy enough, and he seems to be enjoying his time here. Perhaps you should *nae fash* yourself about something where nothing exists."

"Hmm… Perhaps you are right. There is something else that has come to my attention recently, and I have been meaning to speak with you about it. I'm of a mind to find accommodation for Philip in town. Of course, he could still visit out here occasionally, but he would be based in town."

"Why? Does Philip's occupying our spare room present a problem for you? I have to admit I can't see why it would. Or have Wallace Shipping's operations been a bit neglected in recent times as a result of all that's been happening out here? Apart from any of that, I fear Douglas would see such a move as a direct consequence of his presence here and the fact that he has taken over what was Philip's apartment. I'm sorry, Cameron, but you will have to explain your thinking further before I have any definite thoughts to offer."

"No, none of that is a problem. Shipping operations are not being neglected, and we would hardly know Philip was in the house as he spends so much time out and about. You know I would never do anything to make my father feel in any way unwelcome."

"So, then, what is this all about?"

"Well, it seems to me that Philip is showing too much interest in our governess, spending too much time with her. Haven't you noticed?"

"Has Elspeth complained or appeared uncomfortable with the situation?"

"No. No, of course not. But, you know… Well, it's not a healthy situation, and we wouldn't want to cause Jimmy and Annie any concern."

"Cameron Wallace, don't you dare even think about interfering in the lives of those young people. They are adults and, as such, are entitled to make their way in the world as they see fit. If that, at some time in the future, should be as a couple, it would be wonderful. But, if through spending time together now, they discover the way forward for them is not together, that also would be a good thing – and no harm done.

Is this your behaviour our sons might expect when they attain manhood? Will you see it as your right also to interfere in their lives? I'll tell you now, you will not interfere in my stepson's life and, when the time comes, you will not interfere in the decisions our sons make about their lives. I intend our sons will have an appropriate upbringing to ensure that, as adults, they behave as gentlemen and make sensible, well-considered decisions. I warn you, your own marriage is at risk if you do interfere. I cannot abide such bullying and standover tactics by a parent. Now, was there anything else you wanted to discuss with me?

It's unfortunate that Philip is currently occupying our spare bedroom, because that is where you would be sleeping tonight. But, as it is not available, I'll leave it up to you to make your own arrangements about where you will sleep."

Her message delivered, Sarah flounced off to bed, leaving Cameron standing stunned in her wake. With a raft of emotions, including hurt, disappointment and anger, flooding through him, Cameron collected a demijohn of rum from the kitchen and headed out to the stables. That's where Jimmy and Philip found him early next morning, passed out on the wagon.

"Perhaps, right about now, lad, you might disappear and find something else to do for a bit," Jimmy told Philip.

Once Philip was out of sight, Jimmy took a deep breath before venturing in to prod the sleeping bear in its den.

"Come on, Cameron, wake up. The morning is fast away and you haven't been over to check on operations at the mill. Go and put your head under the pump to help clear some of the rum fumes you are exuding. I don't know what you did, but what sort of message does this give the young ones?" Then, softening his tone, Jimmy continued. "So, come on, lad, what did you do to have yourself chucked out last night? Is there anything I can do to help?"

"Huh, even I'm not sure what I did, but whatever it was, it sure upset Sarah."

With a little more encouragement from Jimmy, Cameron recounted the offending conversation from the previous night, ending it with the best statement in his defence he could come up with.

"I thought I was trying to do the right thing, and I fully expected Sarah would support me in my proposal. Instead, all that happened was I was accused of bullying and interfering. In all honesty, Jimmy, all I was trying to do was prevent a couple of very dear young people from maybe making a major mess of their lives. Can you understand my concern for the interest I think Philip is showing in Elspeth?"

"Why would I be concerned? Did you ever stop to consider how Elspeth might feel about Philip's attention? Or how Philip might feel about Elspeth's attention. From what I've seen, it's a two-way situation. I think it's safe to say that the situation you think you're trying to avoid has already progressed far beyond that point. I might be telling tales out of school, but I know Elspeth and her mother are planning a fancy dinner in a few days. It will be the equivalent of bringing the beau home to meet the family… Or, maybe, for the two families to meet before the big announcement."

"The big announcement…? What the… Are you suggesting…?"

"Oh, for goodness sake, Cameron, grow up and stop playing the role of the indignant parent. Your nephew is a grown man and of an age where his thoughts turn to selecting a wife. It would appear that the two young people on our properties have gotten to know one another and liked what they've found. I won't pre-empt what will come of it, but I won't be surprised to hear *a big announcement* sometime soon. Think about it, Cameron. What better time could there be for it to happen other than while Douglas is here?"

"Jesus, Jimmy, have I been such a fool?" Cameron asked, shaking his head in disbelief. "I fear a good deal of grovelling will be required before peace is restored in the Wallace household."

"Aye, you probably are right. But, in the meantime, get yourself straightened up and over to see what's happening at the mill."

Cameron could hear Jimmy chuckling as he watched him walk away, but Cameron remained in the stables. What was he to do? Should he go and apologise to Sarah first before heading to the mill, or might it be better to do it in the reverse order? After a few more moments of indecision, Cameron elected to visit the mill before facing Sarah. By sunset that day, the Wallace household was sailing through calm waters again, albeit with a somewhat stunned and confused Cameron at the helm. A couple of days later, an invitation arrived to attend the 'special dinner' that Jimmy had alluded to that morning in the stables.

Sarah seemed to take an inordinately long time getting ready just to go across to Jimmy's house for dinner. It was time to go, and Sarah still hadn't emerged from the bedroom. Cameron tapped lightly on the door before easing it open. Sarah was still preening in front of the mirror.

"You look amazing, but please, may we leave now?" Cameron asked quietly. "Philip and Douglas have already made their way across and, by now, are probably parked on the verandah with a bevy in hand."

"Yes. Yes, I'm coming. I just want to look good for Philip's special night."

"I don't see the point of all the fuss. Everyone knows what you look like. It's not as though we will be complete strangers at dinner tonight. But you do look amazing, and you will do Philip proud – when we finally arrive for dinner."

Annie and Elspeth had organised for a wonderful dinner to be served. A party atmosphere pervaded the dining room as the diners laughed and enjoyed themselves. Then, in the brief interlude before desserts were brought out, Annie stood up and tapped her glass for attention.

"Thank you. I won't interrupt for long, but I do have something important to share with you. Earlier today, a certain young man now sitting at this table came to see me to ask for my daughter's hand in marriage. He left with my blessing for him to propose marriage to my daughter. I am happy to report she said 'yes'. Tonight, I now ask you to join me in a toast to the newly betrothed couple, Philip and Elspeth.

The dining room was filled with the clatter of chairs as everyone scrambled to their feet and raised their glasses to the young couple. A rowdy few minutes filled with laughter and congratulations followed before, in the traditional way, the ladies retired to the sitting room, while the men, accompanied by a demijohn of rum and their pipes, adjourned to the verandah.

Much later that evening, the Wallace household all walked home together. Philip climbed the stairs first and disappeared off to his bedroom, leaving the other three members of the family to take up the chairs on the verandah.

"How long do you think before the wedding? I don't imagine it will be too long...." Douglas asked. "Despite the risk of out-staying my welcome, I would like to be here for this wedding."

"Has our hospitality been so lacking that you feel it necessary to consider leaving?" Sarah demanded, but Douglas caught the twinkle in her eye.

"Truth be told, Sarah, my dear, I could stay at this place forever. It's not just the hospitality that's wonderful. It's everything about this part of the world and what you've done to it. And, if I am to be really honest, being here invokes strong memories of being a young married man on a Caribbean plantation."

"Right then, now that we know, we won't move to rent out that back apartment anytime soon," Sarah assured him.

Wedding preparations seemed to dominate both households for the next few weeks. There was unanimous agreement that the wedding should happen before the onset of the wet season. That meant, to be safe, the wedding should take place by the end of November at the latest. Wedding planning also gave rise to another problem. Where would the young couple live after they were married? Roddy McDonald and his team of men were again pressed into service.

After some intense debate, it finally was agreed a cottage would be built on Jimmy's Selection. Sarah's initial reaction to the decision was disappointment that her stepson would be moving to live on neighbouring land and not on hers. Although Cameron and Douglas were aware of Sarah's reaction to the decision, they decided that, if they ignored it, she would come around to the idea soon enough. They were right. Soon enough, she saw the wisdom of building on Jimmy's block.

Of course, the other BIG question occupying everyone's mind immediately after the Big Announcement was where to hold the wedding. Cameron questioned what was wrong with the way he and Sarah had gone about their wedding… and was promptly told by the women involved that such thoughts were what they would expect from a man. Nevertheless, in the end, following Cameron and Sarah's example seemed the most logical and practicable way.

"Let's make a list of what's to be done," Annie suggested one evening over pre-dinner drinks.

"Find out when the bishop will be in town to conduct the ceremony, unless you want a magistrate to do it," Jimmy began.

"I'd prefer the Bishop," Elspeth said.

"That's one decision made," Jimmy said before continuing.

"Once you have a date for the Bishop, then you need to book the venue for the wedding luncheon… Oh, and any accommodation that might be needed for, say, the night before and the night after the wedding."

"You will need at least a rough number of guests who will attend the lunch," Cameron added.

"I'm surprised you two men are such experts on organising a wedding," Annie said in genuine surprise. "How did you become so knowledgeable on such matters?"

Jimmy chuckled. "We planned another Wallace wedding a few years ago."

"You keep mentioning a wedding luncheon," Elspeth began. "Why? Shouldn't we be talking a dinner in the evening? And where is the Kirk in which the marriage will be celebrated? There's another thing we need to do. We need to make sure the pipers are available to pipe us to the Kirk, then back to the dinner. And we need to check that they will be available afterwards to play for the *ceilidh*.

When everyone finally stopped laughing, Jimmy and Sarah (in tandem) explained weddings in the settlement.

"For a start, there is no Kirk. The Catholics have one under construction, but for those not Catholic, the Bishop conducts services and marriages in the courthouse during one of his visits to the settlement. That means the marriage will take place in the morning. Guests can't be expected to hang around until the evening to be fed, so there will be a luncheon and not a dinner," Jimmy explained.

"Besides, if it were to be an afternoon or evening wedding, guests would all have to spend the night in town. That might be enough to put many of your intended guests off the idea of attending," Sarah added.

"What about….?" Elspeth began, but Jimmy cut her off.

"As for pipers," he began, "there might be one or two lurking somewhere in the settlement that we could rustle up. But *dinna fash* yourself about pipers. There will be no need for them.

There will be no piping you from the hotel to the courthouse and back again, and there will be no dancing after everyone is fed. Guests won't hang about. Once the luncheon is over, they will leave to be home before dark. Anyone who does intend to stay in town after the event will need to have booked a room at the hotel."

"You both keep mentioning 'the hotel'. Why are we talking about a hotel? Isn't there a nice facility somewhere in town that's suitable for such an occasion?" Elspeth was becoming irritated.

"Aye, Wills' Hotel…." Cameron said. Then, when Sarah fixed him with a fierce glare, he rushed to explain his comment. "I think you'll find we will all agree that Wills' Hotel is the appropriate venue for the luncheon. It could be held in that new brick extension Korah Wills added to the rear of the premises as a venue for public meetings and the likes."

Elspeth looked beseechingly at Jimmy, hoping he might have something better to suggest. He didn't and simply concurred with Cameron.

"Until a couple of years ago, you would have been stuck with the Golden Fleece Hotel as the best venue for your luncheon. Since Korah Wills bought the former Royal Hotel back in 1870, then refurbished and extended it, you wouldn't consider anywhere else."

Annie decided it might be an appropriate time to intervene and, at the first opportunity, spoke up. "It appears we have been given plenty to think about tonight. Let's leave it for now and take another look at everything in the light of day. Elspeth, between all of us, I'm sure we will put together a wonderful wedding day for you." Although most of them felt so inclined, no one actually heaved an audible sigh of relief after Annie's comments.

The next few weeks were a flurry of activity. Jimmy was allocated responsibility for discovering the dates of the Bishop's scheduled visits, and having preliminary discussions with Korah Wills regarding the availability of his hotel's facilities for a wedding luncheon. The two senior women devoted themselves to frocks, decorations for the luncheon venue, and the luncheon menu, while Elspeth's only task at that stage of the planning was to draw up a draft guest list.

Despite Philip's reassurances that Cameron and Sarah's wedding, arranged along similar lines, had resulted in a wonderful day, Elspeth remained convinced her wedding would end up nothing short of a monumental disaster that forever would be remembered for all the wrong reasons. By the time the big day finally arrived, everyone else involved in its planning had long since become quite relaxed about it.

The afternoon before the wedding, Sarah loaded Annie and Elspeth – and their many bags and boxes – onto her wagon and drove them into town to spend the night at Wills' Hotel. Jimmy, Cameron and Douglas followed a little later and checked into another hotel a little further along the street. Philip made his way into town alone and in style in Cameron's recently acquired trap pulled by an equally new little pony. He chose to spend the night onboard one of Wallace Shipping's vessels tied up in the river.

Contrary to all of Elspeth's expectations, her wedding day dawned bright and sunny and accompanied by a light breeze that helped ease the summer heat... And the day ran like clockwork. The ceremony happened on time and without a hitch in front of a packed courthouse foyer. Everyone then made their own way to Wills' Hotel for a drink before sitting down to an amazing feast. With everyone kept well lubricated, the rowdy luncheon continued to almost three o'clock, when the first of the guests, realising how late it was, took their leave.

Tempted though they were to stay in town that night after the wedding, and after considerable discussion beforehand, as agreed, Cameron drove the senior Wallace family members home on Sarah's wagon. Jimmy took himself and Annie home on his wagon. The trap and pony remained in Wills' Hotel's horse yard overnight, ready for Philip to bring his new bride home the next day.

First thing the next morning, Sarah and Annie rushed to the new cottage to open windows and doors to welcome its new residents. Annie gathered a huge bunch of flowers and used an old pitcher as a vase to display them on a small table just inside the front door. Then, the two women made a pact not to go near the cottage for at least a couple of days to allow the newlyweds to settle in peacefully.

After the hurley burley and excitement of the last few weeks, life settled back into a normal rhythm. The newlyweds settled into their newly completed cottage, and Elspeth continued as governess to Angus and Lachlan. The mill's first crushing season came to an end and was toasted with a drop of the first batch of rum from the mill's distillery… And the monsoon weather arrived to kick off the wet season.

From midway through December, it was obvious the 1872 Christmas would be a wet one. The debilitating heat and humidity had built up almost from the day after Philip and Elspeth's wedding. After two weeks of it, the heavy rain that followed came as something of a relief. Douglas had struggled in those oppressive couple of weeks before the rains came, but seemed to adjust instantly once the heavens opened.

Then Christmas arrived. In the week leading up to Christmas, Douglas had witnessed an increased level of activity in the household. He was quite taken aback when decorations were strung up throughout the dining and sitting rooms. But the greatest shock came when Cameron asked Douglas if he would like to accompany him on a Christmas tree hunt.

"Christmas tree…? What is this nonsense? Yes, I am happy to go with you, but I am not sure I understand what it is we are supposed to do."

"We go to a patch of scrub and look for a suitable sapling or low branch of a tree that we can saw off and bring home to put in a pot."

"What for? I mean, what happens to it then?"

"It will probably sit on the verandah and be decorated with streamers and baubles and things to turn it into a Christmas tree."

"I'm a little confused by all this fuss about Christmas. As you well know, Christmas is not a significant event at home."

"Of course, it's not. I had forgotten that Scotland still doesn't mark Christmas in any fancy way. Although, Father, last year, the Bank of Scotland did declare it a holiday for them. Queen Victoria has promoted the idea of Christmas as being a festive occasion and a time for decorations, Christmas trees, and presents. Much of Europe shares her outlook. In fact, that's probably where she got the idea from. Anyway, this settlement is a melting pot of people from many parts of the world and most of those people, with the exception of us Scots of course, are used to celebrating Christmas as a festive time. We liked the idea and have adopted it for our own Christmases."

"Humf... seems a lot of nonsense if you ask me. By all means, go to church if you are that way inclined but, as for the rest of this festive nonsense, it strikes me as a waste of time, energy and money."

"And you are welcome to your opinion, Father, but Christmas will be a festive occasion at our place. You are welcome – nae, you are encouraged – to join in, or you can hide away in your apartment if you prefer. It is up to you."

"So, if a big fuss is made of Christmas here in the settlement, what happens with Hogmanay? Do the Scots here still make a festive occasion of that?"

"Uhmm... Some still do to some extent. Even so, it's quite different from the way it's celebrated back in Glasgow. And, before you ask, the wet season usually has us isolated by then. So, Hogmanay here is not much more than the two households making a bit of a night of it."

"Oh, well, I suppose it is all part of learning what life is like in this part of the world."

"That's the spirit, Father. And, you never know, but you might enjoy it."

Chapter 12

Rust

Suspecting an announcement might soon be forthcoming, Sarah busied herself pulling all her son's old baby clothes out of storage and attending to any mending she found needing attention. Her concern was to have the clothes laundered in readiness should a baby arrive soon, but storms and heavy showers were already an almost daily occurrence. On one miraculous morning, when she couldn't see a cloud in the sky, she insisted the baby clothes be laundered immediately and put out in the sun to dry – before the sun disappeared and the rain came again.

Thanks to the rain, Jimmy and Annie came for pre-dinner drinks only occasionally, and Philip didn't come at all, opting instead to spend time in the evenings with his wife. The evenings on Sarah's verandah remained pleasant affairs, but rather than the rowdy chatter and laughter that had been a hallmark of such evenings, now they were more contemplative affairs enjoyed as family time by the three Wallace family members.

As they enjoyed a pre-dinner drink one evening, Douglas took a wander down memory lane. "I had forgotten what the monsoon season in the tropics was all about, and I struggled to deal with it when I encountered it here. It brought back so many vivid memories of life in the Caribbean, of the place, and of the people. Of course, with the main house being on a rise as it was, it captured any breeze that wandered past. No such relief was available to those down in the fields. At such times, the factory became almost unbearable. I have nothing but admiration for the workers who toiled in those conditions. Now that the wet season appears to have started, tell me how it's likely to impact here on the property."

"I suppose that's a big difference between here and the Caribbean," Cameron began. "In the Caribbean, life continued much as normal when the rains came. The only difference was that it became impossible to work in the muddy paddocks on occasion. Here, the story is very different. Yes, the paddocks become quagmires, all agricultural pursuits are halted, and cattle are moved to the highest parts of the property. Roads are flooded and become impassable and often need considerable repairs once the place dries up a bit. So, in effect, we become isolated here, and that's not such a bad thing. It's a time for catching up on things that have been let slide during the year, and of doing maintenance and other necessary chores perhaps not possible when the place is fully operational."

"While it might sound strange, I'm looking forward to experiencing this wet season," Douglas announced. "Don't ask me to explain why. I don't know why that is. Perhaps it's a further chance to revisit memories of long gone times in the Caribbean with you and your brother and sister growing up there."

"Douglas, are you okay?" Sarah asked quietly. "I mean, are these reminiscences of the good kind, or only the sort that will have us attacking another demijohn of rum?"

"No, I'm fine, Sarah. Your comments intrigue me. Why would you think there were anything but good memories?"

"The party appeared to have become a bit maudlin. I was concerned you might have been heading for a dark place of some sort."

"Perhaps we should put it down to some hidden qualities of our new rum that can take one on long, languid strolls down memory lane. No, I can assure you, Sarah, there are no bad memories anywhere tonight. In truth, I can't remember how long it is since I felt so relaxed… So at home as I do now, and as I have done since I arrived here. Now, how strange is that? I can't explain it, but I don't question it. I'm just enjoying it, every minute of it."

A long silence enveloped the verandah after Douglas's 'confession' as the others present presumably sat exploring their own memories. It wasn't an unpleasant interlude, but nobody complained when Douglas shattered the silence.

"I've been meaning to ask you, Son, who do you have running your distillery? Whoever it is does a fine job, but I'm surprised you found such a talented distiller in this settlement."

"Ah, well, we might have to put that down to luck. Do you remember Tobias, our head distiller in the Caribbean?"

"Yes, of course, I remember him. He was a master of his trade, a champion. I remember when he first started with us. He was no more than a boy and became his father's apprentice until his father became too old and ill to continue working. Then, Tobias took over from his father and it was a seamless transition. Why do you ask about Tobias?"

"My head distiller is also named Tobias. Perhaps it should be 'Tobias Junior', for he is the son of our Tobias in the Caribbean. Like his father, when no more than a boy, this Tobias also was apprenticed to his father. Since our time here, I have seen a number of Caribbean expats arrive in the settlement. The likes of John Dow and Davidson have encouraged some to come, but others are here as a result of their own decision. My Tobias is one of the latter. John Dow knew Tobias had arrived here, and Dow dropped me a wink when he knew I was in the market for a distiller. What is your assessment of his level of proficiency?"

"Like the long line of distillers in his family before him, he is a master of his trade and worth a fortune in any distillery."

Later that evening, as Cameron and Sarah prepared for bed, Cameron noted Sarah appeared preoccupied. It concerned him.

"Sarah, has something upset you tonight?" She looked surprised and shook her head in response. "It's just that you appear to have something on your mind, and I wondered whether everything was all right."

"Oh, I see. Yes, I suppose I have been deep in thought. Those thoughts are centred on your father. I do hope he's okay. I do enjoy having him around, and I'm pleased he's not making any noises about rushing back to Glasgow. But, at the same time, I am a little surprised by his apparent reluctance to leave. Don't misunderstand me. I would be happy for him to stay forever, but I wonder whether his inclination to linger here might be a sign that something is amiss with him."

"Are you suggesting that he might be seriously ill or something of that nature? … That his intention might be to spend his last days here with us? After all, we are the only direct family he has left. It wouldn't be hard to understand if that were his intention."

"I'm probably just being a silly old woman. Let's not say any more about it. Whatever is meant to happen will happen, and we will take that in our stride just as we do with everything else life throws at us."

"Right… Let's not speak on this again unless something happens to warrant it and, in the meantime, let's just enjoy having him around for as long as he's here."

"You are a wise man, Cameron Wallace."

The long wet season seemed like it was never going to depart in 1873. Although it tailed off to frequent heavy showers, it was the beginning of May before anyone believed it was over for the year.

All the cane looked miserable. Although the cane was planted on a slightly more elevated parcel of land than Sarah's home Selection, the paddocks had remained flooded for weeks. Much of the young cane would need to be replanted after being totally submerged for so long, and strong winds had caused havoc in the areas to be harvested that year. Having sat in water for such an extended period, the ground around the stools of cane became a soupy mass. It meant the long, heavy canes simply fell over when the strong winds hit them. Then later, when the sun came out between intermittent showers, the cane lying flat on the ground started growing again and curled up towards the sun. Instead of nice, neat rows of tall, upright cane to harvest, the fields were now a tangled mass of canes laying over and growing in all directions.

"It wasn't a typhoon or cyclone," Douglas observed, "but it might as well have been judging by the state of those paddocks. They will be a nightmare for the cutters to harvest."

He wasn't telling Cameron anything he didn't know. Over the years, the size of the crop to be crushed each season had steadily increased. Prior to the rain, 1873's crop was a considerable increase on that of the previous year. Cameron and Jimmy had discussed commencing crushing operations a little earlier that year to enable the crop to be safely harvested before the onset of the next wet season.

"We are hoping for a cold, dry winter, and the sooner it arrives, the better," Cameron told his father. "It will take some time to dry the paddocks out sufficiently to start reducing the water content in the cane juice, and then we will need a good cold winter to develop the sugar content. On top of all that, we will need a hefty dose of luck if we are to commence crushing in August this year and still achieve the results we want."

"So, a cold winter increases the sugar development in the cane, eh?" Douglas mused. "Well, Lad, that's something we didn't know about in the Caribbean... but then, we didn't have any winter to bother about."

Their 'luck', as Cameron called it, held out. A cold winter followed, and crushing operations for the year began in early August.

Over drinks the night before crushing began, Cameron said he had noticed Elspeth had missed a couple of days of her duties with the boys. Sarah and Annie shared a knowing look but said nothing. When Cameron expressed his concern that the boys' education might suffer if, now that Elspeth was married, she would not be paying proper attention to her role of governess. Sarah shut the topic down by saying that such occasions do occur, and it wasn't a problem because Maggie made sure the boys completed the work Elspeth set for them.

Despite the prospect of a poor season ahead after so much rain, results for the first month of crushing were excellent. But the crop was proving a challenge for the cutters and progress through the paddocks was slow as a result. As they gathered on Sarah's verandah for pre-dinner drinks and to congratulate themselves on what looked like being a profitable season after all, they received further good news.

Philip took the opportunity to announce that he and Elspeth were expecting their first child shortly before Easter the following year. A cheer went up from all those assembled, and Philip was the recipient of a torrent of rowdy congratulations.

Later that night, Cameron again aired his concerns about their boys' education in the light of Philip's news earlier in the evening and demanded to know what Sarah was of a mind to do about it.

"There is nothing to be done about it, Cameron. Elspeth will continue as governess to Angus and Lachlan. There will be a brief break in her duties when the baby arrives, but she will continue to set work for the boys during that period and Maggie will supervise them to see it is done properly. At the end of that short break, Elspeth will return fulltime to her role of governess. While we are on the subject, Cameron, I would have thought you had more to worry about than our sons' education. Such matters have, until now, been my responsibility. Are you now suggesting you think me incapable of appropriately discharging such responsibilities?"

"No. Not at all. I would never do that. It's just that I am concerned about the likely impact of the changed circumstances."

"Then, I suggest you stop being concerned about this matter and concentrate on your own responsibilities. Thank you for your concern, but I assure you everything is in hand here."

A couple of days later, Sarah told Annie of her conversation with Cameron. "Since they were born and until now, he was hardly aware of their existence. Now, all of a sudden, he realises he has two sons and wants to interfere in their education…."

Although Cameron remained unaware of it, the boys' education continued as Elspeth and Sarah had agreed until

Elspeth's baby arrived and again after she resumed work about a month later.

The year was slipping by at a great rate, and the 1873 crushing season was nearing its conclusion. Before long, they would again be making preparations for the onset of the next wet season.

As she dealt with some overdue correspondence at her desk one morning in November, Sarah realised just how late in the year it was. She needed to check their bulk supplies of such items as tea, sugar, and flour. Was it still a bit too early to be ordering an extra bag of potatoes she wondered, and should she check how many pumpkins Cheng Li had stored away to see them through the wet season? Cheng Li was an excellent gardener and kept a tight rein on the small group of his fellow countrymen he supervised, but once the rains came, no amount of miracles would allow vegetables to be grown. At least the chickens would still keep the kitchen supplied with eggs and, with at least one milking cow available, there would always be plenty of milk and butter.

In the midst of such thoughts, it occurred to her that it was nearly a year since Philip and Elspeth's wedding and a little less than that since she and Cameron had discussed Douglas's apparent lack of interest in returning to Glasgow. Sarah made a mental note to revisit that conversation with Cameron at the next opportunity.

A couple of nights later, when just the two of them were sharing a quiet drink before dinner, Sarah ventured to raise the topic. "Isn't it amazing how well Douglas has settled in here? He really has become like one of the family and shows no signs of missing anything of his life in Glasgow."

"Are you tiring of his presence here?" Cameron asked cautiously.

"Cameron, how can you ask such a thing? Douglas was more of a father to me than my own father. We have had a special bond ever since I married into the Wallace family, and he was completely supportive of me during all that rubbish with your brother. I would be happy if he chose to spend the rest of his days here with us. The fact that he has settled in so well here does intrigue me a little. More than a little. In fact, it concerns me quite a bit. I just keep praying that he is all right and that he is not keeping something back from us."

After discussing the matter at some length, they agreed there was little to be done about it other than to enjoy having him around for however long he chose to stay.

Christmas came and went. The wet season set in and stayed until the end of March. Then, at about 3.00AM on the second day of April 1874, James Douglas Wallace entered the world, and his father, Philip, does not remember much about the rest of that day. Both Sarah and Annie were in attendance, and Maggie assisted with what had proved a trouble-free birth. While both the grandmothers went home to catch up on sleep, Maggie stayed on to assist Elspeth with her new baby.

That evening, drinks, followed by dinner, were at Jimmy's house as they gathered to celebrate the safe arrival of a new member of their flock. As they walked home at the end of the night, Sarah noted Douglas's mood had changed. He now seemed thoughtful, contemplative perhaps. What had happened to turn his mood from excited and happy to dark and heavy? Sarah searched her memories of the evening for any clue, for anything that happened or was said that might have caused it. After she came up with nothing, she resolved to ask Douglas about it before he turned in for the night.

The effects of a long day capped off by a touch too much alcohol had Cameron heading straight to bed as soon as they returned home. Douglas hesitated for a moment at the top of the stairs before collapsing into a chair on the verandah. Sarah rushed to him.

"Douglas, I can see you are not all right. What is the matter? Please tell me. Please talk to me about whatever it is."

"It's just an old man dealing with his thoughts, memories – and, yes, recriminations, too. There's nothing to be done or to be concerned about, Sarah, but, as always, having you near lifts my spirits."

"You speak of recriminations. Did someone say something tonight to cause you such discomfort? Please, tell me what it was."

"No, Lass, these are my own recriminations that spring from deep in my conscience, my memories of times long gone and matters that might have been handled differently. Sarah, I have never apologised to you, but I do so now with all my heart. I am filled with remorse and sorrow about the way I behaved. Or, rather, the way I didn't behave all those years ago."

"You have me at a disadvantage. I do not know of your ever having behaved badly. But, for the moment, I'm more interested in what gave rise to these dark thoughts."

"Sarah, they named the baby James after Jane's father. I have almost prayed that he would not inherit the qualities of his grandfather. For my part, back then, I should have tried to prevent your marrying his grandfather, my son, Robert. I knew what Robert was like, and deep down, I suspect I knew he would never change. Then, later, when I realised his behaviour continued beyond deplorable, I should have stepped in to cut him free of this family. I didn't act at all… And I owe you an apology for that."

"Come now, Douglas, this is the rum talking. You owe me nothing, and that child will not inherit his grandfather's characteristics. That baby has two wonderful parents who, knowing about the past, will ensure it isn't replicated in their child. Now, that's enough of such nonsense. It's time for bed."

With that, Sarah hauled Douglas out of his chair and marched him through the house to his apartment. As she lay in bed waiting for sleep to come, she revisited Douglas's words. She became certain of two things. Her life could not be happier than it was now, and that Douglas had given her much over the years and owed her nothing.

Although the wet season had ended, spasmodic showers and storms continued to plague the area. The crop looked at its luxurious best. The high sugar prices in recent times fuelled a boom in the industry. Many new (undercapitalised) players sought to enter the industry. The industry boom was a recurring topic of conversation at pre-dinner drinks.

"Thanks to the current boom, the town is buzzing with talk of who has or who hasn't applied for a loan to make a start in the local sugar industry," Cameron reported on one such occasion. "It appears the banks and other lenders are being swayed to lend money because of the current high prices and generally buoyant state of the market."

"Mark my words," Douglas began, "where there is a boom, a bust will soon follow. It's as well to keep a canny head at such times. You can tell me it's none of my business, but my hope is you have acted wisely, and everything you have here is safe when the next phase happens."

"We have done our best, Father," Cameron answered for the others. "We owe nothing, and our books are well in the black."

"Aye, Douglas, Cameron is right. We have done our best, but we also have been cautious and tried our hardest to insure against the vagaries that have always plagued this industry. If the industry goes bad, we will just have to hope and pray we have done enough to survive whatever it throws at us."

As the 1874 crushing season was nearing its close, returns had already dropped to be about a quarter less than the 1873 season's. The group's comments that evening had taken on a truth beyond what any of them had thought possible.

The sugar industry boom had reached its peak. Prices already had begun a dramatic descent. Doom and gloom pervaded much of the settlement as the possibility of what it might mean became clearer.

While many new players in the Mackay sugar industry became nervous about their financial positions, another more devastating situation was becoming firmly established in the southern areas of the industry.

"I'm hearing that the industry is in trouble down south," Cameron reported one evening. "A pest is believed to have been introduced on plants brought in from overseas. It appears as red blotches on the cane and eventually removes all the goodness from its host."

"That sounds like something I heard about a few years ago," Jimmy mused. "The Hawaiian industry was being ravaged by some mysterious pest that was wiping out crops. Then, in more recent times, I heard about it appearing on other islands closer to us. It stands to reason it would be only a matter of time before infected plants are imported from somewhere and the damned thing is let loose in our industry."

"What do we know about this pest?" Douglas asked. "How does it manifest in the paddock, and what can be done to protect against it?"

"So far, there's only limited information available," Cameron admitted. "It first appears as red patches on the cane plants. The cane begins to look distressed after only a short period of infection. Some are of the opinion that the disease might be of the same family as a fungus or mould that attacks wheat. They have taken to calling it *Rust,* the same name as it is known by in the wheat industry. There has been some suggestion that poor cultivation methods could encourage the spread of the problem. To date, no successful preventative measures have been identified."

"This sounds remarkably similar to an outbreak I heard about that occurred in the Caribbean industry. That was maybe ten years ago now. It was said to have almost totally wiped out the industry in those areas affected," Douglas told them. "There was something similar happened on our island over there some time before that. You would have been quite young children at the time, I think, Cameron. It taught us all a good lesson about not putting all your eggs in one basket. Some varieties were more severely affected than others, while some were not attacked at all."

"Jimmy wanted to diversify the varieties we planted here," Sarah remembered. "At the time, I thought it unnecessary given the excellent results obtained from the Bourbon variety, and we already had put some ground under the Ribbon variety. But Jimmy insisted we plant other canes as well. It seems that foresight might be about to pay off."

"Good work, Jimmy. So, what is the situation here now?" Douglas asked.

"Well, back as early as about 1872, Professor Liversidge was of the opinion Bourbon was the variety at risk," Cameron began. "Bourbon produces tall, thick canes with a high sugar yield. So, it was a hard decision, but we chose to heed what we were being told. We started reducing the amount of Bourbon we had growing and planted no further areas with the variety. We still have a little to harvest next year but, if we are forced to destroy any or all of that, we should be fine. Our thinner, lighter canes like Ribbon, Rose Bamboo, and Raphoe, don't give such good yields but are safe to grow on our riparian lands."

"It appears you have done all that can be done. All we can do now is to sit back, watch closely what develops within the industry, and hope we will come through it in due course," Douglas suggested.

Chapter 13

The Cyclone

A harsh reality for the Mackay sugar industry arrived in 1875. Rust spread through out the crop with alarming speed, devastating the industry. Many new or undercapitalised growers were in financial trouble. Although lenders were mostly sympathetic and did their best to support their clients, some still went to the wall. Who was suffering financial hardship and who had been lost from the industry were regular topics of conversation whenever the group gathered together at Sarah's house.

Although they had little Bourbon variety still growing, Jimmy and the Wallaces still felt the impact of the Rust outbreak. While some of their Bourbon cane was deemed too poor to crush and was cut and burnt, the Bourbon cane that was crushed produced predictably poor results. They ensured there would be no Bourbon variety to worry about by the 1876 season.

Jimmy recounted a tale he heard in town. "Rumour has it that Spiller had five tons of his Ribbon sugar loaded on a punt. On its way to the port, the punt hit a snag in the river and sank. Although the sugar was underwater for twelve hours, Spiller claims to have reclaimed three tons of that sugar. He is reputed to have said that had it been Bourbon sugar, it would have been molasses by the time he reclaimed it."

"Aye, Bourbon seemed like the pot of gold for growers around here, but it has picked up a fair bit of tarnish over the last couple of years," Douglas commented. "Still, it appears knowledge gathered from industries elsewhere paid off for your venture here. I would suggest that the Fraser-Wallace sugar industry partnership might be one of few in the district to survive this Rust crisis okay."

"We haven't been unscathed by it," Cameron said. "Our earnings for the year have dropped considerably, but we managed to remain in the black, while most of the industry sees nothing but red ink."

Changes to the Land Act in 1876 caught the attention of both Jimmy and the Wallaces. As something of a rarity in the Mackay sugar industry, they were in a financially sound position to be interested in opportunities the changes might offer. Their eyes and their interest turned to the north, to the lands between Port Denison and Townsville.

"What exactly do these changes to the Lands Act mean?" Sarah asked. "I mean, what is our interest in what's happening so far from here?"

"Well, it's a bit like what happened here about three years ago, only it was on a lesser scale here, I think," Cameron replied.

"Yeah, but it was the same old story," Jimmy added. "Just a few big-name players took up enormous parcels of land, and in some of those cases, the land wasn't best being utilised. So, the government stepped in and reclaimed large areas of that land. It's now being made available in smaller sized parcels of much the same size as the blocks we have here."

"And I have no doubt there is a whole raft of provisions relating to taking up any of the blocks available," Douglas grumbled. "There always is when the government gets involved."

"No, there's nothing different from what applied here. The blocks available are much the same size, and the residency requirement remains, but the blocks can be first-class pastoral, second-class pastoral, or for agricultural purposes," Jimmy explained.

"What difference does it make?" Sarah asked.

"A lot… As far as your pocket is concerned," Jimmy laughed. "Prime agricultural land costs one pound an acre (£1.0.0), while prime pastoral land costs only half that amount and a block twice the size can be selected. Of course, if you claim the block you selected is only second-class pastoral land, you can select the same size block as prime pastoral and pay only half the price of the prime blocks."

"Half the price of prime agricultural land…? But that means second-class pastoral is selling for only a quarter of the price of agricultural land – five shillings an acre. Can that be right, Jimmy?" Sarah demanded.

"Aye, Sarah. Not only are the figures right, but it also explains why everyone is selecting second-class pastoral blocks… or so they claim," Jimmy confirmed.

"I hadn't looked into the requirements attached to selection of a block," Cameron admitted. "What differences in conditions apply to those northern lands?"

"Residency is the only one. It's much the same as it was here. The selector must reside on the property. The major difference up there is that the selector may appoint a bailiff to live on and manage the place in his stead."

"Oh, the more I hear about those lands, the more I like the sound of them," Sarah said, her excitement evident in her voice as well as her words.

"Are you suggesting someone should venture north to take a wee look at what might be available?" Douglas asked.

"Ah, well, I wouldn't go so far as to say…."

"But I would," Cameron chipped in. "I think, even if out of nothing more than curiosity, it would be worth a look. What do you think, Jimmy?"

Of course, Jimmy agreed and, by the time the night was over, it also was agreed that Cameron and Jimmy would take a jaunt up north to check out what was happening up there. Sarah, always with two feet firmly on the ground, questioned who was supposed to run things here in Mackay while Cameron and Jimmy were on their adventure.

"Philip is perfectly capable," Jimmy assured her, "and it will be good experience for him. After all, he will be taking over running my place soon enough, I don't doubt."

"Yes, but what about the cane and the mill?" Sarah persisted. "I doubt he has enough experience with that, particularly with running the mill."

"No, perhaps not," Cameron conceded. "But the mill management team have all the skills and experience necessary. The same applies to the distillery. Besides that, Douglas will be here to keep an eye on operations. He knows more about cane growing and milling than the two of us put together. So, Father, if you were thinking of going back to Glasgow, you have work to do here for a while yet."

As they made ready for bed later that night, Sarah commented on how surprised she was by how quickly and agreeably major decisions were made within their group. "Cameron, I think the only thing I didn't hear finalised tonight was how soon you and Jimmy plan to depart on your northern odyssey."

"Nothing is definite yet, but probably not until after we organise ourselves a vessel and crew for the trip north."

Sarah lay awake for some time that night. How did she feel about the two men central to her life being away for possibly some months? And how dangerous would it be for them? Just because the natives were causing less trouble around Mackay now days didn't mean the natives in that northern area would be just as agreeable.

Over the next two weeks, Cameron and Jimmy worked at fever pitch. An older vessel of the Wallace Line was resurrected and refurbished a little. Lists were drawn up of the various provisions and equipment they deemed necessary to take with them. Jimmy exercised the electric telegraph to contact an acquaintance near the Burdekin telegraph station to ask him to organise a loan of three horses for the indefinite period of their presence in the area. Then, there was the matter of a crew for their vessel.

Captain Billings, who had gone into semi-retirement, was contacted for suggestions on putting together a crew. It seems that, since he and his wife had settled in Mackay, he had taken on sailing the odd vessel for Wallace Shipping when they found themselves in desperate need of a captain for short-haul trips up the coast. Captain Billings jumped at the chance to take two would-be explorers north to the Burdekin area. He also knew of a few men currently without ships who would crew for him. What Cameron and Jimmy had thought would be the most difficult part of the expedition to organise proved the easiest when they left it all in Captain Billing's hands to organise the boat to be ready to sail a week later.

As the days ticked by, Sarah's foreboding about their trip increased. By the end of the first week, she knew she must deal with it. When a brief period of quiet time to herself presented, Sarah gave herself a good talking-to about her misgivings. She realised that her problems stemmed from the thought of Cameron's absence. After having him by her side for so many years, she had forgotten how to live her life alone. Even Jimmy, who had always been there when she was supposedly living alone, would not be there this time.

"What is wrong with you, Sarah Wallace?" she grumbled quietly. "You will not be alone. There are people all around you, and, most importantly, Douglas is here." As she later told Annie, she set about taking herself in hand and, by that evening, had most of her misgivings under control.

Despite her best efforts, it was a teary Sarah standing beside an equally teary Annie on the river bank to wave the men off as they sailed down the river. A somewhat bewildered-looking Douglas stood ready to load the women onto the wagon for the trip home. Try as he might, his attempts to lighten the mood fell flat. As he would later report to Cameron and Jimmy, he felt desperate when it took at least two days before the women in his charge appeared to return to normal. Sarah later recalled that, over those two days, she frequently wondered how Cameron felt. Did he also feel the pain of separation from her and the children? In her heart, she knew such thoughts would never have occurred to him. She knew the only emotion Cameron and Jimmy felt as the ship set sail down the river was excitement.

One evening, as she sat quietly on her verandah with Douglas, she suddenly realised it was now gone a month since Cameron and Jimmy set forth on their northern odyssey.

"Where do you think they are, and what do you think they have found so far?" she quietly asked Douglas after they sat in silence for a while. "Do you think everything is going well for them? It's the not knowing that is so hard to bear. Anything could have happened to them at any time over the last month… and how would we know about it?"

"They haven't returned. Captain Billings hasn't brought the vessel back into port. There is nothing to indicate they have encountered any difficulties. You must remember, my dear, that the task they set themselves was not straightforward. If something had happened to them, I feel sure word would have filtered back by now. I know Cameron did not give any indication of when they might return. I'm sure that was because they didn't have any knowledge of what they might encounter or how long it might take to complete their quest."

Douglas was right, of course, Sarah told herself as she readied for bed. She should stop worrying. But, she also knew she would continue to unsuccessfully tell herself that until she saw their ship sail back up the river.

Sarah was right. From the moment their ship cast off and sailed down the river, home was not uppermost in Cameron or Jimmy's minds. Although neither of them was aware of it, both men were mentally running through the many lists they prepared in advance of their trip. Had they done everything? What had they forgotten? Should they have thought of other contingencies and prepared for them? But they were underway, and an exhilaration accompanied the gentle motion of the ship.

A fair wind and following sea had them making good time along the coast. The two men took to the deck to watch the coastline slipping past in the distance.

"It's beautiful. We couldn't have asked for anything more," Cameron sighed. "The gods have smiled on us today. It's a glorious day, with wonderful sailing conditions and beautiful scenery to keep us entertained."

"Oh, I had forgotten you are unfamiliar with sailing this part of the coastline," Jimmy said. "I sailed it a few times in the past, and it never failed to impress me. This first leg of our journey to Port Denison is the longest haul at around a hundred nautical miles. The next leg of the journey from Port Denison will be much shorter, maybe only about three-quarters of the length of this one."

"While I'm no expert on the subject, it feels as though we're making good time. Are we likely to be sailing at about ten knots?" Cameron asked.

"Possibly. If we are, we should make Port Denison before nightfall. Spending the night in town before we left was a grand idea. It gave us time to stow everything on board and relax into an early night at the pub. And it made an early departure possible this morning."

"Jimmy, if we make Port Denison before nightfall, might we spend the night on shore rather than on board?"

"That's a possibility, and the crew might like a turn around town as well, but that will be up to Captain Billings to decide."

It was just gone five o'clock when their ship tied up beside the dock at Port Denison. Even at that hour of the afternoon, the harbour remained a busy place. The two men stood on deck for a while, watching the activity going on around them. As soon as the ship was made fast and things settled down again on board, Jimmy and Cameron sought out Captain Billings.

"We have elected to spend the night on shore unless you have some problem with that arrangement," Cameron told the captain.

"No, I have no problems with your being ashore tonight. When might you return to the ship? While I'm not aware of any time constraints, a rough idea of when to make the ship ready to sail again would be useful."

"Our plan is to spend tomorrow in town attending to various business matters. It will depend on how long it takes us to complete that work before we can return to the ship. If it takes us until late in the day to complete everything, we might consider another night in town. Perhaps you and your crew might take advantage of our layover to spend some time in town," Cameron suggested.

By the time they were ready to go ashore, Billings had given his crew leave to go ashore also, but only until ten o'clock that evening. Billings did not go ashore, opting instead for the opportunity the solitude provided to indulge in a quiet bevy and pipe up on deck.

A busy day in town followed a comfortable night in a local hotel. It was always planned to pick up some necessary hardware while at Port Denison and to enquire of the Land Agent regarding the situation with the Burdekin lands. They called to see the Land Agent first thing in the morning and were told he was at a meeting and would not be available until around lunchtime. So, the rest of the morning was devoted to rounding up the hardware they required and arranging its transport to the docks.

Shortly before midday, they returned to the Land Agent's office. He was expecting them and, as it was lunchtime, the men suggested they take the Agent to lunch. Over lunch, they asked all manner of questions about the land they were going to inspect and about the area in question.

"It's a fine area, and interest has been almost overwhelming. My board and I have to identify at the earliest stage those applicants who have little chance, if any, of making a success should their claim be approved. A lot of the best land has already been claimed. That's not to suggest only the dregs are left. There is still plenty of good land to be taken up. If I give you advice at this time, it is to make haste. As I said, many others are interested and they are also undertaking the same quest as yourselves."

After thanking the Land Agent and returning with him to his office to collect the appropriate application forms and other information, the two men elected to return to the ship to check on progress there. Everything they purchased that day had been stowed on board, and the ship now stood ready for departure. After a brief discussion, the two men decided that, rather than spend another night in town, they would remain on board. Soon after they made their decision known, Captain Billings approached them.

"Since you are staying on board, and unless you have more business to complete in town tomorrow, we could set sail on the next high tide."

The two men assured Billings their business in Port Denison was complete, and they were ready to leave whenever he saw fit.

"Right you are, then. It be high tide later tonight. We will set sail in darkness for the next part of the voyage."

As they lay in their bunks that evening, waiting for sleep to come, Cameron murmured, "What time did Billings say it would be high tide tonight?"

"I don't recall he did," Jimmy replied, "but I guess it must be sometime before midnight, or surely he would leave it until the first tide tomorrow and leave in daylight."

Jimmy's guess was wrong by several hours. It was about three o'clock the next morning when movement on the ship woke Cameron. After mentally noting that they were underway, or about to be, he drifted off to sleep again. But neither man slept long after that.

It had been quiet, almost cozy, snuggled up against the dock, but now the ship was making its way gently through the protected waters of the harbour as it headed for the open sea. The Gloucester Passage proved its usual inhospitable self as they entered it. That short stretch of water that runs alongside Gloucester Island is renowned for being unpleasant. It's a place where wind and tide are often opposed to one another.

That night was no different, and the changed motion of the ship woke Cameron again. He swung his legs over the side of his bunk and sat up. Jimmy, already awake, spoke quietly through the darkness.

"Gloucester Passage, I wager. The sea will smooth out again once we are free of the island. No need for concern. Go back to sleep." It sounded like sound advice, so Cameron followed it and crawled back into his bunk.

The anticipated calm sea out beyond Gloucester Island seemed a long time coming as Jimmy lay being tossed about in his bunk. He allowed a few more minutes before deciding something was not quite right and scrambled out of his bunk. His activity woke Cameron again, and he immediately followed Jimmy's example.

"What's happening? Is everything all right? Haven't we gone past that island yet? I expected the sea would have flattened out by now."

"We are well past Gloucester Island," Jimmy assured him, "but it appears we are not in for a fair-weather voyage tonight. I was about to go topside to ask Billings about it. Are you coming with me?"

Once they left their small cabin, they gained a sense of just how rough the sea was. It was difficult to walk through the ship and treacherous climbing the ladder to go topside. They found Billings wrestling the wheel, and with his first mate standing by to help when necessary.

"What the hell have we run into?" Cameron asked. "Is it just a storm that we're sailing through?"

"There was no sign of it when we left Port Denison," the first mate told him. "When the rough stuff hit, we thought it no more than a tropical squall on its way past. Seems that's not the case."

"So, what is the case?" Jimmy asked quietly.

"The glass dropped as soon as we rounded Gloucester, and it's continued to drop as we've made way."

"Has the glass dropped low enough to indicate this is more than just a storm?" Cameron asked.

"Aye, Sir, this be no storm. The glass is saying this be a cyclone."

Jimmy went to stand beside Billings as he struggled with the wheel. "You know this coastline well, Billings. Is there somewhere along here we might shelter until this thing blows over?" he shouted at Billings through the howling wind.

"Nae where at all for many nautical miles, and not even an island we can tuck in behind. We are running along the seaward side of a promontory, out in open water, and any bays along here are merely dents in the coastline that offer no protection. Our only hope is to run through it and then round the cape at its end and tuck in behind the promontory."

"How long before we can round the cape?"

"A few hours yet, Jimmy," Billings replied. "We've dropped all possible sail except for one small canvas."

Cameron, who had come to join the conversation, asked, "Why retain that one? Would it be better to drop that last bit of sail as well?"

"No, Sir, it's important we maintain headway. If we drop that last bit of sail, we will just wallow and that could well bring the end of things. As we are rigged now, we are maintaining slow headway through these mountainous seas, but we are protecting the rigging. If we lose the rigging, we can kiss everything goodnight."

At that point, a huge wave broke over the bow, sweeping all before it and making all those on deck grab for whatever they could to prevent being washed overboard. The first mate came forward and applied his hands to the wheel to help Billings keep the bow pointed into the wind.

Over the howl of the wind and the crash of the waves on the deck, Billings shouted to Cameron and Jimmy, "It's getting worse. Best go below, Maties. Find yourselves somewhere dry and safe while we try to punch our way through this hell."

Going below was easier said than done. It was all about timing. When to let go of one solidly anchored object before dashing to grab the next firm object. Then, Cameron and Jimmy were faced with having to safely negotiate the ladder to leave the deck and reach the dry cabin.

"I know there's nothing we can do to help on deck, but I feel so useless cowering down here in the cabin," Cameron told

Jimmy. "I can't help feeling this is an omen. This cyclone, or whatever it is, has been sent as some sort of warning."

"Warning…? Warning about what, Cameron?"

"About this whole venture we've embarked upon. Maybe the gods are telling us to stop being greedy, that we are lucky to have what we already have. That we should give up this wild idea of more land and go home... if they let us survive to go home. What do you make of our chances? Will we see the sun come up in the morning?"

"That rather depends on whether there is sun in the morning, or if we are still punching our way through the blackness of what the gods have seen fit to throw at us tonight. And, Cameron, I don't believe in omens."

Chapter 14

Cape Upstart

Eight o'clock next morning arrived without any sign of sunshine. The ship still bucked and rolled violently. Waves continued to break over the bow. Everything not strongly secured had been washed off the deck. Cameron's concern turned to Captain Billings and the First Mate. The ship appeared still to have steerage. Someone must still be managing the wheel. A sense of alarm flooded through Cameron.

"Jimmy, I'm telling you it's an omen, a portend of bad things to come if we proceed."

"Cameron, that's enough of this omen nonsense. I told you, I don't believe in omens or any other fancy signs or symbols. So, don't mention omens again. This is nothing more than bad weather. You know, the stuff that happens, usually when you least need or want it to."

"I don't know how much longer we might have to endure this weather, but I am concerned it may be too long for Billings and the First Mate to continue manning the wheel. It's now more than five hours since we departed Port Denison, and for almost all of those hours, those two men have never left the wheel. They must be exhausted by now."

"Aye, lad, they probably are," Jimmy agreed. "But they are seafaring men and will maintain their post and go down with the ship still fighting the wheel, rather than abandon what they see as their duty. There is naught we can do. Maybe pray, if you feel so inclined."

"That's the last thing I feel inclined to do right now," Cameron snapped. "I want… No, I need to do something more positive to help us reach our destination, or at least somewhere safe instead."

Before Jimmy could calm him, Cameron dashed through the cabin and scrambled up the ladder onto the deck. It was no better – or safer – up there than when he had gone below some hours ago, but Cameron carefully picked his way to where the two drenched men continued to struggle to hold the vessel into the wind. Cameron leant in close and almost shouted into Billings' ear to make himself heard above the noise of the wind and waves.

"I might not know as much as you and the First Mate, but can I at least relieve one of you on the wheel?" Billings relayed Cameron's request to the First Mate, who nodded in response to whatever Billings had said.

"Right then, I'll take a short break while you assist the First Mate with the wheel," Billings shouted. "Step up now and slide your hands onto the wheel near mine. I want to see you get the feel of it before I let go."

Cameron did as he was told – and suddenly felt a bit weak at the knees. What had he done? He knew nothing about steering a ship of this size. He couldn't let Billings see that. So, taking a deep breath, Cameron gripped the wheel firmly, and gradually, over the next few seconds, Billings removed his hands. Although Cameron thought he was fairly fit, after only a minute or so at the wheel, he realised he was nowhere near as fit as the two ship's officers. By the time Billings returned after a ten minute break, Cameron was exhausted. But Billings had brought an extra pair of hands with him. Jimmy joined them at the wheel.

Billings took the wheel from Cameron and, after a moment or two, Jimmy took over where Cameron had been. Billings then moved to the other side of the wheel and took over from the First Mate, who quickly disappeared below for a short break. For the next hour, Jimmy and Cameron continued relieving the two ship's officers in turn as they took short breaks.

By a bit after nine o'clock, Cameron felt as though he was about to collapse. As he stepped away from the wheel, he stopped and listened.

"The wind is dropping," he shouted at no one in particular. "Even the waves have stopped breaking over the bow." He watched Billings nod in reply but say nothing.

Soon, they were flying along on that one small patch of canvas. The wind now came from a different direction. The sea was not so angry. When Cameron stepped back up to take another stint on the wheel, Billings shooed him away.

"Go below and rest, Laddie," Billings said. "You've done yourself proud, but we will take it from here. Thanks for your help."

After about half an hour below, another wave of guilty conscience enveloped Cameron, and he went topside again. Captain Billings called him over.

"The weather has abated quite a bit since earlier today. That's the tip of the cape you can see up ahead of us. If it's all right with you, Sir, we will go around the tip and come down along the other side to find a suitable anchorage where it might be safe to spend the night. The way the weather's been clearing, tomorrow should give us a good run for the final leg of the voyage."

"By all means, do that. We could all do with a few hours of quiet rest before we go on tomorrow."

A bit later, Jimmy came up on deck and stood beside Cameron at the railing as Captain Billings tacked around the tip of the cape, skirted around a large isolated white-topped rock, continued along the coastline of the cape for a short distance, and dropped anchor. Nestled in close to the leeward side of the cape, the spine like range running down the centre of the land protected them from the prevailing winds. The water in the bay wasn't dead flat, but its gentle waves lapped soothingly against the ship's hull.

After a tot of rum, a light snack, and a mug of tea, everyone headed for their bunks, except the one crew member delegated to stand the first four hour watch. Before turning in, Cameron took one last turn around the deck. It was three o'clock and almost like having entered another world. While the sky remained grey and angry-looking, it had lightened considerably in the last couple of hours. After dropping a friendly salute to the man on watch as he went past, Cameron hurried below and copied the others' example by throwing himself onto his bunk. It was six o'clock before the first of those on board stirred again. They woke Jimmy and Cameron as they moved through the ship.

Something had changed. It was lighter somehow, Cameron noted as he scaled the ladder to the deck. Jimmy followed him up. Together, they stood at the railing, surveying their surroundings.

"So much for bad omens, lad. What does that tell you now?" Jimmy asked. "Have you ever seen such a sunset in your life before?"

The sky had gone from its previous leaden, threatening appearance to the most glorious sunset imaginable. The sky was bathed in the brightest orange, gold, and red colours, and the surface of the sea in the bay now reflected those same colours.

"Breathtaking… I don't recall ever having seen anything quite so stunning," Cameron said in a voice barely above a whisper. "Perhaps it's a good omen. Such a sunset can only be a portent of good luck. Having survived our 'trial by cyclone', maybe the gods are giving our venture their blessing after all."

"So, I take it you are now happy to continue with our journey and our plans?" Jimmy asked. Cameron nodded. "Good… Bring on tomorrow – and being back on dry land again."

Sunrise the next morning, although dressed in more muted colours, was just as glorious as sunset the night before. An incredibly bright blue sky dotted with pink-tinged clouds stretched out before them as they sailed out of Upstart Bay and bid farewell to Cape Upstart on their way to Cape Bowling Green. The sea, a blanket of low rolling waves with not a white cap in sight, combined with a good following wind, had the vessel making excellent time in the run to the mouth of the Burdekin River.

After handing over the wheel to the First Mate, Billings came to speak to Cameron and Jimmy. For a few moments, all three men stood beside the railing, silently watching a pod of dolphins frolicking in the ship's bow wave. The moment was lost when the captain began what he had come to say.

"We will soon reach the entrance to the Burdekin River. As you know, it's not navigable for a ship this size. I estimate it will be high tide about an hour after we drop anchor in deep water at the mouth of the river. On the top of the tide, it will be possible for the dinghy to enter the river and travel upstream for some distance. We need as much as possible of that you want to take with you to be in the dinghy before we lower it. If you could spend some time working with the crew to ensure everything is as required, we will lower the dinghy just slightly before the top of the tide."

"And so begins the adventure…," Jimmy murmured as he and Cameron went to sort out the dinghy.

As they then waited on the tide, Cameron used the time to go over the next stage of their plan with Jimmy.

"Tell me how the next bit happens, Jimmy. What happens after the crew drops us off and takes the dinghy back to the ship?"

"No, Cameron. We will take the dinghy ourselves and continue up the river by boat until we meet Paddy McPherson, who will be waiting for us with horses. Paddy will then become our guide and will take us to look at land still available for selection."

"What about the dinghy? What happens to that after we meet up with Paddy?"

"Ah, well, there is a bit of a jetty, a small shack, and a horse yard at the place where we are to meet Paddy. That part of the river is not tidal. So, we can leave the dinghy tied up to the jetty, or it can be pulled up onto the bank. Paddy assures me that anything we don't want to carry with us at the outset can be left safely locked in the shack. Although he hasn't said so, I suspect the bit of the set-up along the river is Paddy's own place. He knows this area well now, and we can be guided by what he tells us."

Shouts from the crew brought their discussions to an end. The First Mate rushed over and pointed towards the dinghy. "If you can come now, please, Sirs, they are ready to lower the boat. Please jump aboard so they can get on with it. We don't want to waste too much time, or we'll miss the top of the tide."

It felt like only moments later when Jimmy and Cameron were peering over the sides of the dinghy as it slowly neared the water. Then, the ropes having been cast off, Jimmy hauled up the small sail as Cameron pointed the dinghy at the mouth of the river.

"I don't know how far we can go under sail before we have to start rowing," Jimmy told Cameron, "but I suspect it won't be nearly as far as we would like."

They soon left the tidal reaches of the river, and the dense scrub crowding in along the banks of the river rendered the sail useless.

"Argh, time to break out the oars, lad," Jimmy sighed as he slammed his oar's rowlock into its rowlock chock in preparation for the hard work ahead. "Come on, lad. Grab the other oar and fit it in the rowlock chock ready for action."

A bit under an hour of steady rowing later, a man on horseback appeared at the river's edge. He waved his hat at the dinghy and pointed upstream.

"That's Paddy," Jimmy said. "His camp must be not too far ahead." Horses whinnying quite close by confirmed Jimmy's assumption.

Cameron knew Paddy was an old friend of Jimmy's from the Caribbean, but he had never met him and knew nothing about him at all. As soon as introductions were complete, they engaged in the serious business of deciding how much of the stuff in the dinghy to take with them, how much to leave in the shack, and what to do about the dinghy. Cameron checked the sky visible through a small gap in the overhanging canopy of the trees. The sun in the descent indicated it was well after midday. He wondered whether they would make a start that afternoon or camp at the shack until tomorrow. He didn't have long to wait to find out.

"Right, let's be on our way," Paddy said. "Those two horses (he pointed to two sturdy beasts) are your two pack horses. Let's get them loaded and be on our way."

"How far do you plan to go this evening?" Cameron asked, but kept his eyes on Jimmy as he spoke. Jimmy shrugged, indicating he didn't know.

"Well, if we ever get started, we'll be there just before dark. The sooner we get moving, the better our chances of being able to set up camp for the night while there's still some light available." It was obvious Paddy was running short on patience. To avoid straining the friendship further, moments later, the trio rode out of the horse yard.

After they broke free of the band of scrub lining the river, a vast area of rich alluvial land stretched out before them. With their horses reined back to a walk, Cameron and Jimmy's heads swivelled from side to side as they tried to take in the panorama before them.

"Is this some of the area that has not yet been selected?" Jimmy asked. "It's beautiful land, good for grazing and agriculture. What's wrong with it? Why hasn't it been selected?"

"It's a bit further out," Paddy said thoughtfully. "The selectors preferred to grab those lands closer to existing settlement and other infrastructure. Some of that land wasn't the best available and certainly wasn't as good as this. I have another area to show you tomorrow. In my opinion, it's comparable to this and worth a look. For now, we should make for that small clearing over yonder and set up camp for the night."

"Are we safe to be camped out here at night?" Cameron asked.

"Safe? Safe from what?" Paddy asked.

"Oh, I don't know," Cameron growled. "You tell me... Snakes, crocodiles, natives... Anything else I should be concerned about?"

"Hmm, possibly snakes, but crocodiles are unlikely this far from the river, and the natives in this area have become quite well-behaved."

The next day, Paddy took them to look at the other area of country he thought might interest them. It was further inland and separated from the river by a long, narrow strip of rocky country. Although the land of that second site looked almost as good as the first site's, it lacked easy river access.

After returning to their previous night's camp site, Cameron and Jimmy spent some time discussing the two blocks Paddy had shown them. The next morning, they told Paddy they wanted to do a thorough inspection of that first block as that was the one that held their interest.

"Unless you have some other areas to show us, Paddy, we are happy to ride around on our own if you have other matters to attend to and want to head back to your camp," Jimmy suggested.

Paddy was having none of that. He had been engaged to show them around, and that was what he intended to do.

By the third night back in the camp in the clearing, decisions had been made. That first block that Paddy had shown them was the one they wanted. Then, the hard work would have to begin. The would-be selectors had to peg out their chosen block themselves, recording the various geographical points of the selection as they did so.

"Well, I don't suppose there's any point in putting it off," Cameron began. We need to go back to Paddy's shack to collect all the materials we need to peg out this block, and then we need to roll up our sleeves and get stuck into the hard work."

"What are you moaning about?" Jimmy asked. "Yes, we need to go back to Paddy's camp to organise a few things. Then, his team will bring everything out here and set to work pegging out the block. Where is your problem with that arrangement?"

"Oh, I see. I wasn't aware a team of workmen had been engaged. I spent a lot of last night thinking about the blisters I was going to develop as we slogged our way around the block to peg it out. Jimmy, what other surprises have you up your sleeve? What other arrangements don't I know about?"

"Surprises? I have no surprises. All I did was engage Paddy to show us some country that we might select and to provide whatever else was necessary to be done to comply with the requirements of a Selection Application. I don't think we can fault him on anything so far."

Later, when Paddy went to check on the horses and was out of earshot, Jimmy moved over closer to Cameron as they sat by the campfire. After checking that Paddy was still engaged elsewhere, Jimmy leaned in close to speak to Cameron.

"If our application for this country is successful, we are going to have to meet the conditions of selection. One of those is that the selector must reside on the property. Now, I don't imagine for one moment you're about to set up camp here on a permanent basis. The new Land Act provides for the selector to employ a bailiff who will reside on the property on the selector's behalf. Paddy would make an ideal bailiff… Just a thought for you to keep in mind should the application be successful."

Everything proceeded according to plan. As Paddy's team pegged out the selection, Jimmy and Cameron spent their time exploring the block and drawing up sketches of where fence lines and buildings might go. They made lists of the materials that would be required for fencing and buildings. They discussed stocking the property and where that stock might come from. Two weeks after they had embarked on Paddy's grand tour of prospective lands, Jimmy and Cameron agreed their work there was done. It was time to head back to the ship, supposedly still lying at anchor out from the mouth of the river.

Although the team was still busy pegging out the last side of the selection, Paddy assured them the work would be completed in just over a week. He agreed there was little need for Jimmy and Cameron to linger any longer at the site. Besides, he argued, it was best to get their selection application in as soon as possible and start making arrangements to move stock onto the property. They arranged with Paddy for two of his team to help them push the dinghy off the riverbank and back onto the river when they were ready to depart two days later. To facilitate an early start down the river the next morning, it was agreed Paddy and his two men would spend the night before their departure at Paddy's shack with Cameron and Jimmy.

As they rode towards Paddy's shack, the sky became increasingly darker until, when they were still some way from the shack, a fierce storm hit. While the thunder and lightning were impressive, the rain was the heaviest the men had seen. It continued to fall heavily for several hours before trailing off to a light mist by mid-morning the next day. Their departure was put back a day. After spending most of what was to have been the departure day huddled in Paddy's shack, late in the afternoon, when the rain finally stopped, Cameron and Jimmy ventured outside.

"Jesus, look at that river," Cameron exclaimed. "It's lapping at the stern of the dinghy. If it had come any higher, it would have taken the dinghy away with it."

"Best we tie it up," Jimmy suggested. "At least that way, if the river rises any further, the dinghy won't be washed away."

The open dinghy had sat out on the bank throughout the storm and was now half full of rainwater. "Waste not, want not, eh, Jimmy?" Cameron said as, stripped down to his trousers, he undertook some rustic ablutions using the ready supply of clean, fresh water. Jimmy followed his example. But then, reality dawned. The rainwater had been great to wash in, but it had to be removed from the dinghy before they tried to launch it. That exercise was completed by lantern light that night.

Next morning dawned clear and bright, but accompanied by oppressive heat and humidity. The river continued to run a banker, and the pace of its flow had increased. The good thing about it was, with the river so high, it took little effort to push the dinghy off the bank. Cameron and Jimmy discovered another hidden benefit as soon as they were pushed out into the stream. Now fast flowing and swollen by the runoff from the storm, the river happily took all before it towards the river mouth. No rowing was required. The only need for the oars was to keep the dinghy in the middle of the stream, heading in the right direction, and to skirt around any snags and rocks they encountered along the way.

There was no breeze. The sail was useless. The two men didn't care. They were flying down the river... until they reached the tidal section close to the mouth of the river. They lost considerable speed as the pace of the rushing river was offset by the start of the incoming tide. Nevertheless, the force of the river remained sufficient to shoot them across the myriad of sand bars at the river's mouth.

At what appeared only a short distance from the river, their ship remained anchored in deep water. With no breeze for the sail, there was nothing for it but to start rowing towards the ship – against the incoming tide. Although only a short distance, both men were exhausted when they finally reached the ship and had to call on their reserves of energy to climb the ladder to board it.

Cameron and Jimmy had returned to the vessel with only their personal possessions, everything else they left in Paddy's shack. While the two men went below to stow their belongings, the crew brought the dinghy back on board. A few minutes later, Captain Billings went to talk to the men in their cabin.

"Gentlemen, if you have no other business to detain us here, perhaps we might weigh anchor and begin our return voyage."

A short time later, as they sailed past the tip of Cape Upstart, Cameron dropped it a mock salute and murmured, "See you next time. Better weather and another glorious sunset would be appreciated."

On the seaward side of the Cape, they picked up a good breeze. The return voyage to Port Denison was fast and uneventful.

Chapter 15

The Burdekin

Arriving at Port Denison late in the afternoon, the two men spent the night in a hotel in preparation for a busy next day. Despite the long day, neither man went to bed before a plan of action for the following day was developed.

Their first call the next morning was to the Land Agent's office, where Cameron lodged his application to select the block they had marked out. An inspector would visit the property and submit his report before the Land Board could consider the application. The best time frame the Land Agent could provide for all that to happen was near enough to five weeks. Frustrated but accepting the reality of the selection process, the two men moved onto the next items on their plan and split up for the morning.

Various merchants were to be approached and orders placed for all manner of hardware and equipment, and arrangements entered into for such material to be held at Port Denison until further notice. It was not an uncommon practice, and merchants were used to accommodating such requests. The other important action to be undertaken that day was to engage the services of an Agent, someone who would see to their business in Port Denison as and when it was required.

With those tasks completed, the men returned to the hotel for a meal and to consider their afternoon's program.

"We've done better than expected this morning," Cameron commented over lunch. "Should we both go to talk to a stock and station agent this afternoon?"

"Aye, that's as well. We'll follow the advice we were given this morning about which ones to talk to, and those to avoid. Have you given any more thought to what we might talk to them about?" Jimmy asked.

"Oh, aye, there's been plenty of thought, but none of it has come up with anything new or different. Our prime interest is in what stock might be available from this area and how best to move it to the property. We can't overlook the fact that Townsville is the better place to be discussing such matters. Nevertheless, I'm sure whoever we speak to here will give abundant assurance that they are the right people to handle our business."

"Too true, Cameron. It's possible we may go back to the ship this evening without having made any firm decisions or put any firm arrangements in place here in this settlement. But instinct tells me focusing on Port Denison would be the best move. Still, we don't have to commit to anything today. We can always take the information away to consider it."

In the end, their afternoon produced better results than expected. The second man they talked to about stock, immediately put their minds at ease. Both were convinced, after having queried the man with some locals, that he was the one they would turn to when they were ready to stock the new selection.

The following day, after sailing up the Pioneer River on high tide, while the ship tied up at Wallace's wharf, Jimmy and Cameron secured two rooms at the Wills Hotel for the night. While there, the men took advantage of the establishment's dining room for dinner. As they sat down at their table, Philip marched into the dining room.

"Philip, over here," Cameron called out. "How on earth did you know we had arrived back? We were going to make time over dinner to discuss how we might arrange transport back to our property tomorrow, but now you are here, the problem is solved."

"I didn't know you'd returned," Philip confessed. "I came into town today to take care of a few matters, was delayed leaving home, and then found everything I needed to do took longer than it should have. In the end, I decided the wisest thing to do was to overnight in town and go home first thing in the morning. As long as you don't have too much luggage, you probably will fit on the wagon tomorrow."

After a pleasant meal, catching up on everything that had happened on the property in their absence resulted in a later than expected evening. The two men didn't need to be reminded that Philip expected an early start in the morning.

Although they found themselves perched on an already almost overloaded wagon, Cameron felt an overwhelming feeling of exhilaration as they headed out of town. Soon, he would be back in his own home again with Sarah and the boys. He would be resuming a normal life, at least for a while, and he was surprised at how wonderful that felt.

The excitement their unexpected arrival created at home was wonderful. Cameron's first task on his return was to sit down with his father for a debrief on everything. He was not surprised to learn that nothing had gone awry. Everything had continued as normal without him. While it was good news, it did put a bit of a dampener on his pleasure of his homecoming. It would have been nice to have been missed.

A smooth change over ensued. Without any indication of how he felt about it, Douglas handed over the reins, and Cameron was back in charge. The customary pre-dinner drinks didn't occur that night as both men chose to spend time at their own homes with their families. The following night was a different story. Sarah knew everyone wanted to know every last detail of the men's northern odyssey – and what its outcome meant for the future. Orla was advised there would be seven for dinner.

As soon as everyone settled for drinks, Sarah asked the question she had been wanting to ask since the two men arrived home.

"Tell me about this land you have pegged out. I want to know all about it, so don't leave out anything, please."

After exchanging looks and a brief nod of encouragement from Jimmy, Cameron began reciting details of the block.

"It's prime riparian land with an abundant supply of good water. As soon as our Selection is approved, we will need to make a start immediately if we are to meet the conditions of the selection." Pleased with his description, Cameron smiled at Sarah and sat back.

"No, Cameron, that's not all there is to tell. How much land is involved? For what purpose is it best suited, and what did you claim on the Selection Application? And, for heaven's sake, what is it going to cost?"

Douglas and Jimmy, try as they might, could not hide their enjoyment at Cameron's discomfort. But Sarah wasn't done yet.

"So, Cameron, what is it you are not telling me and appear not to want me to know about? Is it something about the land itself, the selection requirements, or about the cost? I am not some silly little wife to be fobbed off. I'll have all the details, thank you." Sarah's tone left no one in doubt she would not stand for any further nonsense.

"I'm sorry, my dear. I was not trying to fob you off, as you put it. I just didn't appreciate how much you didn't know about everything. Okay, let's see if I can answer those questions. We have applied for an area of twelve square miles of second-class grazing land. The conditions to be met under the selection requirements are much the same as for this block where we live. There are fencing and residential requirements to be met." At that point, Sarah interrupted.

"Second-class grazing land! Why on earth would we want second-class land – and so much of it to worry about? Okay, this is what you have applied to select. Now, what is the cost of this second-class parcel of land?"

"Please let me explain. Our application covers a little over six thousand acres at a cost of five shillings per acre. So, the cost of the land is a bit over £1,500. And, as for it being second-class grazing land, that is simply the classification we chose. It maximises acreage and cost advantages open to us. Prime agricultural land would restrict the Selection to a little over a thousand acres and would cost one pound per acre. First-class grazing land would allow for the same sized Selection, but at twice the cost of second-class lands. I believe I did the best for this family, and I am not unique in what I have done. Most of the lands taken up under this amended Land Act have been selected as second-class grazing land."

"Oh, I see," was all a chastened Sarah could manage by way of reply. But, after a brief pause, she continued. "What about you, Jimmy? Did you also apply for a Selection?"

"Ah, well now, that's an interesting question. With our increasing years, we all need to look to the future. As you are aware, I don't have sons, only a wonderful niece. On my probable not too distant demise, my holdings here will go to Elspeth… and Philip will be charged with their continued operation. In your case, Sarah, you have two sons to consider. How to secure their future here could be problematic with only your current holdings. The Selection in the Burdekin will allow for one son eventually to take over there – problem of inheritance solved."

"Right, so you saw no benefit in a Selection in the Burdekin…."

"Well, not initially."

"You didn't apply for a Selection, Jimmy. I was there. I know you didn't." Cameron said.

"Aye, not initially… But that second block we looked at was too much of a temptation to resist. Before we left Port Denison, I organised a supply of the materials needed for Paddy and his team to complete pegging out that block for me. And the reason I was a little late returning to the ship when we left was because I made a last minute dash to the Land Agent's office to submit my Selection application for that block. Now, I'm just hoping Paddy and his team are able to have it fully pegged out before the inspector comes to check on the application."

Jimmy's confession had the assembled group in fits of laughter. Annie was the first of them to become serious again.

"Brother, dear, if your application is successful, how do you envisage Philip managing to run both the property here as well as the one up there?"

"Yeah, that was the question that delayed my application. Then I thought, well, Philip has one son already. Maybe he should get on with producing another."

Philip looked startled and swung around to face Elspeth, who sat with downcast eyes and crimson cheeks. She gave a hint of a nod, and Philip asked, "Are you sure?" Elspeth nodded again.

"Funny you should suggest that, Jimmy. As it happens, there is another child on the way. Whether it is another son or not… Well, we shall have to wait to see," Philip announced.

Again, the group broke into raucous laughter until Orla sounded the gong for dinner.

As soon as the wagon came to a halt, Cameron sprang down, handed the reins to the stable hand, and sprinted to the house. Bouncing up the stairs, he bellowed for Sarah, who rushed onto the verandah, expecting to see her husband seriously injured or in trouble.

"It's here. It's come through," Cameron shouted at her.

"I'm delighted. Now, please tell me what I am delighted about."

"Our application for the Burdekin Selection has been approved. Now the hard work really begins."

"There is something about that Selection that has bothered me since you told me about it. I don't know why I didn't pursue it with you previously, but now that the Selection is a reality, it becomes important. As I understood from our previous conversations, residency is, as is customary, a condition of the Selection. Does this mean you plan for us, or at least you, to move permanently to the Burdekin? I know that question seems unnecessary. How else can you meet the residency requirement?"

"Well, ultimately, we might choose to move to the Burdekin, but that is not a consideration for now. The amended Land Act allows for the appointment of a bailiff to reside on the property in lieu of the selector. I spoke to Paddy McPherson before leaving the Burdekin. He agreed to take the position of bailiff. His shack on a small piece of land he owns adjoins our selection. He has been living there in the interim while we awaited approval of my application. I will send word now for him officially to commence duties."

"Cameron, I don't mean to be critical, and I'm sure you have thought it through thoroughly, but won't it be nigh on impossible to organise everything to complete the necessary work from so far away from the property?"

"Although we thought it through as thoroughly as possible, I don't doubt contingencies we didn't expect will occur. That's why I ordered all the material we foresaw as being required and engaged an agent at Port Denison to handle affairs on our behalf."

"I see. So, apart from telling Paddy he is now officially our bailiff, what else is needed to make things start happening?"

"After advising Paddy, I need to contact our agent to instruct him to action the list we left with him. He will contact the various merchants with whom we placed orders for various materials and equipment, and will arrange for those items to be transported and loaded onto our vessel for shipment to the Burdekin River. Before he can move anything to the docks, I have to organise a ship to be waiting there."

"Is Captain Billings likely to be making another trip up the coast?"

"He indicated he would be open to another voyage, but I will check on his availability. I might send Cheng Li to ask Jimmy to come early to drinks this evening. We have plenty to discuss tonight."

Over subsequent weeks, Cameron appeared to have little time for anything other than matters relating to the Burdekin Selection. Annie claimed Jimmy was no different. When it appeared everything had settled down, another issue arose to occupy the minds of both Cameron and Jimmy.

"Stock...," Cameron told Sarah. "Now everything is progressing as it should, we need to think about stocking the properties. We enquired at Port Denison about the various options available to us, but the time has come to devote some serious thought to the matter."

"You have a little while to think about it. The fencing needs to be well advanced before you move stock onto the property."

"Aye, and I'm hoping Jimmy has done more work on how we might go about stocking the place."

"What are your options?"

"Move some stock from here… Buy stock at Port Denison – or Townsville – and arrange for it to be moved to the Selection… And that involves working out the best, simplest, and cheapest way to move the stock to the property."

"Ah… I envisage vast quantities of rum being consumed before any of that is settled. I think it's time I asked an important question. When am I going to see this property we selected in the Burdekin?"

"Although I've thought about that, I have to admit I have no answer for you. We can't both head up to the Burdekin, leaving the two boys with no one but Douglas to look after them, and we can't disrupt their education by taking them with us. So, I have no answers for you."

While Sarah knew how difficult it would be for her to visit the new property, she wasn't happy about the situation. Although she knew they were impossible, she eventually put forward a couple of suggestions.

"Sarah, I understand how anxious you are to see the property, but it's impossible for now. Nevertheless, this conversation brings to mind another matter that has troubled me for some months. The boys' education. They have reached the stage where there is nothing more they can gain from a governess. No, don't look at me like that. I'm not criticising Elspeth's ability. Let's face it. Our boys are now twelve and eleven and need to be working towards a higher level of education than Elspeth can provide."

"Don't bother suggesting they be sent away to boarding school. I will not agree to it. I do not want my sons to have to leave home."

"Well, I am concerned that my sons should receive the best education possible. While I hope they will stay on the land and take over from us, I also want them to be well enough educated to be able to follow whatever other career choice they might choose for themselves. It's clear that Elspeth can take their education no further. With another baby on the way, her time with the boys will be limited – even with Maggie in charge of the nursery. Think about it, please, Sarah. Try thinking of the boys' future and not just as a mother not wanting to part with her babies."

Cameron's tone and comments did not sit well with Sarah. Life in the Wallace household took a decidedly frosty turn. There had to be another way of ensuring the boys had a sound education, Sarah told herself, but no possibilities were immediately forthcoming. Over the next few days, Sarah allowed her mind to wander back to her own education and then to that of her brother, who was several years younger than her.

"Of course, that's the answer," she told her empty sitting room. "Find a teacher, just as they did for my brother."

With the problem solved in her mind, Sarah planned to revisit the matter with Cameron that evening. Then, when Cameron didn't return home from the mill until just in time for pre-dinner drinks, she had to curb her impatience until later. Over their evening meal, Sarah told Cameron she wished to discuss a matter of some urgency with him after dinner. He suggested discussing it now, but Sarah was adamant it was too important to be discussed while eating.

As soon as the meal was over, Cameron announced, "Right, then, let's go through to my office, where we can discuss your important matter over a nightcap." Sarah wanted to reply that it was a serious matter she wished to discuss and not one to be made light of, but she bit her tongue – best not to upset him now if she wanted to win him over later.

Once they were settled with their nightcaps, Cameron made an exaggerated gesture to indicate she had the floor and should proceed with whatever she wanted to say. His manner raised her hackles. To Sarah, it appeared he was making light of what she wanted to talk about. That was strange. Cameron had never treated her that way in the past… and she was not about to tolerate it now.

"If you find something important your wife wants to discuss with you so inconsequential, I am perfectly happy to take it to a different audience and follow it through without your involvement. Now, Sir, what is it to be? Before you reply, I will tell you that I am not about to be insulted again by your words or actions. So, think carefully before you say another word."

"Aw, Sarah, I did not mean any insult to you. It was just that it was… Well, it was one more thing on top of everything else that occupied my mind. Of course, I want to hear what you have to say, and to have input if required."

"Fine, but any further nonsense and this conversation will be over."

There was a brief pause while they took a couple of sips of their nightcaps, and Sarah managed to settle some of her ruffled feathers before launching into the conversation she wanted to have.

"Your mention of the boys' education gave me pause for thought about the way my family managed the situation while living on an isolated tea plantation. My mother's education was completed on the plantation, while that of her brother, the son and heir, wasn't. Aged twelve, he was sent back to Scotland for his secondary schooling and then to attend university. At age twenty-one, and after completing a Grand Tour of Europe with his friend, my grandfather brought him home to start taking over running the plantation."

"That was the way of it then, and it remains so now. I'm sure you share my intention that the boys will take over all we have created here – and are creating in the Burdekin. Is there a problem with that?"

"No, as you say, that is the way of it, and it is what I would hope to see happen. But, the reason I tell you about my uncle is because I fear what happened with him could happen here. After being sent to Scotland, he never returned to the plantation until after he turned twenty-one, and then only after his father cut off his allowance. His return was a disaster. He knew nothing of running a plantation, hated the lifestyle, and missed his city life and friends."

"How was the situation resolved?"

"My grandfather was determined to continue the family tradition. He sacked my father as the plantation manager, and we went to live with Great Aunt Bess in Glasgow. Grandfather tried training his son to manage the place. It was hopeless. My grandmother knew her son was a wastrel and his training wasn't working. Grandfather was doing all the work. He was old and not well. His health started to fail. My grandmother stepped in and told him she was leaving the marriage and going to live in Glasgow alone, if he did not stop what he was doing. A long story happened, but eventually, we returned to the plantation, and my father again became manager. Grandfather allowed his son to go back to London and paid him an allowance for twelve months while he became settled and began earning an income. At that time, Egypt was a place of exploration and adventure. My uncle and his friend went to Egypt on an adventure and died in a sandstorm."

"It's a sad tale, Sarah, but I'm not sure I see the relevance to our situation."

"My parents learnt from my uncle's experience. I wasn't sent to Scotland for my secondary education. When my brother, who is several years younger than me, was to begin his secondary education, he wasn't sent to Scotland. Instead, they employed a qualified male teacher to continue my brother's education and oversee his proper upbringing at home."

"I know your brother now manages the tea plantation, so your parents' approach appears to have worked."

"Yes, it did."

"I've heard all you said, Sarah, and I think you want me to take something from it. What do you want me to do?"

"Employ an appropriate secondary teacher for our sons."

"May I think on this for a while?"

"No. If you do not agree to take action now, I will see to the matter."

At the start of the next year, Mr Rigby took up his position as the boys' teacher.

Chapter 16

Scottish Banks Crash

By the middle of 1878, much had been accomplished on the Burdekin Selections, but not before another important visit by the selectors.

The wet season proved an ideal time to make plans for the next excursion to check on progress in the Burdekin. In April, and not without some misgiving on Sarah's part, Douglas joined Cameron and Jimmy on the voyage north.

"Cameron, at Douglas's advanced years, is it wise for him to be gallivanting about in what sounds like rough country?"

"Surely, that is something Douglas must decide for himself. He seems eager to go with us. I will keep a close eye on him while we are away to ensure nothing happens to make us regret it."

After spending the night at Wills' Hotel to be able to catch the early morning tide the next day, Philip waved the three men off in the early morning semi-darkness as their ship, with Captain Billings at the helm, slid silently down the river and out past Flat Top Island. Fairweather and a constant breeze gave them a good run up the coast. Again, they elected to spend the night in Upstart Bay before heading on to Townsville. It was late afternoon when they arrived, but the boat was soon rocking gently at anchor with waves no bigger than ripples lapping at the hull.

Douglas went in search of his two companions and found them leaning on the railing on the top deck. Jimmy called out to him.

"Come up and join us, Douglas. This part of the world is amazing. It has the bluest of blue skies during the day and the most startlingly brilliant sunsets in the evening."

"Those colours filling the sky are amazing," Douglas agreed. All three men lingered at the railing until the last of the glow left the evening sky.

Next morning, in the half-light before dawn and while the three men remained in their bunks, Captain Billings and his crew had the ship on its way north again. The men didn't linger long at Townsville. As arranged, a team and wagon loaded with various equipment was drawn up on the wharf ready for them. After sending Captain Billings on his way back to Port Denison to collect a few head of cattle, the men climbed aboard their wagon and headed for the Burdekin area, where they met Paddy at his shack.

After showing Douglas the river, Paddy took them to his proudest achievement since their last visit, the completed first stage of the homestead on Cameron's Selection.

"It's still only two rooms and a detached kitchen," he explained, "but you should find it comfortable enough to sleep in. My wife is preparing dinner and will call us when it's ready."

There wasn't time for anything other than to freshen up and take a wee dram of rum before Paddy's wife announced dinner was ready. Paddy joined them for dinner, and during the meal, plans were put in place for the next couple of days.

After an early morning breakfast, the four men rode out to inspect Cameron's Selection. They rode past areas still heavily wooded with gums, acacias and palm trees, and cleared areas now well-grassed. They admired fence lines running straight and true and inspected the various water sources. At times during the day, they met small teams of men engaged in scrub clearing or fencing and chatted with them over a mug of tea. As twilight descended, in a small clearing, after a light meal cooked over an open fire, they slept under the stars. Cameron was pleased Sarah was not there to witness that night. It would have increased her concerns for Douglas's safety.

About half of the next day was spent riding over Cameron's Selection before heading over to Jimmy's Selection to check on progress there and for a chat with Jimmy's bailiff. By nightfall, they were back at the small clearing and preparing for another night under the stars.

On the third day, they crossed more of Cameron's Selection, but as they headed back to the homestead, there remained a vast area that Douglas had not ridden over. They stopped beside a waterhole for a quick cold lunch and a mug of tea before continuing towards the homestead. As they swung up into the saddle again, Douglas sighed.

"I have to admit I am looking forward to a comfortable bed and a homecooked meal tonight. I still struggle to take in the enormity of this place and its vast isolation. From here, Glasgow seems almost on another planet."

Back at the homestead, after they freshened up, Cameron and Douglas had the luxury of a few quiet minutes alone after Jimmy and Paddy rode off to look at something along the riverbank.

"Well, what do you think, Father?" Cameron asked as they sat sipping their wee drams. "Was selecting this property a wise move?"

"Son, I'm surprised you need to ask. It's amazing country. Rich, alluvial soil and good water supply. What more could you ask for? Aye, there's still a mountain of work to do, but I'm impressed with what's been achieved. What will be your main focus on this place for the immediate future?"

"Extending the homestead will be high on the list. The building behind us now is no more than the front room of the eventual homestead. Bedrooms and other facilities will be the next extension added. While work will be continuing here at the homestead, work clearing and stocking the property will continue. We plan to have substantial herds in place by the Land Agent's inspection later in the year."

"Will that inspection determine whether you've met all the conditions required under the terms of the selection?"

"Aye, at the time of the inspection, we need to be able to demonstrate the appropriate levels of stocking and fencing have been achieved and a substantial dwelling constructed. We have completed more fencing than required and, although it's not particularly impressive at the moment, what already exists of the homestead is sufficient to meet the requirement. The only aspect we must give some priority to is moving more stock onto the property. At the moment, the herd is barely big enough. I'd like it to be considerably more substantial before the inspection. I don't know whether you noticed it during our short visit to Jimmy's Selection, but work on his property is progressing in much the same way and at the same rate as on my block."

"So, both of you will be looking to move stock here over the next few months. Do you foresee any problems with that?"

"Not really. Nothing is easy up here, but it can be done. Jimmy and I will have to work out from where to source additional stock and then determine the best way of moving them onto the property. Father, I'm sensing you're concerned about something, but are holding back mentioning it. If something is bothering you, please discuss it with me. What's on your mind?"

"Sheep… That's what's on my mind."

"Eh? What about sheep?"

"Why are there so many sheep on the properties up here? This land isn't meant for sheep. Even the number of sheep on properties in Mackay amazes me. This is tropical country, not sheep country. So, why are there so many sheep about?"

"I suppose it's fair to say that settlers stuck with what they knew best, and sheep were what they knew from back in their home countries. The number of sheep in Mackay has decreased over the years, but some persist with them. It is too wet up this way for sheep to be successful, and the spear grass plays havoc with their fleece, but there are those who won't accept the truth of it."

"Hmm… That's human nature, I suppose. Nevertheless, it intrigues me that you are concentrating on cattle and not on sugarcane. This land of yours is ideal cane country, yet you are rushing to cover it in cattle."

"Again, it's all about the conditions and requirements attached to selecting the block. Yes, it is agricultural land and will be ideal for cane growing in the future, but it has been selected as second-class grazing land and, therefore, the land must be seen being used for that purpose at the time of the inspection a little later this year. After that, things will change."

"If you signed up to use the land for grazing, how can you then change what you do with it without breaking some rule or other that puts your retaining the place in jeopardy?"

"Ah, well, it's all about how the system works and how you work the system. Once the inspection at the end of the first year is deemed successful by the Land Board, we are then able to pay the remaining lease fees and convert the land to freehold. Once that is achieved, we can do as we see fit with our property. As with most things in life, much of what we want to do – plan to do – depends on timing. No sugar industry as such has been established in the Burdekin yet. We believe one grower further down the river has a small paddock under sugarcane. I have no real knowledge of it, or what he plans to do with it, as no mills have been built in the area."

"Right; I agree waiting a while before planting any cane might not only be necessary but wise. At least you're not messing around with sheep."

"We never had sheep on the plantations we owned in the Caribbean. There were a few cattle, but no sheep. So, there was nothing that inclined us to become involved with sheep now."

Their discussions came to an end with the return of Jimmy and Paddy, and a few minutes later, they were being called into dinner. An early night followed as they planned to set off for Townsville early next morning. There, they would return the team and wagon to its owner before boarding their ship for the voyage home. Soon after setting sail from Townsville, the two men went to discuss a change of plans with Captain Billings. Instead of sailing directly to Mackay, they would now call into Port Denison and possibly overnight there.

Again, the gods smiled on them for the trip to Port Denison, where Jimmy and Cameron spent some time in discussions with their agent about procuring stock for the Burdekin. The agent told them that a herd being driven from the Gulf country was expected to arrive at Port Denison later that day.

"Like as not, it will be dark before they arrive. They will be put into the yards near the wharf. If you're staying overnight, you could inspect them in the morning," the agent told them.

While the two men secured rooms at their customary hotel, Douglas elected to spend the night on board ship rather than in a hotel and spent a lively night in the company of Captain Billings and some of his crew. It was lunchtime the following day before Cameron and Jimmy returned to the ship. As soon as they were on board, the crew cast off and the ship was Mackay bound once more.

Below decks, the trio sat down to a light lunch, during which Cameron and Jimmy told Douglas of their morning's work.

"It was well worth staying over to look at that herd this morning," Cameron said. "There were some excellent looking beasts amongst them, and they hadn't lost as much condition as I expected on the long drive down from the Gulf country."

"From your comments, am I to understand you have purchased additional stock?" Douglas asked.

"They were too good to pass up," Jimmy replied. "And this morning's efforts will result in the stock held on our properties being well above the selection requirement."

"To sum up our current situation, Father, I think we can feel confident our first annual inspection will be trouble-free."

As a result of the unscheduled stopover at Port Denison, they tied up at Wallace shipping's wharf on the riverbank at Mackay a day later than anticipated. Their arrival was greeted by an anxious Philip, who later explained why he had been so anxious.

"You were expected to return yesterday. That was the arrangement you put in place before you departed. Yesterday morning, I sent Cheng Li into town with the wagon to collect you. He returned on dark last night with an empty wagon. I don't suppose there's any need to describe the level of anxiety that pervaded all three households last night following your nonreturn. As soon as I could get away this morning, I brought the wagon into town again and, after attending to a few matters, hung around all day in the hope that you might return before dark. I was about ready to give up and go home when I saw the ship enter the river. What do you want to do now? Do you want to travel home in the dark or spend the night in town?"

The trio elected to travel home in the dark, rather than leave their households still anxious about their return. After their abject apologies and brief explanation of what happened, Jimmy took the reins and urged the team on its way out of town. Mixed emotions greeted them at home. There was initial relief as they all scrambled off the wagon, but that was soon replaced by anger at the men's lack of consideration for those waiting at home for their return. The anger soon dissipated and was replaced by relief and curiosity. Only a brief explanation was offered while the welcoming group stood around the wagon but, when the travellers returned to their individual homes, more detailed explanations were required.

Most of the next day was spent reassuring people and settling households back into their normal routines. The big news that greeted them on their return was that the Wallace clan had increased by one. Phillip and Elspeth's baby had arrived the day after the trio had sailed for the Burdekin. They named the little girl Alfreda. It was a name that intrigued Annie as it was one that had never been used on either side of the baby's family for as far back as Annie could discover.

Cameron and Jimmy spent a good deal of time with Philip the following day, catching up with everything that happened during their absence. The group did not gather for pre-dinner drinks that first evening back. It provided Cameron and Douglas with further time alone before dinner. After sitting in silent companionship with their bevvies and pipes for a few minutes, Douglas took advantage of the situation.

"There's something I've been meaning to mention to you but, somehow, the time was never right, and I never got around to it. I thought you should know, I have disposed of the last of my property in Glasgow. My solicitor there handled the sale for me."

"If I am honest, that does come as a surprise. May I ask what your plans are for the future? I have to admit that, since about five minutes after you arrived here, I have been expecting you to want to return to Glasgow."

"Well, I suppose my future rather depends on whether you and Sarah can accommodate my continued presence here for however much longer I have on this earth. I had decided some time ago that this was where I wanted to end my days, if not here with you, then somewhere here in Mackay. Nothing of importance to me remains in Glasgow. Having disposed of my businesses, including Wallace Shipping to you, all that remains of my family is here on this property. Being here, and in the Burdekin over those few days, took me back to my days on the plantations in the Caribbean. It revived all the happy memories of my time there and, somehow, that seemed to indicate this is where I should remain."

"I hope you have some understanding of how disappointed we would be if you chose to live anywhere else but with us. You will always have a home here."

"Be that as it may, Sarah also has to have a say in the matter."

"By all means, talk to her about it, but I know her response will not differ from mine. Ever since she joined the Wallace family all those years ago, she has considered you more of a father than her own parent. Further, if I am being honest, I have to admit to a degree of relief and comfort from knowing you are not suddenly going to announce you are returning to Glasgow."

"Another thing has happened that you will need to be aware of at some time in the future. Around the same time as I sold the last property, I had reason to believe Scotland's financial situation was not in the best of health. I previously asked my solicitor to arrange the transfer of certain of my accounts to the London branch of the AJS Bank. After the sale of that last property went through, I asked him to transfer any remaining money in Scottish banks to that same London bank. The most recent information I have is that the City of Glasgow Bank has collapsed. I don't know whether my solicitor was successful in transferring all my funds out of that bank, or if some remained there at the time of its collapse and, if so, how much."

"You don't appear too concerned about the possibility you have lost money when the bank crashed."

"A Scotsman not concerned about losing cash…? That's something you are unlikely to encounter any time soon. Of course, I hate the thought of losing any, but if there was a loss, it should have been quite small and not of major significance."

"How could such a situation arise? All the banks were flush with capital, including the City of Glasgow Bank. What happened to trigger the crash?"

"Too generous with their lending… It seemed everything was going so well. All the markets were buoyant, and prices for many exports were increasing. That encouraged unrealistic lending. I guess nobody took the time to look beyond the boom times – to think about the bust that would follow when the bottom dropped out of the market."

Sarah joined them. As she settled into her chair, she noticed the gloomy atmosphere that cloaked the verandah.

"What has happened? Why are you both sitting so glum and long-faced? Come on, I need to know what is going on, especially if it is bad news."

"No, my dear, there was no bad news being shared out here. Well, maybe a little doubtful news, perhaps, but all the rest was good news," Cameron tried to reassure her.

"And since when did good news turn you both into something resembling stone statues? But, all right, if you insist it is good news, I definitely want to hear it, and you should be eager to share it with me. Will I consider whatever it is good news?"

"Douglas has severed his final ties with Scotland. He has disposed of his final property in Glasgow," Cameron told her.

"Oh, that is sad. Douglas, has something terrible happened back home to bring about this situation?"

"Quite the contrary. It's a decision that began some time ago, and this was the final step to take. So, I'm sorry, Sarah, but it looks as though you will be stuck with me in your back apartment for the remainder of my days on this earth – unless you would prefer I establish alternate long-term accommodation elsewhere."

"You will do no such thing. We love having you here. After you took me in under your roof for so long all those years ago, what we have to offer hardly seems fair recompense."

"Thank you, but you owe me nothing. It was me and my operations that gained from your presence and involvement."

"Are you not telling us something, Douglas?"

"Like what, my dear?"

"Are you unwell? Mention of your last days has me anxious about your wellbeing."

"Of course, I'm not ill. But, as I'm sure we are all aware, I am no longer a young man and it stands to reason my time on this earth must be drawing to a close. It is appropriate that I put my affairs in order before I encounter my demise and others find themselves burdened with sorting out my affairs. Now, I will hear no more talk about such matters."

As the middle of the year approached, both Jimmy and Cameron's thoughts focused on their Burdekin Selections and their first annual Land Agent's inspection. One afternoon, as Cameron rode home from the mill, Jimmy stopped him along the track.

"If you have time, there's something I wish to discuss regarding our Burdekin blocks. I would prefer to discuss it with you privately for the moment, rather than bring it up at our usual evening drinks."

"This sounds ominous. Ride to the house with me so we may discuss it in comfort."

"Uhmm… perhaps we might find somewhere a little more private? It's not that I wish to keep anything from Sarah but, for now, I would prefer this to stay between us."

After handing their horses over to the stable hand to take care of, the two men entered that part of the stables where the wagon was housed. As Jimmy jumped up to perch on the end of the wagon's tray, Cameron moved a couple of bales of hay to reveal a demijohn of rum and a couple of mugs.

"Shall we…?" he asked, waving the mugs at Jimmy.

"Oh, definitely, I should think."

"Right, now, what is this clandestine matter you wish to discuss with me?" Cameron asked as he vaulted up onto the wagon to sit beside Jimmy after handing him the mugs to hold.

"It's not clandestine. It's more of a problem with it being nothing more than a half-baked idea at the moment. Maybe talking it through with you will help clarify my thinking. Once that happens, I will be happy to discuss it with the others.

"I see. The intrigue deepens. Come on, don't keep me wondering any longer. Tell me what's on your mind."

"Well, as you are aware, the time is fast approaching for our first annual inspection of our Burdekin Selections. Once that has happened, my thinking is to move to the Burdekin and set myself up on the block for an extended stay. I want to be there to organise and oversee the changes we want to implement on those blocks."

"If the annual inspection is successful… don't forget that none of our plans can be initiated until and unless that happens. All that aside, you might need to explain your thinking a little more before I understand what it is you are really proposing. What exactly do you mean by an *extended stay*? Are you telling me you plan to relocate and live up there permanently?"

"Well, no. That's not the thinking at the moment, but if needs be in the future, that could be the case."

"What about all you have here… Annie and Elspeth and her children? Do you propose moving them to the Burdekin as well, or will they remain here?"

"I don't have any answers, Cameron. That is why I sought to discuss the matter with you before anyone else knew of it.

I'm not a young man. Setting up the Burdekin lands as we want them might be my last big challenge on this earth. So, what say you? May we discuss my ideas?"

"Good God, is everyone suddenly concerned with dying? No, don't look like that. It was a hypothetical question. Of course, we must discuss this matter… just as soon as I top up these mugs."

Chapter 17

Burdekin Cane

The annual inspection date for the Burdekin selections came and went without any communication received from the Land Agent. Nevertheless, Jimmy and Cameron pushed ahead with planning the next stage of development of the lands.

"It will be too late to plant cane now," Jimmy moaned.

"Does it matter much whether we plant now or later?" Cameron asked. "There isn't an established sugar industry yet, so we have plenty of time to make our move in that direction."

"If it drags on too long, the wet season will be upon us again, and it will be next April at the earliest before we can plant."

"There is plenty to do before then. Ground has to be cleared and worked up ready for cultivation before we can plant."

"Before we left last time, I left instructions with Paddy regarding the initial area we need cleared. That probably has happened by now, or is well under way. I suggested it might be wise not to start working up the ground until the inspection had been done. We don't want the inspector to think we are turning the place over to agriculture."

"Good move, Jimmy. But, for the moment, I guess there is nothing much else we can do to progress our plans. Have you spoken to Annie or any of the others about your plan to move to the Burdekin for a while?"

"Not yet; I wanted to have an idea of when I might leave before I talked to people about it."

"Are you expecting opposition to your plan? How is Annie likely to react to being left alone?"

"She will be fine with it. After all, we are only brother and sister, and have lived apart for most of our adult lives until Annie came here to live with me. Anyway, she has Elspeth here and a couple of grandkids to fuss over now. I don't expect my plans to upset Annie too much, if at all."

The waiting and anxiety would continue for many weeks before relief finally came.

It was mid-September when Cameron galloped up the track, handed his reins to the stable hand, and bounded up the stairs, yelling for Sarah. Expecting the worst and ashen-faced, Sarah rushed onto the verandah, only to be enveloped in a bear hug by her husband.

"Exciting news…," he shouted.

Sarah eased herself away from him a little to allow herself to breathe before asking, "Oh, I love exciting news. Now, what is it that I'm to become excited about?"

"It's through. We finally have confirmation it is through."

"Sit down, Cameron. Take a deep breath. That's good. Now, please, slowly explain to me what is through and why it is such exciting news."

"No, I can't sit. I must find Jimmy. There is mail for him, too. It will be the same news as I received."

"You may go to find Jimmy after you tell me about this good news."

"Our Burdekin blocks have passed inspection. Now, we can move forward with our plans for the land up there. Oh, God, we are going to be so busy for a while, but first things first, I must find Jimmy. I'll tell you everything there is to know about our plans later."

With that, Cameron bounced down the stairs again and jogged to the stables. Still confused and a bit shocked, Sarah leant against a verandah post as she watched Cameron gallop off in search of Jimmy. As she turned to go inside, a thought occurred to her.

"Douglas will know," she snarled as she marched through the house to knock on Douglas's door.

"Sarah… Is everything all right? You look somewhat flustered. What has happened?"

"Are you aware of their plans?" she demanded. "Do you know anything of what that pair are up to?"

"I can assure you I have no knowledge of anyone's plans, other than my own, perhaps. Which 'pair' are we talking about here? Have your sons been up to something that concerns you?"

"Not the boys, Douglas. I'm talking about Cameron and Jimmy and some plan they have."

"Sorry, dear lady, I can't help you there. They have not confided in me. I don't know of any plans they might have, but whatever such plans might relate to seems to have caused you a degree of anxiety."

"Ignore me, please, Douglas. I'm probably just being a silly old woman. It's just that Cameron and I have never had secrets from one another. We've always shared everything, and now it seems he and Jimmy have some major plan they are about to action and I know nothing of it."

"Calm yourself, Sarah. I'm sure there is no mischief afoot… And, the right approach at drinks this evening might elicit all the details you desire."

"You're right, of course. Thank you, Douglas. I'm sure there will prove to be no cause for concern – once I know what that pair are about."

"Don't take offence, please, Sarah, but do you trust your husband?" Although shocked by Douglas's question, Sarah managed to assure him she trusted Cameron implicitly in all matters. "Then, relax and let that trust guide you in this matter. Let it help you find the best way to broach the matter this evening. I also would like to know what is being planned!"

Cameron returned just in time to freshen up before Jimmy wandered over to join them for pre-dinner drinks.

"Are we celebrating something tonight?" Douglas asked as they settled into their chosen chairs on the verandah. "We seem to be gathering a bit earlier than usual."

"Will Annie be joining us?" Sarah asked before anyone could respond to Douglas's question.

"Ah, apologies; no, she is dining with Elspeth and Philip this evening."

"And, yes, Father, we are a bit earlier than usual tonight, and yes, I suppose it is a bit of a celebration."

"Wonderful… Please enlighten us further," Douglas said with just a hint of sarcasm in his voice.

"Today, Jimmy and I received confirmation our Burdekin Selections had successfully passed this year's Land Agent's inspection. It means we can now move on with our plans for those blocks."

"I would be interested to know more about those plans," Sarah said.

"We had to pass that first inspection successfully before we could do anything. Now, we are free to move towards freeholding the lands. After that, we can move from grazing to agriculture," Jimmy told them.

"What exactly does that entail, and how long is it likely to take before it's accomplished?" Douglas asked.

"Our first move is to apply to the Land Board to pay the balance of monies owing under the terms of the selection. Once we have paid those monies, we can apply to change the blocks to freehold," Cameron explained.

"That process could take until the end of the year, depending on when the Land Board meets. In the meantime, however, once we have paid over those selection monies, we are free to start growing cane without fear of further inspections or contravening the rules governing Selections," Jimmy added.

"So, when do you propose paying that money to the Land Board?" Sarah asked.

"No time like the present," Cameron quipped. "We will go into town tomorrow to make the necessary arrangements regarding money and application documentation."

"And then you sit back and wait… Until when? The end of the year, perhaps?" Douglas asked.

"God, no. There's too much to do to be sitting around doing nothing," Cameron said. "While we are in town tomorrow, we will look to purchase two wagons and two teams to take up to the Selections. Over the following week or so, Jimmy and I will load the wagons with various pieces of equipment and a quantity of cane to use as planting material."

"Who will drive those wagons to the Burdekin?" Sarah asked, although she already knew the answer.

"Ah, well, yes… Jimmy and I will be making another trip up north, overland this time," Cameron answered sheepishly. "Father, it means you and Philip will be running everything here while we are away."

"And how long might that be?" Sarah demanded.

"I can't be sure at this stage, Sarah, but I will be returning as soon as possible. It is Jimmy's intention to stay on up there for some time to oversee the various works to be undertaken, but he intends being back here before Christmas. In both our cases, the timing of our return will depend on the arrivals of Wallace vessels at the Morris Creek Landing."

"We probably should plan on meeting the ships at the Morris Creek Landing," Jimmy suggested. "It will be best to have a firm plan before we leave here."

"What about Annie, Jimmy? Does she know about your plans?" Sarah demanded.

"No, not yet. I was waiting for a more definite timeframe to be available before I mentioned it to Annie."

"How do you think she's going to react to the news that she will be left here alone for some time? I know the thought of losing Cameron for such a period of time would not sit well with me."

"Annie is my sister, not my wife. Our sharing the same house is a recent innovation after having spent separate adult lives. I doubt she will object to the arrangement or miss me much. Besides, she is besotted with her grandchildren and is constantly getting under Maggie's feet in the nursery."

With little else that could be said on the matter, and with the atmosphere becoming a little tense, Jimmy took the initiative to leave early. The Wallace household remained subdued for the remainder of the night.

Next morning, Douglas tapped lightly on Sarah's sitting room door. "May I have a few minutes of your time to discuss something that's been on my mind since last night?" he asked.

"Of course, come in. Sit down. Your mind is not the only one being occupied by the events of last night. What is it you want to talk to me about, Douglas?"

"Please don't think I'm interfering, Sarah, but a thought that came to me just before I fell asleep last night might be worth your consideration. And, please hear me out before you start raising objections. I believe it worthwhile to give some thought to allowing the boys, both Angus and Lachlan, to accompany Cameron and Jimmy when they head overland to the Burdekin. The boys have spent their whole lives here at the homestead, having everything done for them, everything taken care of for them. They have not had a chance to learn to do things for themselves. The trip up north would provide a good learning experience."

"Douglas, are you suggesting the boys have been coddled too much?"

"Not at all. All I'm saying is that the boys have never camped out under the stars, have never made tea over an open fire, or spent days on a track through the bush. They are good horseman, and they've learnt to fish and shoot, but there are so many other things they have yet to experience."

"What you say is true, and I am aware of that. Many of the skills they have gained in recent times are thanks to you and Jimmy. Angus can now handle the pony trap as though he was born to it, and both boys can drive a team hitched to a wagon. That much is down to you and your time spent training them. Over the years, Jimmy has made sure the boys know how to shoot and fish, to recognise the various birdlife and know what's edible and what's not, and to understand not just cattle, but also cane growing. While I might not show it, I am grateful for the training the boys have received, and I do recognise the opportunity the overland trip to the Burdekin would provide to further their self-sufficiency."

"I'm hearing a 'but' about to be delivered," Douglas said with a shake of his head.

"It's not that I don't want them to go, Douglas. Please accept that. My concern is for their education. They both are still young and we have employed Mr Rigby to ensure they receive the education we want them to have without our having to send them away to school. This overland trip Cameron and Jimmy are planning will involve some weeks, even for Cameron. I am loath to interrupt the boys' education for such a period of time."

"Is that your final comment on the matter?" Douglas asked quietly. "If your mind be made up accordingly, I will not raise the matter again."

"No, the matter is not closed yet. I will think on it before I make a decision. But I do want you to understand that it will not be an easy decision to make. Please leave it with me to ponder."

Alone in her sitting room, Sarah admitted to herself Douglas's suggestion was excellent and one she would dearly love to endorse. She knew that, as young lads, Robert and Cameron had spent much time with the workers on the Caribbean plantations and in the mill. The learning gained in those years was now evident in Cameron today. Apart from being able to run the plantation and the mill, he was an excellent horseman and a skilled bushman. She knew she wanted that for her sons as well. Now, if only she could see how to achieve it without disrupting their schooling.

Early in the afternoon, as he went past the homestead on his way home from town, Philip dropped off the mail he collected in town. As soon as the boys' lessons finished for the day, Mr Rigby collected his letter from amongst the mail left on the hall table. A few minutes later, he approached Sarah as she sat on the verandah, working on her embroidery.

"Begging your pardon, Mrs Wallace, may I have a moment of your time to discuss a serious matter that has come to my attention?" he asked quietly.

"Is there a problem with one of the boys, Mr Rigby? Please don't hold back. Tell me exactly what has happened."

"Oh, apologies for worrying you, but I have no problem with the boys. It's this letter I received today that bothers me," he said, showing her the envelope. "My sister wrote to say our mother is poorly. The doctors say she has little time left to have to suffer her illness. I know I have not been here long, and appreciate the inconvenience I may cause, but I come to ask if I may take some time away from here to visit my mother in Brisbane – before it is too late?"

"How distressing for you this must be, Mr Rigby. Of course, you must go to your mother, and as soon as possible, as you suggest, before it's too late. I'm sure the boys' education won't suffer unduly over a few weeks without you. Please speak to Mr Philip Wallace to arrange a berth on Wallace Shipping's first available clipper to Brisbane. Please advise me of your arrangements as soon as they are in place."

About an hour later, Mr Rigby returned to inform Sarah he had accepted a berth on the clipper ship departing for Brisbane tomorrow, and asked how he might be taken into town to board the ship. She told him she would organise something for him and that he should pack tonight and be ready to leave quite early in the morning. She assured him she would have more definite information for him after dinner that night.

Sarah felt elated. She abandoned her embroidery in favour of gazing out across the paddocks while she marshalled the thoughts swirling around in her head. With Mr Rigby off in Brisbane attending his dying mother, the boys' education would be on hold for the duration of his absence. That left no impediment to the boys' accompanying their father and Jimmy on their overland trip to the Burdekin. By the time they gathered for drinks that evening, Sarah's mind was made up. The boys would be going on the wagons to the Burdekin with the two men. Now, all that was left to do was to convince Cameron that's exactly what was going to happen.

After allowing the initial few pleasantries and general comments about the day everyone had spent, Sarah stepped in to move the conversation in the direction she needed it to go.

"So, gentlemen, are you any closer to establishing exactly when you might head north? I noticed there was some significant shopping done today, and assume the two new wagons and teams are for your trip north and that the other four new horses might be going with you as well."

"Ah, yes, dear, I was going to speak to you later this evening. We believe it will take us another couple of days to have everything in place, but in three days – or possibly four at the latest – we will be ready to leave. Does that create any unforeseen complications on the home front?" Cameron asked.

"None whatsoever. In fact, it couldn't suit me better. Mr Rigby leaves in the morning to attend to a family matter of some urgency in Brisbane and will probably be absent for a few weeks. It has come at a serendipitous time. With Mr Rigby's absence, there will be no schooling. So, Angus and Lachlan will be free to join you on your trip north. It will be a wonderful learning experience for them as, so far, they have no knowledge of camping out and all of its attendant technicalities and problems. While I am happy for you and Jimmy to work out how this will happen, I had thought that one boy could travel on each of the wagons, and each day they would swap wagons."

"You have caught me unawares, Sarah. I… Er, I don't know how to respond," Cameron stammered.

"I don't understand your problem. Surely, your only response could be that you welcome the opportunity to teach the boys something of that aspect of life. Jimmy, do you see a problem with the arrangement that perhaps I've overlooked?"

Jimmy slid a sly glance at Cameron before answering. "No, I can't say I foresee any problems with such an arrangement. I must admit, I agree with your comments that it would be good for the boys to do this trip."

"Oh, well, that appears settled then," Cameron snarled. "It appears we need to tell the boys they are coming with us and make sure they are prepared for what lies ahead."

"As their father, I know how much this will mean to you, and I envy you how rewarding you will find this experience,"

Douglas said quietly as he fixed Cameron with a steely glare.

Later, as the Wallace family members prepared to go in for dinner, Cameron caught his father's arm and held him back a little until Sarah had disappeared inside.

"I'd like a word with you about interfering in my family's affairs," he snarled at his father.

"No, Son, it is I who have need of a word with you. Your behaviour tonight was both appalling and childlike. You're unhappy about being taken to task by Sarah, although only mildly, for not keeping her informed of your proposed arrangements. That's bordering on unforgivable, and she deserves better. And, you are a bit put out that your wife is making decisions regarding your sons' upbringing, while you have hardly given them a thought since they were born. You have been perfectly happy for others to take responsibility for producing offspring you can be proud of without as much as lifting a finger to be involved in achieving that. And now, you choose to belittle Sarah's efforts in that direction. Make no mistake, Son, on this occasion, your pride is fouling your judgement and influencing your unforgivable behaviour. Now, what was it you wanted to talk to me about?"

"Er… Uhmm… I …uhmm …was wondering what you thought of the idea of the boys accompanying us on this trip. Do you see any reason why they shouldn't?"

"It's a marvellous idea. It will be a precious opportunity for you to spend time with your sons, and I'm sure the boys will love every minute of it."

Douglas, Sarah and Mr Rigby dominated conversation over dinner, while Cameron confined his contribution to the odd comment here and there. When the matter of Mr Rigby's travel into town the next day was raised, Douglas felt justified in making a suggestion.

"As I assume you won't have too much luggage, Mr Rigby, perhaps Angus could take you in the pony trap. What do you think, Cameron? The lad is quite capable of undertaking the task."

"The pony trap? Are you sure he knows how to handle it?"

"Probably better than you or I. Although both boys have a feel for it, Angus almost appears to have been born to it."

"Well, if you think it would be safe enough, I suppose it will be all right. I do have to take the wagon into town tomorrow. Depending on what time Mr Rigby's ship departs, he could ride in with me," Cameron suggested while carefully avoiding his father's eyes.

"My ship doesn't leave until the midday's high tide," Mr Rigby volunteered.

"There you are then," Douglas began. "Problem solved. Mr Rigby and you, Cameron, can ride in on the wagon, and Angus will drive you. It will be his chance to show you how well he handles a team." As he finished speaking, Douglas beamed at Cameron, who replied with a wry smile.

"That's a wonderful idea, Douglas," Sarah chirped. "The lad has been dying to show his father what he has learnt."

Defeated, Cameron smiled at Mr Rigby. "Well, Sir, it seems your transport has been arranged. After an early breakfast, we will leave here at about six o'clock."

No one lingered after dinner. Douglas thought it wise to abscond before Cameron again sought to take him to task. Sarah, while pleased with the way all matters were handled by the end of the evening, was not feeling too kindly disposed towards Cameron. She retired to her sitting room briefly before deciding on an early night. Cameron found himself sitting alone on the verandah with his nightcap. It allowed him time for reflection.

As Sarah prepared for bed, he knocked softly on their bedroom door before opening it just wide enough to fit his head in.

"Excuse me, Mrs Wallace, may I ask if I am allowed to sleep here tonight, or if I should retire to the spare room?"

"The answer to the question rather depends on what you have to say to me."

"If I may come in, the words I have for you will be my most abject apology for my behaviour tonight, and to ask your forgiveness."

"In that case, you had better come in and get on with it."

While all went according to plan the next day, its most important feature was a major shift in the relationship between Cameron and his sons. As Jimmy later reported to Sarah and Douglas, although it took Cameron a while to settle properly into his role as both parent and teacher, he eventually blossomed into it. Jimmy believed the thing that really opened Cameron's eyes to how capable his sons had become while he wasn't looking was how well they managed tasks he thought them incapable of performing. According to Jimmy's report, the two boys drove the wagons for most of the journey, with the adults relieving them only for short spells.

Chapter 18

The Boys

With Cameron, Jimmy and the two boys away, Douglas and Sarah enjoyed the peace and quiet of evenings alone. On a balmy night a couple of days after the wagons headed north, Sarah and Douglas took their nightcaps out onto the verandah. After a few moments of sitting in the silent darkness admiring a starry sky, Sarah eased into the conversation she wanted to have with Douglas.

"Douglas, I know something has to change if my boys are to develop into the men I want them to be, but I don't know what that change might be. I want them to be the same competent and considerate men as their father. How did you achieve it with your sons?"

"You are asking someone with no insight into such matters until he realised his own shortcomings in that regard. It pains me to admit my sons are not the product of my parenting."

"I know Cameron is busy, and he is excelling at running our businesses. But he seems not to know he has two sons who need his guidance and teaching. If it were not for the time you and Jimmy have spent with the boys, they would not be able to do any of what they can now."

"Sarah, your sons are a product of their upbringing. No, that's not a criticism of you or all you have done for them."

"Thank you. I should hope not. I've tried to ensure they have had the best of care and education from nursery maid, nanny, governess, and now their teacher, Mr Rigby. What more should I have done? Where have I gone wrong?"

"You have just told me where the problem lies. Sarah, think back to your own childhood. Were you close to your mother?" Sarah shrugged, and Douglas continued. "You would have had someone who cared for you, a maid of some sort. How were your days structured?"

"Yes, Maisie was with me from when I was a small child. She was with my mother before me. And then there were a number of governesses along the way. After breakfast, the rest of the morning was spent in the classroom, or we might take our lessons outdoors on a nice day. After lunch, there might be another hour or so of lessons before I was free for the rest of the afternoon. Of course, when I was little, I was forced to have a rest in the afternoon, but I soon outgrew that."

"How did you spend the rest of your afternoons?"

"Sometimes, I rode my horse around the plantation. Otherwise, I played with the workers' children and went swimming in the creek with them. One of the gardeners taught me how to handle a wagon and team, and how to shoot."

"Your mother didn't disapprove of such activities?"

"I doubt she knew they were happening. She helped my grandfather run his business and spent most of the day in the office with him."

"So, you spent part of your days outdoors engaged in various activities that might not necessarily be seen as fit for a young woman?" Again, Sarah shrugged and then nodded. "Can you see how your sons' lives differ from yours?" Sarah gave a weak shake of her head. "Your boys have spent most of their formative years indoors being looked after and coddled by women. I know this is the way of the world today. Rearing your children this way is a sign that you are doing well and can afford it. But is it in the best interest of the men you want them to be? I think not."

"Then, explain to me, please, how your two sons gained the skills and knowledge they possess and grew into the men they became. What did you do to achieve that?"

"Me? I didn't do anything… and that might be the best thing I could have done. From childhood, they spent their time out in the fields and in the mill, mixing with the workers, both expats and indigenous. They were the people responsible for the way my sons developed. They were not coddled by their mother nor spent their days cooped up with female carers. They were outside learning to be men… And none of that they obtained from me. I was too busy running my empire, just as Cameron is now. Cameron is desperate to prove to you that he is every bit the manager his older brother was, and is determined to care for and provide for you in a way Robert never did."

"Your words make it so clear, Douglas. I can't understand why I didn't recognise where the problem lay before this. But how do I fix it?"

"It's simple. *Loose' your apron strings, My Girl.* Loosen those strings, send them outside, and set them free. They will absorb so much so quickly from others. It will astound you. And, yes, some of what they learn you may wish they had not learned. But, that is life."

Sarah sprang out of her chair and rushed to wrap Douglas in a hug. "Thank you, Oh Wise One. I am so glad you are not returning to Glasgow. Now, you can teach me how to let go of my sons."

Having left the wagons and Jimmy at the Burdekin Selections, it was almost five weeks later when Cameron and the two boys returned to Mackay by ship. Sarah took the wagon into town to collect them from the docks and a few supplies from the general store. On leaving Port Denison, they encountered bad weather that continued to pound them all the way to Flat Top Island. None of them had slept a wink on that last leg of their voyage home. The three tired and exhausted passengers on board the wagon generated almost no conversation. Then, after a wash, all three took to their beds for the rest of the day.

Douglas and Sarah were sipping their pre-dinner drinks when Cameron emerged from the bedroom and came out to join them on the verandah. Although a little subdued at first, he soon came to life and was eager to talk about their northern adventure. And Sarah had a barrage of questions to help him focus and remember details.

"The trip went well. We made excellent time along the track and reached our blocks sooner than anticipated. Paddy had done a good job of clearing the plot we wanted ready for planting. As requested, he had held-off working up the ground until after the Land Agent's inspection. When we arrived, it was almost ready for use."

"Did any of that cane you took from here survive the trip?" Douglas asked. From the outset, he had been sceptical about the viability of cane taken by wagon from Mackay to the Burdekin.

"We threw two canes away because they were starting to look a bit withered. The others wrapped in the wet hessian survived and remained in perfect condition on our arrival. Planting commenced the day after our arrival. The billets had already started to shoot by the time we left."

"Is it likely to be ready for use as plant stock next year?" Sarah asked.

"No, probably not by early in the year, but it might be ready in time for a late planting around August or September. Either way, we would be lucky if it were ready for a harvesting season in 1880. Our belief is that we won't see a crop harvested off those lands until 1881."

"Given that this is only the end of 1878, it seems a long time to wait for the first harvest," Sarah commented. "It will be costing us money in the meantime in terms of care and attention to maintain the crop."

"I wouldn't expect you to be too keen to rush into your first harvest up there," Douglas began. "There is no point in harvesting it if there is nowhere to crush it. Until it's crushed, it doesn't make any money."

"Do we have to erect another mill between now and when that crop is ready for harvest," Sarah asked, her concern evident in her voice.

"That is not our intention," Cameron reassured her. "Interest in a Burdekin-based sugar industry is increasing. There is talk of at least one mill being erected in the near future. We think the timing of our crop is about right for us to approach others about crushing it. We envisage a similar arrangement as we had here with Spiller and Pleystowe until our mill was operational. So, we are not in any rush to start harvesting cane."

"What other progress has occurred since you were last there?" Sarah asked.

"Well, I think you might be most interested in the homestead. As you might remember, a 'substantial' dwelling had to be constructed on the land by the time of the first inspection. The word 'substantial' might be a bit misleading. In many cases, a two-roomed sawn log construction passed inspection as a dwelling. By the annual inspection, my block boasted a dwelling comprising a dining room, sitting room, two bedrooms, and a detached kitchen. There was no question of its meeting the requirements. When I was last there, only the dining and sitting rooms had been built, so quite a bit has been added since then. Nevertheless, the homestead is a long way from being completed. The plan is to add another two bedrooms and a smaller sitting room, as well as an office. Construction of the extra bedrooms is underway at the moment."

"Perhaps I might have expected some input into the design of the homestead," Sarah suggested, her voice dripping with sarcasm.

"No doubt you would have enjoyed contributing to the design of the new homestead, but it would have been difficult to achieve and almost impossible in the time available. Before you become too put out about your lack of input, let me reassure you. The new homestead will be nothing more than a mirror image of this one. For the foreseeable future, the only difference between the two buildings will be the rear apartment wing currently occupied by Douglas. There are no immediate plans to attach a similar extension to the new homestead in the Burdekin, although it is understood that there might be a need to do so in the future."

"Anything else of note you might care to share with us?" Douglas asked. "Oh, and I've been meaning to ask, how did the boys find the trip?"

"Ah, the boys… Yes, that is another story worth telling. Both my sons amazed me with their abilities. They handled the teams drawing the wagons like expert horsemen, and they are impressive in the saddle. On one occasion, when we made camp early, Jimmy suggested the boys might find something for the pot for dinner that night. The boys set off with the rifles. After they were out of earshot, I asked Jimmy what he was playing at. He just laughed. I feared dinner would be slim pickings that evening, but I sold the boys short. They returned with an ample supply of ducks for the pot. Jimmy delighted in teaching them how to prepare the birds for cooking. We dined well that night."

"Speaking of dinner…" Douglas began, "is dinner perhaps running a little late tonight? I don't recall having heard the gong but it's gone our usual dinner time."

Douglas had no sooner finished speaking than Orla sounded the gong. As Douglas and Cameron stepped through the door, Lachlan almost crashed headlong into them. Angus managed to come to a halt before crashing into Lachlan, but it was not the most dignified arrival.

"Boys, that is no way to behave," Sarah barked. "Please allow the adults to continue through to the dining room, and then you two may fall in behind. Cameron, please lead the way through to the dining room so we may all be seated before our dinner goes cold."

Bewildered and shaking his head, Cameron did as instructed. Moments later, all five members of the Wallace family were seated at the huge dining room table. Everyone remained silent while the staff bustled about dishing out dinner. As soon as they left the dining room, Cameron could contain himself no longer.

"Sarah, we appear a larger contingent than usual at dinner tonight."

"Perhaps, but this will be our usual number henceforth."

The firm look Sarah gave her husband told him not to pursue the matter at that time, but he made sure they didn't linger long after dinner. Back in their room later, Cameron demanded to know why the boys had joined them at table.

"They are of an age when they should be taking their meals with the adults. How else will they learn appropriate mealtime behaviour? If the separate meals prepared for them continue to be eaten alone in their room, they will never be fit to assimilate into the adult world. And, while we are discussing our sons, having them sit at our table is not the only change that will occur for them. They will be encouraged to go outside more often, to become familiar with the properties and how they operate, and to get to know the workers."

"Our sons are still children. And, I would have thought such matters were for me to decide."

"Cameron, you are never here, and you have taken no part in the boys' lives before this. I understand how busy you have been, and the fact that it occupies all your time is not a problem. But, it meant you had no hand in their upbringing. As a result, you are unaware of their capabilities or their shortcomings. If it were otherwise, you would not have been surprised by their skill as horsemen or with handling the wagons. No, I'm sorry, Cameron, but changes must happen. They have been coddled, mainly by women, for far too long. It's time they learned to be boys who are soon to become young men, because that is what we need them to be in order to take over from us all we have put in place for them."

"I need to think on all of this."

"You may think on it for as long as you like, but it will not interfere with, or prevent the changes that have been put in place. No, Cameron, there is nothing more for you to say. If your dignity and ego were not blinding you, it would be obvious to you that this is what needs to happen. Right now, making it right for my sons is more important to me than whatever might be bothering you. It will happen… or there may well be other major changes to follow."

Sarah spent the night alone, Cameron having elected to take himself off to the spare room… where he hid out to sulk whenever he was home over the next few days. Douglas had noticed the change in the household arrangements but chose to ignore the situation. At the end of the second day of Cameron's nonsense, and just before everyone arrived for drinks, Douglas detoured to the kitchen.

"Good evening, Orla. Has Mr Cameron ordered a tray again tonight?"

"Yes, Mr Wallace. He will take his meal in the spare room again this evening."

"No, Orla, he will not be needing that tray. Mr Cameron will be joining us at table tonight," and as he walked away, Douglas murmured, "or he will starve until he does."

After speaking to Orla, instead of joining the others now starting to arrive for drinks, Douglas went to the spare room and knocked on the door. Without waiting for a response from inside, he opened the door and marched in.

"Get up off that bed, Son, and stop carrying on like a spoilt schoolboy. It's time you grew up and realised others have been carrying your load for far too long. You didn't know anything about your sons because you hadn't spent time with them. That's okay. We all understand how busy you have been, and we appreciate everything you have done. But you still think of those two boys as the bairns you brought into the world all those years ago. Get over yourself and accept that others are more *au fait* with the lads, and are better equipped to develop their path to manhood. The first thing you can do is to stop embarrassing your wife and me by hiding away in here to sulk."

Having said his piece, Douglas turned on his heel and marched out to the subdued, smaller than usual group gathered on the verandah, who all looked up expectantly as he strode out.

"I see Elspeth isn't with us tonight," he commented as he pulled over a chair. "Is she all right?"

"She is, but Alfreda hasn't settled all day. Elspeth and Maggie are exhausted," Philip told them.

Conversation was cut short at that point by the appearance of a somewhat sheepish-looking Cameron, who quietly dragged a chair over to sit beside his wife.

"Apologies for my late arrival… Things on my mind," he said quietly.

Although the rest of the drinks interlude remained subdued, Sarah detected no real tension among those present.

As 1878 raced towards Christmas, Angus and Lachlan, settled into their new way of life and seemed to be thriving on it by Jimmy's return from the Burdekin three days before Christmas.

He delivered glowing reports of progress on their Burdekin blocks. There was now an impressive block of plant cane. Extensions to the homestead on Cameron's block were all but completed, and a start had been made on increasing the homestead on Jimmy's block. Jimmy also shared the latest gossip regarding cane in the Burdekin.

"John Scott, on that block of his he calls *Norham,* still has a small paddock of sugarcane growing. It's rumoured that Robert Graham is preparing to plant cane in the coming year. There's also a story going around about a chap named Macmillan who is looking to take up land on which to plant cane, but I don't believe he has taken up anything yet."

"So, interest in a sugar industry in the Burdekin appears to be on the increase," Douglas commented. "Has there been any talk of a mill being erected by anyone? It's all well people wanting to plant cane, but little point in it if nothing can be done with it once it's ready for harvest. I imagine that, until someone plants considerable acreage, there will continue to be no talk of a mill for the area."

"My understanding of Jimmy and Cameron's intentions for their blocks is to put considerable ground under cane," Sarah began. "Might we also be faced with the problem of a crop ready to harvest and nothing that can be done with it? Surely, we are not planning to erect another mill just to service our own needs?"

"No, not at all," Jimmy assured her. "We are unlikely to be putting any acreage under cane until sometime in 1880. Our thinking is that, by then, others such as Graham or Macmillan might have responded to their own need for a sugar mill and have progressed in that direction."

"Well, now that you're home again, Jimmy, what are your plans for the future?" Douglas asked. "I appreciate you have every confidence in your bailiffs, but will they continue unsupervised until you are ready to enter the next phase of development on those blocks?"

"The wet season will be upon us within weeks, if not days. There will be little to do here or in the Burdekin while the wet weather prevails. Sometime after that, possibly around Easter next year, I will again travel to the Burdekin. Beyond that, I have no other plans. Cameron, do you have anything to add?" Jimmy asked.

"As you rightly noted, the wet season is about to set in. It seems pointless to make too many plans at this stage. My approach is not to plan anything until after the rain has gone and we have a better idea of what needs to be done up there. I would add that I see little point in my travelling back and forth for no particular purpose other than to check on the bailiffs. As my father pointed out, I have complete confidence in my bailiff, Paddy McPherson, and will continue to maintain regular communication with him."

"I should like to see those Burdekin lands at some time," Philip said quietly. "While they are not my concern, and I have plenty to do here to keep me occupied, from all I've heard about those blocks, I yearn to see them for myself."

"And so you should," Jimmy responded. "We must see what can be arranged after the wet season has left us."

"…And after Elspeth approves his leaving her alone with the two children for some period of time," Annie said firmly and made everyone chuckle for a moment until Philip replied.

"Surely, there can be no problem with my being away for a while. It's not as though Elspeth would be left alone. She has all of you in close proximity, and she has Maggie full-time to help with the children."

"Perhaps it's time we went home for dinner," Annie suggested, "and, young man, on the way home, I will explain to you a few facts relating to married life," she told Philip.

"Oh dear," Sarah whispered as they watched Annie leading Philip by the arm towards home, "I believe by about now, Philip will be regretting having made such rash comments." Those left on the verandah dissolved into laughter until the dinner gong brought it to a halt.

As soon as the gong sounded, Douglas, aiming for discretion, scrambled out of his chair and, murmuring something about being famished this evening, headed for the dining room. On his way, he was joined by the two youngest family members. After being seated for some time at the table, the two boys began to fidget and shot questioning glances at Douglas until he felt compelled to say something.

"It appears your parents have been momentarily delayed. I'm sure they will be along shortly. None of us will die of starvation in the meantime."

The boys exchanged a look that Douglas couldn't quite interpret before Lachlan drew himself up in his chair and asked quietly, "And will they both be joining us tonight, Grandfather?"

Wrongfooted and at a loss as to how best to answer the question, Douglas made a show of pretending to ponder the question while he tried desperately to come up with a satisfactory reply. Just as he was about to admit to the boys that he wasn't sure and couldn't give any guarantee that both their parents would be joining them, Cameron came in with Sarah on his arm. He breathed a silent sigh of relief and relaxed back on his chair. Orla, who had been an unseen observer of the dining room proceedings, miraculously appeared and began dishing out dinner as Cameron and Sarah took their places at the table.

"You boys must be starving after we were so late arriving for dinner. I know I am, " Cameron quipped as Orla placed plates in front of the two boys.

Douglas raised a cautious eyebrow in question at Sarah who gave him a smile and a hint of a nod in reply. He breathed a gentle sigh of relief. Disaster averted, and peace reigns once more, he thought as he tucked into his meal.

Later that evening, Cameron knocked on Douglas's door. "May I come in to indulge in a slice of 'humble pie'?" he asked nervously. Douglas smiled and gestured for him to come in. "I've come to thank you, Father, for rescuing me yet again from myself. Thank you for your stern words earlier tonight. If I'm honest, I'll admit I had seen the error of my ways but couldn't quite bring myself to do what I knew should be done. Thank you… and thank God you have chosen to remain here with us. Having you around may one day save me from ruining my marriage and my relationship with my sons."

Chapter 19

Plans

As soon as it appeared the 1879 wet season had departed, Jimmy again packed his bags and boarded a Wallace vessel for the Burdekin. His stay this time would take him through to the end of September, and his return generated much excitement. It was an enthusiastic gathering that welcomed him home at pre-dinner drinks on his first night back.

"Here, Jimmy, get this into you," Cameron said as he shoved a large measure of rum at his friend. "You will need it to keep lubricated while you answer all the questions I know are about to be thrown at you."

"Is there no rest for me?" Jimmy replied with a twinkle in his eye.

"None whatsoever, and I will lead the inquisition," Cameron told him. "Now, if you would be so kind, your report, please, on all things relating to progress on the Burdekin lands."

"There is nothing but good news to report. Everything is going much as we intended. We have a good crop of cane to use as planting material next year, and clearing of the land continues on both blocks in readiness for our agricultural endeavours next year. The homestead on your block is all but complete and a fine home it is, too. Meanwhile, the homestead on my block still has some way to go before it's completed. Even in its present state, it provides comfortable accommodation. Both our bailiffs have indicated they are happy to continue in our service and, based on their performance so far, we would be fools not to keep them on."

"What of sugar industry developments up there, Jimmy?" Douglas asked. "Is interest in sugarcane continuing to increase, and has there been any talk of sugar mills being erected?"

"Those topics continue to keep gossip swirling around up there. It's been confirmed that Robert Graham has planted cane on his *Lilliesmere* property. You might recall that Archibald Macaulay had applied for a substantial block. He has cancelled his application, but I've no idea why. Archibald Macmillan has taken up the land forfeited by Frederic Gordon. He named it *Airdmillan,* and has cleared and planted six hundred acres with cane. So far, I have heard nothing of planned sugar mills, but speculation has it that one of the large planters, possibly Macmillan, must have intentions in that direction. That's enough from me. What has been happening here in my absence?"

Cameron and Douglas exchanged looks before Cameron endeavoured to answer the question.

"Not a lot to report, I'm afraid. Life has gone on much as usual in your absence. There is one interesting story doing the rounds at the moment. It appears Spiller is currently away from Mackay. Rumour has it he has taken himself off to Tasmania, or some such place, to deal with an ill health problem. Almost as a footnote to that rumour is the comment that he might be interested in disposing of his Pioneer Plantation and its mill. As I said, it's mere speculation at this stage. So, I suppose it's a case of waiting to see what develops."

"Hmm… That is interesting. I did hear something newsworthy just before I left the Burdekin that might add weight to those stories. I heard that Spiller's bank manager, Henry Brandon, had been showing a bit of interest in Burdekin land. Of course, there could be a totally different explanation – if it's true. But, it might be worth keeping an ear to the ground to be aware of what's happening."

"Jimmy, now you are home again, how long do you intend to grace us with your company this time?" Sarah asked.

"That's a good question," Annie commented. "It's one I would like the answer to as well."

"Ahh, I see a female conspiracy here," Jimmy said as he fidgeted in his chair. "I'm sorry to disappoint you, Ladies. I don't have an answer for you. The best I can tell you is that I have no immediate intention of returning to the Burdekin. But, I reserve the right to change my mind at any time and without prior warning." His chuckle told them his final comment was just a tease.

"I anticipate we both will need to spend time in the Burdekin when we are ready to put those cleared lands under cane. Given your experience of climates and other conditions that prevail in the Burdekin, when do you consider the best time for planting?" Cameron asked.

"In loose terms, some time after Easter might be best. The wet season will be over by then, and it would allow ample time for planting to take place and the young cane to emerge before winter settles in. If we plant too close to winter, some of the billets might not come up."

"Are we set up and ready for planting?" Douglas asked. "I mean, are the necessary equipment and labour already available, or is there more to be done in that regard before planting can take place?"

"We will not be the only landholders looking to plant cane at that time. I had casual conversations on the matter with other landholders in the area with similar intentions. The suggestion was that, by pooling our existing labour resources during the planting period, there should be more than enough for our needs."

As people started making noises about going home to dinner, Douglas observed, "It sounds as though life can settle down and run smoothly, both here and in the Burdekin, until at least after Easter next year… And that might be a good thing for all concerned."

Hogmanay had welcomed in a miserable start to 1880. Torrential rain continued through the month and then turned nasty. For several days from January 26, the whole of the Queensland coast was lashed by gale force winds and heavy rains. All ships remained in port until the seas settled down again. Flooding was widespread in coastal areas all along the coast including the Mackay area. While no damage occurred on their Mackay properties, other than tall, heavy canes tipping over in the soggy ground, the situation in the Burdekin was unknown. All forms of communication were down and remained so for several days.

Watching the heavy rain pour down became a regular pastime. On one such occasion, as Cameron and Sarah shared a quiet moment on the verandah, Sarah heaved a loud sigh.

"Will this weather never end this year? I know we need the rain, and that the first months of each year are devoted to the annual wet season, but this year, I am truly sick of it. Mould is growing on everything and continues to grow no matter how diligent we are about cleaning it away. Is it likely to impact your planned trip to the Burdekin after Easter?"

"The flooding we've experienced here in Mackay probably is being replicated in the Burdekin area. Even once the rain stops, it will take some time for inundated lands to become dry enough for cultivation. All we can do at this stage is wait to see what Mother Nature does over the next couple of months. It's been a while since we've been able to get into town. How are our supplies holding out?" Cameron asked.

"Our supplies of everything are sufficient for a bit longer yet, but I hope we don't have to wait too much longer before we are able to restock. Speaking of flooding, my thoughts turned to that new bridge across the Pioneer River. It's only been there just over two years after the previous one was damaged by flood. That new one they built ended up costing double the amount they allowed for it. If this new one is damaged and has to be replaced again, I'm not sure the Council's coffers could stand the expense."

"We should thank our luck that we are on the south bank of the river, the same side as where the town is located. It means we have little need to cross that river except on rare occasions."

"Cameron, there is something I've been meaning to talk to you about. Would this be a good time?"

"It's as good a time as any. We are both sitting here with nothing much else to do. What is on your mind?"

"I've been thinking about the boys' education."

"Do we have a problem with Mr Rigby?"

"No, not at all. He does an excellent job, but the boys are growing older. Later this year, Angus will be fifteen, and Lachlan recently turned fourteen. How long should we continue their education? At what age should they begin becoming involved in the running of the properties?"

"That's a good question, but it's one I haven't given any thought to prior to your asking it. Is it something that must be decided now?"

"Perhaps not immediately. My concern is for Mr Rigby. I wouldn't want him to go on thinking his tenure here will continue for some time into the future when our intentions are contrary to that. I would hope to give him ample notice of when his services might be terminated."

"Well, I think we should continue with their education until at least the end of the year, but we will need to consider what we do after that. So, I would suggest advising him that he has a position until the end of the year, but that may be subject to review in the new year."

"I'm sure Angus will be fine to finish his education this year. I am concerned that Lachlan might still be a little too young but, as you suggest, we will review the situation at the end of the year."

It was well into May before Cameron and Jimmy headed north again. Reports received from the Burdekin suggested the ground remained far too wet to plant cane. There were also reports that some of the low lying blocks along the river had suffered significant flood damage.

"Reminds me a bit of that early settlement of Wickham that was founded near the mouth of the Burdekin River and was completely wiped out by flooding some years ago," Jimmy commented as they sat going over their plans for their next trip north.

"Aye, I don't doubt there are a few unhappy selectors up there at the moment. It's a relief to know we chose wisely and our blocks are above flood levels. Although, Paddy McPherson might not be too happy. His shack on the flat area on the river bank was inundated, but no real damage occurred, I believe."

A couple of days later, Annie and Sarah stood on the wharf waving to the men as their boat eased down the Pioneer River and out to sea.

"Any idea how long they will be away this time?" Annie asked as they settled themselves back on the wagon.

"None at all. I did try to have Cameron give me an indication of how long he might be away, but it was a waste of my time. But I doubt I will see Cameron again for at least another couple of months. It's likely there will be a delay in getting the planting under way because the ground will still be too wet – or sour from having been wet for so long. Either way, the fields will need some work before they are in the right condition for planting to occur."

"Well, you may well see Cameron back here in a couple of months, but that doesn't mean Jimmy will return with him. You and the boys, and the whole operation you have here, will lure Cameron back as soon as possible. I doubt Jimmy will feel the same need to return. In fact, I'm almost sure he will see his priority as overseeing whatever is happening on those blocks in the Burdekin. Besides, Jimmy doesn't have to worry about anything here. Philip looks after everything for him now and, if Philip has a problem with anything, he can always ask Cameron or Douglas for help. No, I think it will be some time before I see my brother again."

"Annie, are you unhappy about Jimmy being away so much?" Sarah asked cautiously. "I know that he thinks you won't even miss him when he is not here. Have you told him how you feel about being left alone so much?"

"Good God, no. He would think I'd lost all reason. After all, I'm only his sister, not his wife, and we lived separately for most of our adult years. I know it sounds odd for me to say I miss him now, but I've grown accustomed to having him around for company and to care for him. He is getting too old to be roaming around up there on his own with no one to take proper care of him."

While everything Annie said made sense, Sarah knew Jimmy probably would not see it that way if he was made aware of her feelings. All Sarah could do in response was to make conciliatory noises.

A couple of months proved wishful thinking on Sarah's part. It was in the last days of August when Cameron boarded a vessel for home. Jimmy was not with him. Cameron later told Sarah in confidence that, while Jimmy would be home for Christmas, it was unlikely he would return much before then. Sarah's heart went out to her neighbour, and she mentally vowed to increase the time she spent with Annie until Jimmy was home again.

One night soon after his return, when Cameron was spending the night in town after spending all day attending to Wallace Shipping Line business, only Sarah and Douglas sat on the verandah with their nightcaps. After a few minutes contemplating the clear Spring sky, Sarah decided to seek Douglas's help with something troubling her.

"Douglas, I'm probably way out of line discussing this with anyone, and you probably do not wish to be troubled by it, but I need your advice. It's about Annie – and Jimmy's increasingly long absences from home. Would you mind if we discussed it for a few moments?"

"Of course not. I had wondered how Annie was coping with being left alone so much. I'm sure Jimmy isn't consciously neglecting her but, nevertheless, it is neglect on his part."

"What's to be done about it, Douglas? I know there is little you or I can do to right the situation, but do you think there is anything I might do to help Annie cope with his absence? It's almost as though she is pining for him, and it tears at my heart to see her like this."

"Well, it's not surprising Jimmy's absences are wearing a little thin with Annie. She becomes lonely when he is away. I know it's not like he spends all day every day at the house when he is here, but they do spend time together every day. It wasn't so bad for her for a while. Elspeth's bairns kept her interested and busy, but spending so much time with them became intrusive. You are the only other person around to talk to and she is aware you are a busy woman. Do you know if Jimmy has made any remarks about maybe moving to the Burdekin to live?"

"No, I've not heard of any such comments. Would that be possible? I mean, would the set-up he has established up there be suitable as permanent accommodation? And is it likely Annie might be comfortable living there?"

"Oh, aye. It was a fine homestead I saw being constructed on Jimmy's block, and I hear it has now been completed. I doubt it is intended for his bailiff, as a fine cottage also has been constructed for him and his wife. The homestead would be comfortable enough for Annie, but she would be just as isolated up there as she is here – and maybe even more so. It appears the thought of Jimmy – and possibly Annie – leaving here troubles you. Is there more I should know?"

"I hadn't given the matter any thought until now. Of course, Jimmy is a free agent and may do whatever he chooses. It is just that he has been a fixture in my life – my rock, if you will – since I arrived here. That's not to suggest I have any misgivings about Cameron's abilities. Quite the contrary, but Cameron and Jimmy have become close friends and partners in many things. We both would miss him terribly. The thought of his moving away does create nervousness in me, a bit like when you first move out of your childhood home. The thought of Annie also disappearing from my life is something I do not want to contemplate."

"Perhaps the day will come, and possibly sooner than you expected, when you may have to accept one or other of those scenarios. What about you and Cameron? Has there been no talk of the future of that Burdekin block... or the substantial homestead Jimmy reported as now complete?"

"Obviously, the Burdekin block is intended for one of the boys, Lachlan probably, but that is some way off yet. Neither of the boys is nearly old enough to be thinking of their future in those terms. It was only the other day that Cameron and I were discussing how much longer we should avail ourselves of Mr Rigby's services."

"And your decision was….?"

"To think about the matter between now and the end of the year. While we want to give Mr Rigby plenty of notice of our intentions, we want to ensure our sons have the best education for the future. I would welcome any thoughts you might have on how much longer we might continue with Mr Rigby."

"Let's see now… By the end of the year, Angus will be fifteen and early in the new year, Lachlan will turn fourteen. From what I have seen of Angus, unless he holds some secret desire to attend university, he is ready to begin taking on responsibilities on the plantation. As for Lachlan, he is a different stamp of a lad. Although he is the younger of the two, he has a more adventurous streak. He is the one who gets himself into scrapes all the time. I would not expect him to be in the least interested in a university education, and I suspect he is now only going through the motions of gaining further education with Mr Rigby. Oh, he is behaving himself properly in class, but I doubt his interest is there."

"It sounds to me as though you are suggesting both my sons are ready to begin pursuing their adult destinies rather than spending more time in a classroom. If I'm honest, I am half of the same mind myself. I must try to broach the subject again with Cameron before much more time elapses."

A few days later, just such an opportunity presented and Sarah seized on it. As they enjoyed a quiet night on the verandah after dinner, Sarah eased into the conversation she wanted to have.

"Cameron, I know it's only a few days since we last discussed the subject, but I would like to revisit the matter of our sons' education. Is this a good time to do so?"

"As good a time as any. It sounds as though you've had some fresh thoughts on the matter, so please share them with me."

"Without knowing exactly why I think this, I believe Lachlan may be wasting his time in a classroom. He is an adventurous spirit and needs to be out in the wide world learning about what goes on out there, rather than what Mr Rigby is trying to teach him. I also wonder whether being out on the property amongst the workers might help curb some of his restless, adventurous nature."

"I see… And what are your thoughts about Angus and his education?"

"Angus is quite different from Lachlan. He seems to enjoy his time in the classroom with Mr Rigby while, at the same time, showing a real interest in how the plantation works. Unless he holds some private ambition to go on to further education, I suspect he would come into his own if he were to be allocated responsibilities on the plantation."

"You are indeed a wise woman, Mrs Wallace. I find your thinking much aligned with mine. As we are in agreement, then, sometime in the next few weeks, we should have a word with Mr Rigby regarding the termination of his services."

"Yes, I believe that is the best approach. Once we have spoken to Mr Rigby, then at some appropriate time thereafter, we should sit down with the boys to explain our plans for their future."

"Right, that is the plan. In the meantime, I must give some thought to how the boys might be utilised on the plantation once their education ceases. I suppose I've always had it in the back of my mind that one would spend more time with the sugarcane and the mill, while the other spent his time here with the cattle and other agriculture. Of course, they will both need to understand fully both sides of our enterprise, but I think that's how I see the beginning of their involvement on the plantation. Now, are there any other important matters you wish to discuss before we turn in for the night?"

"No… Well, yes, there is one other issue I would like to discuss sometime when it's convenient."

"You have my undivided attention as we sit here alone on this cool and silent evening. Tell me about this other issue."

"This conversation stems from thoughts I've had about the possibility of Jimmy – and Annie – moving permanently to live on his Burdekin block. As you have reported, there is now a fine homestead on your block up there, and I'm wondering what your intention is for that house."

"Has Annie said something about moving to live on the Burdekin Selection?"

"Goodness, no, I've never mentioned it to her. It's just that Jimmy also has built a considerable homestead on his block and, as he is spending increasing lengths of time up there, might he plan to relocate and live in that new homestead? If he were to do that, I suspect Annie would go with him."

"Jimmy has not mentioned anything in that regard to me, but as you say, it is a likely possibility. I agree. Annie would insist on going with him, even though it would mean leaving her precious grandchildren behind. There is no question about Philip being able to manage Jimmy's interests here, but I am concerned about how you would cope if both Jimmy and Annie left here."

"So am I. Jimmy has been a major part of my life in this country and Annie has become a close friend. While I would still have Elspeth and her children nearby, I would miss Annie's company. What about your new homestead, Cameron? What's to become of that now it is built? I understand what our long-term plan is for the Burdekin property, but what about in the immediate future?"

"You do ask awkward questions, Sarah Wallace."

"Awkward…?"

"The need to devote some thought to the future of our holdings, both in the immediate future and long-term, has been on my mind for a while. I think I subconsciously labelled it 'too hard' and pushed it to one side, all the while feeling guilty about not having dealt with it. I would ask for your forbearance for a bit longer while I try to get my head around the issue before we discuss it again. I promise you, we will discuss it soon, and we will have at least some rough ideas in place by the time we have that difficult conversation with Mr Rigby. Do we have a deal?"

Sarah nodded and smiled while thinking to herself that she would spend the next little while ensuring Cameron's thought processes focused on the matter.

Chapter 20

Burdekin Crushing

Late September saw Cameron preparing for another quick trip to the Burdekin. This time, he and Jimmy planned to take a loaded wagon overland to their Selections. Cameron would then bring the empty wagon back to Mackay, while Jimmy stayed on for a bit longer. How long continued to remain a mystery by the time they left, and Sarah noted Annie's increasing displeasure as the men's departure approached. Discretion suggested she should wait until later to discuss it with Annie.

For the first couple of nights after the men left, only Douglas and Sarah sat on the verandah for pre-dinner drinks. On his way home from the fields, Philip advised Sarah that he and Elspeth would not be joining them in the evening for a few days as Elspeth was not feeling well. He assured Sarah it was nothing serious. Elspeth just was feeling tired and a bit run down. No word was received from Annie regarding her non-attendance, but there was never any need for people to advise whether they would be there or not. Nevertheless, the fact that Annie had not been seen out and about since Jimmy left concerned Sarah.

"I am concerned about Annie," she told Douglas on the second night when Annie didn't join them. "Despite the risk of intruding, I will go across to see her some time tomorrow. She wasn't happy when Jimmy left, and I suspect those feelings have festered in her for the last couple of days."

"Mind how you go, Sarah. I'm sure I don't need to remind you that Annie could be in a fragile state and might not welcome company. Still, attempting to spend some time with her tomorrow is a sound move to make."

By the time sleep came that night, Sarah had resolved to take a batch of scones across to Annie for morning tea tomorrow, and she made a mental note to ask Orla first thing in the morning to bake them for her.

Nothing went according to plan the next day, apart from Orla having been organised to bake the scones. As Sarah busied herself to go across to Annie, Mr Rigby knocked on her sitting room door. He looked nervous. Sarah felt her pulse rate increase. Had something happened to one of the boys? She sprang up off her chair and rushed to greet him.

"Do come in, Mr Rigby. Please, take a seat and tell me what I can do for you. Is everything all right with your two pupils? I hope they are not playing up and giving you a hard time."

"Oh no, Mrs Wallace. They are fine and they are wonderful students, never a handful at all. No, there is something else I need to discuss with you, something I find difficult."

Sarah tried to remain calm and hoped the smile on her face looked genuine and did not mirror the anxiety she felt. After kind words of encouragement, Mr Rigby continued.

"As you will recall, I required some time away from here when my mother took ill and subsequently passed away. I regret to have to tell you, once again, family matters are impacting my life. Soon after my mother's death, my brother-in-law, my sister's husband, fell ill, and nothing the doctors tried made any difference. About six weeks ago, he died suddenly. It was all over and done with long before I knew about it, but my sister has been struggling ever since, not only financially, but also with grief and loneliness. I heard of a couple of positions for teachers at a new secondary school in Brisbane and, on the off chance I might qualify, sent in my application. I was surprised to discover my application was successful and I have been offered a position from the start of next year."

"Congratulations, Mr Rigby. It appears life might be falling into place for you. Have you shared your good news with your sister?"

"Not as yet. I only received news in yesterday's mail, and I have been battling mixed feelings ever since. Obviously, this new position allows me to return to Brisbane and live with my sister while teaching at the new secondary school which is close to where she lives. But it also means terminating my position here and abandoning your sons' education. I will understand if you do not allow me to terminate my contract here, but I hope you may see your way clear to allow me to return to Brisbane in time for Christmas."

"Mr Rigby, of course, you must take up your new position and be there to help your sister cope with what life has thrown at her. We are a resilient bunch of people here on this plantation and we will work around your departure. But, Mr Rigby, there can be no question about your leaving prior to Christmas. Of course, you should go then and must take up your new position. I wish you well with your future, as I'm sure the rest of this household will do also when they learn of your departure."

After a few more pleasantries and inviting Mr Rigby to join her in a cup of tea and a scone for morning tea, the next half hour was taken up with discussions about where the boys were at with their education and what Mr Rigby considered might be their next move in that direction. Then, it was time for Mr Rigby to return to the classroom, albeit a little bit later than usual. It was far too late to take the remainder of the scones to Annie for morning tea. It didn't take long to think of an alternative. She would take herself across to see Annie now to invite her to come to lunch.

Sarah almost skipped through the house on her way out to knock on Douglas's door. He looked surprised to see her and raised his eyebrows at her in question.

"If you've not yet had morning tea, would you care to join me in my sitting room for tea and scones?"

"You look quite pleased with yourself. It intrigues me. I would love to accompany you to your sitting room, and I warn you I will want to know all the details of whatever has transpired."

"Douglas, it was such a relief when Mr Rigby came to see me this morning," Sarah began once they were settled in her sitting room. "Cameron and I had agreed to terminate

Mr Rigby's employment at the end of the year, and we had agreed he should have plenty of notice so he had time to put the rest of his future life in order. As Cameron had actually engaged him, my thinking was that Cameron would have the difficult conversation with him. It hasn't happened, and now Cameron is away for goodness knows how long. I was plucking up the courage to speak to Mr Rigby myself when he came to see me this morning to hand in his notice."

"Sometimes the gods smile on us," Douglas chuckled, and Sarah recounted details of her conversation with Mr Rigby.

"So, I take it there has been agreement that, from the start of next year, the two young Wallace lads will start learning about work on the land, instead of foreign languages and complicated mathematics."

"That was the agreement, and Cameron was to devote his thoughts to how that might occur. So far, I haven't heard more on the subject, and I fear there has been little more thought given to it. I hope he is ready to deal with the matter when he returns. I certainly will be asking him difficult questions about it."

"I do understand your concerns in this regard, Sarah, but I believe you will find they are unfounded. It is not such a difficult problem as you imagine and, if Cameron allows the boys some say in the matter, it will be no problem at all. You forget they are no longer children. They have been spending more time out and about on the plantation with the workers, watching the mill in operation, and they know what interests them most. Allow them to tell you what they want to do and run with it, but don't relinquish control of how it happens. Now I think on it, and now I know of Mr Rigby's imminent departure, I also might have a word with Cameron when he returns… Nothing serious, mind, just a nudge to help him see how to go forward with this."

"What would I do without you, Douglas? But I really must make a move. I am going across to see Annie to ask her to lunch with me. Wish me luck. It will be wonderful if it goes as well as the rest of my morning."

Sarah's buoyant spirits crashed when Annie answered the door. Annie's red, puffy eyes and red nose clearly indicated she had been crying. Sarah rushed in and wrapped her arms around Annie.

"Come, sit and tell me what has you in this state? Has something happened to Elspeth or the children? Come on, Annie, talk to me, please."

"No, it's nothing like that. Everyone is fine as far as I know. It's just me being a silly old woman. Nothing for you to worry about, Sarah."

"Well, I am worried. I came to ask you to come to lunch – or afternoon tea if you prefer. With the men away, it's nice to have another adult to talk to and better still if it is another woman. Is it Jimmy's absence that's behind those tears?"

Annie blew her nose, stood up and paced around the room for a few moments before collapsing back onto her chair. After a couple of deep breaths, she returned to Sarah's question.

"What I am about to say won't make any sense to you, Sarah. It doesn't make any sense to me." Another deep, heartbreaking sigh before she continued. "I know Jimmy has his own life to lead, and I'm only his sister, but I miss him when he's not here. I was used to living on my own until I came here, and now I seem to have become used to having Jimmy around. It's obvious he doesn't miss my company, or he wouldn't be away so often for so long… Or maybe he would take me with him, at least on some of his trips up north. The last couple of days, I've been giving serious thought to returning to Glasgow to live."

"Glasgow… What is there to draw you back to Glasgow? I thought you didn't have family left there."

"I don't. Elspeth and Jimmy are all the family I have left, and the grandchildren, of course. As much as I hate Glasgow, it's not so isolated as here. There are places to go and things to become involved with if you so choose. I had friends back home, mainly made through the business, but they all had their own lives to live and several of those have now passed on. I know I'm not painting a very glamorous picture of life in Glasgow but, at the moment, I'm remembering it as having more appeal than what I have here. Please don't take offence at my words, Sarah. You have been a wonderful friend, and I enjoy your company, but you have your life to lead, too, and I am loath to intrude too much into that."

"You don't intrude. I enjoy your company and, like you, I would find myself yearning for the company of another woman if you were not here. Returning to Glasgow does not seem like a sound move to me. But spending time in the Burdekin with Jimmy on his new block might not be the solution either. Has he talked about moving up there permanently at all? And, I suppose, the big question is, has he ever given any indication that he would want you to go with him?"

"Not directly… I mean, he hasn't come straight out and said that he plans to move to the Burdekin to live full-time, but I've picked up it is his long-range intention. After all, why else would he have spent so much time and effort in building a comfortable homestead just to have it sitting there idle and unoccupied? As to whether he plans I should move with him or not, I can't say I've ever had any clues as to his thinking on that."

"Let me put a theoretical scenario to you. If, when Jimmy came home this time, he asked you to consider moving to live at the Burdekin with him, would you go?"

"Oh, it would be so hard to decide. I would be torn between leaving my daughter and grandchildren here and continuing to live alone, or moving with Jimmy to live somewhere possibly even more isolated than here. We would need to discuss it at some length, and then I would need to devote considerable thought to the possibility."

"None of that is difficult to understand. I sometimes feel a bit unhappy about the length of time Cameron spends away from us, but my situation is different. There are the two boys to consider and their education, and one of us needs to be here to keep a hand on running the business. I know Douglas is here and he could manage the business if we were both away, but he is an old man now. I don't think he needs to be left here alone and in charge of two teenage boys. Family commitments do tend to get in the way, don't they?"

After chatting about family relationships for a couple of minutes, Sarah asked, "Well, Annie, are you joining me for lunch, or would you prefer to wait until afternoon tea? It's just that it is almost lunchtime and Orla will be wondering where I am and whether I'll be back for lunch."

"Lunch sounds wonderful. Shall we go?" With Douglas, Mr Rigby, and the two boys joining them for lunch, Annie was not short of company, and Douglas stayed chatting with the two women until well into the afternoon.

Later that night, as Douglas and Sarah sat sipping their nightcaps on the verandah, Sarah shared with Douglas some of the comments from her visit with Annie.

"It almost broke my heart to see her so sad and upset and to know there is nothing I can do about it other than to just be there for her."

"What about you, Sarah?" Douglas asked. "How do you feel about Cameron's absences? Are you coping with the frequent times you spend apart?"

"My situation is very different from Annie's. I have my boys and their education to consider, and also the business here. Apart from that, I am not alone. I have you, another adult, for company."

"Cameron has built a fine homestead on his Burdekin block, or so I'm given to understand. If he came home this time and announced that the pair of you were moving to take up permanent residence in the Burdekin, how would you feel? How would you answer?"

"I don't know. I've never given the matter any thought. I suppose I haven't considered it because it's too much of an unrealistic situation to waste time thinking about. When the boys are older, our situation may be different, but I can't see that being for some time yet."

Although she watched Douglas closely as she spoke and for a while afterwards, he showed no reaction to her words. It was confusing and almost an anti-climax when the topic just died at that point. She would revisit that conversation in her mind several times before too much longer.

As if in accordance with some pre-ordained calendar of events, Mr Rigby departed in December. Christmas and Hogmanay came and went. The wet season arrived on schedule and continued into April. The wet season provided opportunity for Cameron and Philip to establish a plan for integrating Angus and Lachlan into operations on the plantations. After that, 1881 continued in what appeared to be something of a normal pattern. Around the middle of the year, Jimmy and Cameron again travelled north to check on the condition of the cane crop.

Last September's planting had produced an excellent crop of plant cane, but the men's focus was on the crop approaching maturity. The latter would be ready for harvest within a couple of months, but a problem remained. As they sat beside an open fire out front of Cameron's new homestead, the two men discussed the matter and their available options.

"We can't allow the crop to sit there until this time next year," Cameron stated, "and there is no indication the situation will then be any better for us than it is now. So, what options do we have, Jimmy?"

"Aye, it can't be put off any longer. We do have to make some decisions about the cane that's ready for harvest. I don't believe leaving it stand until next year is the right move. Anyway, by this time next year, that new plant cane will also be nearing maturity and require harvesting."

"I agree. We can't just leave it. It has to be cut now, but the question is what to do with it once it's cut. I'm afraid I don't have any bright ideas on that subject. Other than burning it or seeing if the cattle will eat it if smashed up, I don't know what else to do with it. The annoying part about it is that we always knew this might happen. Despite the growing interest in establishing a sugar industry in this area, we always foresaw there could be a problem with what to do with the cane that was already in the ground."

"The erection of a sugar mill was never in our plans for up here. I knew mills would be slow to appear, but I am surprised there hasn't been more enterprise in that direction. There is a farmer a little further along from us, who was setting up a horse mill to crush his own cane. I don't know whether it's operational yet, but it might be worth finding out about it. Perhaps there is an opportunity, at least for this year, to enter into some sort of arrangement similar to that we had with Spiller for our first crushing season at Mackay."

"Worth exploring the possibility, I should think, particularly as we have no other options. Perhaps you might ride over to have a word with the grower in question before we devote any further thought to what to do with that cane."

"Cameron, I've got nothing needing my attention tomorrow. I'll ride over to check on the progress with the horse mill and, if appropriate, have a chat with him about an agreement to crush our cane."

Next evening, when they again took their places beside the open fire, Jimmy took command of the conversation as soon as they sat down.

"I went to see the chap with the horse mill today and managed to put in place an arrangement similar to that we had with Spiller for our first Mackay crop. The only problem with his set-up is that he can't do anything with the juice produced when the cane is crushed."

"So, he has made no provision for boiling the juice he extracts from the cane? Is that what you are telling me?" Jimmy nodded emphatically. "What does he plan to do with the juice from his own cane? By the sound of this, I'm not sure we should even consider having him crush our crop."

"No, I didn't say he hadn't done anything about processing the juice. He knows the next stage of the process is the one that will result in a cash flow. He just doesn't know how to do it. He has acquired a pan and other bits and pieces for processing the juice, but doesn't know how to set it up or how to use it."

"Might there be an opportunity for us in there somewhere?"

"Now, we are speaking the same language. I suggested we might be able to help with that process… for a reasonable consideration in return."

"And, what might constitute 'reasonable consideration'?"

"Ah, well, it would mean having our cane crushed would cost us next to naught."

"Definitely reasonable…," Cameron said, nodding his approval. "And just how might this plan of yours work, Old Friend? I'm sure you have some devilish plan in mind."

"Right, I have, and it's not too complicated. I will spend time at his plantation setting up the equipment. From my brief inspection of everything he has acquired, all that's needed is already there on site. So, I will set it up and run it for the first little while to ensure it performs satisfactorily. He will receive some basic training while that happens. Then, you will free up Paddy McPherson to take over from me."

"Paddy is my bailiff. What am I supposed to do about this place while he is up there turning juice into sugar? Anyway, why would Paddy be of any use to the operation?"

"You forget that I knew Paddy in the Caribbean, and I know that he had experience in sugar mills there. With a bit of a refresher course, he will be fine, and my bailiff and I will oversee work on your plantation in his absence."

"Hmm… might be all right, I suppose. I'll think on it before I agree. Right, it sounds as though you believe you have everything in place for the cane to be crushed and the juice to be turned into sugar. What happens after that? How does the end product be turned into cash? This year probably won't produce a big tonnage of sugar, but carting it to the nearest port to ship it to market will be costly. Is there a plan that takes care of the end product?"

"Oh, aye, our enterprising colleague has a plan for that and already has sounded out a few potential buyers. I believe it will work well enough."

"It seems that everything that is now in place is the best we can achieve this year and probably is more than I had dared hope for. We'll need to have a word with Paddy, of course, to ensure he is up for the arrangement you have in place. Any idea when the horse mill set-up will be ready to start crushing?"

"I figure it will be July or early August before we have tested everything and are right to become operational. I just remembered some other news I picked up today. It appears that chap Macmillan over on Airdmillan Plantation has begun construction of a sugar mill. A couple of other people I encountered while I was out and about confirmed the story. While nobody knows exactly what his plans are, common opinion has it that the new mill is unlikely to be operational next year. It will more likely be 1883 before it becomes operational."

"Not surprising that he felt compelled to do something about a mill. He has a significant area under cane. I can't image what he plans to do with his crops until his new mill is operational but, with sugar prices so high and continuing to increase, I don't doubt he will be pushing to have it working as soon as possible."

"Yeah, prices at the moment offer a golden opportunity to recoup some of the money we have poured into our two blocks. It would be nice not to have to continue diverting money from our Mackay operations to fund what is happening up here."

Chapter 21

Moving North

The following evening instead of their usual 'wind down' beside the fire, they invited Paddy McPherson to join them in a drink and to hear Jimmy's plan for him to help boil the juice from that year's crushing. Paddy expressed his concern that, now a long time removed from the Caribbean, he might no longer be up to the job. After Jimmy explained the plan in detail, including how it also incorporated a 'refresher course' for Paddy, and Cameron assured him he was happy for Paddy to be absent from the property for however long that year's crushing required, Paddy agreed.

"Paddy might have to convince his wife it's the right thing to do," Jimmy chuckled. "She might not be at all happy if he moves to stay up the road for the duration of the crushing season."

"That brings something else to mind, Jimmy. While you appear to have this year's crushing under control, we need to keep an ear to the ground for any other mills likely to be constructed close by. Airdmillan is a bit too far away to be of any use to us."

"There are a couple of whispers I will try to follow up."

"With everything now in place, I'm of a mind to head home early next week. How long do you plan on staying up here this time, Jimmy?"

"At least until this year's crop is processed, so it could be October before I leave here. Actually, I'm thinking of moving to live up here permanently. Not immediately, of course, but maybe after the next wet season."

"Have you discussed that with Annie?"

"Annie? No. I doubt that would cause her any concern, so I hadn't thought to discuss it with her until I had decided what to do and when to go."

"Had you considered whether Annie would want to come with you or not?"

"Annie wouldn't be interested. She is settled in Mackay, close to her daughter and grandchildren."

"Perhaps you should ask her about it, instead of assuming your assessment of the situation is correct."

Jimmy gave Cameron an enquiring look before conceding maybe he should talk to Annie about it before making any final decisions in that regard.

On his return to Mackay, Cameron was a touch disappointed and maybe a little put out to discover everything at home had gone on perfectly in his absence. The situation regarding Mr Rigby was sorted in his absence, and his sons were doing so well in the allocated duties on the plantations, Philip had given them increased responsibilities. Douglas had kept a close eye on operations and had stepped in quickly to avert a couple of situations that could have turned nasty.

"I could stay away forever and no one would even know I was missing," he lamented to Sarah as they readied for bed on his first night back.

"Is that what you think? Well, I would miss you. In fact, I do… And I am not the only one who struggles to cope with these long absences in the Burdekin that seem to be becoming increasingly a part of life."

"Who else? Oh, Annie…."

"Yes, Annie has become so unhappy, she is talking about returning to Glasgow. I would hate to see her go, and I know she will regret the move if she does. If only Jimmy could see how she feels…."

"Hmm… perhaps something might eventuate in that regard. Let's see how things work out when Jimmy returns. Good night."

It was late October before Jimmy appeared again. His appearance shocked Sarah. Jimmy looked tired and worn out. He looked an old man. No matter how hard Sarah tried to ease her mind on the matter, she failed. Of course, Jimmy was an old man now. He was several years older than Cameron, and she and Cameron could no longer be considered young. But it wasn't just Jimmy's appearance that concerned Sarah. She felt sure something wasn't right with him. At her first opportunity, she broached the subject with Cameron.

"Perhaps you're fussing unnecessarily. I'm sure Jimmy is fine," Cameron tried reassuring her. "Things have been a bit hectic up there over the last little while and Jimmy was kept busy. Our first Burdekin crop was ready to be crushed and Jimmy was heavily involved in making sure everything was operational in time for a start to the season. He's probably just a bit tired, nothing more."

Her conversation with Annie a couple of days later confirmed Sarah's earlier assessment of Jimmy.

"He's not well, Sarah. He's being difficult and won't let me look after him properly, but he is not well. He seems to have picked up some sort of influenza type virus while he was up north… and, of course, did nothing about it at the time. He had a fever when he arrived home. I've managed to bring it down a bit, but it is still a bit high. Whatever it is seems to be hanging on. It has left him a bit weak. I've sent a message to Dr McBurney asking him to call in next time he is out this way."

"Things do seem harder to shift once you gain a bit of age. I suppose seeing Jimmy so rundown has made me see our lot with new eyes. Cameron and I are not getting any younger, and I suddenly realised how old Douglas is now. He never seems to age, but he has chalked a lot of years. I can't bear to think of life or this place without him."

"Don't think such thoughts, Sarah. Douglas is well and as fit and agile as he ever was. Yes, like the rest of us, he is getting older, but I wager he will be around for quite a while yet."

By Christmas 1881, the annual monsoon season had already established itself. Under Dr McBurney's care, Jimmy slowly regained his strength and returned to something more closely resembling his old self. The wet season, when there is nothing to do but sit and watch the rain come down, provided Jimmy with a further long period of rest to fully recuperate. It wasn't until then that the question of another trip to the Burdekin arose. Mindful of Cameron's earlier careful comments, Jimmy sought to discuss the matter with Annie.

"Sometime prior to the middle of the year, I'll be needing to travel to the Burdekin again in order to ensure everything is in place for our 1882 crop to be crushed. Do you cope well enough when I am not here?"

"No, I do not cope well with those situations at all. I have no doubt you would prefer to remain at your Burdekin block fulltime and probably only feel compelled to return here because of me. Is that not the truth of the matter?" Annie demanded.

"Well, I wouldn't put it quite like that, but I suppose, there is an element of truth in what you say. Certainly, remaining up there would suit me better than having to travel back and forth so much. But I still have responsibilities here, and I need to take care of you as well."

"You could take care of me up there just as well as you do whenever you are here. And, if I were to be there with you, I would not be constantly worrying about what is happening to you and if you are all right. An alternative I have been considering is returning to Glasgow. In that case, you wouldn't have to return here on my behalf. You wouldn't have to worry about me at all."

"Do you really want to return to Glasgow?" Jimmy asked, somewhat taken aback by Annie's words as an uneasiness developed within him.

"Of course not. If I loved Glasgow so much, I wouldn't have come here in the first place. I've come to feel you don't want me around, that I am nothing more than a burden around your neck. Better I make my own way back in Glasgow than that."

"Good God, woman, I don't know what I would do without you. I've become so used to having you around to take care of me. I find my time in the Burdekin difficult without you."

"Then, take me with you and let's settle into that new homestead of yours."

"There are things to be put in place, of course, but can we agree to be ready to relocate to northern lands by the start of June?" Jimmy asked, a grin splitting his face.

At pre-dinner drinks a couple of days later, Jimmy told the assembled friends that he and Annie would be relocating permanently to live on his Burdekin block. Sarah felt her heart sink. She immediately spun around to look at Elspeth – who showed no reaction to Jimmy's announcement. It was obvious it wasn't news to Elspeth. That made sense. Of course, Annie would have informed her daughter of their plans before they were shared with the rest of the group. Nevertheless, Jimmy's announcement put a dampener on things and the remainder of the evening became a subdued affair.

Later that night, Cameron again revisited the subject and, with extreme caution, endeavoured to assess Sarah's reaction to it. He even went so far as to solicit her thoughts on following Jimmy and Annie's example.

"I should like to see your land up there, Cameron. While I accept we must continue to consider our responsibilities to our sons for some time yet, a little part of me envies Annie her northern adventure."

"Don't envy her. Come with me." Cameron's excitement was clear in his voice and on his face.

"But the boys…."

"The boys spend all day out working on the plantations. They have the household staff to look after their needs here at home and Douglas and Philip to guide them and look after their wellbeing. You wouldn't be saying farewell forever. You could make return visits as you saw necessary. I think Annie would welcome another woman's presence close by."

"I will think on it, Cameron, but one thing about it does bother me. Is it fair of us to leave Douglas to look after our sons? He is an old man who has already brought up his own family. Does he need to be lumbered with ours now?"

Cameron roared laughing. "The boys spend more time with Douglas than they do with us, and he looks forward to it. I'm sure the boys consider him something akin to the Font of All Knowledge. They absolutely adore him… and he, them."

By the end of the week, and only after discussing the matter with her mentor, Douglas, Sarah told Cameron she would move to the Burdekin with him. The discussion that followed saw them agree that they would set up home together in the Burdekin towards the end of the year and before the wet season set in again.

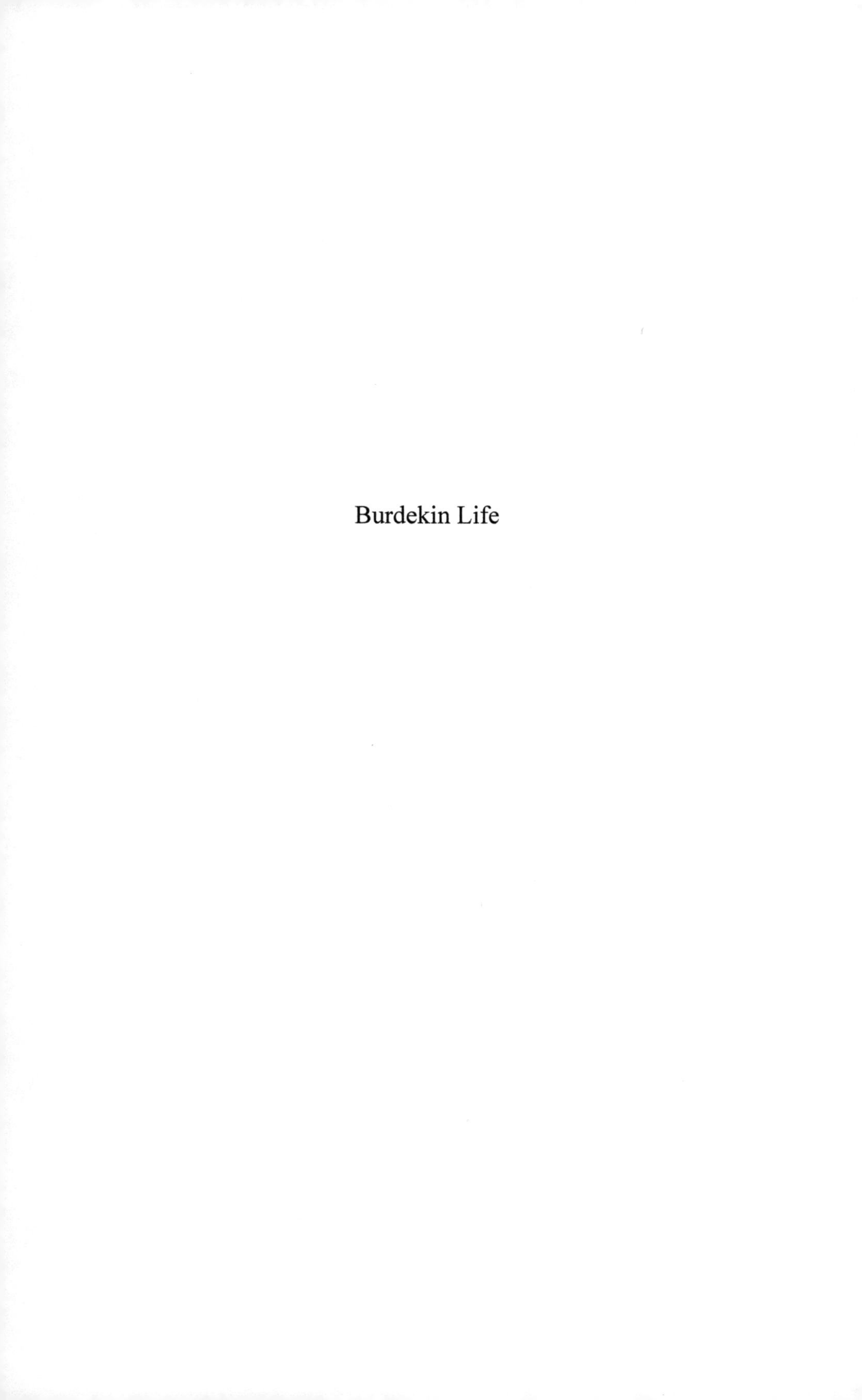

Burdekin Life

Chapter 22

A New Home

By the time Easter Sunday 1882 rolled around, Annie was settling into her new home on Jimmy's Burdekin block. Mrs Langton, the wife of Jimmy's Bailiff, took charge of the detached kitchen as soon as Annie arrived, and within the first month, the women had become firm friends. In a letter to Sarah written some weeks after Annie had settled into her new home, she bleated to Sarah about the lack of opportunity for hiring domestic staff. She warned Sarah that, when Sarah moved to the Burdekin, unless she packed a housemaid along with the rest of her belongings, Sarah would be doing her own housework just as Annie was now.

After a bit of persuasion by Sarah, Cameron agreed a trip to the Burdekin around the middle of the year might be beneficial to Sarah's planning for their relocation later in the year.

"Perhaps a short stay on the property might help with planning what needs to be organised for our major move later in the year. It will give you a feel for the place and the furniture and other bits and pieces that need to be brought up with us."

"That will be extremely useful for me," Sarah agreed, "but the logistics of moving our belongings to the site are a mystery to me. Will everything have to be transported on drays, or is there a better way of transporting bigger items, such as large pieces of furniture?"

"All you need to concern yourself with is gathering together all that needs to be taken to the Burdekin. Then, Philip and I will look at the best ways of transporting which items."

"How about June?" Sarah asked.

"June?... What about June? Are we talking about some woman or the month?"

"Oh, Cameron, focus, please. We were talking about a trip for me to see the house I will be living in come the end of the year. I'm suggesting June might be a good time for the trip. It won't be too hot or wet, and it will allow me plenty of time afterwards to prepare for moving up there permanently."

"I see. Yes, we will go in June, but it will be the end of June. By then, this year's crushing should be about to begin."

Rather than waste the weeks available before they left for the Burdekin, Sarah kept herself busy sorting out the obvious things they would need for their new home. The spare bedroom became a storage area for household linen and kitchen equipment and utensils, and Sarah's wardrobe came in for a cull as she disposed of older clothing and replaced it with newer versions.

As she explained to Orla, "Goodness knows how long it might be before it's possible to acquire new clothing once we move up there."

"What about the staff, Mrs Wallace? Will we be moving with you?"

"I do apologise, Orla. In the midst of all that's happening, I had overlooked talking to you about the future. I suppose the big question is whether you wish to move north with us or would prefer to stay here."

"Well, if there is a choice, Ma'am, I would prefer to stay here… unless you happen to be taking Cheng Li with you when you go."

"Cheng Li? No, I don't believe there is any intention of taking him away from the work he does here. Is that important to you in some way?"

"Begging your pardon, Ma'am, but yes, it is important, and if that is the case, I would prefer to stay here. You see, with your permission, Cheng Li and I would like to marry. I was going to mention it to you earlier, but you were so busy with everything, I decided it could wait."

"Good Lord, you don't need my permission to marry. You are a free person like the rest of us, and so is Cheng Li. You both will remain a vital part of the continued operation of this place, and those who remain in this house will still need a cook and a housekeeper. I do hope you and Cheng Li are planning to marry before I move north."

"Thank you, Ma'am. Thank you. We had hoped it would be soon. I will talk to Cheng Li today and, hopefully, we will decide on a date."

When Cheng Li went into town the next day to collect supplies, he booked the first available date for their wedding. Orla advised Sarah of their arrangements after dinner that night.

"I don't wish to pry into your affairs, Orla, but is it to be a Christian ceremony or something else?"

"We are both Christians, Ma'am, so there is no problem in that respect. I do need to ask, however, whether we might be permitted to be married here on the property? The Reverend Tanner says he would be happy to conduct the ceremony here."

"Oh, that would be lovely. Yes, you must have it here so the people who know you both so well can attend. We can plan it together."

"Thank you, Ma'am, but may I be so bold as to ask one other question?" Sarah nodded and gestured for her to ask it. " Will Cheng Li be allowed to live in my quarters with me after we are married?"

"Of course, you must be together. What is the point of being married if you are not together?" As Sarah finished speaking, the germ of an idea had formed. She knew she would be discussing it with Cameron before they went to bed that night.

Cameron, somewhat taken aback by this latest development when Sarah told him of it, asked, "Are we all right about this marriage? I mean, is it likely to cause us any problems? What if there are children? How will that work?"

"Goodness me, Cameron, what is all this about? Of course we are all right about Orla and Cheng Li being married. As for children, although Orla is getting along a bit in age now, I suppose it is still possible there might be children. And, if there are, they will accommodated here on the plantation along with any others that are born here."

"Right, then that is taken care of and we can now sit back and wait for the wedding."

"Not exactly everything has been taken care of, Cameron. Orla and Cheng Li are my staff and have been with me since I arrived here. I see them almost as an extension of the family. I would like to do something for them as they start this new phase of their lives. I would like to provide them with a small cottage to live in, rather than have them crammed into Orla's quarters for too long."

"Are you sure about this?" Sarah nodded, and Cameron continued. "Yes, it is the right thing to do. You are a generous woman, Mrs Wallace. Not too many employers around here would do likewise. I had better take myself off to have a chat with Roddy McDonald tomorrow. The sooner the cottage is built, the sooner they will be out of Orla's cramped quarters and living comfortably."

The wedding day arrived, and everything was set up under a couple of large shady trees in readiness for the big event. Reverend Tanner was late arriving. The ceremony got underway about twenty minutes later than planned. Cameron watched his wife with increasing amusement in the lead-up to Tanner's arrival and, later, shared his observations with Sarah.

"One thing about Orla's wedding, she did not want for an anxious mother-of-the-bride fussing around her on her big day. It was fascinating to watch you fulfil that role. I don't know what you will be like when our sons marry, but I am a bit pleased we don't have a daughter who has to live through a repeat performance of your behaviour today."

"What do you mean by 'my behaviour'? As you said, Orla did not have her mother here today, or any of her family for that matter. I felt for the woman and wanted her day to be as memorable as possible – for all the right reasons and not the things that went wrong. It was the least I could do for her after all her years of service. In my early days here alone, Orla was more than just my housekeeper."

"Who was that woman Orla brought over and introduced to you soon after the ceremony finished?"

"Mrs Walters… Orla asked me yesterday what I was going to do about household staff when I moved to the Burdekin. I had to admit that I was a bit concerned about the matter as I did not think it would be easy to find such staff where we would be situated. She introduced Mrs Walters to me as a possible cook and housekeeper. She has been the cook at one of the big houses in town until recently when the owner and his family returned to England. She is a widow, and it appears she has no qualms about moving to the wilds of the Burdekin."

"So, you appear to have scored yourself a cook. Now, what about a housemaid? Have you done anything about one of those?"

"No, not yet, but I did mention to Mrs Walters that I would have to try to find one before we moved. She mentioned a young lass who she thought might be interested in the position, but she would talk to the girl first before taking it any further. At my first opportunity, I will ask Orla if she knows anything of the girl Mrs Walters mentioned."

"You seem to have the staffing arrangements well in hand. What other staff will you try to employ before we leave here?"

"We will need a gardener, but I assume you already have someone employed in that capacity, or someone who could become the gardener."

"Hmm… Yes, I could have someone who would be ideal. I'll have a word with him when we are up there. I must admit, I currently use him in another capacity and am a bit reluctant to relinquish him from that position to become your gardener. Still, an alternative employee could materialise in the meantime, much as Mrs Walters has."

A few days later, an opportunity presented for Sarah to talk to Orla about the possible housemaid Mrs Walters had suggested. Sarah reported the outcome of that conversation to Cameron that night.

"Orla spoke highly of the lass Mrs Walters mentioned and said that she thought the girl would welcome such a position with me. The other piece of good news… Well, possible good news… came when I mentioned that, apart from domestic staff, I also needed to find a gardener. Orla suggested Cheng Li might be able to help in that regard, and she would mention it to him tonight."

"He probably has someone from his own community he might recommend."

"She did hint that the person she thought Cheng Li might recommend had some familial connection to Cheng Li. Anyway, I trust Cheng Li's judgement and I don't believe he would knowingly do me a bad turn."

On his way home from work the next day, Cheng Li stopped at the homestead and asked to speak to Sarah. An excited Sarah shared her good news with Cameron as they took their places for pre-dinner drinks later that evening.

"Cheng Li came to see me this afternoon to recommend a gardener for the Burdekin property. The man he recommends is a family member of sorts, a cousin or nephew perhaps, and is aged in his thirties. He assures me the man in question would welcome a job similar to that Cheng Li had when I first arrived. The man's name is Ming Wei. Cheng Li says he would not recommend the man unless he believed him to be good enough for the job. It would be too much of an embarrassment for Cheng Li if he recommended someone who turned out not to be good enough. So, after Ming Wei comes to see me, and I determine that he is the man for the job, you won't have to worry about giving one of your workers to me for the gardener position."

As October approached, Sarah's emotions ran riot. While she was excited about seeing the Burdekin property and setting up a new home, the thought of leaving all she had in Mackay behind tore at her. She had spent so much time and effort – and money – setting up the plantation here and turning the homestead into a home. Then there were the friends she had made over the years, including the likes of Roddy McDonald and his wife. And there were Philip and Elspeth and the young family – Sarah's two grandchildren – who she also would be leaving behind. But Annie had gone north and left her daughter and her grandchildren behind. If Annie could do it, Sarah told herself, she could do it too.

Of course, there were the two boys to consider, and Douglas. The thought of leaving them behind, and not knowing what was happening with them, pulled at her heartstrings. What if something happened to one of them? By the time she knew about it, the event would be long gone. And what about Douglas? He was not getting any younger, and it can't be denied that his time on earth was running out. If his end came while she wasn't there, she would never forgive herself, not only for not being there for Douglas, but also for not being there to support the boys at that time. There was no point in talking about such things to Cameron. To him, such thoughts and anxieties were nothing more than women's frailties.

It was early November when Cameron announced the time had come. He had the men bring the wagon up to the house to start loading those items earmarked for transport to the Burdekin. A couple of wagon loads were taken to the docks to be loaded onto a Wallace vessel for the journey north, while a small amount of material remained to accompany Cameron and Sarah on their voyage.

Life was hectic, and amidst the hurley burley of packing, clearing out cupboards, and generally preparing to leave, Sarah still found time secretly to shed a few tears. It wasn't that she changed her mind and didn't want to go. It was the wrench of leaving home – again. In her experience, such a move had never proved a joyous occasion, and it was perhaps the only thing that had reduced her to tears over the years. Although she knew that once she was on the ship and she was on her way to starting a new adventure, such nonsense would depart and be replaced by excitement and anticipation, it didn't help.

And then, they were boarding the ship, with their two boys, Douglas, Orla, Cheng Li, Philip, and Elspeth, gathered together on the wharf to see them off. There were tears, both on and off the ship, and Sarah sobbed uncontrollably as the ship slid down the river and out to sea.

A fair wind and flat sea saw the vessel make good time to Port Denison. Although Sarah wasn't aware of it when they left Mackay, Cameron had several matters to deal with while in Port Denison, and it meant spending the night in that town.

"You have a choice, Sarah, between spending our time here on board, or spending it exploring the township, and we could spend tonight either on board or in a hotel. What would you prefer to do?" Cameron asked as their ship tied up at Port Denison.

"I think I might like to explore the town while we are here, but I would prefer to spend tonight on board. It would mean a lot less fuss and bother than packing a bag to stay in a hotel for the night. Would our staying on board tonight create a problem for the crew?"

"Not at all, but I am a bit surprised by your choice. I expected you would want to explore the town, but I also thought you would opt for a night in a hotel. But I see your point about fuss and bother. I, too, will be happy to spend the night on board. It will also be easier in the morning when the captain wants to leave Port Denison on the early morning tide."

Things did not quite go to plan next morning, and they were later than anticipated leaving the port. The delay resulted in their having to spend an extra night on board, tucked in behind the Cape at Upstart Bay. They dropped anchor late afternoon when the sun was still high in the sky. Cameron took Sarah up on deck.

"Take a look at the sky, Sarah. See how blue it is? You will get used to seeing such blue skies up here, for this is the nature of the Burdekin blue sky."

"It is an intense blue, bluer than I've ever seen a sky before. This looks like a lovely spot. Does our voyage continue for much longer?"

"No, not far. We will weigh anchor at first light in the morning before being delivered to Jimmy by lunchtime at the latest."

Cameron took his wife up on deck again at sunset. "If we wait here for a while, we will be treated to a kaleidoscope of colours as the sky turns from blue to the darkness of night. See how the sky is already adorning itself with a hint of gold. If you keep watching, you will see the sky become ablaze with reds, oranges and gold as the sun makes its way across the sky to drop down behind those distant hills on the mainland. I think it plans to put on one of those spectacular, breathtaking displays just for you tonight."

Later, as they prepared for bed, Cameron mentally debated whether he should say something to Sarah. Sarah had been quiet, almost withdrawn, since being up on deck to watch the sunset. He was concerned she might have been having second thoughts about leaving Mackay. Sarah's comments as she climbed into her bunk put his mind at rest.

"I have no idea what to expect when we reach your block, but what I have seen in this part of the world so far has stunned me. It is so beautiful. I know the place where we will live will be quite different from this bay with all its beauty, but it has given me a feeling that what is to come will be just as impressive – although different, perhaps. I can't wait to see my new home."

They made good time from Cape Upstart, and well before lunch time, they were perched atop Jimmy's loaded wagon and heading for their homestead. Sarah chattered incessantly to Jimmy from the moment they set off. How was Annie? Had she settled in okay? Was she missing the grandchildren too much? How far away from their place was Jimmy's homestead? How difficult would it be for Sarah and Annie to spend time together? After travelling only a short distance, Cameron felt obliged to intervene.

"Sarah, perhaps you should give Jimmy's ears a rest. Perhaps leave your questions until we are home and you've settled in a bit. I know you're anxious to see Annie again, and that will happen soon enough. In the meantime, please give Jimmy's ears a rest... and mine, too."

Jimmy laughed and winked at Sarah. "Don't you be paying him any attention. You ask all the questions you like, but you have to accept that I might not know the answers to any of them. And there probably will be some I wouldn't dare answer, because they will be for Annie alone to answer… And Annie will probably have more than a few questions for you, as well."

Although she tried to comply with Cameron's instructions, Sarah found it impossible not to ask questions – until their arrival at the homestead stunned her into silence. Waiting at the bottom of the stairs to greet her were Ming Wei, Mrs Walters, and Molly, the new housemaid.

"How…? When…?" Sarah stammered. "Oh, this is so much more than I expected. I don't know how you managed this, but it is wonderful. Am I going to be just as surprised when I go inside?"

"Well, there will be no surprises if I tell you about it," Cameron said. "I think the best thing you can do is to go upstairs and answer those questions yourself."

The front room had been set up much as the front room in the Mackay homestead was. Sarah realised that either Mrs Walters or Molly, or both of them, had visited the homestead at some point and taken notes on the way Sarah had set up its main rooms. And, perhaps, Annie had some hand in ensuring things were just right for when the lady of the house arrived.

Annie arrived while Sarah was still exploring her new abode. After Jimmy dropped off Cameron and Sarah, he returned home on the spare wagon to collect Annie. She arrived carrying a bunch of flowers from various flowering plants in the surrounding bush.

"Begging you pardon, Mrs Wallace, but I took the liberty of inviting Mr Fraser and Miss Annie to join you for lunch. I will dish up as soon as you are ready," Mrs Walters told Sarah.

"It smells delicious, Mrs Walters, and we wouldn't want it to get cold. Perhaps, if Molly will lay the table, we could eat now."

During the few minutes before they were seated at the dining room table, Sarah, accompanied by Annie, continued exploring the rest of the house.

"Am I mistaken, Annie, but it seems larger – so much more spacious – than the Mackay homestead?"

"Ah, well, there was no Roddy McDonald up here. So, when the builder was given a sketch of the layout for the new homestead, he added his own measurements to it. This is how it turned out. The same man was responsible for our house as well, and I have to say he did an excellent job. It's really a piece of expert craftsmanship, just as this one is."

The guests didn't linger long after lunch. A couple of Cameron's workers had arrived to unload the wagon and carry the goods upstairs where, under Sarah's supervision, everything was placed where it needed to be unpacked. There was a rest before afternoon tea, and then Sarah filled in the rest of the afternoon unpacking and putting things away until it was time for pre-dinner drinks with Cameron.

As they sipped their drinks, Sarah confided to Cameron, " I almost don't know what to do with myself after tomorrow. I still have a little unpacking to do, and I want to rearrange a few things, but after that, the house will be perfect and there will be nothing more for me to do."

"Is that a complaint, and already so soon, my Dear?"

"No, just an observation. I was unaware the staff would be here before me and would have the house set up by the time I arrived. My expectation was to arrive to a huge workload waiting for attention, and that is not the case. I think my choice of staff for here was excellent."

"Judging by lunch and those scones for afternoon tea, Mrs Walters is every bit as good a cook as Orla, and I, for one, am probably in danger of overeating. It will necessitate spending more time in the fields to keep excess weight at bay," Cameron commented. "Oh, and I must tell you before I forget. Jimmy has been teaching Annie to drive the wagon so she can visit you from time to time. Their house is too far away for a quick stroll as was the case in Mackay."

Chapter 23

Drought

Life for Sarah quickly settled into a measured routine of meals, cups of tea, and strolls in the grounds surrounding the homestead. She took care of most of the office work for Cameron and caught up on her personal correspondence. She had promised herself she would write to the boys every week. Although there often was little enough happening worth writing about, Sarah stuck to her self imposed regime. Sadly, she soon learned the boys felt no such reciprocal responsibility. Their letters to their mother were a major surprise when they arrived.

When they stopped at Port Denison on their way north, a hot rumour doing the rounds of the settlement intrigued Cameron. He decided to ask Jimmy if the same story was circulating in the Burdekin area.

"It seemed the talk of Port Denison was about the new town for the Burdekin. Do you know anything about it?"

"Aye, it's caused a bit of fuss up here as well. As I understand it, Lymburner completed a survey of a government town in about April of this year. Premier McIlwraith insisted it be named 'Ayr' after his birthplace. Then, in August, the Bowen Land Office sold the first lots in the new town. According to local gossip, there was quite a bit of interest in purchasing town blocks.

"Hmm… I suppose it had to happen sometime, given the way the area has been developing and expanding. Anything else of interest happened recently that I should know about?" Cameron asked.

"You probably are aware that John Spiller sold his Pioneer and Ashburton holdings in Mackay at the end of last year or early this year. Then, earlier this year, Spiller moved all his labour and staff here and started developing a new Pioneer Plantation on the lands Henry Brandon bought in his and Spiller's names. Their combined holdings comprise over 5,000 acres."

"That is interesting. Is there anything else to report on that matter?"

"As a result of Spiller and Brandon's activities, a town has been established on part of Bannister's land opposite the new Pioneer Plantation. I believe George Moss is opening a hotel there that will include accommodation for travellers. No surprise, I suppose, that the town has been named 'Brandon' and Moss's pub is named 'Pioneer Hotel'."

"We should keep an eye on that Brandon township. It's a bit closer for supplies than Ayr is for us. I might make it a priority to check out what is available at Brandon. Any further major sugar industry developments here?"

"Macmillan has 800 acres of cane planted on Airdmillan and has already laid tramway in the fields. He supposedly plans to put thousands of acres under cane. Construction of his sugar mill continues and is expected to be ready for its first crushing season next year. The only other thing I should tell you is that I have negotiated the same arrangement for the crushing of our cane again next year. I don't think there's much else of any significance that's happened to tell you about. "

"While I know not much is produced each season, I am curious about what happens to the sugar and molasses produced from our crop each year. The money coming in from it is good, so it must be being sold somehow somewhere."

"That chap with the horse mill who crushes our cane is an enterprising operator. Most of the sugar he produces is sold directly to landholders within the local area. Selectors and their wives are happy to be able to buy bags of sugar locally, and at a cheaper price than from commercial suppliers. I believe he sells the molasses to selectors as supplemental stock feed. His small amount of sugar not sold locally is shipped to market through Townsville."

"Let's hope the sugar price continues its spectacular rise, or at least remains at the level it's at now."

"Ah, that reminds me of something else I did hear today. Although it's unconfirmed, the word is that a couple of other sugar mills are about to be erected in the Burdekin. I'm told that James Mackenzie has ordered a mill, about half the size of the Airdmillan mill, to erect on his Seaforth lands. They have formed the Burdekin Delta Sugar Company. John Davidson, who we know from Mackay, is a shareholder. Seaforth's near neighbour, Kalamia, also has ordered a mill similar to the one ordered by Seaforth."

1883 proved a year of establishment and consolidation. The wet season that arrived at the end of 1882 seemed determined not to hang around for too long. Sarah complained it felt more oppressive than the wet seasons she remembered at Mackay. But, once the wet season disappeared, it left in its wake months of drought.

Many of those starting out in the sugar industry struggled to keep their cane alive. Not long before the 1883 crushing season began, Cameron and Jimmy discussed the drought over a drink at the end of the day.

"Today, I took a ride up to make sure everything was ready for the horse mill to begin crushing cane on schedule," Jimmy said. "Along the way, I saw a lot of droughted cane. The upside of that is that the horse mill owner wants every stick of cane we have. He has lost quite a bit of his own crop due to the drought and will struggle to make as much sugar and molasses this year as last season."

"We are lucky to have those springs keeping our crops going," Cameron commented. "And we should be thankful Ming Wei learned his trade well from Cheng Li. The channelling his team put in to bring water to our crops has saved this year's income for us."

"Aye, it saved everything. I had forgotten how Cheng Li had employed a similar approach one dry year in Mackay but, as you say, we are lucky Ming Wei remembered what to do."

"I have been keeping an eye on the flow from those springs on our blocks. Flows have decreased but haven't reduced sufficiently to be a cause for concern. Nevertheless, I think careful management of that supply might be in order, if we are to survive unscathed until the end of the year when the next wet season should arrive."

"Yeah, I have already told my men to take care and not waste it by allowing it to run everywhere because they are not keeping an eye on things," Jimmy told Cameron before changing the subject. "I'm of a mind to take a wagon into that township of Brandon tomorrow. I thought it about time I checked out what it might have to offer us on properties out this way. If the basic necessities are available there, it will save us the long runs into Ayr."

"Good thinking. I'll come with you. It will be a good opportunity to see what is happening around that area."

"Ah, that reminds me of something else I learned while I was out and about today. I had it on good authority that, at the beginning of May, Spiller and Brandon had sold their lands that comprise the Pioneer Plantation to a Scottish partnership. Then, later in the same month, they were granted Certificates of Fulfilment over all those lands. So, the 5,000 acres or so of Pioneer Plantation are now freehold. And there's another bit of news about that plantation. They are erecting a mill bought from Walkers of Maryborough."

"Now, that could be of interest to us. Perhaps they might like to buy our cane once their mill is up and running."

"Could be a possibility, and something worth looking into, anyway. Another piece of news that attaches to all this is that Pioneer has established a wharf at Barratta Creek to bring in their mill's machinery. Machinery was shipped to Townsville and then brought down from there on lighters that are able to come up the creek to the wharf. Perhaps we should enquire about whether we might be allowed use of their wharf on occasion."

"Sounds to me like a ride into Brandon tomorrow will be worth our while for all the other things we might be able to do while we are in that area. By the way, do we know who the head man is on Pioneer Plantation? It will be helpful to know who to ask for."

"I was told George Russell Drysdale is the boss. I think he might be one of the shareholders and is their man on the ground here to manage their operations."

"Right… Well, let's hope Mr Drysdale is at home and will see us when we call on him tomorrow."

The following night, after having been out and about all day, Cameron shared details of their day's activities with Sarah after she asked about the Brandon township.

"It is just an embryonic township, but will be useful for some things. Jimmy purchased a couple of rolls of fencing wire while we were there. After we finished at Brandon, we went over to the Pioneer Plantation."

"Pioneer Plantation… isn't that John Spiller's land?"

"Not any more. Soon after Spiller moved to the Burdekin, he and Brandon sold their lands to a Scottish conglomerate of family connections. One of their number … I suppose they are all shareholders … Anyway, one of them, George Drysdale, now runs the plantation. They are erecting a mill that is scheduled to commence crushing in August next year."

"Might that be a better option for having our cane crushed?"

"We thought so, too, and raised the matter with Mr Drysdale. We have an agreement in place for our cane to be crushed by Pioneer next year."

"You said it wasn't scheduled to start crushing until August. Won't that be a bit late in the year? I know an August start to the season isn't a problem now, because the horse mill doesn't have a large crop to crush. Pioneer's cane, plus ours, will give their new mill a fair sized crop for their first crushing season. What happens if they are unable, for whatever reason, to commence crushing operations in August as scheduled?"

"Jimmy and I discussed that on our way home. We agreed that, once the wet season is over at the start of next year, we will have another conversation with Drysdale to be sure all is still on schedule."

"How did Pioneer's crop look? I've heard you and Jimmy discussing the effect of the drought on the local industry."

"Pioneer's more mature cane is badly affected. It has yellow leaves and shrivelled stalks. Their young cane is doing better, but it is obvious it is stressed. Something interesting we saw at Pioneer was the well they sunk in a bid to obtain water to save their crop. Drysdale said they found an excellent supply of good underground water and are now trying to work out how to pump it out onto their crop."

"Did you tell him about what we do here to keep water up to our various crops?"

"No, what we do isn't relevant. Ours is a totally different situation, and we didn't want to waste anyone's time talking about irrelevant matters."

"It seems your day away from the property produced plenty of rewards. It will be interesting to see if some form of relationship develops with the management of Pioneer Plantation."

The next event to create a stir within the Burdekin sugar industry made history in July 1883. Airdmillan Mill, the first 'proper' mill in the Burdekin, crushed its first cane. It was unfortunate that its first crushing season coincided with a severe drop in the sugar price.

For the rest of the year, life in the Burdekin seemed to follow the same preordained script as that in Mackay, with planting and crushing seasons occurring on cue before preparations for the annual wet season became the focus. The only thing missing from their previous life in Mackay was the regular nightly pre-dinner drinks with their group of friends. Annie and Jimmy joined them occasionally, and on a few occasions, Cameron and Sarah went across to Jimmy's house for drinks. With such an orderly progression, the year seemed to be sliding past at an incredibly fast pace until it was December again, and the signs were there for an early start to the monsoon season.

January 1884 and the wet season it brought with it would soon become etched in the memories of many people. On the night of 29 January and the morning of 30 January, a tropical cyclone struck the Queensland coast. Almost every building in the town of Bowen was damaged, along with significant infrastructure. Vessels at sea along the coast north of Port Denison found themselves in trouble. The *Silvery Wave,* on its way to Mackay, was found by the British India Steamer *Duke of Argyle* in the Whitsunday Passage with its distress flags flying. The *Duke of Argyle a*lso rescued four sailors from the lugger *Cordelia* on her way to the Torres Strait for the pearl shell trade. It was assumed the Cordelia was abandoned and went down.

The cyclone also wiped out telegraph lines between Bowen and Clare in the Burdekin. While repairers fairly quickly managed to repair the line from Clare to Inkerman, sixteen miles of line between Inkerman and Bowen were completely wiped out. Repairers worked at full speed to restore services by way of makeshift repairs.

Other centres were also affected by the cyclone, although none quite as severely as Bowen. The unfinished mill buildings on Pioneer Estate were damaged, and severe flooding occurred. Mackay also suffered severe flooding. No lives were lost, but some of the Burdekin cane crop was lost due to flooding. Paddy McPherson's shack on the river bank, although now empty, was all but washed away when the river rose higher than ever seen before.

"Better keep an eye out for crocodiles," Paddy warned Cameron and Jimmy as the trio rode to inspect the properties. "The flood would have brought them further up the bank. They could be wandering anywhere along the river flats now."

"A bit more culling required, Jimmy? What do you think?" Cameron asked.

"Aye, it wouldn't hurt to eliminate any who happened to think they had found new ground to inhabit. This stretch of the river had been relatively free of crocs, and I'd like to keep it that way."

"There were no' many crocs in this area because their skins were a useful way of supplementing one's cash flow. I am aware quite a few were removed from this part of the river over the last few years," Paddy explained.

"We might still have a look around," Cameron said and Jimmy nodded his agreement. "Oh, if we do manage to cull a few, Paddy, I'm sure you will know of someone who might want to skin them," Cameron added and gave Paddy a knowing wink.

After the cyclone, 1884 settled down to become almost a standard type of year. The only significant difference that year was that Jimmy and Cameron sent their cane to Pioneer Plantation's mill to be crushed after its first crushing season started only five days later than planned in August.

Sugar prices had continued to fall and many of the struggling growers just entering the sugar industry found themselves in trouble. For Cameron and Jimmy, the year ended on a sound note. They still did well out of that year's crop, next year's looked even better, and they had entered into a long-term agreement to supply their cane to Pioneer Plantation's mill. The relatively docile wet season that arrived at the close of 1884 remained that way as it ushered in the new year.

Although 1885 began with no disasters and full of promise, developments back home at Mackay would soon impact the lives of those in the Burdekin.

In March, Sarah watched Cameron sorting the mail as she arranged flowers in a vase in the front room. The next time she looked up at him, he held one of the letters he just opened in his hand. Sarah knew, from the look on his face as he read the letter, it contained no good news.

"Cameron, what is it? Have you received bad news? Who is it from? Cameron, talk to me, please."

"I had expected a letter from Father. He has religiously written every week to keep me up-to-date on what has happened and how things are progressing, but it's a couple of weeks now since I've heard from him. Then, today, this letter from Philip has arrived. I'm afraid it's not good news. He says my father has become quite frail over the last couple of months. While Douglas claims he is fine, Elspeth suspects he is ill, possibly seriously ill."

"We must go back to Mackay, Cameron. How soon is the next ship likely to be available?"

"There will be one heading south from Townsville on Friday. I'll send word to book our passage and for them to collect us from the Morris Creek landing. That gives us two days to prepare for the voyage and, as I understand it, that vessel is not scheduled to call in at Port Denison. So, we should have a relatively quick trip back to Mackay. I must tell Jimmy. He and Douglas go back a long way together. They became great friends during the Caribbean days. I don't doubt this news will take the wind out of his sails as well."

Lachlan was waiting on the wharf as the lighter brought them up the Pioneer River. Sarah climbed up to sit beside Lachlan, while Cameron settled himself amongst the bags of potatoes and flour and rolls of fencing wire already occupying space on the wagon. There was scant conversation as they headed for the homestead.

When the wagon pulled up in front of the homestead, Sarah gasped. Douglas was dosing in a large wicker chair on the verandah. While he looked peaceful enough, his overall appearance shocked her. Douglas was now a shadow of the man he had been. He seemed to have aged at least a decade in the two years since she last saw him. After tiptoeing through to their bedroom to dump their bags, Sarah went in search of Orla.

"I've just put the kettle on, Ma'am. Would you take tea on the verandah or in the sitting room?" Orla asked.

"Oh, on the verandah, I think," Sarah said before turning on her heel and heading back out to where Douglas continued to snooze.

The rattle of teacups as Orla put the tray down on the table disturbed Douglas, who blinked blearily at Sarah and Cameron.

"Good God, what a surprise. It's not my birthday, is it?" he demanded. Cameron shook his head. "No, I didn't think it was. So, what brings you here without a word in advance?"

"You do, Douglas," Sarah said. "You are the reason we are here. I was going to ask you how you are – but I won't. I know you won't give me a truthful answer, and it's obvious you're not well."

"I am just old, Sarah, and my time on this earth is running out. So, your unexpected visit at this time could be quite serendipitous."

"Don't say such things, Douglas. We are all growing older. There is no getting away from that fact, but I need to know if you are ill."

"You've just identified the heart of the matter, my dear. As you say, we are all growing older and, for me to have my youngest son as old as Cameron is now, I can be nothing more than ancient. I have expended much more than my three score years and ten on this earth, so there can be no railing against what must come next... And what comes next may well be soon. Don't be sad, Sarah. I've had a wonderful life. I have a wonderful son and daughter-in-law and more grandchildren than I ever thought I would have. The family I leave behind is well-placed to carry on into the future and be able to live the life they want comfortably. An old man can ask no more, and I don't. I am just so grateful for everything I've had and everything I've had opportunity to do. Now, that's enough of this maudlin stuff. I want a current update on life in the Burdekin."

They chatted for an hour or so until Sarah noticed Douglas was becoming tired. She suggested he go to his quarters for a rest before dinner. Cameron agreed with her and told his father he would go to find Philip and catch up with the latest news about the plantations and the mill. In truth, as soon as Douglas went to his room, Cameron rode across to the mill to discuss its operation with the staff. It was on his way back to the plantation that he caught up with Philip and spoke with him until it was time to get ready for dinner.

Although Cameron and Sarah made sure conversation, jokes and laughter brightened dinner that evening, a melancholy undercurrent prevailed. As soon as dinner was over, Sarah took the two boys aside for a quiet talk before the three of them joined Douglas and Cameron on the verandah for a nightcap. Of course, the boys were aware of Douglas's situation. They were no longer children. Angus would soon be twenty, and at the start of next year, Lachlan would be nineteen. Nevertheless, at that moment, Sarah would have given anything to be able to spare her sons the sadness that must soon envelop the family.

Douglas's spirits lifted no end about four days later when another surprise visitor arrived. Jimmy and Annie arrived in Mackay that morning and Philip was waiting at the wharf to collect them. As Jimmy quietly told Cameron later, he could not let his old friend slip away without seeing him again one more time, and without having had the chance to say goodbye.

A little over a week later, and just as Jimmy and Annie were preparing to return to the Burdekin, Douglas slipped away peacefully in his sleep. There can be no describing the sadness and grief Sarah felt, but she shared it with Cameron, who had lost his father. Douglas was buried on the plantation in a place that Douglas had once said was the most beautiful spot he'd ever had the privilege of enjoying. Jimmy and Annie stayed on for another few days after the funeral. During that time, long and in-depth conversations were held between Jimmy, Philip, Cameron and Sarah. By the time Jimmy and Annie were ready to leave, there was agreement all round on how the Mackay operations would continue now Douglas was gone.

"I suppose we all realise there would be little change necessary," Cameron said. "After all, Douglas had wound back his involvement over recent months. While it was a comfort for us to have him here to watch over our sons, they are now young men and don't need someone holding their hand. But, Philip, I hope you will see your way clear to be available to them should they need someone to talk to now they don't have Douglas."

After both boys and Philip assured Cameron and Sarah they would be just fine and everything would continue as it always had, Jimmy and Annie returned to the Burdekin. Cameron and Sarah stayed on for another fortnight before returning north. Douglas's passing was not the only noteworthy event of 1885.

"Airdmillan Mill, the first mill to crush in the Burdekin, has closed," Cameron announced on his return from a trip to Brandon. "It's only about twenty-five months since it started operating and already it has been forced to close."

"It's a sad day for this area's industry," Sarah commented.

"Aye, it is that," Jimmy added. "I hear it is all down to a shortage of labour. Securing sufficient labour to service both the needs of the plantation and the mill had become increasingly difficult."

"Then, added to that, Premier Griffith's announcement this year that employment of South Sea Islanders would cease in five years rang the death knell for the mill," Cameron added.

"Aye, finding enough labour for the crushing season would be nigh on impossible," Jimmy agreed. "Rumour has it that bits of the defunct Airdmillan Mill already are being cannibalised by Pioneer Mill and some of the Mackay mills."

Alfred Knobel, a sugar boiler expert in the Icery method of producing white sugar, who had worked at various sugar mills in the Mackay district, was employed by Pioneer from the commencement of their crushing operations. Knobel applied the Icery method to produce Pioneer's earliest sugars, and he also produced raw sugars. In 1885, the first shipment of any size of raw sugar to be sent from a Queensland mill to England was raw sugar from Pioneer Mill shipped to London direct on the British India vessel *Merkara*. Pioneer Mill's operation and its production of sugar continued to improve over the years from that first eleven-week season in 1884 that produced 635 tons of first and second sugars. By 1886, Pioneer, like all the plantations, was heavily in debt and struggling with increasing running costs. At the start of 1886, George Drysdale's brother,

John Drysdale, a skilled engineer, arrived at Pioneer to work with their consulting engineer, Henry Braby, to turn around the fortunes of the Pioneer Mill that was down on its knees, like all the other mills, as a result of depressed sugar prices and scarcity of labour.

For the Wallace and Fraser clan, life in the Burdekin settled back into its orderly routine… at least for another few years.

The Next Generation

Chapter 24

Lachlan

Life on the Burdekin properties continued in an orderly, largely uninterrupted way for the next few years. The townships of Brandon and Ayr expanded, the population increased, and Pioneer Mill continued to move onto bigger and better crushing seasons.

In November 1886, Angus attained his majority. Sarah could not allow his twenty-first birthday to pass without being there to help him celebrate it. Despite Sarah's pleading, Cameron did not return to Mackay for the occasion, having repeatedly told her he could not be away from the Burdekin property at that time. There was no such problem in January 1888 when Lachlan turned twenty-one. His birthday, occurring in the midst of the wet season, meant no one was going anywhere.

Then, in mid-1888, Jimmy dropped his bombshell when they dined together one evening.

"I seem to be tired all the time these days. I fear my age is catching up with me."

"We none of us are getting any younger, Jimmy," Sarah responded.

"Aye, that's true, but I have a few years on you and Cameron, and I think the time is fast approaching for me to step back and put my feet up. And Annie has missed out on so much of her grandchildren growing up."

"That's stuff and nonsense, Jimmy," Annie retorted. "When have I ever said I was missing the grandchildren?"

"Nah, you have never complained, but that hasn't stopped me feeling guilty about it. Anyway, I believe the time is right for me to slide into the background, put my feet up, and while away whatever time I have left doing whatever takes my fancy. My plan is to return to Mackay and for Annie and me to move into the small house we built for Philip and Elspeth when they were married. The homestead is far too big for us now, and Philip and his tribe seem to occupy it comfortably."

"Jimmy, you have never given me any clues as to this line of thinking," Cameron said. "Has there been something in particular that's led to this resolve?"

"No, nothing in particular. I've been feeling and thinking about it for some months now. Don't worry. I haven't rushed a half-baked decision about this. It's well considered, and Annie and I have discussed it at length."

"I can't imagine life without you, Jimmy. You've been with me ever since I arrived in this country. You helped me become established here, gave me advice and kept me grounded when things went wrong," Sarah said. "And Annie, you are my closest friend. I will miss you more than I can say."

"Regardless of what's being said here, you must do what you need to do," Cameron said. "We will support and help you achieve that in any way we can. Are there any other details you can share with us?"

"Well, yes, there is a matter that I need to discuss with you – the pair of you – and whether or not we return to Mackay much depends on how those discussions play out."

Jimmy was encouraged to share details of his proposed relocation to Mackay and how he saw them having any role in that process.

"Right; you both will realise that I can't just walk off the property here. Yes, my bailiff, Fred Langton, would remain here, but it would need someone to manage the place and oversee the running of the property. That's where you two come into the planning. Probably since I bought the block here in the Burdekin, my thinking has been that one of your sons should take over from me up here. Now, Angus, being your eldest son, I understand you would see Angus taking over all your holdings in Mackay. Philip and Elspeth would continue with my Mackay plantation until such time as Philip felt inclined to retire, and then his son would take over from him. That leaves only one of the next generation who might take over my land up here from me, your younger son, Lachlan."

"Lachlan…? I'm sorry, Jimmy, but I don't see what you're suggesting here." Sarah said.

"If you can see your way clear to free Lachlan from his duties in Mackay, I hope he will take over my place up here. The offer I make is not some short-term arrangement. My intention is that this property will eventually be his. So, as you can see, two things need to happen. First, you have to agree that he is free to move up here on a permanent basis and, secondly, that he is willing and happy to do so. I understand you will want time to think on this, but I ask that you don't take too long about it."

"That is a most generous thing you are proposing, Jimmy," Sarah whispered. "You are right. Cameron and I do need to discuss it. I can tell you now that I support your proposal up to a certain point, but not entirely."

"Sarah is right, Jimmy. While it is a generous offer, it cuts across our plans for Lachlan and this place. We have two sons, and the logical thinking is for Angus to take over our Mackay interests when the time comes, and for Lachlan to take over this place in the Burdekin. None of this has been discussed with the boys yet. So, while we would be happy for Lachlan to take over running your place when you return to Mackay, I would see it only as an interim measure for some period of years."

"Argh, that won't work for me. I need to know that whatever I put in place will ensure the future of my holdings here."

"Jimmy, you have a grand nephew. As I understood your earlier thinking, Elspeth would inherit the Mackay property and Philip would run it for her, and your grand nephew, James, one day, would take over this place. Has something changed in your thinking?"

"Perhaps, at the time, I did not know or accept how old I was and, therefore, didn't realise I would need to put other plans in place much sooner than anticipated. Annie's grandson, James, is just a child and will be for some years to come. I need to retire now and need a more readily available solution."

"You are wrong about James," Cameron said quietly. He is going on fifteen years old now and spends much of his time, when free of the classroom, out in the fields with the men. His interest is in the land. The word I had while in Mackay was that he is well advanced in his training to run this place."

"While we don't know what Philip and Elspeth's plans are for James's education, it is likely he will have no more than perhaps another year of schooling ahead of him. Might I suggest an alterative plan that could work well for everyone involved?" Sarah asked.

"Please do, Sarah. I am open to any plans that allow me to sit back and put my feet up."

"Okay, Jimmy. Here's what I suggest might work. If Lachlan is interested, he moves up here now to run your place. Then, when James completes his education, and with his parents' approval, he moves up here to complete his training for the future under the guidance of Cameron and Lachlan. After a few years, we, too, can retire, and Lachlan will take over this place as we planned, while James takes over your block. Of course, this is just a suggestion at this time, and Cameron and I would still need to discuss any such arrangement before we could give it our approval. You would need to think on it as well."

"How fast time goes by without you noticing," Jimmy mused. "I had forgotten James was growing up and would soon be a young man. As always, Sarah, you are brilliant. I have no doubts your suggestion would be best for everyone – if all parties involved agree. But, as you say, you and Cameron must discuss it before you give me a firm answer."

"It doesn't look like it's going to take too long to discuss at all," Cameron chuckled. "I also think the proposal for Lachlan to run your place here until James is old enough to takeover is a sound approach, and it's a proposal I feel confident Lachlan will grab with both hands. That plan has the support of both of us, Jimmy, but the final decision is down to Lachlan. Does your thinking include how you might go about making it happen?"

"As a matter of fact, it does, and it involves the pair of you inviting Lachlan to visit you up here for a week or two. I'm sure it won't take that long to know one way or the other how he feels about it. If he is in favour of the proposal, he can return to Mackay to prepare to relocate to here, while Annie and I prepare to return to Mackay. Is there more we need to discuss, do you think?"

Cameron, Sarah, and Annie shook their heads in unison, but their only reply was silence. What else needed to be said? After a few moments, Cameron broke the silence by stating that he would send an invitation to Lachlan the next day.

Later that night, after the guests had departed, the Wallaces spent some time discussing and analysing Jimmy's proposal. While they both agreed it was a wonderful opportunity and relieved any concerns they might have regarding how, in the future, to bequeath their Mackay properties to their sons in a way that was fair and equitable.

"Do you believe Lachlan will accept the offer?" Sarah asked quietly. "He is his own man now. Whatever we do, we must not allow him to feel we are pressuring him one way or the other in this matter."

"Apart from the fact that Lachlan is our second child and that all the protocols that attach to Angus's position as the elder are being maintained, I genuinely believe Lachlan will jump at the opportunity. He has a different nature from that of Angus, more outgoing and adventurous in some way. I suspect he will see the offer as his first major challenge, the first major challenge of his manhood, and that prospect will excite him to the core."

While Lachlan thought the invitation a little odd, he found no clue as to why it should arrive so unexpectedly. He sent an immediate reply that he would arrive in two weeks. He spent the whole time almost driving Philip and Angus mad with questions and discussions about how much change he would find in the Burdekin now. While the two weeks slipped by in a blur for Philip and Angus, it seemed to drag on for a lifetime for Lachlan until he finally was waving goodbye from the lighter as it made its way down the river and out to the steamer that would take him along the coast to Barratta Creek.

Cameron collected his son from the Barratta Creek wharf. As they drove off in the pony trap, he told Lachlan, "I have to tell you that we are not going directly to the plantation. Ming Wei, our gardener, our equivalent of Cheng Li, asked me to deliver a basket of eggs to the general store in Brandon. We won't be there long, but it does take us out of our way a bit. Still, think of it as a sightseeing tour of the country up here."

Their stop in Brandon was just long enough to visit the general store and handover the basket of eggs to the young lass at the counter.

"Thank you, Mr Wallace. We sold the last of our eggs this morning, so these have arrived just in time to save us the embarrassment of having to say no to customers. Shall I record them on your account as usual?"

"I'm glad we saved the day for you. Yes, please, on my account as usual. See you the next time we are in town. Bye…." As Cameron started to walk out of the store, he realised Lachlan wasn't with him. "Are you coming, Lachlan?"

"Eh? Oh, yes. Sorry, I wasn't paying attention."

While Cameron raised a questioning eyebrow at his son, he said nothing. But he thought, *possibly paying too much attention,* and a grin began to tug at the corners of his mouth.

After allowing Sarah to fuss over her son for as long as Lachlan and Cameron could stand, Cameron rescued his son.

"Come, Lachlan, I'll give you a quick tour of some of the property before we return for lunch. Sarah, please let staff know we won't be back for morning tea."

"This is quite different country, isn't it?" Lachlan commented after an hour or so of touring the place. "I see you do some things a little differently up here, like the irrigation installed here. There is still very little irrigation used in Mackay, and what is used there differs from the system installed here."

As they rode back to the house for lunch, Cameron did his best to explain the difference in growing conditions between the

Burdekin and those in Mackay, and how their simple irrigation system operated. After they had eaten, father and son took their cups of tea out onto the verandah to relax for a while before continuing Lachlan's tour of inspection.

"You are well into the harvest already up here," Lachlan observed. "Isn't it still too early to be crushing this year's crop? In Mackay, harvesting still doesn't begin until late August or early September."

"That's another difference between the two locations. Up here, the cane is quite mature by the middle of the year and, once it's had a bit of a cold snap on it to improve the sugar content, it's best to harvest it as soon as possible. Pioneer Mill always starts its crushing season early and came in for a load of criticism when it first adopted the practice. Their crushing season starts in June and sometimes as early as May, depending on what the growing conditions were like that year. It appears to work well, and we haven't had any problems with such an arrangement."

An hour or so was spent riding over more of the property before Cameron made a suggestion.

"Ah, we find ourselves close to the boundary between my block and Jimmy's. As we are here, I suggest we ride over and impose on Annie for afternoon tea. I know they are both looking forward to seeing you again. So, prepare for another dose of much fussing."

Much later, as they rode back to the homestead to freshen up before dinner, Lachlan commented, "You weren't wrong about the fussing," he chuckled. "Anyone would think they hadn't seen me in a lifetime. It is good to catch up with Jimmy again, though. I've always enjoyed his company, and over the years, he has taught me so much."

"It's likely you will be seeing a lot more of Jimmy now that you're here. If I think on it, he and I actually spend quite a lot of our time together. In fact, it's not unlike the way we were in Mackay, except we don't have a mill to worry about here."

About a week after Lachlan's arrival, he and Cameron again had afternoon tea with Jimmy and Annie. They reminisced and relived old times together until most of the afternoon had slipped away.

"We should be on our way," Cameron announced. "As we were only supposed to drop in to invite you and Annie for dinner tonight, Sarah will be wondering where we are. We'll see you in time for pre-dinner drinks in keeping with our time-honoured practice."

Sarah had a quiet word to Annie as they walked into dinner. Then, as soon as dinner was over, Sarah and Annie retired to Sarah's private sitting room.

"I hope you don't mind, Annie, but I knew Cameron wanted a 'men's only' session after dinner tonight. I think this is when they're going to talk to Lachlan about taking over when you and Jimmy return to Mackay. If their discussions go well and swiftly, we may be invited to join them."

Out on the verandah, and with each of the men armed with a hefty tot of rum, Lachlan learned of Jimmy's offer to take over the running of his block when he and Annie moved back to Mackay. If anyone had held any concerns about how the proposal might be received, such concerns soon disappeared. While Lachlan jumped at the opportunity, he held some reservations.

"This is the most generous offer, Jimmy, and I want to grab it with both hands here and now. But I am concerned about Mackay. My absence will leave only Angus and Philip to manage everything we have in that place. I'm not sure I have the right to abandon them like that in such a selfish way. Philip's son, James, does help out a bit, but most of his time is devoted to his education, and he is still quite young. Would it be fair of me to abandon Angus and Philip?"

"We would not have extended this offer to you if, for even one moment, we had thought your absence might jeopardise operations in Mackay," Cameron tried to reassure Lachlan.

"Your concerns are commendable, Lachlan," Jimmy said, "but quite unnecessary. Every aspect of the Mackay operations has an excellent manager or foreman to oversee it. Angus and Philip will not be running the place alone. I will be there and, yes, I plan to ease back and put my feet up and relax, but I'm not about to go out onto the scrap heap. With or without their approval, I intend to continue to help out with the running of Mackay operations as necessary for a bit longer yet."

"So, what say you, Son, will you accept Jimmy's offer or not?" Cameron asked with a silly grin plastered across his face.

"Oh, yes, please… And how soon can all this happen?"

The sound of loud laughter from the verandah was soon followed by an invitation for the ladies to join the men. Five people on the verandah drank a toast and shook hands to seal the agreement.

"This is fantastic," Annie began, "but how soon is it all going to happen? I need to know how much time I have to do everything that needs to be done to facilitate our relocation."

"Well, Lachlan has another week here before he returns to Mackay," Jimmy told Annie. "We have agreed Lachlan will move up here at the end of September, and two weeks later, we will return to Mackay. How does that suit you, Sister Dear?"

One day, late in November, Sarah caught up with Cameron as he came in for lunch.

"I saw Lachlan here earlier this morning and thought he might be joining us for lunch. I assume that is not the case?" Sarah asked.

"No, he only called in here on his way to ask if we needed anything from Brandon."

"So, Brandon – again. Our son appears to have a lot of business to do in Brandon and frequently, I have observed. Is this something we should be concerned about?"

"Probably not. It is a young man who has found something there that has caught his interest… Smitten by a crop of copper-coloured curls might be the best way of describing it."

"What? Lachlan is chasing after some girl in Brandon? And you are all right with this?" Sarah flared indignantly. "Who is this woman, and how did he meet her?"

"Relax, Sarah. It likely will come to nothing. It's probably nothing more than a young man doing what a young man does at his age. I assure you the girl is beyond reproach, and nothing untoward is likely to occur."

Sarah remained sceptical. A few days later, she surprised Cameron at breakfast. "Is there anything you need collected from Brandon?"

"Err, no, I don't think so. Why would you be thinking of going into Brandon?"

"Oh, just a few things I want to pick up. I'll see you sometime after lunch."

Cameron found her at home again when he returned for afternoon tea. "Well, what do you think?" he asked as Sarah poured their tea.

"About Brandon…? Yes, I found what I went for."

"That's not what I asked. You know what I meant by my question?" Sarah shrugged and started to shake her head, but Cameron's hard look made her rethink her response.

"Aw, okay. Yes, stunningly attractive and well-spoken. I can understand Lachlan's interest. Do you think something serious is developing there?"

"Would it matter if there were?"

"Of course not, but it would be good to know about it rather than be taken by surprise by whatever might come next."

"My advice, Sarah… Relax. Nothing is likely to come of anything any time soon."

Late in 1889, the question of James's moving to the Burdekin to work with Lachlan came up for discussion at Mackay on the occasion of a visit by Cameron and Sarah. While Philip and James were all for James to head north immediately after the forthcoming wet season, Elspeth was adamant her son should finish his education first. Elspeth won out, and James had to endure another year with his tutor before his mother untied her apron strings. So, late in April 1890, after a cyclone caused damage in Townsville and Ayr and the Burdekin River again flooded cane lands in March, James (now aged sixteen) arrived in the Burdekin and moved in to share Jimmy's former homestead with Lachlan.

The two lads continued to get along well as they always had done, and Annie's domestic staff ensured they were well looked after. James quickly adjusted to the differences in the Burdekin industry, and life settled into a steady rhythm without interruption or upset until late in 1891. One afternoon, Lachlan called at the homestead as Sarah and Cameron partook of afternoon tea out on the verandah.

"I'm going to be away for the night, and I'm a bit concerned about leaving James on his own. Please, would you mind just keeping an ear to the ground in case anything happens?"

"I hardly think James needs us babysitting him. He's no longer a child, but we will keep an ear out in case anything should crop up," Cameron said.

"Where are you off to?" Sarah asked. "Where do you plan to spend the night?"

"Oh, I'll probably take a room at the hotel in Brandon. Anyway, I must be off. See you tomorrow," Lachlan called up to them as he dug his heels into his horse.

"Lachlan, where...."

"Let it be, Sarah," Cameron told her. "He no longer has to tell you what he is doing or where he is going. If he wanted you to know, he would have told you when you asked him the first time. Don't interfere."

"Interfere in what?"

"I don't know. But when a man reaches twenty-one years of age, his mother no longer has the right to ask such questions."

The tone of Cameron's voice warned Sarah there was no more to be said on the subject. While Sarah heeded the warning, she was determined to take up the question with Lachlan the moment he returned. Fortunately for Lachlan, he did not call at the homestead on his way home – or, perhaps, it was a strategic move on his part. Anyway, it was several days later before he encountered his parents again when he called on them to ask for advice.

"A few days ago, I was invited to come to dinner at the Donald's home, and later, I spent the night at the hotel in Brandon. I would like to repay their hospitality. I know etiquette demands it, but I'm not sure how to go about it. I know my cook and other domestic staff would do me proud, but inviting the Donalds to dinner with me and James seems highly inappropriate. I'd welcome your advice on what I should do."

"The Donalds, are they the parents of that lass, Bethany, who works at the general store?" Sarah asked. Lachlan nodded. "I take it there was some special reason – some special occasion – for your invitation?"

"Uhmm… Ye-es, you might say that. It was an opportunity for the Donalds to meet me."

"Why would they wish to meet you?" Sarah asked and shot Cameron a hard look when she heard him chuckling.

"Well, I had asked their daughter, Bethany, to marry me, and I needed to ask Mr Donald for her hand in marriage. She told her parents of the situation and suggested it might be an opportunity for them to meet me and get to know me… And hence the invitation."

"And…?" Cameron demanded. "Don't leave it there, Son. How did it all go?"

Lachlan fidgeted on his chair for a moment before replying. "I suppose I'd say it went very well. Bethany and I are to be married straight after Easter next year. So, you see, not only would I like to repay their courtesy, but I would also like for you to meet Bethany and her parents."

"Quite right, too," Sarah said emphatically. "They must come to dinner and then stay overnight here in this house with us. I shall deliver a formal invitation to Bethany to take home to her parents."

"If you have finished being proper about all this, Sarah, perhaps it's time we congratulated Lachlan on his engagement,"

Cameron suggested. "I can't say it comes as a surprise. I think it was heading in that direction from the moment you arrived in the Burdekin. Bethany is a beautiful young woman, and you appear to have chosen well, but I would like to know something of her parents before they come to dinner. Perhaps we can all liaise on developing this arrangement we are about to put in place."

Chapter 25

Changes

The year 1892 was a year of changes. On Friday, April 22, Lachlan and Bethany Donald were married in a ceremony on Pioneer Plantation, where her father was employed as a foreman. After a luncheon in a marquee set amongst the trees, Cameron drove the couple to the wharf at the Barratta, where they boarded a steamer for the trip to Mackay.

That night, after dinner at the homestead, Sarah said, "It's just like old times, all of us sitting here like this. Jimmy, I'm so glad you and Annie were able to join us for the wedding, and I know it meant a lot to Lachlan, too. How long will you stay with us?"

"Maybe a week or so," Jimmy replied. We will spend some time with James, of course, but we will also be on hand to help out here."

"Help here with what?" Cameron asked. "We don't send our guests out into the fields to have them work for their supper."

"Don't be a pratt, Cameron. There's plenty to do if you are to be out of this place and back in Mackay by the time the newlyweds arrive back from their honeymoon. It won't do to have them return, expecting to set up home in this house, and find the pair of you still here. Remember, we have been through this and know how much work relocating to Mackay involves. You helped when we were going through it. Now it's our turn to reciprocate."

"Sarah, will your cottage be ready for you to move into when you return?" Annie asked. "It looked all but complete when we left, but I don't know what it was like inside."

"Angus says it will be another couple of weeks, or maybe a month before it's ready. Thank you, Jimmy, for talking Anguss into joining us up here for the wedding. He will catch the steamer back to Mackay the day after tomorrow. After that, James will be on his own in your old homestead."

"Ah, well, he needs to get used to it," Jimmy said. "Soon, you will be gone, and there will be no one here until Lachlan and Bethany return. When do you anticipate leaving here?"

"In about three weeks," Sarah told him. "Lachlan plans to be away about a month, so we will be gone in plenty of time for the staff to give the place a good clean and tidy before the new residents move in. Most of our belongings will be shipped next week, and Angus will store them in Douglas's former apartment at the rear of the homestead."

"Cameron, you're being very quiet. You seem a bit withdrawn," Annie suggested. "Is everything all right? A wedding is supposed to be a happy occasion, but it doesn't seem that way for you."

"It's not right, is it?" Cameron stated flatly.

"What's not right?" Sarah demanded. "Are you suggesting something is not right about Lachlan marrying Bethany? What do you know that I don't, and why haven't you mentioned it before this?"

"It's not right that Lachlan is married before Angus. Angus is the older and should be the first to marry. It's the natural order of things."

"I've never seen such a rule written anywhere," Sarah retorted. "And I've never heard such nonsense. Angus will marry when he is good and ready, and not in accordance with some spurious preordained schedule. It may be quite some time before he contemplates such a major step as marriage. I am unaware there is a special woman in his life yet... Unless you know differently, Jimmy."

"No, I can't say I do. He did show a bit of interest in a lass from one of the properties up our way. I don't think it was anything serious. It didn't last long, and then she left with her parents when they returned to England. Regardless of any strange ideas you might have about it, Cameron, you would have to agree young Lachlan has done very well for himself," Jimmy said.

"Aye, he has, Jimmy," Sarah agreed. "And, Cameron, you'll not be harassing Angus about marriage when we return to Mackay, or you will be having me to deal with. Is that clear?" Cameron gave her a wry smile in reply.

After what felt to Sarah like three weeks of absolute chaos, she and Cameron were back in their Mackay homestead.

On their second night back, Angus asked, "Why is the new cottage being built? Who is to live in it? Or, is it intended that, now my parents have returned, I should live in it?"

"Why would you think that, Angus," Sarah asked. "That is to be our home, and you will continue to live here in the homestead."

"Why wouldn't we all live in the homestead? If having me around bothers you, I would be more than happy to move into Grandfather's apartment out the back."

"Your presence wouldn't bother us but, after you have been living here on your own for so long, we thought you would prefer it remained that way."

Discussions of the matter continued over the next couple of days before it was resolved that they would all live in the homestead and Angus would occupy the rear apartment. When Sarah caught Angus alone a couple of days later, she added a footnote to that agreement: *only until such time as you marry, and then this house will be home for you and your wife, and future family.*

Robert Angus Wallace was born to Lachlan and Bethany in May 1893, and Hamish Cameron Wallace arrived in mid-1895. Soon after Hamish arrived, Sarah took a renewed interest in the cottage they had built on her Mackay Selection before she and Cameron left the Burdekin.

The cottage had remained 'not quite finished properly' (as Sarah told Annie) for about three years when Sarah took a renewed interest in the place. Quietly, she arranged for the place to be finished and a few extra comforts added. It was just before the onset of the wet season at the end of 1895 when Cameron noticed work had been carried out at the cottage. After a quick inspection of the place, he asked about Sarah's interest in making the place ready for occupation.

"Cameron, Dear, open your eyes. All the signs are there. Have you not noticed them?"

"What signs? I haven't noticed anything out of the ordinary. Perhaps you should explain them to me."

"I suspect it will not be long before we are again witnessing a Wallace wedding." Cameron gave his wife a startled look. Before he could say anything, she continued. "For some time now, Angus has been developing a strong relationship with a young woman, and I think it might be fast approaching time for another wedding."

"By relationship, do you mean something inappropriate, something I need to have a word to him about?"

"Good heavens, no… And don't you dare say anything to him, Cameron Wallace, or you will suffer the full force of my wrath. Leave them be to work things out for themselves."

In the weeks leading up to Christmas, the weather grew increasingly humid and oppressive. One night, Sarah found it impossible to sleep and took herself out onto the verandah in the hope of finding at least a hint of a breeze. While she sat there silent and unmoving in the darkness, a horseman rode up, unsaddled and turned his horse into the yard, before making his way silently around to the rear of the house. Sarah's immediate thought was to wake Cameron and alert him to a possible intruder. She sprang up out of her chair, but something stopped her.

What if that horseman was Angus? Why would Angus be out riding around at that hour of the night? Then, common sense suggested he hadn't been just 'riding around' but was returning from somewhere specific. Of course, it was possible they had trouble at the mill, and Angus had gone to deal with it. Or was it an assignation of a different nature? The answer to that question came the following evening.

Over dinner that night, Angus announced, "I am to be married early next year. I proposed a few weeks ago and finally had the opportunity to speak to her father last night. We haven't set a date yet but, if it doesn't happen before the wet season sets in, we will have to wait until after Easter. Well, say something, please. I had hoped you would be happy for me."

"We are, I promise you," Cameron stammered, "but we also are stunned by this sudden news. May we know the name of our future daughter-in-law?"

"Eh, what? Oh, didn't I say… Sorry… I am to be married to Isabella Montgomery, daughter of Richard Montgomery, who has a Selection a couple of miles along the road from here." He had no chance to say more before Sarah, who had raced around the table, wrapped him in her arms.

"I am so happy for you both. I had a little to do with Isabella and her mother before we relocated to the Burdekin. We must invite them over… Perhaps at Christmas. What do you think, Son?"

"That's a wonderful suggestion, Mother, if a bit late. I took the liberty of inviting them when I was there last night. They will be joining us for Christmas lunch."

A few moments later, Sarah's face lit up with excitement. "Had you thought about being married on New Year's Eve? We could make a grand Scottish night of it. How do you think the Montgomery family might feel about that?"

"New Year's Eve? I don't know. It has never come up in conversation. As I recall, Mrs Montgomery is Scottish, but I don't know about her husband."

"Oh, he is, too, and he still has the brogue to prove it. I suppose a wedding on New Year's Eve could appeal to them. It certainly appeals to me," Angus added with a grin.

"Right; first thing in the morning, I am off to call on Mrs Montgomery."

"Wouldn't the protocol be for someone to speak to Mr Montgomery about it?" Cameron interjected.

"Och, no. We women will discuss it and, if Mrs Montgomery agrees, she will organise everyone else in the household accordingly. That's the way things get done quickly and effectively. Now, this evening, before I go to bed, I need to make a list of things to be done before the wedding."

Next morning, Sarah was saved a visit to the Mongomery farm when Mrs Montgomery arrived on her doorstep. After Mrs Montgomery apologised for arriving unannounced, Sarah said how she had intended to call on her that morning.

"Angus shared his good news with us over dinner last night. I knew it was up to us to make a start on the necessary arrangements. I wondered, Mrs Mongomery…

"Maude, please, Mrs Mongomery is such a mouthful."

"Thank you. Maude, and I am Sarah. Now, I was about to ask you how you felt about a New Year's Eve wedding and whether we might be able to arrange one in the time available."

"Oh, that would be wonderful. And, if the rain holds off, it will be over and done with before the wet season sets in to delay things until at least Easter. Of course, we have enough time. Do you have some suggestions to offer?"

"There is one thing, though, Maude. Reverend Tanner won't provide a proper Scottish ceremony, but I still intend having a quaich with a dram of whiskey for the bride and groom … if I can get one here in time," Sarah said.

As Cameron and Angus rode home for lunch, they passed Maude Montgomery heading into town. "Now, where do you suppose she has been this morning," Cameron asked tongue in cheek. "No doubt we will hear all about it over lunch."

Once lunch had been served and the staff had left the dining room, Sarah began. "Right, Angus, you are to be married on New Year's Eve here on the plantation. Mrs Montgomery will speak to Reverend Tanner this afternoon to confirm his availability. We will have to arrange a carriage to take him safely back to town after the ceremony. The evening's events will be in a marquee over in that cleared area near the trees. We anticipate there will be twenty to twenty-five guests. We worked out a draft menu for the wedding breakfast, and I will discuss that with staff later today."

"Are you sure this is possible in the limited weeks available to organise everything? Angus asked.

"Of course, it's possible. Now, one of your responsibilities, Cameron, is to delegate someone to organise a dark haired stranger for *first footing* at midnight. Angus, you need to consider where you will spend your wedding night, bearing in mind it will be after midnight before you are free to leave. Oh, and Cameron, you need to talk to Roddy McDonald about organising pipers for the evening. Now, the other thing we need to think about is some sort of floor suitable for dancing. Perhaps you and Jimmy might give that matter some thought, Cameron. And there will be invitations to deliver as soon as they are ready."

"Is Isabella comfortable with all these arrangements? I mean, it doesn't give her much time to do whatever it is brides need to do before their wedding."

"Well, I'm sure she will be all right with it. Once, Maude – Mrs Montgomery – confirms the Reverend Tanner's availability, she will apprise her daughter of her wedding arrangements. So, by this evening, everything should be well underway."

Despite everyone's doubts, the wedding went off without a hitch. Even the engraved silver quaich arrived in time to take its place on the little table, ready for its part in the marriage ceremony. Guests numbered thirty, three pipers organised by Roddy did an excellent job during the wedding part of the evening and then later when the dancing began. As needs must, the wedding was a new (Australian) version of a Scottish ceremony.

A small table sat beneath an arch decorated with flowers and ribbons. On the table were the documents to be signed after the ceremony and the silver quaich complete with its dram of whiskey. This is where Reverend Tanner, Angus and Lachlan, as his best man, waited for the bride, after Angus had spent the day at Jimmy's house. The skirl of the pipes marked the start of the ceremony. The piper led Mr Montgomery, Isabella, and her maid (Claire, a friend) from the homestead to where the groom waited impatiently. After the brief ceremony, the newlyweds sipped from their quaich before the bridal party moved to sign the various documents.

The ceremony over, guests made their way to a marquee some twenty five yards away to await the start of the wedding feast. Again, led by the piper, Angus and Lachlan led Isabella and Claire the 'long way around' to the marquee. The 'long way' involved crossing a small wooden bridge over a pool formed by a spring on the property. Halfway across the bridge, Angus stopped and tossed a silver coin into the pond.

"Sticking with tradition," he told Isabella, "crossing water on our wedding day is for good luck for the future, and the coin is for an extra dose of good luck."

Then, it was on to the marquee and a wedding feast not too far removed from the traditional version. The piper led the bridal party to the top table, and the feast began. Later, the *ceilidh* began and the dancing continued to midnight, when the tradition of *First Footing* took place. Soon after midnight, the happy couple slipped away unnoticed to the homestead to spend their first night as a married couple. A stable hand loaded Mr and Mrs Montgomery into a carriage borrowed from Philip and drove them home.

As soon as the actual ceremony was over, Reverend Tanner had been loaded into the pony tap and taken back to town by one of Cheng Li's men. And Cheng Li had organised an excellent man who rode up at midnight, collected his shilling, drank his dram of whiskey, and departed again on horseback. The dark-haired, dark-eyed bride looked stunning in her self-made wedding dress. The makeshift dance floor Jimmy had organised for the *ceilidh* proved a hit with guests.

"Tonight went better than I dared hope for," Sarah admitted to Cameron as they strolled back to their cottage. Tomorrow will be another busy day to clear all that area again."

In the midst of everything else taking precedence at the time, Sarah and Cameron managed to move into their cottage to leave the homestead free for the newlyweds. All through the day of the wedding, Cameron kept forecasting it was about to start raining, and he was right… Rain started to fall about ten minutes after midnight to help usher in the new year. Being well aware of the perils of trying to travel at that time of the year, the newlyweds had elected to spend their wedding night at the homestead and loosely planned a belated honeymoon for some time after the wet season.

The day after the wedding, Cameron and Philip took Lachlan, his family, and James into town to board a steamer for the Burdekin. On the plantation, after organising a few of the men to clear away the aftermath of the wedding, Jimmy and Annie in their cottage, and Sarah and Cameron in theirs, sat back to recuperate. After the hurley burley of the previous few weeks, and although exhausted, all four of them felt justifiably proud of what they had achieved.

"The next generation holds the reins now, Cameron," Sarah murmured as they sat on their cottage's verandah the next evening. "Together, all of us have done an excellent job of ensuring everything is in the best of hands, and that gives me immense pride and confidence."

Over the ensuing years, the Wallace clan increased by three more through the efforts of Angus and Isabella. Their first son was born around Easter in 1897, a second son arrived in mid-1899, and their daughter, Moira, made her appearance towards the end of 1902.

By the time Moira arrived, Lachlan's elder son, Robert, was almost ten years old and already causing his father concern, and more than a little anxiety about his future. Lachlan's two boys, while looking almost identical, possessed completely different personalities. It was Robert's adventurous, devil-may-care approach to life that Lachlan struggled with. Even as a ten year old, Robert was constantly getting into scrapes and falling foul of the field supervisors for some of the capers he got up to. By contrast, Hamish was polite, studious, and fast becoming the apple of his father's eye. Sarah constantly warned Lachlan against favouring one child over another – usually every time she heard of Robert's latest escapade. As the years went by, it seemed Robert never lost his lust for adventure and somehow remained a constant source of his father's wrath and misgivings.

During a reflective interlude one evening, Sarah sighed deeply and murmured to Cameron, "We have been very lucky, Cameron. Our lives could have been so different. We have both experienced great sadness, but out of that sadness, we forged a new and blessed existence here in a new country. Now, the younger generation carries on the legacy we established, while we sit back and observe their efforts with pride. Apart from the loss of your father a few years ago, there have been no tragic events to mar the life we have made here. And, for me, the recent birth of my granddaughter – my true granddaughter – is the icing on the cake."

It wasn't too much later that those words came back to haunt Sarah on the occasion of Jimmy's death in 1903. In the winter of that year, he had caught some flu-like virus that he never seemed to shake off completely and finally succumbed to it at the beginning of November when he was aged eighty-eight. On his death, Jimmy's Mackay plantation passed jointly to Annie's daughter, Elspeth and her husband Philip, and Jimmy's Burdekin land passed to Annie's grandson, James.

For Sarah, the loss of Jimmy, who had been her rock since their meeting so long ago in Glasgow, was traumatic. He had been the one who had encouraged her *to grasp every opportunity when it presents.* She had adhered to that philosophy ever since, and it had always stood her in good stead, but now her mentor was gone. It caused her to take a look at her own life. She and

Cameron were no longer young and it stood to reason they would not have too much time left on this earth.

Given that fact, what else – what more – could she do before her demise? Nothing immediately came to mind, but it was a question that became a fixture deep in the back of her mind. For the moment, all she could think to do was to stay close to her family, her sons and grandchildren so they would have sound memories of both her and Cameron to take forward with them into their future lives. And, for her part, it would provide her with the most rewarding time of her life.

Life rolled on for the Wallace clan, untroubled by many of the vagaries that plagued the Australian sugar industry and ruined the lives of many of those involved in it. It appeared the only blight on the entire countenance of the Wallace family was the many escapades of Lachlan's son, Robert. Over the years, he seemed to be able to discover or invent even more ways of causing his father embarrassment and grief. At age fourteen, he was sent off to boarding school in the hope it might help quieten him down a bit.

After two years, when it was obvious that had failed to curb his wild spirit, putting him to work on the plantation seemed the only other option available to Lachlan. He proved he knew plantation life inside out and was a capable and willing worker, but his adventurous spirit still managed on occasion to raise the ire of his father. But troubling times extended beyond the fences of the Wallace's Burdekin plantation.

Although many changes and developments had occurred over the years in terms of communications, transportation, and improved living conditions, the world seemed unsettled in many ways, and forebodings of increased unrest in some areas were persistent.

Annie's death in 1910 left Sarah feeling bereft for weeks. They had forged such a strong friendship almost from the moment Annie had arrived to join Jimmy in Mackay. Annie had helped bring Sarah's youngest son, Lachlan, into the world, and later, both women had shared the joy of being grandmothers to Elspeth's children. And Sarah recalled Annie's pride and joy whenever she spoke of James, his wife, and their two sons, Annie's great grandsons.

While it was a fact that she and Cameron were younger than Jimmy and Annie, Sarah again wondered how much longer she and her husband had left. Should something happen suddenly, were their affairs in order? Had they done all they needed to do to ensure their plans, hopes and ideals for the future would hold true after their passing? It was something she and Cameron must discuss but, so far, any attempt to discuss such matters with her husband had been brushed aside.

"Well, the time has come when he WILL sit down and discuss these matters with me. I have been far too lenient with him in the past," Sarah told her reflection in the mirror as she brushed her hair.

Chapter 26

Endings

As Sarah closed her diary for the 1914 year, a tear trickled down her cheek. She reached for the length of black ribbon that lay stretched across her desk and wrapped it firmly around the book before tying it securely.

"Let there be no more such years, please, God," she murmured as she placed the diary in a gap on the bookshelf beside her desk.

Cameron had died not long after Easter in 1914. In a couple of months, he would have turned 93. No one should have been surprised when, having reached such an age, he passed quietly and unexpectedly in his sleep, but nothing prepares those left behind for the death of a loved one. Over the weeks that followed Cameron's death, Sarah tried to accept it as the natural order of things, and sought to reconcile herself to her own impending demise. A solemn pall that seemed to hang over the plantation for months did nothing to revive her spirits. Then, a letter she received in September of that year almost tore her apart again.

It was a letter from Lachlan. She recognised his handwriting and, as she ripped open the envelope, she realised it was not yet time to receive the next weekly letter from her youngest son. That realisation made her stomach tighten. She tore the letter from the envelope.

Dear Mother

It is with a heavy heart I write you today. After all that has happened this year, I would avoid you further worry and concern if it were possible.

Late last month, we received a letter addressed in Robert's hand. He had seemed not himself for a few days. I suggested he might take a short holiday, and he agreed. We understood he had taken himself off to Mackay for a couple of weeks, so a letter from him came as a surprise, but a worse surprise followed. Robert had not gone to Mackay. He had caught the train to Brisbane, where he signed up to join the 2nd Australian Light Horse Regiment that was formed at Enoggera on 18 August. Before he left here, Robert wrote the letter telling us of his intention to enlist, but to avoid any fuss and opposition to his plan, he did not post the letter until after he was in camp in Brisbane.

A second, hastily penned letter from Robert arrived today. It was posted shortly before they left Brisbane to join the fighting in the War. Robert and his regiment sailed for Egypt on 25 September, four days before we received his letter.

I imagine mail from overseas will be sporadic from now on, but I will endeavour to keep you posted as information comes to hand.

Given Robert's approach to life, we should not be surprised by his latest escapade. It would appeal to him as an opportunity for the biggest adventure ever. Let's hope and pray he returns to continue to worry us with his escapades in the future.

Your loving son, Lachlan.

The subsequent months proved difficult for Sarah. She spent her days constantly tense and worried despite a letter from Robert received early in 1915. As she discussed Robert's latest news in a quiet moment with Angus, Sarah stopped speaking abruptly. It was a few moments later before she continued.

"It was the name, you know. That was the cause."

"Sorry, Mother, I don't understand. What do you mean by the name was the cause?"

"That name, Robert, should not have been given to that child. Both your father and I jokingly said at the time that we hoped the name didn't bring with it the spirit of its previous Wallace family recipient. There is nothing from the last Robert Wallace anyone would want to carry forward to today's generations, but it seems his spirit has indeed attached itself to the name."

"Mother, I don't believe that for one moment. Lachlan's son has always been his own man and lived his life accordingly, albeit somewhat differently from the rest of us, and very differently from what Lachlan would want. He always was a high-spirited young lad. While his enlistment might smack of just another adventure to those of us here, I believe Robert would have been driven by more than that. Yes, adventure might have been a part of his motivation, but I believe the real driving force behind his enlistment would have been a sense of duty."

"Do you believe that, Angus, or is it no more than an attempt to make me feel better?"

"No, I believe it. Somehow, Robert and I became close. While the rest of you see Robert as reckless and a constant source of worry and anxiety, I knew a different lad. One who possessed high moral standards and beliefs. Someone who could not stand by and watch someone being downtrodden and abused by someone else. His enlistment is completely in keeping with the man I know him to be."

"What if we lose him, Angus? What if he doesn't come back?"

"We must trust in God, Mother. And if, Heaven forbid, he should not return, we should try to remember that Robert was doing what he wanted to do, what he believed was the right thing for him to do. I believe he followed your philosophy. He seized what he saw as an opportunity for the greatest adventure of a lifetime. It presented, and he seized it."

If only I believed those noble words, Angus thought as he made his way back to the homestead from Sarah's cottage. If I feel so badly, what must Lachlan be going through? And, if there is a God, I hope and pray he is merciful enough to spare my mother the loss of her oldest grandson.

Perhaps God, fate, or whoever, heard Angus's plea for mercy for his mother that day. Three weeks after Angus's conversation with his mother, Sarah passed away. Although she was 92, to everyone, it felt as though she had been taken much too soon. They, and particularly Angus, had occasion to revisit his earlier plea.

Later that year, Lachlan received the dreaded communiqué. Robert was dead. He and his mount had been killed in one of the regiment's early offensives. The news of Robert's death had a tragic sequel a week later when Robert's last letter home finally arrived in the Burdekin.

After receiving news from Lachlan of Robert's death, Angus sat on his front verandah with only his memories for company. Through the darkness and sorrow of those memories, one shining thought broke through. Although it had been difficult to accept at the time, Life had been merciful after all. It had spared his mother the heartbreak of knowing her oldest grandson would not be returning from the war.

A couple of days after receiving news of Robert's death, Angus succumbed to some strange urge to sit amongst his mother's things that remained undisturbed in the cottage since her death. As he sat at Sarah's desk, his eyes fell on her 1915 diary. It had been written up until the day she died. With tears trickling down his cheeks after reading her last few entries, he went to add the diary to the others residing on her bookshelf. The 1914 diary, bound closed with black ribbon, caught his eye.

In Sarah's sitting room, he rummaged through her sewing basket until he found what he needed. Angus snipped off a long length of black ribbon, took it and bound up Sarah's 1915 diary before adding it to the bookshelf beside its 1914 companion.

One day, this cottage must be cleaned out, he told himself, but that won't be for some time to come. While this cottage remains as it is, the spirit of my mother will continue to reign over us, her family, and all of this Wallace empire. Now, she, too, lies out there beside my grandfather and my father. It's as though the Wallace dynasty will never leave this place. They will remain here, keeping watch over us.

"Somehow, for me, that provides a sense of reassurance," Angus whispered to the cottage as he stepped outside and locked the door behind him.

The End

Also by the Author

Revenge is not Enough
Harbour Plaza: built on dreams
On the Way to Istanbul
An Unsuitable House
A Land Too Far
Paradise Interrupted
Unwelcome Mail
By Any Other Name
House of Secrets
A Life of Tea and Sugar

About the Author

KAYLA DANOLI spent her early years traipsing around Australia and then Europe with her parents, and then completed her tertiary education in England before returning to Australia. There were a variety of jobs in various parts of Queensland before eventually making her way towards the coast. She now lives in a small coastal town on the Queensland coast where she works part-time on a charter vessel.

In the early days after settling in that small town, to fill in her spare time, both when at home and while on cruises, she started scribbling down her ideas for stories. These days, she writes whenever time permits. Her *Harbour Plaza* series, previously released in 2015 as monthly eBook episodes, was updated, extended and released in 2016 as the *Harbour Plaza: built on dreams* compilation. *Revenge is not Enough,* also released in 2016, was her first full-length novel.

A Life of Tea and Sugar was Kayla's tenth novel and was the precursor to *A Life of Seizing Opportunities..*

Discover more about Kayla and her work by visiting
www.eaglemountbooks.com.au/kayla-danoli

or contact her at
admin@eaglemountbooks.com.au

www.ingramcontent.com/pod-product-compliance
Lightning Source LLC
Chambersburg PA
CBHW040217170726
48295CB00014B/710